Aunt Killer

Jeneva Johns

DB-Books
Mansfield, Ohio

Although this is a work of fiction, the childhood incidents and the experiences with viral encephalitis are real but fictionalized for the sake of the story. Names and characters are fictitious, and any resemblance to actual persons, living or dead, are entirely coincidental.

All rights reserved. No part of this book may be reproduced or transmitted in any form or by any means, electronic or mechanical, including photocopying, recording, or by any information storage or retrieval system, without permission in writing from the author.

Copyright © 2001 by Jeneva Johns

Published by DB-Books, a division of DB-Systems, Inc.
733 Westview Boulevard, Mansfield, Ohio 44907

Publisher's Cataloging-in-Publication
(Provided by Quality Books, Inc.)

Johns, Jeneva.
    Aunt killer / Jeneva Johns. -- 1st ed.
    p. cm.
    LCCN 2001090943
    ISBN 0-9711307-0-1 (hardback)
    ISBN 0-9711307-1-X (paperback)

    1. Man-woman relationships--Fiction. 2. Encephalitis --Fiction. 3. Virus diseases--Fiction. 4. Phenylketonuria--Fiction. 5. Memory disorders--Fiction. 6. Florida--Fiction. 7. Ohio--Fiction. I. Title.

PS3560.O337A96 2001   813'.6
                      QBI01-700774

Printed in the United States of America
1 2 3 4 5 6 7 8 9 10

First Edition 2001

*To my husband, Don,
who was there for me during my illness,
helped me recover, and encouraged my writing.*

To all who have survived encephalitis.

Aunt Killer

~ 1 ~

Rural, north central Ohio – August 17th

"I can't take much more of this," Eva muttered.

Alone in her Chevy Blazer, Eva Johnson watched a red sports car in the rearview mirror. It had been tailing her in a dangerous game of taunting tag: racing forward, dropping back, and then slipping across the hot pavement like a snake.

Again the red Pontiac Firebird nudged closer, drafting like a racecar. Now, only inches separated their bumpers.

"Why doesn't he pass?" After tapping the brake, Eva pulled over. "There's plenty of room and no traffic. So pass!"

With its horn blasting, the sports car swung into the left lane of the Ohio country road.

"What's he doing now?" In the mirror, Eva watched the red car whip across the road. "This is a poor place to speed. It's not the Daytona raceway, you know."

With its horn blaring, the sports car pulled closer. Through its dark-tinted side window a light flickered, but no face was visible. Screeching, its wide tires skidded across the hot pavement and onto the berm, spewing debris into the air.

Stones smacked her Blazer's windshield, pinging as they hit. Gravel hurled in the open window, stinging Eva's arm.

A cloud of dust obscured the red sports car racing past.

I was hoping the fresh country air would help me ditch this headache, she thought as she closed the window. *Nothing else seems to be working.* From her purse, Eva Johnson pulled out a prescription bottle and swallowed another white capsule with a swig of Coca-Cola. A checkmark recorded when she took her medication. With her failing short-term memory, notes were Eva's only way to remember.

"Let's see, what do I need to do today?" Eva glanced at the big yellow note taped to the steering wheel. "Should I really file a restraining order against Jim? If I do, he'll go ballistic. I can almost hear him shouting. Will he get violent, again?"

Eva scanned the horizon. Beyond was a wide Ohio valley with grain fields, ripening in the August sunlight. On the far sides were low rolling hills, shrouded in a late summer green. *Hooker's Green*, she mused. *It's my favorite watercolor green. Luscious.*

Down the road, the red car spun around and headed back.

"Trouble," Eva muttered. "I don't want to deal with any more road rage. I came out here to get away from Jim and his – what's the word? Obsession, stalking, intrusion. Whatever, he's driving me crazy. I told him to leave me alone. He's nuts to think I'd marry anyone like him. I would never do that. Never, never, never."

Whipping the steering wheel right, her Blazer turned sharply onto a familiar looking side road. Flicking on the CD player, the relaxing sounds of piano notes and breaking waves on a beach reminded Eva of her childhood at the ocean. Her sea-blue Blazer rumbled south, cutting across the rural Ohio valley.

"It's time to go home. The restraining order will have to wait until tomorrow." After glancing at the speedometer, her foot hit the brake. "Slow down, girl. Don't want your name in the newspaper. It would make a juicy heading, 'Art professor arrested for speed.'

I'd get a lot of ribbing at the next faculty meeting. And what would my church group say? Oh, my gracious, what's wrong with me?"

In front of her, an Amish buggy pulled over. Two children peeked out with beaming smiles.

Slowing her Blazer, Eva carefully pulled around the buggy and waved at the children. In a distant field, a group of Amish men worked in the hot sun. All similarly dressed in dark pants, light shirts, and wide-brim hats, the men were busy erecting a new barn near one of their multi-family homes.

They're lucky, Eva mused. *Maybe smart is a better word. They keep their life simple and slow. I'll bring my next semester's watercolor class out here to paint. It'll be a pleasant change for my students. They're always in too much of a hurry, like that pesky red car behind me.*

In the rearview mirror, Eva studied the rapidly approaching car, now following her down a different road. *That looks like my niece's sports car. But then, most sports cars are sleek and red.*

Her Blazer bounced over a rut. "Don't do that. My head feels like it's going to explode." Rubbing her forehead, Eva felt the heat boiling inside her skull, hotter than the afternoon sun.

It's summer. This can't be the flu, Eva thought, straightening her stiff neck. *Besides, I get a flu shot every year. I should have some immunity to it. And it's been over three weeks, ... I think. I've lost twenty pounds and still the doctor hasn't found out what's wrong with me. And, if he thinks it's a simple sinus infection, why does he want me to have a CAT scan of my brain?*

Again the red Pontiac Firebird pulled behind her Blazer. It didn't pass. It kept pace. Close, too close.

Trying to ignore the car, Eva concentrated on the country lane. *I thought this was the road home. I don't remember that bridge. But then, my memory has been on the fritz for ... well I don't recall how long. Anyway, that's south, ... south, I know home is that way.*

Honking, the red sports car nudged closer.

Is car-tag some new teenage game? She pulled over. *Now pass and leave me alone.*

Whipping into the left lane, the red sports car slowed, matching her speed. Its dark-tinted window slipped down. Jarring music blasted out, sounding like war drums. No face appeared. Only a hand was visible. A metal object slipped into the light.

Light flashed off a gun barrel.

Eva glanced left. "It's a ... gun!"

A blast erupted. The side window cracked. A bullet hissed passed her head. Another shot erupted. Pain stabbed her left arm. The steering wheel jerked right.

Her Blazer slid off the road. With a thud, the right wheels sank into the open ditch, flipping the Blazer sideways.

"Hang on!" Eva shouted, gripping the steering wheel.

Metal ground against stones, crumbling and twisting it.

Rolling down the embankment, her seatbelt snapped tight.

Twigs broke and weeds flattened. The Blazer tumbled over and over, steel groaning under the torque.

Grinding yielded to the squishing of mud. Another roll splashed the crumpling metal into the creek far below the bridge.

The sudden jolt of hitting a boulder triggered the airbags. With a flash of billowing white, the airbag surrounded her head, protecting it from the final impact. For Eva, there was a moment of silence before the blackness consumed it.

* * * *

A twig snapped. Afternoon had turned into early evening.

Eva's head jerked. Warm red liquid ran down her forehead and cool water trickled between her fingers. Her eyes opened to fuzzy shapes and faint moving shadows. The ringing in her ears sounded like a phone urgently calling.

I better get home. It's getting late. She pushed aside the airbag and unbuckled the seatbelt. Slowly, Eva crawled out.

In the creek, a startled deer ran from its evening drink.

Dazed, Eva stood in the shallow stream and studied her strange looking Blazer. *Look at it. It's all muddy. What happened? Where am I?*

A redbird called to its mate, singing: Pretty, pretty, pretty. A chipmunk scampered across the rocks of the stream, shallow from an August dry spell.

Eva crawled back into her crumbled Blazer. *I hope my CD didn't get broken and I better get my keys. You never leave your keys in the car. Someone might steal it. ... And where is my purse. I need another headache pill. Boy, do I ever need one right now.*

Back outside, she popped two white capsules in her mouth and dipped her cupped hands in the trickling stream. Eva studied the water seeping through her fingers. Light glittered off it like sunshine rippling across the ocean at daybreak. *I wish I were home. Which way is home?*

Walking away from her crumpled Blazer, Eva ambled upstream towards the setting sun. A piercing pain stabbed her left arm and her vision blurred. For her the accident was not recallable, wiped out by the concussion of the sudden impact of stopping and the illness fogging her mind.

Stopping in the middle of the stream, Eva rested on a boulder. A turtle, the size of a fifty-cent piece, ambled across a sandbar. "I remember the baby turtles running across the beach. ... Come on little fellow, time to be getting home." Pulling a watercolor brush from her art box, she touched the turtle. Instantly, its legs pulled in and its head disappeared into the shell. "Well, I guess you are home. You carry it with you." Eva sighed. "I wish I could disappear like that."

It's getting late; I have to get home, she thought. *Which way is home?* Creek water trickled between her muddy walking shoes. *I live on the high point. Home is uphill.*

Two miles upstream, the creek banks dropped lower and Eva stepped up, into a field of knee-high soybeans. Their green leaves swished against her legs and the warm earth smelled rich. On her left arm, a thirsty mosquito drank its fill of warm blood trickled from a wound.

I have to get home. The sun is on the horizon. Her weary legs crumpled and Eva sank to her knees. *I better rest for a minute.*

The big, red summer sun sank below the Ohio horizon, setting the sky ablaze with intense colors like an impressionistic painting.

Summer sunsets are so vivid, Eva thought, *flaming orange, blood red, and violet. Reminds me of Turner's painting of the sunset over the ocean. There are even some billowing black clouds. Looks like a storm is brewing. I better get home soon.*

Sitting in the field, Eva watched the light drain from the western sky. Behind her was Interstate 71, heading south. Ahead of her, home was over the next hill. It would soon be dark.

Home. Rubbing her forehead, Eva Johnson wondered what could be waiting. *Do I really want to go home?*

~ 2 ~

Evening – August 17th

Blood! Eva's heart pounded at the thoughts swirling through her mind. *How did I get hurt? Did I fall on my walk home? Where have I been? Why can't I remember what happened to me? I know my memory is fried, but this is ... what's the word? Frightening.*

A white bath towel, stained with blood, dropped into the washing machine, powdered soap followed, and the lid dropped shut. "Blood," Eva mumbled, switching through wash cycle. "Cold water. It takes cold water to wash out bloodstains; every woman knows that. But if that doesn't work, I'll use it for a car towel."

Pushing the cold wash button, Eva stared at the door to the attached garage. "Where did I leave my Blazer this time?" She asked the churning washing machine. "You're right. I probably left it in Kroger's parking lot again. It's not the first time and the way my memory is these days it won't be the last. I'll just walk back out there and get it, later. Right now I'm too tired. I need a nap and it has to be time for my medication. My head is pounding."

In the laundry room, the washing machine sloshed, rinsing out the bloodstains from the towel like the memory of Eva's accident had been erased by her mild concussion. Neither event had time to set and there would be little evidence either had occurred.

In the background, there was ringing. "Is that the phone or just my ears?" Slowly, Eva wandered down the hall.

Stepping into the living room, she heard the answering machine click into action, give directions, beep, and record.

"Aunt Eva. Are you there?" Maggie's frantic voice paused for a second. "Call me as soon as you get in. It's really important! I need your advice, Aunt Eva." A click ended the message.

Sinking into the sofa, Eva stretched out. Her body lay motionless, aching like a bad case of the flu. Only her thoughts continued to ramble. *Maggie, now what's up? Every time you ask for advice, what you really want is your Aunt Eva's money. What is it this time, another deposit for a new apartment? Or did you change jobs again and need a little cash to tide you over?*

A flash of heat rolled through Eva and she sat up. "Money. Where did I put it? If I lost that box, I'm out twenty five thousand dollars. That's my traveling money. It's my ticket to freedom and away from Jim. He'll never find me. Cash leaves no trail."

Fear fueled her muscles into action. After searching her desk, Eva hurried into the kitchen. Beside her blue backpack were a set of car keys, her novel, and the missing box. Inside it were twenty-five small Ziploc bags, each containing a thousand dollars.

"I don't need to take the box." Eva laid the sacks of hundred dollar bills aside. "I'll be able to live on this for quite a while. Even at a thousand a week, I'll have twenty-five weeks of freedom from Jim. By then he'll understand I want him out of my life. Forever." She sighed in relief. "A smart man should be able to get that hint."

Ringing echoed down the front hallway. "Maggie must be desperate." The answering machine picked up the call as Eva stepped into the living room. A soft woman's voice whispered. "Just a reminder. Our next women's investment club meeting will be at the church tomorrow at seven."

After jotting down a reminder note, it was torn up. *No need,* Eva considered. *I'll be long gone by then. But maybe I should call and tell them I can't make the meeting. ... No. Jim could be the guest speaker again. If not, he will surely ask one of them where I've gone. And I can't ask my church friends to lie for me. Still, I don't want them to worry.*

Reaching for the phone, she noticed the answering machine's message-waiting light blinking and pushed the play button.

"Eva." Jim's voice snarled. "I dropped my ... some important papers in your raspberry patch. Get them. I'll be over later. Be there! Remember what I told you." The recording went dead.

"What's he talking about? What papers?" Her finger trembled pushing the erase button. "Wish this could delete him from my life. Then I wouldn't have to run away from my lovely home."

Eva looked around the spacious living room filled with reminders of her parents. A collection of mementos and photo albums were all that remained. Her mother had been killed when Eva was twelve and her father passed away a year ago. Now at twenty-seven, she was alone in the big house her father had built.

"There is no reason to stay." Eva talked to herself, more often now that a fever burned in her brain. "I should call Detective Galloway again. He should be back from Lake Erie by now. Paul will know what to do. At least he can give me some advice." Pushing the redial button, she waited. When a police recording answered, she hung up. "I hate talking to machines."

After flipping on her CD player, Eva flopped back on the sofa. Her body lay dead still, but her mind reviewed her options. In the background, the song words from "The Boxer," repeated over and over. Part of its lyrics engraved deeper and deeper in Eva's subconscious: "Going home."

Napping on the sofa, her wet blond hair dried and in the background the washer clicked off. But the music continued to repeat its hypnotic message as Eva slipped into a dream. Images of the frozen Siberian tundra at sunrise flashed in her mind. It was a refreshing dream for a fevered mind and outside the air conditioner hummed on high in the hot August night. In the western sky, storm clouds loomed and distant lightning clawed at the sky.

Inside, the music was interrupted by a loud crash. The tinkling of shattered glass hitting the marble floor echoed down the hall.

What was that? Her heart shuttered. A wave of goose bumps rippled down her arms and a cold chill rolled through her. *Was that part of my dream?*

Another thud. Then the smashing of more glass and hitting the marble floor it shattered again.

Who's breaking in? A burglar? Or is it Jim? ... I have to get out of here. Her feet were one step ahead of her thoughts. In the dark, Eva grabbed her backpack and stuffed in the sacks of money. The bag's zipper ripped open a cut. Blood trickled down her hand, dripping onto the floor.

Behind her, something beat against the back door.

More window glass cracked.

The back doorknob rattled.

In the living room, the song repeated, "running scared."

Dashing to the front door, Eva paused only to flip on the security alarm. Her blood streaked the wall, smeared the doorknob, and dripped across the front porch.

The security patrol will call the police.

If I stay, ... I'll get killed.

~ 3 ~

Lightning streaked the night sky. Thunder rumbled. Wind whipped paper across the parking lot. Billowing clouds let loose with drenching rain. A few midnight shoppers fled to safety.

Having walked to the nearby mall searching for her missing Blazer, Eva took refuge inside the Kroger store to wait out the storm. A thunderclap rattled the windows. At the checkout counter, Eva Johnson watched a gust of wind sway the light poles and the beating rain obscure the rows of cars.

My poor, lost Blazer will be well washed by the time I find it, she thought. *Wherever it is. I was sure it would be here. This is generally where I leave it. ... Why do I keep forgetting things?*

Eva kept her bandaged hand in her pocket, out of sight of the checkout clerk. Her other scrapes and bruises had been taken care of after her shower at home. "I should be getting home."

"Lady, wait until it lets up. If you get hit by one of those lightning bolts, you'll be fried like our crispy chicken." The clerk sacked a bottle of Motrin and a box of bandages. "Why don't you take your travel magazine back to the deli and wait until the storm passes? No rush, we're open all night."

Resting for a bit sounded good to Eva. Her body ached.

The panic of leaving her home had subsided. *If there were a problem,* Eva considered, *I would have heard police sirens before I reached Kroger's. There were no sirens. That shattering noise must have been in one of my weird dreams; they're so real.*

"Something wrong?" The clerk asked, ripping off a receipt.

"Do you have a pay phone?"

"Down that way. But don't use the phone when it's lightning. You could get zapped." Looking at Eva, the clerk handed her the receipt. "You look a little banged up. Did someone hit you?"

"No. I just took a tumble when I was out hiking." The story sounded acceptable and Eva didn't want to admit to a stranger that she had no idea what happened to her. And she was glad her long sleeves and slacks covered most of the bruises. "I'm okay, really."

Back in the deli, Eva settled at a remote table and chair, out of the way of the night clerks restocking shelves. As the pages of her travel magazine flipped, the lettering began to blur and her head rested on a photograph of sand dunes along a tropical beach.

Home, Eva thought. *Tomorrow morning, I'm going to my childhood home. No one can find me there. No one will miss me here. Everyone is gone, and I, too, will soon be gone.* The sound of rain pattering on the roof lulled her into a deep sleep.

Shifts changed. Shelves were restocked. Floors were swept. The smell of fresh coffee and breakfast rolls filled the air.

"Morning." The cheerful voice of the deli assistant woke Eva. "Looks like you could use some strong morning coffee."

Eva's head rose from the magazine. "Morning?"

"Yes. Want an orange-glazed roll to go with your coffee?"

Although Eva's appetite had vanished weeks ago when the headaches started, she took a roll and her coffee to the checkout. In front of Kroger's, she got on the city bus. As they drove through the parking lot, Eva looked for her lost sea-blue Blazer.

I'll go to the police station. Make out a missing car report and see Detective Galloway. Eva glanced at her bandaged hand and felt the bump on her forehead. *On the other hand that may not be a good idea. Paul will ask me tons of questions when he sees me. I can't hide how I look from a detective and I don't want to tell Paul I don't remember how I got hurt. ... He'll think I'm crazy.*

Minutes later in the downtown bus terminal, Eva listened to Detective Galloway's police recording and hung up the phone.

An Amish family stood at the ticket counter. A cute little girl peeked from behind her mother's skirt. Standing in the doorway, a young Amish boy fed the pigeons outside in the rain.

"You folks from Holmes County?" the ticket agent asked.

Nodding, the bearded Amish father paid for his ticket.

Home, Eva thought. Stepping to the Greyhound ticket counter, she put her backpack down. *That's an idea. Take the bus home. I don't need my Blazer. I can sleep on the bus while they drive.*

"You going to Holmes County, too?" The ticket agent asked.

"No." Eva watched the Amish family step on the bus. "I want a ticket for Daytona Beach, Florida."

"Round trip?"

"One way."

"Cash or credit card?"

"Cash." Eva pulled a hundred dollar bill from her backpack.

"If you hurry, you can catch that bus to Columbus. You'll make connections there." The agent handed over her ticket.

Outside, Eva dashed through the pouring rain. Near her, a startled flock of pigeons took off and flew south. *I wonder if they're homing pigeons,* Eva mused. *How do they find their way home without a map? Do all animals have a homing instinct?*

Sirens wailed. Lights flashed. A police cruiser slid around the rain-slicked corner followed by an unmarked detective's car.

The bus door hissed closed behind Eva, cutting off the noise and shutting out the dreary rain. Slipping into a window seat, Eva glanced outside at the road sign: South to I-71. *Home,* she smiled.

I'll call Detective Galloway when I get there. Holding her aching arm, Eva closed her eyes. *Maybe by then I'll know how to explain my problem with Jim and remember what happened to me. Remember, that's the wrong word. Forget. ... I just want to forget.*

~ 4 ~

Daytona Beach, Florida – Dawn, August 19th

"Oh God. Look at that." Eva hesitated, standing in the bus' doorway. "That's something I could never forget."

"It's just the ocean." The bus driver glanced out the open door. "Y'all getting off? I can't sit here all morning."

Stepping off, the door closed behind her, then opened.

"Ma'am, y'all left your book." The driver tossed it to her.

With her novel in hand and the backpack on her shoulders, Eva wandered down the concrete beach ramp. Three motorbikes roared past, heading towards the Atlantic Ocean forty yards away.

Pain radiated through Eva Johnson's skull and her forehead felt like an electric burner left on high. Her viral illness was taking its toll on her mind. Sitting in the sand, she concentrated on the one thought that comforted her. *Home. It's good to be home again.*

Inhaling the salty air, Eva wiggled her toes in the soft cool sand of her childhood home, Daytona Beach. Sitting down, she yawned. *Even after sleeping most of the way down, I could use a nap. Twenty-four hours and a thousand miles on a bus are tiring.*

Overhead, a passenger jet roared, banked, and headed north.

I should have flown down. But I'm afraid my sinuses would have exploded. And ... and I don't want anyone to find me. Maggie will have to get along without her Aunt Eva. And as long as no one knows where I am, Jim can't find me. ... I need time to think. Think. Eva laughed. *Only God knows how scrambled my thoughts are right now. I pray He doesn't tell anyone what's going on in my hot little brain. Maybe a long dip in the ocean will cool it.*

An alarm clock rang inside her backpack. *It's time to take my medicine. I don't want a headache, not today.* Eva took out one white capsule from her backpack and downed it with a sip of Coke. *I don't know why I keep taking these pills. They don't cure my headaches. But the doctor insists I take all of them.*

Sitting in the dry beach sand, Eva watched the seagulls flock around a woman feeding them, holding scraps of bread high in the air. Chattering, the birds swooped low to grab the bread and then land on the beach to devoured their treat. Sandpipers scurried across the wet sand, pecking for tiny tidbits, as they dashed in and out with the baby waves, growing pancake thin before they slipped back out to sea. A Frisbee sailed past with a leaping dog in pursuit.

I've missed all this. Daytona has always been my favorite home. Eva stared east, watching the sun rising over the flat horizon of the Atlantic Ocean. It reminded her of a dream.

Next to her backpack, Eva curled up in the soft cool sand and closed her eyes. *I just need a little nap. Then I can continue my journey. I wonder how far it is to the West Indies? I want to see my childhood home. ... Home.* A tear ran down Eva's cheek. *With a thousand miles to protect me, I'm safe here. No one can find me.*

* * * *

"Hey, lady. Wake up. ... You can't sleep on MY beach."

"I was just resting my eyes." With her lovely dream shattered, Eva looked up at a scruffy man with his hands firmly planted on his hips. "I don't see anyone's name written in the sand."

"Look, lady, don't give me no hard time. This here's MY spot. Everybody knows this is where Joe's bike rental sits. Right here!"

His foot stomped the sand and he waved to a trailer backing up. It was loaded with bikes. "Move or y'all be part of that there sand."

Bikes. That's what I need, a bike. Eva stood, dusted off dry sand, and put her hands on her hips. "I was here first."

"Come on, lady. Get off my sand before I call the cops."

"Fine with me. Call them. They won't see your name written on the sand either. But –" She eyed the assortment of bikes sitting on the trailer inching closer to her, backing-beeper warning.

"But what?"

"If you make it worth my while, I'll give you this spot."

"Look, lady. This IS my spot." His feet slid deeper into the sand. "Get out of the way before my fool son runs over you. He ain't no good at backing and I don't want blood on my sand."

Eva watched the red taillights. "I'm not moving. Either make a deal or there'll be blood on this sand."

"Stop, you idiot!" He shouted at his son and turned to Eva. "A deal? Well, I suppose y'all could use some wheels. That's a heavy looking backpack." He rubbed his chin. "Tell you what; I'll rent you a bike, half price for one day. Deal?"

"I bet one of your competitors would give me a better deal for this prime location." Eva looked down the beach at the other concession stands setting up. "Looks like it's going to be a busy day at the beach. Today, this sand is worth its weight in gold."

"Okay, I'll let you have a bike for a day, free." He rolled off a simple motorbike. "Let me see your driver's license."

Eva searched her backpack. *Did I forget my driver's license and credit cards? I'd lose my head if it weren't attached. Well, I'll just have to use cash.* She pulled a hundred dollar bill from the bottom of the backpack. "I plan to be here for a while. I'd like to buy a bike. How much is that one?"

"A peddler? Well, this here is a dandy one." Grinning, he pulled off a shiny new bike. "Three hundred dollars. Dirt cheap."

"No. It's too fancy." Eva walked to the front of the trailer and patted a simple little girl's bike, scratched and dented but with a sturdy wire basket and old-fashioned fenders over the wheels. It reminded her of her childhood bike and she was fond of sea-blue. "I'll give you fifty for this ugly-blue rambling wreck."

"Lady, that there's got new tires." He pulled it down and dusted it off. "That's worth at least a hundred."

Eva rubbed her forehead. "It looks like it rolled over a cliff. I'll give you sixty-five for it."

"Seventy-five. Not a dime less."

"Seventy and one of those wide brim hats."

"Smart. By noon, your Yankee-white skin will be lobster red without one of my dandy shade hats. But, that'll be seventy-five bucks with that there expensive imported sunbonnet."

"It says Hong Kong inside this hat. Seventy dollars, not a dime more." From the rack, Eva picked out a wide-brim straw hat similar to what the Amish men wear but this one had seashells glued to the hatband. "Do we have a deal?"

"Yep. One bike and one hat for seventy bucks." He stared at her. "Did you run into a door or someone's fist?"

"Just rolled over a little cliff. That's all." Eva looked down.

"Sure." He counted out the change, holding back five. "Y'all need a good lock. Five bucks. And that's a steal."

"Okay. But give me one with a key lock. I have trouble remembering combinations." Eva tucked her blond hair under the wide-rim hat and slipped on her sunglasses, adding to her disguise.

A glance in the little mirror tied to the concession stand startled her. *How did my forehead get so banged up? How could I forget something like that?* She could faintly hear the buzz of her synapses hissing hot inside her brain, making strange connections or none at all.

"Lady, you drive a hard bargain." He rolled the old blue bike to her. "I'm short one son today. Want a job?"

"Not today." Eva looked south. "I'm going home."

With her backpack in the wire basket, Eva walked her bike towards the ocean. Her childhood memories began there, where the sky, sea, and land met. She was home and safe for the moment.

Staring at the sun just above the horizon, her thoughts meandered. *What am I going to do without my Ohio driver's license? I think I left it and my credit cards on the desk so I wouldn't forget. But, when I heard the back window breaking, I must have panicked. ... All I remember is running out the front door and south down the road. I was so frightened.*

Standing in the shallow water, the current pulled sand from under her feet, beginning to bury her toes like any lost item left too long on the beach. The ocean's tinkling echoed in her ears like shattered glass hitting the marble floor of her Ohio home.

Who was breaking in? What were they after?

My money or me?

~ 5 ~

Early morning, farther down the beach

"Who killed her?" Mark Reining leaned against a beach patrol car, talking to Bob, an officer and one of Mark's students.

"Good question, Professor Reining. We don't know that or even who she is … was. Chief thinks it was for her money." Bob paused to listen to a radio dispatch. "That's my section of beach. Have to go. … Good luck fishing." Bob flipped on the siren.

Beach traffic pulled over for the cruiser. But early morning beachcombers hardly noticed as they searched for shells. Beyond them in waist-deep surf, fishermen were casting out their lines.

Mark glanced north, up the beach, where a woman's body had been found. Images of his sister's murder flashed in his mind and his body chilled in the warm morning air. *It's been two years since Susan was killed.* Mark vividly remembered his sister's death. *And it still haunts me. Anytime I hear about a woman being murdered, my blood runs cold. How can a man be so brutal?*

Professor Mark Reining watched Bob's cruiser roll up a beach ramp. With the conversation cut short, Mark would have to wait until his morning class to get the details about the murder from Bob. Teaching law enforcement officers gave Mark access to privileged information on local criminal cases, and being an ex-Secret Service agent gave him connections to national crimes.

Standing in the shallow water, the current pulled sand from under Mark's feet, burying his toes.

"If you don't move soon, you'll be part of the beach." Fritz put down a fishing tackle box. "Mark, something wrong?"

"No, Dad." Mark stepped into the surf. "I was just thinking about today's lesson. I need a different angle."

"How about a little bait to go with it."

"My lecture is about missing persons, not fishing."

"Well, my lesson for the day is, you have to put bait on your hook before you can catch a fish." Fritz pointed to his son's empty hook. "I promised your mom we'd have a nice mess of fish for dinner. If we go back empty handed, she's going to make one of those fluffy cheese casserole things."

"Cheese soufflé?" Mark cringed as he grabbed a handful of bait. "Mom knows how to pressure a fisherman."

"Let's get cracking. Take a gander north. She's trouble."

Wading out, Mark scanned the northern horizon. Dark clouds sliced a line between the dark blue ocean and the pale morning sky. "Maybe she won't come this far south."

Fritz shook his head. "Nope, she's coming our way. I can feel it in my bones. She's going to be a humdinger."

Mark glanced back towards his parents' home beyond the sand dunes. Near the wooden walk stood an old ship's mast with a storm warning flag barely flapping.

"The wind is almost calm." Mark waded out through the quiet surf. "Has the marina issued a storm warning already?"

"Nope. They wait until I put my flag up."

"Looks like that storm front will roll in about dinner time." Having grown up on the beach, Mark was good at judging storms.

"More like seven thirty." Fritz was even better at predicting the movement of squall lines. "That northeaster will be packing a mean punch. It's a spin-off from the storm that smashed through the Midwest, then bounced off the tropical depression near New England. And now it's aiming at us."

Casting out into a slue, Mark studied the water. Even for morning, it was unusually calm, as if the north running current was leery of rushing into the path of the approaching storm. *It looks almost like glass,* Mark mused. *It's so peaceful. But a storm like that one can whip the sea into lathery foam.*

Only their fishing line disturbed the quiet water and nothing even nibbled at the bait. After a while, even an experienced fisherman rans out of patience and fishing tricks.

Fritz pulled in his line. "Mark. I don't like the looks of this."

"What's wrong?"

"The fish aren't biting and I hate the thought of eating that cheese fluff for dinner." Fritz cast his line the other direction.

In the distance, a blue bike ambled south beside a small figure. Slipping past it was a police cruiser, heading towards Mark.

"You're on your own, Dad. I don't want to be late for my class." Mark pulled in his line. "We'll fish again this afternoon. I have only one class today and they cancelled the faculty meeting."

The beach patrol car pulled to a stop.

"Been trouble on the beach?" Fritz asked his son.

"That's Bob. He's in my morning class. Probably wants to discuss the final project." Mark waded towards shore. He didn't want to tell his father about the woman killed up the beach. That would remind his dad of Susan's death. It was time to forget the tragedy of his sister's murder.

On the beach, Bob sat in his cruiser listening to the police radio. "Professor Reining. They brought in the woman's nephew to identify her body."

"That can be traumatic." Mark leaned closer. "Any suspects?"

"Yep. They locked up the nephew," Bob shook his head.

Mark leaned closer. "Why did the nephew kill his aunt?"

~ 6 ~

Afternoon – South Atlantic Avenue

"Someone killed their aunt?" Eva gasped at the newspaper's headline. "Why would anyone kill their aunt?"

On a little bench in the shade of a burger stand, Eva rested. Glancing over the newspaper, she watched hungry tourists rush inside for a quick lunch and then dash back across the road to the beach. It was a perilous journey across South Atlantic Avenue with heavy traffic and inattentive drivers.

Morning had slipped into afternoon. Only the travel alarm in her backpack had kept track of the time. The ringing alarm and her headache, pounding louder than the morning surf, were reminders for her to take her medication and to rest.

After swallowing the white capsule and recording when it was taken, Eva returned to the news article. The details of the crime were disturbing and one item in particular was unsettling.

They think the nephew killed his aunt for her money. Eva's mind felt a chill and it wasn't from the ice cold Coke being held to her feverish brow. *That's a really sick thing to do. Why didn't he just ask his aunt for help? Or did the aunt get tired of helping?*

The news article was sketchy on the prior night's murder and how the police knew the nephew did it.

"Aunt Killer." Eva reread the headline. "That's a chilling title and even a more frightening thought. Who would kill their aunt?"

Sitting on the concrete bench, Eva glanced around. No one seemed to notice her talking to herself or even her existence. *Good,*

Eva thought. *I knew a tourist town would be a good place to get lost in for a while. No one can find me here. I'm safe from Jim. And I don't even think I'll call Maggie.* Again, Eva glanced at the headline, "Aunt Killer."

One of her niece's remarks disturbed Eva. *When Maggie came for her birthday money, why did she make that comment? It startled me at the time but I ignored it. ... Why did Maggie say that after I'm gone she'd take care of all my bank accounts? I may be a little ill but I'm hardly on my deathbed. At twenty-six, I plan to be around for a long time unless ... unless I'm killed.*

Trying to settle the queasy feeling in her stomach, Eva munched a few fries and sipped Coke. A breeze tumbled a discarded burger wrapper across the pavement and into the sand near the dumpster. A cat's paw reached out and snared the paper.

With its tires screeching on the hot pavement, a police cruiser pulled into the burger stand's parking lot. A beach patrol officer got out and walked to the black Jeep pulling in behind it.

Munching a fry, Eva studied the man who had caught her attention. "The suit and tie seem a bit formal for a jeep but it suits him," Eva mumbled. "The police officer looks like he's explaining something. The other man must be a detective: a handsome one at that. He reminds me of ... of someone."

Before she could recall, the Jeep pulled away.

"Should I call Detective Galloway?" Shaking her head, she answered herself. "No. I'll get his recording again. Paul's a busy detective. Anyway, by the time I get back, Jim will be out of my life. Right now it's time to enjoy myself. ... When's low tide?"

Flipping open the newspaper, she skimmed the tide chart for the times for high and low tides. *What's the date?* Eva wondered. *This shows the tides for the nineteenth through the twenty-fifth. But that can't be right. It's the end of the month. Memorial Day is next weekend. I think.*

The newspaper's date read August nineteenth. Shaking her head, Eva read it again. "Can't be," she whispered rubbing her forehead. "Where did the summer go? What happened to June? Surely I couldn't have forgotten my birthday. I'll be twenty-seven and I'll get my full inheritance then."

A weak "meow" answered.

"Princess?" Eva turned, even knowing it couldn't be her cat.

A furry head peaked from under the dumpster, sniffing before it slinked out into the sun. Carefully, the cat stepped over a sandspur plant and towards the smell of fish.

"Here kitty, kitty." Eva held out a piece of her fish sandwich.

Eyeing the fish, the shorthaired cat walked past at a safe distance, stopped, strolled back, and sat down in front of Eva.

"Good girl. You have to be careful of strangers." Eva stripped the breading off and left the fish on the wrapper. "It looks like you're nursing kittens. You could use a good meal yourself."

As soon as Eva backed away, the calico cat approached the fish and began to eat. "You remind me of my cat, Princess, although she has ... had longer hair. My Princess was killed. The vet said she ate ant poison and –" Eva's eyes watered.

"I don't keep ant poison around," Eva told the stray cat. "It couldn't have been an accident and I never let her run loose; she had no claws to protect herself. So, who would poison my cat?"

Another sip of Coke cleared her throat. "The only person I know who hates cats is ... Jim. He's allergic to almost everything. So, be careful of the food you eat, momma cat. There are some bad people around and you can't tell who they are by their looks. I should know. ... That's why I'm here."

A horn blared. The cat dashed under the dumpster.

"Here kitty ditty; I mean kitty, kitty." *What's wrong with me? My words are getting scrambled. Am I losing my mind?* Eva moved the last few scraps of fish closer to the dumpster. "Don't worry, momma cat. I'll buy you some more fish. Money. I need change. This burger place doesn't take traveler's checks or hundred dollar bills. I need a bank." Eva flipped open the notebook and read her scribbling: *bank is south of burger stand.*

Hopping on her bike, Eva headed south. Three blocks away, she parked in the shade beside the bank. With her blond hair tucked neatly under her hat and the wrinkles smoothed out of her blue slacks and white blouse, Eva tugged open the heavy bank door. *It's nice and cool in here. I'll take my time here.*

Scanning the lobby, she noticed the security cameras. *I should put my money in this bank. It looks safe. And I don't know where I'll be staying tonight. I've always wanted to sleep on the beach. Just curl up on a sand dune and sleep under the stars.*

"Ma'am. May I help you?" The smiling teller asked.

"I would like some change for a hundred."

"Do you want fifties or twenties?"

"Three twenties, two tens, and –" Eva looked up trying to calculate how much that was. "Make the rest ones." She watched the teller count out the change. *What's wrong with me? I'm good with money. Why can't I figure out how to change a hundred?"*

"One hundred." The teller scooted the pile of bills closer.

Eva glanced at the bank vault. "Do you have any small safe deposit boxes?"

"Only the large ones are available. Would you like one for six months or a year?" The teller slid a form across the counter.

"I'll take one for a year." Eva printed her name on the top part of the form. "I'll leave the address blank until I find a place."

"Yes ma'am." The teller nodded. "This way, please."

Inside the vault area, Eva signed the signature card and unzipped her backpack. *It was a little dangerous carrying all this cash but I was afraid a bank transfer would leave a paper trail for Jim to follow. With no trail, I'm safe. No one can find me.*

Eva glanced over her shoulder. No one was in sight. *I wonder if twenty-five thousand dollars is enough?* Pulling out snack size Ziploc bags filled with one hundred dollar bills, Eva stuffed them in the empty burger bag.

She slipped three hundred dollars into her pocket. *I'll just keep out enough cash for a few days. … Days? What day is it? What do I care? It's summer and I'm home. Well almost. I still haven't found the West Indies.*

The last item out of the backpack was a heavy blue box. Smith & Wesson was printed on it and inside was her father's .38-caliber revolver. *Should I keep my dad's gun with me? No – Yes – No. Better leave it here. It's safe here and I surely don't want it stolen.*

The gun slid into the safe deposit box along with a stack of envelopes. The lid closed and Eva slid it back into its shelf. The safe deposit box key was added to the chain with the bike lock key.

Leaving, Eva studied the bank lobby, trying to remember it.

"Don't forget to stop back and give us your new address. Have a nice afternoon, Ms. Johnson." The teller smiled.

Outside the bank, Eva turned her bike north and rode towards the burger stand. Cars zipped by on South Atlantic Avenue.

"I could use another Coke with lots of ice to put under my hat. That should cool my brain for a few minutes." Talking to herself, she peddled faster. "And I'll buy momma cat another fish sandwich and maybe some milk."

Down the street, a horn blared and brakes screeched. With a thud, something tumbled into the curb. A car sped away.

Eva stared at the accident and peddled faster. "Oh no. Please, God. Don't let it be the momma cat. Not her."

Cars rushed by, not noticing the little lump of fur in the gutter.

Before the bike stopped, she hopped off, letting it tumble into the sand. Eva knelt beside the momma cat lying motionless in the gutter. Touching her, there was no cry of pain, no motion, and no sign of life. In the gutter, blood oozed into the sand. The cat's neck was snapped and its skull cracked.

"Come on, momma cat, open your eyes." Trying hard not to believe the cat's fate, Eva kept petting it, hoping it was just stunned and would move again if stroked. "Please don't die. Your babies need you. Wake up momma cat."

But Eva's subconscious knew there was no hope for the mother cat. No amount of petting could bring the cat back and the kittens would slowly die of starvation without their mother.

Tourists leaving the burger stand looked the other away. Cars zoomed by, blowing sand into the puddle of blood.

Sobbing, Eva carefully lifted the furry calico body and carried it into the shade, laying it beside the dumpster. With a broken board, Eva dug a proper grave, like the one she had made for her own beloved Princess, killed weeks before by ant poison. The Florida sand was easier to dig than the dense Ohio soil but her hands ached the same and Eva's heart weighed just as heavy for this little stray as for her own pedigreed cat.

"Poor momma cat." Weeping, Eva looked at the dumpster. "Don't worry, I'll take care of your kittens. I promise. I know what it's like to be all alone in the world without your parents."

Eva rubbed her forehead, echoing the pain of her head hitting her Blazer's steering wheel. Pools of water filled her eyes. Her arm throbbed and her chest ached with each sob. A queasy sensation, like rolling down a steep hill, gripped her stomach. Vague feelings fought to be remembered but Eva's feverish mind couldn't grasp them; it was fighting for its own survival. The memory of her auto accident was lost in the growing fog of her strange illness.

"Here kitty, kitty." Talking to herself, Eva pulled sand from under the dumpster. "I have to find them. I won't leave them to die, all alone."

~ 7 ~

Red taillights flashed. A backing-beeper warned. Forked tongs lowered towards the dumpster, banging its side.

"Hey, you. Get away from there!" A big man munching an unlit cigar leaned out of his garbage truck.

Eva pulled her head out from under the dumpster. "Wait!"

"Got no time. I'm running late." His arm waved. "Move away. If that dumpster slips, you'll be squashed flatter than a cockroach."

Eva ran to his window. "Please wait. I have to get the kittens out from under the dumpster."

His lips rolled the cigar. "Kittens?"

"A car killed the momma cat. I'm trying to find her kittens."

"Your cat?"

"No. But I can't let the kittens die of starvation." Eva looked up at his rugged face. Sweat rolled below his stained ball cap.

"Stop crying, Missy. I'll take a look see." He grabbed a flashlight and turned off the motor. Giant boots stepped into the sand. "If they're not in the way, I'll just lift the dumpster off them. I'll have them out in a flash. You'll see."

"The momma cat came out on the other side but I heard the kittens meowing back there, in the corner. I can't reach them."

"Not a good idea to reach under these things. No telling what's lurking there." After banging on the side with his scarred hand, he kneeled in the sandy trench she had dug. The flashlight shined into the corner where hungry meows echoed.

"Do you see them?" Eva peeked underneath.

"Yep. Them kitties are way back there. No problem. They're away from the edge. I'll just lift this bucket, nice and easy."

"Can I help?"

"Missy, I've been doing this for years. Don't need no help." He flipped the flashlight into the bib of his overhauls. "Just stand over there and watch a pro in action."

Back inside his garbage truck, he slowly backed up and realigned it. Like a fine seamstress, he threaded the lifting forks into the eye of the brackets. Slow and steady the heavy dumpster lifted up. Holding the container a foot off the ground, he leaned out the garbage truck window. "Do you see them little kitties?"

"Yes, they're over here."

"Wait. I have to make sure there's nothing else in that stuff." After putting the dumpster down out of the way, he hopped out and grabbed a broomstick mounted on the truck's side. Like mixing a batter of cake, he swirled the stick through the trash, breaking up lumps of paper. "Surprising how much sharp stuff winds up under these things. Don't want your little hands getting all cut up."

In the corner, meows cried from inside a discarded hamburger patty box. From under a torn napkin, two heads lifted and moved towards the light but their eyes were still closed. Stepping into the trash, Eva scooped them up. "There are two of them. Poor babies. Don't worry, I'll find you a home."

"Don't look at me." The garbage man bent over and stroked the kittens. "If I bring home any more strays, my wife says I'll be sleeping in the dog house." He laughed patting his bulging belly. "And, I don't fit anymore."

"Thanks for saving their lives. Can I pay you for your time?"

"No, Missy. You'll need your money to feed those hungry kitties." He stepped back. "Enough chitchat. I've got my rounds to finish. Tis the season of summer trash."

"Thanks again." She hugged the two kittens: one the color of sand and the other a calico like the mother cat. Moving into the shade, Eva watched the garbage man empty the big trash container, swing it back into place and drop the emptied dumpster into the sand with a thud. With a screeching jerk, the prongs pulled free and the truck rumbled away. A hand waved from the window.

"Well, kitties, we're on our own. How about some milk for you and a nap for me?" After placing the kittens in her backpack, Eva flipped open her tablet of notes. "That place where I bought my newspaper had milk. Now where's that number-store?"

A few minutes and a short bike ride later; Eva was wandering the aisles of a Seven-Eleven store shopping for cat supplies.

With the kittens in her backpack, she whispered to them. "We have canned milk, an eyedropper, a basket for your bed, and … darn, I forgot to get Motrin. I'd forget my head if it weren't attached. Now that's an idea. I'd feel better without it. There could be advantages to losing your head." She laughed.

In the home remedy section, the labels blurred and the print seemed to vibrate. "I think my flu is back. My body aches all over," Eva mumbled rubbed her forehead. "If I could massage my brain, that would make it feel better."

A man beside Eva glanced over his glasses at her. Shaking his head, he chuckled and quickly moved to another aisle.

"Don't take it personal, kitties. He just thinks I'm acting a bit crazy. … Bet he never had a headache like this."

"What'd you say?" Asked the checkout clerk.

"Coke. I'll take a bottle of Coke. A big cold one."

"Diet or Regular?"

"Regular. That diet sweetener gives me a smashing headache." She handed him a twenty. "Make sure it's regular Coke."

Fifteen minutes later, Eva rode down a concrete ramp to the beach and headed south. Cars with blaring radios passed and noisy motorbikes rumbled among the traffic cruising the beach. Seagulls screeched as they flew overhead.

"Kitties, we need a quiet place to nap. How about the sand dunes down there near those beachfront homes? Look! ... Look at that. A flagpole ... well, actually it's a ship's mast rising from the sand dunes. But it looks familiar, I think." Eva aimed her bike towards the flagpole. "We'll stop there. Both of you need to eat and I'll feel better after I have a little nap."

Her feet peddled faster and her mind slipped into neutral. After a time, the wheels sank into the soft dry sand near the dunes and stopped. "Sea oats. I've always liked them. They remind me of my early days on the beach. And that flagpole looks familiar. Maybe the West Indies is around here somewhere."

Carrying her bike, Eva walked over the sand dune and parked it on its kickstand. "This is a good place. We can't hear the noisy beach traffic and we're out of sight of the home behind us."

The kittens meowed.

"Y'all sound hungry." Eva lifted them from her backpack and put them in their new basket lined with a soft, fluffy hand towel. She popped open a can of condensed milk and fed the kittens with an eyedropper until they dropped off to sleep, their little bellies bulging.

"Nap time." Eva gently laid them back in their basket and covered it from the sun. "We need some more shade. It's not good to be in the boiling midday sun. Only tourists do that." With a flap, she unfolded a white sheet and draped it over the bike, making a crude tent. Clothespins secured the fabric to the bike fender and she clipped the other end to the rope on the old flagpole.

Above her, a storm warning flag flapped.

An alarm rang inside the backpack, reminding her.

"Okay, I'll take my medication." Eva scooted into the shady tent. She swallowed a prescription capsule and two Motrin with a swig of Coke. Growing groggy from the medication, she took off her sunglasses and curled up beside the kittens. The cold Coke bottle lay against her hot forehead.

In the northeast breeze, the dry sea oats waved like tan flags stuck into the crest of the dunes. At first, Eva watched the sea oats swaying and then she looked down their tall slender shaft to the sparkling grains of dry sand tumbling across the dune.

It is so peaceful and quiet here. The blowing sand looks like snow drifting in a blizzard, so cold and stinging. With her head sinking into the soft sand, her eyes closed and her muscles became motionless. Images of a familiar dream flashed in Eva's mind. *I remember this dream. It's the Siberian one. It's my favorite.*

I can feel the cold creeping through my body, into my bones, and slowly freezing me. I'm lying on the sparkling snow and look east to the pale sun rising over the flat Siberian horizon. It's so beautiful, so quiet, and I feel no pain, just tranquility. In the distance, the Ice Palace is waiting for me, shimmering like sparkling diamonds. I want to go but my body won't move.

I feel a tear roll down my cheek and watch it freeze before it hits the ground. On impact, the droplet shatters into millions of pieces, each sparkling with a rainbow of colors. I watch them blow towards the Ice Palace. I want to go with them.

Beside me red blood oozes into the pure white snow. No one is left in this frozen place but me, and I, too, will soon be gone. I exist only in my mind; free of the pain and filled with serene blissfulness. My soul is moving towards the sparkling Ice Palace. I feel myself slipping to the other side.

~ 8 ~

Late afternoon at the beach – August 19th

"You look troubled. What's eating you?"

"Nothing's wrong, Dad." Mark Reining sat at the dining room table of his parent's oceanfront home, developing a lesson plan for a hypothetical police case to challenge his class. The *Daytona News Journal* was open to the article about the prior night's murder. But after his morning class, Mark had gotten more details from Officer Bob White at the burger stand. They were grim details about an elderly aunt being killed by her only nephew. Greed had driven the nephew and stupidity got him caught.

Mark laid the "Aunt Killer" article aside. Murder was not the topic for his summer quarter, missing persons was the subject. But Mark found nothing in his clipping file to spark an idea for a new lesson. *If nothing's wrong, why can't I think of a new case study?* Mark wondered. *The students can learn the basics by just reading the books. I want to teach them to develop a gut level feeling for –*

"Something's gnawing at you." Fritz poured a cup of coffee for his son and slid it across the table. "You've been sitting there, staring at that blank computer screen for an hour, and haven't typed a word. So what's your problem?"

"Professor's block."

"What in blazes is that?"

"It's when a professor can't think of how to reach his students. My mind is a total blank. I've run out of ideas." Mark powered off his laptop computer, flipped it closed, and stared out the front windows at the sand dunes. The sea oats waved in the northeast breeze like a friend calling and the storm warning flag flapped from the top of the ship's mast flagpole.

Maybe I should get another job: a crew hand on a shrimp boat or a construction worker. Good physical labor, just muscle and sweat. No lessons to prepare, no papers to publish, no faculty meetings, and no grumpy academic deans.

Fritz pushed his chair back. "Son, when I'm out of ideas, I go fishing. Especially since I didn't catch a decent fish this morning. We may have to eat that cheese fluff for dinner."

"Cheese soufflés. No way!" Mark frowned. "We better hit the surf. Those fish should be hungry by now."

Beside Mark, an old bucket with a dog-chewed rope handle dropped on the floor. An eager tail lashed against the table and big, brown eyes stared up from the tan fur of a German shepherd.

"Did you hear the magic word? Fishing." Mark slipped the collar and leash on his dog. "Okay, Rex. You can come. We need someone to guard the bait from the seagulls. And we'll have time for one game of keep-away before dinner."

"Lets get moving. Your mom will be home in a couple of hours." Fritz handed Mark his lucky fishing hat. "You know, if you're tired of being a professor, we could always buy a boat and take tourists fishing."

"I didn't say I was tired of teaching." Mark walked out the door and across the deck towards the ocean. The breeze was stronger than usual and the storm warning flag was flapping.

Fritz walked behind his son. "Looks like that northeaster is fixing to blow in. We'll have to batten down the hatches tonight."

Mark looked north. Cutting across the tropical blue sky was a dark squall line with flashes of lightning. "As soon as the wind shifts this evening, she'll roll in, full steam!"

Dry sand blew across the walk's weathered wooden planks.

On the sand dunes, sea oats bent in the wind. In formation, a flock of pelicans headed towards the calm Halifax River and a safe harbor on one of the low sandy islands near the inlet.

Rex dashed ahead with his leash trailing behind.

"What's your hurry, boy? The fish will wait for us." Mark watched his dog, sniffing the ground intently. "What's wrong, Rex? Did something stray across your sand?"

"Be careful of those land crabs." Fritz laughed. "The last one nipped your paw. I guess old police dogs have a nose for trouble."

Sniffing the sand, Rex disappeared over a sand dune.

"Rex," Mark called. "Rex!"

Whining, he returned, sand stuck to his snout.

Mark reached for the leash but Rex pulled away, barking. "Did you find a new toy to play with?"

"If we can't eat it for supper, we're wasting our time." Fritz paused by the edge of the wooden walk.

"Come on Dad. Let's check it out." Rex is too excited for it to be another land crab."

"Can't be very big. I don't see any tracks."

With each gust of the northeast wind, sand blew south as if it was trying to escape the approaching storm. Beach grass rustled and wild morning glories began to close their blooms.

Rex stood on a dune, eyeing what lay below.

"What'd you find? ... A bike?" Handlebars sparkled as Mark walked to the top of the sand dune. "Hey, Dad. Check this out."

Fritz looked down. "A bike and a body. Is it dead or alive?"

A small body laid curled in the shade under a sheet clipped to their flagpole and stretched over a blue bike. A straw hat covered the face and a beach towel covered the body.

Mark stepped closer. "It's been here for some time, the tracks have been covered by the blowing sand, and it hasn't moved yet.

Could be a teenager stoned on drugs. Better let Rex check it out. Rex, go boy."

Although his days of being a police dog were over, he still remembered his training. Circling, he watched the body for sudden movements or the sign of a weapon. Investigating, Rex sniffed the backpack for that distinct smell of drugs. His ears twitched, his head snapped left, and his nose moved closer to a faint sound.

"Is that wagging tail a police dog signal?" Fritz kidded.

"Yep, that's a code K-9. A wagging tail and twitching ear mean approach with caution. ... Here, take my cell phone. We may need the beach patrol if that kid gets violent. Never can tell what someone on drugs will do." Mark walked down the sand dune and cautiously stepped in front of the body. There was no sign of a weapon, but most of the figure was covered with a beach towel.

"Hey, kid. Wake up."

Something under the fabric moved. Rex hopped back.

That's no kid. Mark studied the legs sliding out from under the beach towel. *She has nice legs, perfect except for the bruises. Must have fallen off her bike a few days ago.*

"Lady, wake up!" Mark watched a straw hat lift from the sand. "Don't you know it's against the law to sleep on the beach?"

"I wasn't sleeping." Eva Johnson slipped on her sunglasses and slowly sat up. "I was just resting my eyes."

"Must have been a long nap. Your tracks have vanished."

"I walk lightly." Eva pulled her hat down and tied the strings under her chin. "Looks like the wind is picking up. Do you think a northeaster is brewing?"

"Could be." Mark pulled Rex back. "Sounds like you're from around here. Do you live nearby?"

"Does this sand dune belong to you?"

"It belongs to my father. ... I'm Mark Reining." He reached for her and pulled her up. *Must be a nice breeze under there. Her hand is cool. And, she seems a bit shy, hiding under that hat and big sunglasses. I wonder if she's a celebrity of some sort. ... Not likely. They wouldn't be sleeping on the sand or riding an old bike.* Mark smiled at her. "What's your name?"

"Eva Johnson. I apologize for falling asleep on your sand." She dusted off her rolled up navy-blue slacks. "It's just the little ones needed a nap after eating and I must have dozed off."

On the ground, something wiggled under the towel. Whining, Rex pulled at his leash, trying to get to it.

"Little ones?"

"Yes. Very little ones. Just a few weeks old. Twins. I think your dog wants to play with them." Eva patted Rex's furry head. "Good boy. Remember, they're just babies."

"He's good with children." Mark pulled Rex's leash tighter.

"They're kittens." She pulled back the towel, revealing a sandy colored kitten and a spotted calico.

"Oh. Well, he's good with cats too. Aren't they too young to be away from their mother?"

"She was killed in a car accident. I couldn't leave the kittens under the dumpster. They needed someone to look after them, 'til I can find them a good home." Eva picked them up and turned to Mark. "Would you like two adorable little kittens? Your dog seems fond of them."

"Mark," Fritz called. "I'm going on down to the beach. Looks like we'll need extra fish for dinner."

"Right. I'll be there in a few minutes." Mark glanced at his father, who was nodding his approval. *Dad is too trusting when it comes to strangers.* Mark turned to Eva. *But she looks harmless and very attractive, but a bit thin. She could use a good meal.*

The sheet flapped as Eva unclipped it from her bike.

"Eva, would you join us for dinner? We're having fresh ocean fish." Mark held out his fishing rod.

Folding the small sheet, Eva glanced towards the house. "I wouldn't want to impose on you guys."

Mark listened to her soft voice. *Sounds like she's a little nervous about eating with strange men. In our old fishing gear, we must look a bit scruffy.* Mark kneeled beside Rex, rubbing his dog's head. "It's no imposition and Mom would enjoy having a woman to talk with. Also, those kittens will be getting hungry and there's a big pitcher of milk in the refrigerator."

Eva hugged the kittens. "They could use some fresh milk."

"Then I'll give them a nice big bowl of milk for dinner. In the meantime, you can wait on our deck. There's a big lounge chair up there and an umbrella for shade."

Packing up her gear, Eva studied the ocean. "It's low tide. That's the best time to look for shells. I always find some nice ones on the edge of the shallow slues."

"Here, let me help you." Mark pushed her bike over the sand dune. "What kind of shells do you collect?"

"Sand dollars and angel wings are my favorite. They're both so fragile and yet, somehow, they manage to survive the pounding surf. That amazes me." Eva tucked the kittens into the backpack and tied it inside the wire basket on the back of her bike.

Mark watched. *She's as pale as a sand dollar and looks as fragile as angel wings. Eva must have a tender heart to match. Most people wouldn't bother with two stray kittens.*

"Are you and your dad fishing for Mullet?"

"We're not choosy. Whatever strikes the hook, we reel in. It adds variety to the menu." Mark studied her. *I wish she would take off that hat and big sunglasses. I'd like to see the rest of her face.*

After reaching the hard sand, they walked around the passing cars to the water's edge. The sound of traffic and the pounding surf filled the awkward lull in their conversation.

Stopping beside the bait box, Mark pounded a stake deep into the sand and leashed Rex to it.

Eva looked south. "The traffic on the beach has picked up."

"Low tide is the best time to drive on the beach. It's wide and firm as long as you stay out of the soft sand and the ocean." Mark pointed at two motorbikes splashing through the waves. "That's a dumb thing to do. If the patrol spots them, they'll get a lecture."

Eva shook her head. "I once saw a tourist park his car in the surf and wash it with buckets of salt water. The tide was rolling in and pulling sand out from under the tires, sinking them. It took two tow-trucks to pull his car out of the surf. The ocean almost won."

"Yep." Mark chuckled. "One of my students is a beach patrol officer. Bob has some astonishing tales about the crazy things people do at the beach and the things they leave behind."

"You're a teacher?"

"Actually, I'm a professor." He pulled an object from his hatband. "Here's my card."

Smiling, Eva studied it. "Do you always carry a business card in your fishing hat?"

"Only the waterproof kind. They come in handy. If someone looks like a potential student, I give them one of my university cards." Mark pulled bait from the bucket. "Are you interested in taking any college courses here in Daytona?"

Eva looked up the beach. "I'm interested in finding some seashells before dinner."

"Dinner. Well, in that case, I better hit the surf and start fishing." Mark backed into the ocean.

She looked at his card again. "Mark. Good luck fishing."

Wading into the surf, he watched Eva strolling north along the water's edge with her bike. *This will be an interesting evening. She strikes my fancy. Petite, cute, and a little shy.*

"Watch it." Fritz put out his arm, stopping his son. "You're walking into my line."

"Are the fish biting?" Mark cast out beyond the breakers.

"Two nice ones so far." Fritz showed off his catch. "You know, that little lady you found reminds me of you and your sister. Always rescuing strays and injured creatures: cats, seagulls, and crabs. Even that dumb hammerhead shark."

"Yeah. I'll never forget Mom screaming when she found it swimming in her bathtub." Mark chuckled. "Good thing you returned it to the ocean. I think Mom would have fried it if you wouldn't have saved that little rascal's life."

Fritz pulled up his fishing line with an empty hook. "I have to confess, I used it for bait. I didn't think the world needed any more hammerhead sharks. Bad for the tourist business."

"But they don't attack swimmers."

"Makes no difference. A shark is a shark." Fritz baited his hook. "But I have no objection if you want to ask your lady friend and her kittens to supper."

"I already invited her to dinner." Looking north, Mark spotted Eva wading in a shallow pool of water near the shoreline. Bending over, she pulled something from the water and seemed to study it before putting it in her pocket.

"If you spend all your time watching her, we aren't going to have anything to feed her."

"Right. I'll catch a big one for her. She looks like she could use a good meal." Mark cast his line further out into the ocean.

"Son, you need bait if you want to catch something."

"I'm not trying to catch her. I just invited her to dinner, that's all. Just dinner."

"I was talking about your hook. You'll need to bait your hook if you're planning to catch anything. No bait, no fish, no dinner."

Mark reeled in the empty hook. "Just practicing my cast."

"Right. How about doing it with a baited hook. You did remember to bring some bait with you, didn't you?"

"Of course. You make it sound like I'm some moonstruck kid. She's just coming to dinner." Mark glanced up the beach and watched Eva walking her bike along the shoreline. *She seems so at home on the beach. I wonder if she lives nearby. ... That's an idea. I'll take her home in my Jeep so I can find out where she lives. By the time we finish dinner that storm will be rolling in. Can't let her ride her bike home in a thunderstorm. ... By the time the evening is over, I'll know all about Eva Johnson.*

Watching his son, Fritz reeled in his line and another fish. "You seem as interested in Eva as Rex. He's watching her too."

Guarding the bait box on the beach, Rex pulled at his leash.

A sports car pulled away and someone tossed small firecrackers at the nearby seagulls. In panic, a flurry of soft, gray wings took flight. Feathers fluttered to the ground.

The crack of exploding gunpowder echoed down the beach like gunfire.

~ 9 ~

Booms erupted from the exploding firecrackers as they rolled across the beach. Panicked seagulls took flight; feathers fell.

Was that a gunshot? Eva jerked her bike's handlebars. Wisps of gray smoke carried the stench of sulfur. *I smell gunpowder.*

A sports car splashed through a wave. More firecrackers spewed out of the side window. Two exploded and the others sank into the surf, like depth charges.

Don't those guys know it's not the fourth of July yet? Its only June ... I think. Eva rubbed her forehead. *Or is it July? No, can't be. Crazy girl. How could I forget my birthday? My memory isn't that fuzzy. Is it? Anyway, I remember my childhood at the beach and it's summer. I'm glad to be home. Home again.*

A flock of gulls flew past and landed on a low sandbar.

Good idea. The sandbar will be safer. Carrying her bike, Eva waded through the shallow water between the beach and the sandbar. *A slue*, she thought. *Is that the right word? A slue is the valley area between two sandbars. I remember playing in the warm water of the slues as a child.* Eva studied the aquamarine water. *Slue rimes with blue. ... Slue has to be the right word.*

Small fish darted between her feet. "See those, kitties? Those are baby mullet fish. They like to play in the warm water of the slue. But don't worry, the tide will be back."

After parking her bike on the sandbar, Eva moved the sleeping kittens into the shady corner of the backpack. They were too young to be interested in fish, even minnow sized mullet.

"We'll just rest here for a few minutes." Talking to the kittens, Eva looked down the beach and spotted two fishermen standing chest high in the ocean beyond the breakers. "I wonder if he's catching any fish. You know, he seems like a nice guy. He's a teacher like me. What's his name? Where did I put his card?"

Searching through the backpack, Eva found his waterproof business card. With her Bic pen, she made a hole in it and slipped it on the chain around her neck. "Now I won't lose his card. I don't want to forget Mark's name during dinner. Mark Reining. That's a nice name."

Reaching down, Eva pulled an olive shell from the soft sandy bank of the shallow slue and studied the lines on its smooth surface looking like a fisherman's net.

Eva glanced back at Mark casting his fishing line into the ocean and down at his business card. *Professor Mark Reining. He's so ... what's the word? Handsome, cute, rugged ... no, manly.* Eva blushed. *My, my let's not get carried away. He only offered to feed my kittens. Just southern hospitality, that's all.*

Eva stroked his business card dangling on her key chain. "Professor Mark Reining. I should be able to remember that; maybe and maybe not." She laughed, opening the palm of her left hand, revealing two notes. "Feed kittens" was printed on the top of her palm and "find home" was written on the bottom. In black letters, the ballpoint pen added a new note between them: Mark Reining. "Good. Now if I forget at dinner, I can just sneak a peak at my hand. What would I do without notes?"

With her bike parked behind her, Eva sat on the damp sandbar and put her feet in the clear water of the slue. "That feels good; just the right temperature. Not too hot, not too cold; just right for Goldilocks." She pushed her blond hair up under her straw hat.

Looking at the still water of the slue, Eva studied the odd image in the reflection. *Why can't I remember?* Eva pondered.

How did I get that awful bump on my forehead? Was it when Jim shoved me into the raspberry patch? Did I file that restraining order against Jim? And what will he do when he finds out?

Her troubling thoughts sank back into her unconsciousness as she focused on a little school of fish swimming below. Silvery light shimmered from their sides, sparkling like sequins.

This is where my memories begin. Eva glanced down the beach towards the Ponce de Leon Inlet. The past was a comfort to her. Thoughts of her childhood surfaced to fill the void left vacant by her fuzzy short-term memory that now resembled Swiss cheese with small holes like the Amish make.

I remember walking in the shallow waters of the inlet. I was spellbound by all the life around my feet. Baby crabs, small fish, and pretty little shells. It was low tide and I waded way out through the slues and over the sandbars. It was awesome discovering so many little creatures living in the giant ocean.

Minnow size fish darted behind her legs and paused a moment to nibble plankton in the shady water before moving on. Shadows crossed the water. Overhead a long line of pelicans glided south towards the inlet.

"It's good to be home." Eva inhaled the salty air as the warm breeze rippled the rim of her straw hat. Behind her, a ringing mixed with the pounding surf and echoed the throbbing inside her skull. "Better take another pill. Don't want to have a headache before dinner. Dinner with Mark Reining." She smiled and opened her hand, checking her memory against the name written on her palm. It matched. "See, kitties, I can remember – at least a few things. I just have to work much harder at it these days."

Walking back to the bike, she turned off the ringing travel alarm, reminding her to take her medication. A sip of warm Coke washed down the white capsule.

Water trickled across the sandbar. The tide was turning.

"Better get back to the beach side. The two of you are too young for swimming and I don't want to be late." She looked up the beach. The salty haze hung like fog, softening the late afternoon sun. On the northern horizon, a dark band of clouds billowed high in the tropical blue sky.

A wafer-thin wave washed over the sandbar. Eddies of sand swirled in the peaceful warm water of the slue. The influx of cooler ocean water sent the schools of fish scurrying to the safety of deeper areas to wait for the returning tide.

Eva carried her bike back to the beach. "Time to move on, kitties. Which way shall we go? I wanted to go to the inlet today, but we'll get caught in that storm. The rain won't bother me but I know y'all will hate to get wet."

Meows echoed from inside the backpack as if agreeing.

Eva read the note written on the palm of her hand – *Feed kittens – Mark Reining – Find home*. "Okay, kitties. You want to go to Mark's place for dinner. I'm not hungry but the two of you could use a fresh bowl of milk. And maybe Mark can help us find my home." Looking south, she spotted two fishermen in the surf and headed towards them as she repeated Mark's name.

Cars meandered slowly up and down the beach. Wearing hats, an older couple ambled past with the aid of canes. A jogger with sweating bronze skin dashed around the elderly couple.

Three young children played at the water's edge. The youngest piled sand around his massive fort, making a wall of sand. A girl collected shells in her pail and the older boy dashed through the slue, chasing fish. Their mother sat on a beach chair reading a book while her husband typed on a laptop computer.

Eva pulled two objects from her pocket and walked over to the little girl. "You can add these to your collection. They're called netted olive shells. See the fine dark lines look like a fishing net."

The wide-eyed girl took them and carefully laid them in her pail. A shy smile beamed on her face and she ran to her parents.

Eva watched the girl showing her mother what she had found. *That's about the age I was when I discovered the wonders of the ocean. These are the days she'll always remember.*

A reddish sports car weaved through the beach traffic. From its open windows, jarring music roared out.

A wave of panic swept over Eva. Hopping on her bike, she rode south towards Mark who was wading in from the surf.

Splashing through shallow water, the car chased seagulls off the sand. The horn blared and voices shouted as hands banged against the side of the car.

"Those guys must be drunk." Peddling faster, Eva watched the sports car circle around and head towards a dog near a bait bucket. A head leaned out the sports car and a hand pointed at the dog.

Barking, the tan German shepherd yanked at its leash.

They're heading towards – the dog. Mark's dog. Peddling fast, Eva rode between the approaching car and the dog.

"Stop!" She yelled.

Laughter roared over the blaring radio. Firecrackers flung out. A hand emerged from the side window, aiming something.

"Hang on!" Eva slammed on the bike's brakes. Firecrackers exploded around her. Paper stung her bare legs. The bike's front tire hit a hole, snapping the wheel left, flipping it. Her body rolled onto the sand and the bike followed, landing on top of her. Her legs tangled under its frame and the handlebars hit her forehead.

The barking of a dog echoed in her ears as Eva passed out.

~ 10 ~

Dashing out of the surf, Mark raced towards Eva. Lying on the sand, her bike was on top and her legs tangled under its frame. Instinctively, Mark reached to his side; but he was no longer a Secret Service agent and there was no gun for defense.

The smell of gunpowder hung in the air.

Yanking at his leash, Rex barked at the car circling back.

Watching the car, Mark knelt beside her. "Eva, are you okay?"

There was no answer.

Hanging out the sports car's windows, three teenagers shouted obscenities and hurled beer cans and firecrackers in the air. The crack of explosions sounded like gunfire.

As the car lurched forward, Mark stepped in front of Eva. He could not pick her and the bike up at the same time. Mark glanced back at the approaching car, which was heading towards Eva.

Firecrackers hurled from the car rolled towards them.

Mark dropped to the ground, his hands spread for pushups but with Eva's body beneath his chest, shielding her like a Secret Service agent would defend the President. Exploding bits of paper stung his back. A beer can rolled towards them and blew up, showering thin aluminum fragments on the beach.

Flinging sand from its tires, the sports car swerved and cut back into the normal beach traffic.

With the car gone, Mark looked at the slender body lying quietly beneath him. "Eva, are you okay?"

After rolling off Eva, he carefully untangled the bike from her legs. A gust of wind tumbled her straw hat down the beach.

"Eva?" He brushed her blond hair back from her pale face blemished with a bruise on her forehead. *That isn't a new injury. Something hit her head hard. What happened to her?* "Eva? Eva, are you hurt?"

"I'm okay." With a wobble, she lifted her head from the sand and sat up. "I just ... have to ... catch my breath."

Frantic meows cried from the backpack in her bike's basket.

"The kittens. Where are the kittens?"

Having broken free of his leash, Rex was tugging at the backpack. With gentle nudges he tumbled the kittens out onto the wet sand, complaining about the rude awakening and the water.

"The kittens are okay." Mark steadied Eva. "How about you?"

Eva glanced at the kittens beside the bent wire basket. "Fine. But my bike looks like it needs some help."

"What happened?" Fritz rushed up.

"Give me the phone, Dad."

"I already called 911." Fritz handed the cell phone to Mark. "They're on their way."

Up the beach, sirens wailed. Nearby, cars slowed and beach walkers ambled over to investigate.

Fritz knelt beside her. "Are you okay, Eva?"

"I just fell off my bike. That's all. No need for everyone to fuss over me." She pulled her knees to her chest as she sat on the sand. "I can take care of myself. I'm fine."

"But what happened?" Fritz asked.

"A car pulled too close." Looking dazed, she rubbed her forehead. "And ... and I thought I saw a gun."

"A gun?" Mark looked down the beach at the sports car weaving through traffic. "Are you sure?"

"I thought I saw a gun barrel pointing out of the red sports car." She nodded. "I was afraid he was going to shoot your dog."

"Dad. Check Rex."

Mark turned towards the approaching sirens. *I have to warn the beach patrol,* he thought. *Stopping that car is going to be dangerous.* He hit the redial button on his phone. "This is Mark Reining. ... Oh, it's you, Dixie. Tell your beach patrol officers there may be a gun in that maroon sports car they're pursuing down the beach. A witness reported seeing a gun."

Mark stepped away from Eva to answer the police dispatcher's questions. "No, Dixie. I didn't see a gun. I only saw firecrackers and beer cans. ... Right. Tell Bob I'll be waiting."

Clicking off the phone, Mark watched Eva rubbing her forehead. *She seems a little shaken up. I'm sure those were just firecrackers she heard. She probably thought they sounded like gunfire. Someone like her wouldn't know the sound of a gun.*

Kneeling beside Eva, Mark looked for visible signs of blood. There were splotches of wet sand on her long sleeved, white blouse, but no visible wounds. "Did you get hit with anything?"

"I'm all right, really. Just got whacked by the handlebars."

The rescue squad screeched to a halt.

"How did you get that bump on your forehead?" Mark asked.

Turning, Eva looking north. "That storm is getting closer. I better get the kittens inside before it rains."

"After the paramedics check you, I'll take you home. Where do you live?"

The paramedics dropped their bags of equipment on the sand. One medic slowly straightened her legs, checking for broken bones or pulled muscles. The other medic took Eva's blood pressure and pulse as he talked to her.

Mark listened to them asking Eva questions and rattling off her vital signs. *Doesn't sound good. She is repeating herself. She sounds confused and could have a mild concussion from the bike hitting her head.* Mark was familiar with medical terms; his mother was a recovery room nurse at the Halifax Hospital. Listening to the paramedics, he knew Eva needed some medical attention.

The medic flashed a light in her eyes. "When you fell, did you lose consciousness?"

Eva blinked. "No. I just –"

"Yes." Mark interrupted. "She was unresponsive when I got to her. Check her for wounds. She thought she saw a gun in the car. And she could have been hit by exploding firecrackers or pieces of the beer can that blew up near us." Mark watched the medics examine her as she brushed sand off her blue slacks, looking as if she was embarrassed by all the attention.

A crowd of beach spectators watched. Some eagerly gave information to the beach patrol officers. One man handed them a Polaroid photo of the suspect car as his children hid behind him.

The paramedic noted her painful response to his touching Eva's arm. "No obvious gunshot wounds, but we'll tell the doctor to check for them." Nodding to Mark, the medic checked Eva's blood pressure again. "93 over 65. It's dropping. The doctor will need a few x-rays. We have to take her to the hospital."

"No." Eva pulled her arms close to her sides. "I don't want to go to the hospital. I'll take care of myself. Just give me something for my headache and a few bandages."

A stretcher scooted beside her.

"Eva." Mark knelt next to her. "The paramedics are just doing their jobs. A doctor needs to tell them you're okay."

She looked at the stretcher. "But it's a long way over to the Halifax Hospital. It'll take me hours to walk back."

Mark watched her holding her side, taking shallow breaths. *She needs a couple of x-rays and some medical attention. She shouldn't be so stubborn about getting medical help.* Gently, Mark touched her shoulder. "It'll just take the doctor a few minutes to check you. And I'll pick you up afterwards."

"No. I don't like hospitals. Besides, I'm fine."

"Eva. I'll have my mom meet you at the hospital. She's a nurse there. You don't need to be afraid. It'll just be a quick check up." Mark helped the medics move her to the stretcher. "I'll pick you up and we'll have dinner at my place."

"That reminds me." She glanced at the note written on her left hand. "I have to feed the kittens. So I can't go to the hospital."

"Dad will take care of them." On Mark's nod, the medics carried the stretcher to the rescue squad. "We'll take care of the kittens and your things."

"But, I'm fine, really. There's nothing wrong with me." Her arm waved, and black and blue marks showed from under the sleeve as it slid up. A spot of blood oozed from a dry scab near the bump on her forehead. "I just rolled over a cliff."

"Cliff?" Mark looked at the flat, sandy beach where she fell and back at the paramedics, shaking their heads.

"Sir, we need to go." The paramedics slid the stretcher into the back of the rescue van. "Don't worry. The doctors will take good care of her."

As the doors closed, Eva covered her eyes. With its siren blaring, the rescue van headed towards the beach access ramp.

As Mark watched it pull away, a rusting white car with no doors pulled next to him. "Professor Reining, we could use Rex's help. He used to be one of our top dogs in running down wayward drunks. We may need him if these dudes take to foot."

With his tail wagging, Rex hopped in the back seat on command. His ears twitched, his head poked into the front, and his tail wagged. For a retired police dog, sirens mean excitement and work to be done. Rex loved a good chase.

Sliding in the passenger's seat, Mark studied the modified car with two surfboards mounted on top of the roll bars making an odd roof. "Bob, is this some sort of undercover beach patrol car?"

"We're short one cruiser, so I volunteered my dune buggy. I get to wear cutoffs on the job that way. The chief doesn't want to be embarrassed by having a uniformed officer in this dune buggy." Bob shifted gears. "Dispatch said you reported a possible gun involved with the firecracker kids."

"All I saw were firecrackers and exploding beer cans. But Eva thought she saw a gun." Mark buckled his seat belt. "There were three, possibly four drunk teenagers in the maroon sports car. We need to get them off the beach before they hurt someone else."

"Don't worry, Professor. We have them boxed in. There's a cruiser at each beach ramp." Bob pulled a portable siren from under his seat. A flip of his left hand plunked the siren on top of the surfboard and he flicked on its flashing light but not the sound. "We're slowly herding the suspects south to the corral."

"The corral?"

"Yep. It's something new we're trying. The chief went to a Texas dude ranch on his vacation. Need I say more? Anyway, just beyond the last beach ramp we've set up a roadblock. No one can drive forward and there's no place to go, the ocean is on one side and the soft sand dunes on the other. We'll drive in from their rear, closing the corral door."

"Sounds like a creative approach to law enforcement."

"Yep. You know the chief. He'll do most anything to make sure the tourists are safe and still get his suspect. I helped him fake that auto accident to rescue the kidnapped woman from a motel a while back. It was better than the movies. Almost made me want to become a stunt driver."

Mark looked at all the parked cars on the beach. Near them sunbathers laid on towels, children dug in the sand, and teenagers played volleyball; all of them unaware of the danger. A high-speed chase after a drunk driver on the beach could be lethal. "Does this new corral procedure work?"

"It worked in practice." Bob pulled around a slow moving van blocking his view. "Haven't tried it in a real situation."

"That's them." Mark pointed at the maroon sports car weaving through traffic, pulling close to parked cars. Bare-chested teenage boys leaned out the side window and whistled at the pretty girls, sunbathing. Being ignored, the driver pulled back into traffic.

"Good. They're heading towards the last exit and the corral." Bob radioed to the patrol cars silently slipping in behind him.

Mark reached to his side. But there was only a bag of bait in his left pocket, no weapon. *Old habits die hard. It's been almost two years since I left the Secret Service and I still reach for my gun. Maybe I should join the beach patrol auxiliary so I can carry a gun. ... No, that's not practical. A professor doesn't need a gun.*

Watching his student, Bob, reminded Mark of how he had been: eager, overconfident, and trusting in the law to protect the innocent – too trusting. Trust cost Mark's sister her life.

~ 11 ~

Ahead, lights flashed on a line of police cruisers blocking the beach near the Ponce de Leon Inlet. The massive boulders of the jetty formed a barricade for both the sea and for vehicle. There was no way around the jetty. And the access ramp to the right was barricaded. The ocean was to the left. Behind the maroon sports car, cruisers drove four abreast, closing off any escape.

"Now we'll close the corral." Bob flipped on the siren. All the other police vehicles responded with their wailing sirens.

The sports car spun in a circle near the forward line of police cruisers. Firecrackers and beer cans showered from its windows.

"Those cans may be filled with firecrackers." Mark grabbed Rex's collar. "Now what are those idiots doing?"

Fleeing, the sports car swerved towards the jetty, splashed through a shallow slue onto a sandbar then headed north.

"Hang on Professor." Bob floored the accelerator. "I have to cut them off. This is MY beach. These dudes are mine."

"Watch the slue!" Mark grabbed the dash.

Salt water splashed inside.

Rex growled.

Bob whipped the steering wheel right. On the narrow sandbar, they headed south.

The sports car raced north towards them.

Mark braced himself. "Now!"

Bob yanked the steering wheel right. A shower of wet sand and water spewed up from the tires, blurring their visibility.

The sports car veered into the surf. Salt water sprayed from its sides. A wake followed behind it. An incoming wave rolled over its sleek hood, smashing against the windshield. The maroon sports car stopped dead in the water.

Mark hopped out. "I'll approach from the back."

"Wait!" Bob jumped behind his car with his gun aimed at the suspect vehicle. "These dudes may be armed and you aren't. This is no time for Secret Service hero stuff. We'll wait for the troops."

Uniformed police officers rushed towards the surf with their weapons firmly clenched in both hands, pointing at the sports car.

"Everyone, out of the car," an officer shouted. "Keep your hands above your heads."

Several bags were flung out the window and fell into the surf.

Yanking at his leash, Rex growled.

"You're right, Rex. Looks like they're dumping drugs." Mark unclipped the leash from his dog. "Fetch."

Leaping through the surf, Rex snatched a bag in his teeth and raced back with the evidence, dropping it beside his master.

Mark opened the plastic bag. "They're dumping marijuana."

"They've got drugs." Bob shouted to the other officers. "They probably are stoned out of their minds. Armed and stupid."

"Out of the car," officers shouted as they approached with their weapons aimed.

Three teenage boys crawled out the windows and staggered through the surf with their hands high. A large wave smacked them in the back. The short one slipped under the surf.

"Go, Rex." Mark waded into the surf. In front of him, a head popped out of the water and sank again. Mark grabbed the teenager's long hair as another wave broke over the kid. Mark lifted the teenager's head out of the foaming surf.

"We'll take him." Two officers grabbed the teenager.

Already on the beach, the other teenagers were sprawled on the sand with their hands cuffed behind their backs.

Rex snatched another bag and returned to the beach.

"Bob, I'm going to check the back." Mark waded towards the car. "I'm sure there were four of them."

"Wait!" Bob shouted.

A wave snacked Mark as he touched the sports car. He knew anyone stoned on drugs could be dangerous and a gun could make them lethal. Mark peeked inside. A foot bobbed in the back and the car was flooding. *He could drown*, Mark thought. *He's just a kid.*

"Professor!" Bob pushed past. His arms snapped into the window and he aimed his gun into the back seat. "Damn!"

Mark looked inside. In the back, a tall lanky teenager was out cold with his arms around a big, brown teddy bear with a pink bow. "Looks like he missed all the action. We better get him out before he drowns in his sleep."

After pulling the fourth teenager and his teddy bear to the beach, they laid him next to a stretcher. Two tow trucks backed up and an officer attached chains to the sports car's back bumper.

"Professor Reining, this would make a good case study for the class. Drugs, beer, explosives, a high speed chase with a splashing end, and a teddy bear for a prize." Bob laughed.

"No, this quarter we're studying missing persons, not teenage stupidity." Mark watched Rex jumping at the sports car's trunk. "I think we've missed something in there."

"Probably more marijuana stashed in the trunk. Let's take a look." Bob turned to a fellow officer. "Get some crowbars. We need to pry the trunk open."

Mark walked to the driver's side, leaned in, and yanked out the car keys. "This will be faster."

Unlocking the hatchback, Rex hopped in and yanked at a blanket covering more plastic bags and a large lump.

"Damn. Another body." Bob's gun whipped out and pointed inside. "Hey guys, we got another one."

"Careful, Bob. The kid can't be more than thirteen."

"Old enough to pull a trigger."

"He doesn't look good." Mark touched the kid's neck artery. "I can't feel a pulse. Better get him out fast."

Mark and Bob pulled the fifth teenager through empty beer cans, bags of marijuana, and girly magazines. Officers carried the unconscious teen to the beach and laid him next to the other four.

"We'll take him." Squatting beside the boy, the paramedic examined the unconscious teenager reeking of marijuana and beer. "Better get this one to the hospital. He's slipping away fast."

Ringing echoed in Mark's shirt pocket. Startled, he pulled out his cell phone. "Hello. ... They what! ... Are you sure? ... Yes, I'll tell them. I'll be over right away."

"Sounded like bad news, Professor. What's wrong?"

Mark glared at the row of handcuffed teenagers. Sprawled on the sand they looked like beached baby sharks. "Did you find any weapons in the car?"

"Not yet. Why?"

"The x-rays showed a bullet in Eva's arm."

"A bullet?" Bob gasped. "She was shot on my beach?"

"You'll have to charge them with attempted murder."

"Professor, no need to tell us our job. If they still have the gun, we'll find it. I'll keep Rex for the search." Bob took the leash. "What caliber was the bullet?"

"Eva was sent down to have a CAT scan." Mark hopped in the back of the rescue squad. "They haven't removed the bullet yet."

~ 12 ~

Fluorescent lights flashed by as Eva looked up from the moving gurney and the dots blurred on the Halifax Hospital's ceiling tile. Trying to avoid the queasy sight, she pulled the sheet over her face.

A nurse pulled the cover back. "We're almost there."

The nurse's soft voice was comforting, but the surroundings looked sinister even to an adult. Lying on a gurney, Eva felt it swerve around another corner in the rat-like maze of hallways. As they passed each doorway, Eva stared into the brightly lit rooms. Diabolical looking machines consumed them and they seemed to murmur eerie greetings. Other gurneys rolled out of doorways with motionless patients looking like life had been drained from them.

"I want to go home." Eva pulled the sheet over her eyes.

"They're just going to do a CAT scan. It's like a big camera." The soft-spoken nurse walking beside the gurney pulled the sheet back. "There's nothing to worry about, Eva."

Easy for her to say, Eva thought as she studied the nurse holding her hand. *I don't want my brain photographed. Besides, there's nothing wrong with it. Just because I can't remember what year it is doesn't mean anything. The year isn't important to me. I live by the seasons. I know it's summer.*

Her head rolled to the side and Eva's thoughts rolled on. *But surely the doctor is wrong. It can't be August. It has to be June. I couldn't have forgotten my birthday and the whole summer. ... No, no. This has to be a nightmare. Like a what's his name, King, horror story. The doctors have to be wrong. I know I'm okay. It's just these sinus headaches.* She touched her forehead, feeling the heat boiling inside her skull.

"Eva, we're going to move you over," the friendly nurse whispered. She and a technician moved Eva onto the machine's cold, vinyl bed.

"I don't need a CAT scan. I just have a sinus headache. Just give me a couple of Motrin and I'll go home."

"The doctor needs a few pictures of your head before he can give you any pain killers. It's standard procedure."

Lying on the machine's platform, Eva jerked her neck sideways to look around. The ominous gray object behind her didn't resemble any camera she had ever seen. Consuming the other end of the platform and most of the room was a giant metallic doughnut-shaped ring. It hummed like it was hungry.

The smiling nurse repositioned Eva's head. "I'm going to put pillows beside your head so it won't move. Now, lie still while they're taking your picture. Maybe you can give one to Mark."

Opening her left hand, Eva looked at the name written on it, Mark Reining, and at the nurse's name tag, Reining. "Mom?"

"Yes, I'm Mark's mother. He called and asked me to meet you." Nurse Reining straightened the sheet. "Mark is on his way over. He'll be here soon."

"Miss Johnson." A medical technician leaned over with a large hypodermic needle. "I'm going to inject a contrast liquid into your veins so we can get a better picture. You'll feel a warm sensation as it flows through your body and your kidneys will feel hot for a bit. It's perfectly normal."

A hypodermic needle pierced Eva's skin like a giant mosquito. She watched it inject a large quantity of liquid into her arm. A sudden, odd warmth rushed thorough her body. But in her brain the liquid was cooler than the fever burning inside her skull.

"Just relax and don't move." The lab technician tucked the pillows tighter beside Eva's head. "The platform will slide through the ring and you'll hear it turning as it takes the photographs. We'll be in the control room watching." Both the lab technician and Nurse Reining retreated behind a thick door.

Slowly, the platform inched backwards, sucking the bed and Eva into the massive, gray metal doughnut.

Eva's muscles relaxed but not her thoughts. *They must have Valium in that concoction. My muscles seem to have melted and my veins feel warm like liquid sunshine is flowing through them. Solar power or is it nuclear in this case? I wonder if they still use radioactive iodine. I hope I won't glow in the dark. ... If this procedure is so safe, why do the technicians hide in that glass control room? ... What's that noise?*

The big silver ring hummed with a rushing sound like a steady ocean breeze. Metallic clicking noises ticked at slow intervals as the ring rotated, shooting photographic beams through sections of brain tissue and skull.

In the control room, slices of Eva's head showed on the monitor. A doctor's fingers pointed at each new image forming on the screen. In a normal patient the circle of skull bone showed white, sinus cavities were black, and soft brain tissue was gray. Notes were recorded on hospital records for further review.

Under the machine, Eva lay motionless but conscious. *This is awfully expensive equipment to be using just to look for a sinus infection. So what are they really looking for? A brain tumor? Cancer? A cerebral aneurysm? No, there is no fever with them. No, a fever has to prove it's just a stubborn sinus infection. Surely they won't find anything. I can relax. I just have a fever.*

Her thoughts dissolved into a tranquil bliss. Eva's mental circuits for worrying were burning out along with her short-term memory.

~ 13 ~

The doors to the Halifax Hospital emergency room banged open. Paramedics rolled a stretcher down the hall. Voices rattled off the patient's condition to waiting doctors. The fifth teenager from the beach lay motionless on a gurney with an IV dripping fluids into his veins and an oxygen mask over his mouth. Beer reeked from his almost lifeless skin.

A nurse stepped behind a man backing from the emergency squad's stretcher. "Mark."

"Mom." Mark Reining spun around. "Where's Eva?"

"She's down this way. Mark, why did you come in with the rescue squad?"

"It was the fastest way to get here." Mark looked down the hall at the doctors treating the teenager. The ride in the back of the rescue squad with an unconscious teen stirred up memories Mark had worked hard to forget. It was inside such a van that he had last touched his sister's hand before she died. Susan's life slipped from Mark's grasp and guilt over his sister's death still gripped him.

I should have protected her. Sis and I were always so close. Why didn't she tell me? Why did she hide her boyfriend's abuse? No, that's wrong. She tried to tell me in her quiet way. I'm to blame. I was too busy being a hotshot Secret Service agent. The early warning signs were there; I should have seen them. If I would have taken charge, I could have saved Susan.

"Mark, you look a little pale. Were you injured?"

"I'm okay." He smiled for his mother. "Now, where's Eva."

"Down there." Nurse Barbara Reining pulled her son aside. "First, we need to have a little talk."

Mark recognized that tone in her voice. Being an ex-Secret Service Agent and now a college professor didn't exempt him from his mother's questions. Mothers are always mothers. "Talk? Is something wrong, Mom?"

"I want to know a few things about this Eva friend of yours. She had very little money in her pockets and no identification. No driver's license, no credit cards, and no insurance card."

"Sounds like the hospital is worried about getting paid." Although his mother worked upstairs in the recovery room, Mark was still angry at the treatment his sister had gotten the night she died. "Well, have Dad check Eva's backpack for her wallet. Wouldn't want the hospital to miss their all important paper work."

"I've already called him. He checked. There was no billfold or identification in her backpack. So, just who is this Eva Johnson?"

"I'm sure Dad already told you. We found Eva sleeping on our front sand dunes." Mark looked at his mother's tightening lips. "Why don't you ask her? What's wrong?"

"We did. She told us her name was Eva Johnson and she lived at the West Indies. But there is no West Indies motel on South Atlantic Avenue and no phone listing for her."

"Well then, we'll just have to ask her again." Mark grabbed the curtain separating him from Eva.

"Wait." His mother pulled him back. "We tried. Her answers are vague and she's confused. She thinks its June, not August. And Eva doesn't even know what year it is."

"What? Eva doesn't know what year it is?" Mark stared at the hospital curtain around Eva. "Are you saying she has amnesia?"

"Not clinical amnesia. She knows who she is."

"She hit her head when she fell off her bike. Maybe she's just a little dazed." Mark studied his mom's face for her reaction.

Frowning, his mother shook her head. "Falling on beach sand wouldn't account for that or all the old bruises on her body. It looks like she's been in an accident, mugged, or beaten."

"Beaten?" Mark closed his eyes, trying not to see the images of his sister's beaten body. "How bad is Eva hurt?"

"Eva has multiple bruises and a bullet in her left arm."

"I can't believe she was shot. I didn't see any signs of blood on her arm. I thought she mistook firecrackers for a gunshot."

"You wouldn't have noticed. The bullet wound is several days old." Barbara pointed to her arm. "It's lodged in the soft tissue of Eva's upper arm. The doctor thinks the bullet passed through something to slow it down." Nurse Reining shook her head. "Bullets do strange things when they enter the human body."

"What caliber is it?"

"Small, but they're not sure. They haven't removed it yet."

"What are they waiting for? Insurance papers?"

"Calm down, Mark. You're beginning to sound like your father. The doctors wanted to look at the results of the CAT scan before they removed the bullet. It's been there for a few days; a few more minutes won't make any difference. Besides, they can't give her a sedative without the results of the CAT scan."

"Why a CAT scan?"

"Many reasons; her response to light, her foggy memory, and her blunt head trauma," Barbara explained.

"What did they find?"

"Nothing." A doctor stepped from behind them.

"Doctor Williams, you remember my son, Mark."

"Yes, Barbara." The doctor held large sheets of x-ray film. "Eva Johnson's CAT scan is inconclusive. No signs of a cerebral hemorrhage or a tumor. And there is no visible brain damage; however, I noticed a slight swelling of the brain."

Mark studied the doctor, tapping the x-rays. "Eva fell from her bike onto the beach. Would that account for her confusion?"

"Not likely. And that wouldn't explain her other symptoms. Eva has a fever, memory problems, and a severe headache. She said she hadn't eaten much, but her blood sugar level is normal and her blood protein level is elevated. That makes me suspicious."

As a Secret Service agent, Mark had learned to read facial expressions. Watching faces in crowds was his business and interpreting body language gave clues of potential danger. Mark studied Doctor Williams clenching Eva's CAT scan negatives as he gave a contemptuous look at a passing doctor. "Doctor Williams, what's wrong with Eva?"

"The other doctors don't agree, but I think Eva's symptoms are remarkably similar to those of viral encephalitis."

"Viral encephalitis?" Mark watched his mother cringe as she turned towards the nursing station. "How serious is that?"

"Depends on which virus is involved. With the milder strains, the mortality rate is about five percent and in more virulent strains the mortality can be forty percent or higher."

"How do you cure viral encephalitis?"

"We don't." Doctor Williams looked down. "Most viruses, like the flu or the common cold, are confined to the body: nose, throat, or lungs. The brain is protected from bacterial and viral infections by the blood-brain barrier. Most of the time that is. But when a virus does pass through that barrier into the brain, we call it encephalitis. We have only a few anti-viral medications. And there are many different viruses that cause encephalitis."

"Do you know which one Eva has?" Mark asked.

"No. Our tests are very limited and sometimes we never know, especially if it's one of the arboviruses. And with no cure, there's no great need to identify the virus involved."

"If there's no cure, what's the treatment?"

"Supportive care. Eva's body will have to kill the virus."

"Are you going to hospitalize Eva until she recovers?"

"That will take time. Hospitals only treat encephalitis patients when they're in a coma or having seizures. Since it not contagious, homecare is the best for them. This illness can be a bewildering experience and hospitals are frightening to a confused person. And for the most part, patients can take care of themselves, under supervision, of course." Doctor Williams glanced at his watch. "I'm sorry, I have a surgery scheduled."

Mark watched Doctor Williams strut down the center of the hall with his white coat flapping. Others gave the tall doctor a wide berth and nodded politely as he passed.

"Mark." Nurse Reining stepped beside her son. "I'm worried. We haven't been able to find Eva's family and they're going to release her after they remove the bullet. She's in no condition to wander around alone."

"Don't worry, Mom, I'll find her family."

"Professor Reining." Bob ambled down the hall, his police badge flapping. "Guess what? That innocent thirteen year old in the back seat had a .22 pistol tucked inside his teddy bear. If I would have gotten shot by a teddy bear, the chief would never let me become a detective. Damn. ... Uh, excuse me, Mrs. Reining."

"Armed teddy bears? What's this world coming to?" Nurse Reining shook her head. "I'm going upstairs to get my things. I won't be long. Mark, don't let Eva leave alone."

"So, Professor, was your lady friend shot with a .22?"

"They haven't removed the bullet from Eva's arm yet."

"It's not that busy in here. What's the hold up?" Bob asked.

"They wanted to make sure Eva didn't have a concussion."

"From falling on the beach?"

Mark glanced at a tray of instruments swishing past. "She was injured before she fell on the beach. Mom said it looked like Eva had been in an accident, mugged, or beaten."

"Mugged?" Bob whipped out a notebook. "I'll have to get to the bottom of that. The chief doesn't take a cotton to anyone messing with our tourists. Did she say who did it?"

"Her memory is fuzzy. She doesn't know what date it is."

"Heck, we all lose track of time."

"That explains why you're usually late to my class." Mark stepped out of the way of a lab technician. "Eva's case is different. She thinks it's still June and doesn't know what year it is."

"Amnesia?" Bob asked. "Is she a Jane Doe?"

"No. She knows her name is Eva Johnson and where she is. The CAT scan ruled out a brain tumor and severe concussion. Doctor Williams suspects Eva has viral encephalitis."

"You mean that Nile fever that killed those birds last year?"

"That was West Nile encephalitis. The doctor didn't mention that one, and I don't remember reading about that this year."

"Sounds like she's pretty sick." Bob wrote a note. "But I'll still need to get her statement. A shooting is a shooting."

"Bob, I need to have you track down her family. She said she lived at the West Indies on South Atlantic Avenue, but there is no such place and her name isn't in the phone book."

"Probably just unlisted. Lots of single women have unlisted numbers." Bob pressed redial on his cell phone, calling police headquarters. "I'll have her phone number and address, pronto."

A nurse approached. "Either of you named Mark Reining?"

"I'm Mark. What is it?"

"Eva Johnson asked for you. She's refusing treatment. You're the only one she'll talk too. We could use your help."

Mark followed the nurse. "Have you removed the bullet yet?"

~ 14 ~

"You've got the wrong patient. I was NOT shot. I just fell off my bike." Sitting on the emergency room table, Eva Johnson pulled the sheet around her shoulders, arms welded tight against her body and her fingers strangling the fabric between them.

"Now, Eva, stop struggling."

"Her blood pressure is going up. BP 140 over 110."

"We have to remove that bullet. You'll hardly feel it."

Eva turned away from the clamoring voices and tucked her chin next to her clenched hands. In a hodgepodge of uniforms, strangers crowded around, moving in nervous jerks. Everything seemed unreal. The medical staffs' touches were cold and clinical. Multiple conversations blurred into confusing mumbles.

"We'll have that bullet out in a minute. Don't fight us."

Fight, Eva thought, scanning the bodies pressing close. *I can't fight. They outnumber me. Besides, they have weapons. Just look at them. They have a whole tray full of knives.*

A cart screeched closer with a tray of cold steel instruments: scalpels, scissors, and clamps. Next to them was a hypodermic syringe, and its needle looked threatening.

"Ms. Johnson. This is an x-ray of your arm. The bullet is that spot, right here." A doctor tapped the negative. "It has to come out. Do you see it?"

Eva squinted at the x-ray held up to the glaring overhead lights. "Looks more like a rock than a bullet. Besides, I think that arm belongs to someone else. I don't recognize it."

"That wound is going to get infected if we don't take the bullet out. Now stop being so stubborn."

"Am not!" Eva watched a nurse reach for a large hypodermic. "What's that for?"

"We're going to give you a tetanus shot. It's required for all deep puncture wounds."

A needle pierced Eva's skin with the finesse of a bloodthirsty mosquito. Her arm jerked back. "I'll skip the rest of this."

A male nurse pried her arm free. "Ma'am, if you relax your muscles, it will be a whole lot easier."

"BP 145 over 115."

"Relax, this won't take long."

"You haven't been listening. You've got the wrong patient. I just fell off my bike." The sheet slipped from Eva's arm. "It wasn't me who got shot. The kid was aiming at the dog. Surely I would know if I had been shot. How could anyone forget being shot?"

"You aren't the first person to be shot and not know it. Now relax. We'll have it out in a jiff."

"I don't want any emergency room surgery." Eva struggled. "I've seen those ER programs on TV. They roll in a half dead patient, chop him open, blood oozes all over, and in the next scene the doctors are eating pizza and singing Christmas carols."

"That's just TV stuff. We're professionals. So just relax!"

A scream shrieked from the other side of the curtain confining Eva. A young man's voice pleaded for his mother.

"That doesn't sound like acting to me." *It's time to flee,* her mind warned. *This is crazy. That's not a bullet in my arm. My mind is a bit fuzzy, but I couldn't have forgotten something like that. How could anyone forget being shot?*

The memory of the gunshot from the red sports car running her off the road had been lost. Both the concussion from the sudden stop and viral encephalitis had fogged her ability to remember.

Eva pulled her foot free. "I don't need any medical help. I can take care of myself. Where are my clothes? I'm going home."

Hands held her on the examining table. Voices, snapping orders for instruments, mingled with side conversations and everyone seemed to ignore the patient. They had work to do: recording her assorted bruises, abrasions, and injuries. Photos were taken. The police required accurate records of all bullet wounds.

"Relax, Eva." A glint of a knife flashed in the doctor's hand.

"Ask him. ...Mark. He'll tell you. I only fell off my bike."

"BP 150 over 120." A nurse grabbed Eva's ankle.

Metal rings on the side curtain screeched as it was pulled back. "Doctor. I'm Mark Reining. You wanted to see me."

"Mark!" Eva squirmed. "Tell them I just fell off my bike."

The doctor glanced at the clock, then at Mark. "We could use your help. If you could get her to cooperate, it'd speed things up. We can't take all day digging out one little bullet."

"You will take as long as needed to treat Eva." Mark's voice cuts sharp. "That's your job."

Eva opened her clenched fist to read the name written on the palm: Mark Reining. *He'll help me get out of here. Then I can go home. He should know where the West Indies is. He can take me there, or anyplace for that matter. This place frightens me.*

"Mark, please tell them I just fell off my bike. I wasn't shot."

"Eva." Mark stepped beside her and looked at the x-ray the doctor was tapping. "There's something in your left arm. Could be a piece of a shell."

"Seashell?" Eva reached for Mark. For her, the others in the room seemed to fade into the curtain surrounding her treatment area. Their medical babble sounded like white noise. Only Mark's friendly face was familiar and comforting. "I did fall on the beach. It could be a piece of a small olive shell."

Mark stroked her right hand and nodded at the doctor. "Or that shell could be an Atlantic auger. Let's have the doctor get it out. Then we'll know what it is."

"Okay. He can take it out. I'll add it my collection." After a needle prick, Eva felt a relaxing sensation roll through her taut muscles, loosening them with sedation. Not warm like during the CAT scan, but at least soothing. Time seemed to pause.

"Blood pressure is dropping, 130 over 95."

Metal instruments clanged leaving the tray. A scalpel flashed out of Eva's sight. The medical staff moved closer, cutting through cracked blood and dead skin to the metal object buried in the soft tissue in the back of her upper left arm.

Studying Mark's face, Eva's thoughts rambled. *Strange, this Mark Reining reminds me of my great grandfather. A broad head with well proportioned features and kind eyes. My dad always said you could judge a man by his eyes. A person's character circles their eyes like the iris rings the pupil. Look into a man's eyes and you'll see his soul, Dad told me. And this Mark has friendly blue eyes. They're a beautiful aquamarine.*

Eva's eyes blinked from exhaustion. Pumping stress-related chemicals through the body required a lot of energy, and that was in short supply after weeks of illness. Eva was losing ground to the virus battling inside her mind.

"BP 115 over 70."

"There it is." The doctor grinned. "See, I was right."

Looking over her shoulder, Eva squinted at the dark object. "What kind of shell is it?"

"9mm." The doctor shook his head. "A rather common shell these days."

"Looks more like a rock than any seashell I've ever seen. Could be a clump of coquina." Eva looked at Mark. "Do you know what kind of shell it is?"

Mark nodded. "I've seen those before. But we'll give it to Bob. He'll have the lab identify it. Eva, you should stay here overnight for observation."

"No way! I can take care of myself." Squirming, Eva's feet slipped over the treatment table. "As soon as I get dressed, I'm out of here. Would you take me home?"

"Sure. Where's your home?" Mark held her arm.

"I live at the West Indies."

"Where's that?"

"It's on South Atlantic Avenue, just beyond the bend."

"We should call your family and tell them we're on our way."

"I don't have a family here."

"Then let me call one of your friends." Mark glanced at his mother approaching, carrying medical supplies.

"I'm on my own, like the kittens. But, if you have something else you have to do, I can take a bus home." Eva slipped off the table and grasped Mark's arm for support.

"Take it easy. It will take a while before that local anesthetic wears off. You should stay with someone tonight."

"I can take care of myself." Eva reached for her clothes that someone had laid beside her. "Mark, you'll have to leave. I need to get dressed."

Nurse Reining pulled the emergency room curtains closed as her son stepped out. "I'm Mark's mother. Remember, we met earlier, during your CAT scan. Mark is right. You shouldn't be alone this evening. We have an extra room and I would feel better if you stayed with us until you're back on your feet."

The emergency room gown dropped to the floor. Eva slipped into her navy-blue slacks, one unsteady leg at a time. With effort, her arms navigated down each long sleeve and Nurse Reining buttoned Eva's white cotton blouse.

"Come and stay with us this evening." Nurse Reining pulled the curtain back and steadied her patient's steps.

Taking Eva's other arm, Mark walked her towards the exit. "You're coming to stay with us."

"Thanks for the kind offer." Eva studied Mark's eyes trying to read the character written around them but their image blurred into two seas of soft blue, swirling around puddles of lamp black. "I don't want to impose. Really, I can take care of myself."

Outside the emergency exit, a black Jeep pulled up. Officer Bob White slid out and tossed the keys to Mark. "I'll call you later, Professor Reining. We'll need her statement about who –"

"Later, Bob. She needs a little rest first." Mark steadied Eva.

Nurse Reining climbed in the back with a pillow, sheet blanket, and a bag of medical supplies.

With a surge of sedatives swishing through her veins, Eva wobbled and then stepped into the Jeep. She was growing oblivious to her surroundings and didn't care where she was going.

Only a glance at her hand reminded her of her obligation: feed kittens. "Where did I leave my backpack? I have to feed the kittens. They're orphans, you know. Poor babies, they have no family." Eva continued to ramble. "I couldn't leave them to starve to death under the dumpster. They're too weak to take care of themselves. Someone has to look after the lost souls of the world."

Mark turned his Jeep towards the peninsula and his home.

"I'm going to take the kitties home." Eva's voice began to fade. "Home to the West Indies."

~ 15 ~

"Mark! ... What are you doing?"

"Mom, don't sneak up on me like that."

"You sound guilty. Did I catch you in the act of snooping?"

"No, I'm looking for some identification." Mark piled Eva's possessions on the dining room table. Everything was neatly stored in zip-style plastic bags of assorted sizes and packed tightly inside her backpack. "How's Eva?"

"Sleeping. She's exhausted, but the IV that Doctor Williams sent along will help her feel better by morning. I still think Eva should have stayed in the hospital. But maybe she couldn't afford to pay." Barbara watched her son searching Eva's backpack. "I didn't raise you to snoop through people's belongings."

"I'm not snooping. I need to know more about Eva Johnson. Surely there's something in here that will tell me who she is so we can notify her family or friends. Someone must be looking for her." That thought concerned Mark for several reasons.

"Let's wait until morning. By then she'll be feeling better and she can tell you herself."

Mark found a bag of seashells tucked in Eva's backpack. "I'm not sure a good nights sleep is going help. You didn't hear Eva arguing with the doctors, insisting she hadn't been shot. Even when they showed her the bullet, she refused to believe it."

"Well, Doctor Williams said she has viral encephalitis. A high fever clouds anyone's thinking and this virus is worse."

"That's why I need to find out who she is, tonight."

Barbara pulled a chair next to her son. "Surely we can wait until she gets better. What's your rush?"

"The bullet they found in her arm. That's the rush. Someone shot her and she doesn't remember it. That means she won't know who did it or why." Mark glanced up at the family portrait on the dining room breakfront. It was the last photo of his family before his sister, Susan, had been murdered. "That means whoever shot Eva is still out there. Looking for her."

"Oh Mark! Don't say things like that. She doesn't look –"

"Mom." He glanced at his mother staring at the family photo. "Looks have nothing to do with it. Anyone can be a victim."

Distant thunder rumbled. Outside, palm branches tossed as the evening wind shifted, pulling the storm close to the beach.

"Where's your father?"

"He's out battening down everything before that northeaster blows in." Looking up, Mark saw the palm trees swaying outside the dining room window, streaked with ocean spray. "It hasn't rained in days. The salt will be thick on the transformers. One of them is bound to blow when they get wet."

"I already have the hurricane lamps out. I hate hearing the transformer arcing, knowing it's going to explode any minute." Cringing, Barbara watched her son opening the bags of Eva's possessions. "Do you really have to snoop through her things?"

"Yes. Her – " Mark swallowed the word – life.

No, he thought. *I don't want to upset Mom. No need to get melodramatic. But, Eva's life could depend upon knowing what happened to her, who did it, and why. Without a memory, Eva can't defend herself. Not knowing who shot her, she could walk into the killer's hands. ... I have to make sure that doesn't happen.*

Mark glanced back at his sister's photo.

"Her what?" Barbara asked her son.

"Eva's private things, Mom. Would you look through them for some identification." Not looking at the pastel fabric and lace, Mark held out the clear plastic bag as if it contained secret stuff.

Barbara took it. "I don't think she has her name and address written on her lingerie like she was going to summer camp. But at least I can tell your dad you didn't get into Eva's panties."

"Mom!"

Laughing, Barbara unpacked the garments. "I swear Mark, you're blushing. You're almost thirty, surely you've seen a lady's lingerie before."

Ignoring the wisecrack, Mark unzipped the backpack's side pockets and removed the contents: a travel alarm, a packet of white capsules, Motrin, and vitamins. Inside another pocket were canned milk and an eyedropper.

Barbara unfolded the silky garments. "Interesting."

"Did you find an ID label on ... one of those things?"

"Identification of what kind of person she is. A nurse can tell a lot about a persons from their under garments. Eva has expensive but conservative lingerie. Feminine but not showy. They're not the kind you wear man hunting. And they're not skimpy enough to flash at an unsuspecting President. ... No. They're the kind of lingerie a refined lady would wear."

"That's a lot of information from such small bit of fabric. I really didn't want a dissertation. Just wanted to know if they were a unique brand. Something I, ... we, could track down."

"You're out of luck there. They can be bought in any better dress shop." Barbara repacked them. "Did you find anything?"

"She brought a CD. Music for meditation is an unusual choice for someone her age. I've never heard of *The Mystic Sea*. Eva seems to have a fixation on the ocean." Mark flipped the plastic CD case over and read the back side. "The write-up says it will relax your mind."

"Might as well check out her taste in music." Mark walked over to his CD player, slid the disk in, and pushed the play button. The soft rush of an ocean, gentle waves breaking, seagulls calling, and string instruments blended. Violins, piano, and subtle sounds merged with the soothing rush of timeless surf. The melodic music echoed from the speakers.

"Sounds more peaceful in here." Fritz stepped in through the living room door.

"Close the door, Dad. It's raining."

"Gee, I hadn't noticed." Fritz slipped off his dripping raincoat. "The first squall line just rolled in. It's going to be nasty when the main storm hits. Barbara, we'll need the hurricane lamps tonight."

"I already have them out, dear. You know, you could always fix the emergency generator."

"I'm not in the business of doing the electric company's work for them. Anyway, lamp light is more romantic." Fritz winked at his wife. "And what are the two of you doing with Eva's things?"

Mark stared at the small pile of conservative clothes, a few possessions, and the music CD but no CD player. "Trying to find some identification."

"I already looked." Fritz sat in his big captain's chair at the other end of the dining room table. "There's no wallet in there. And that backpack has me puzzled."

"What do you mean, Dad?"

"Well, if she lives nearby, why is she carrying a backpack with clothes? And if she's vacationing, she doesn't have enough clothes or money."

"Good point." With the music playing slow, crisp, piano notes, Mark looked at the plastic CD case. "She could live in Orlando where this music was recorded and just came to the beach to get away from … from it all. I'll check the recording company. She may work for them."

"What's everyone's hurry? We can ask her in the morning." Fritz swiveled around in his captain's chair and looked into the night storm. "Everything will be clearer in the morning."

A curtain of rain slapped the windows. Jagged lightning stabbed into the ocean as if spearing creatures hiding in the deep sea. Thunder rumbled outside. Inside, the soft music of harps and seagulls calling mingled in a mystical hum from the CD player.

From the bookcase, Barbara retrieved her nurse's guide of diseases and flipped it open on the dining room table. "The two of you should read this section on encephalitis. It lists the causes and symptoms as well as the care Eva needs. It will help explain some of her actions today and what she may be experiencing."

Mark pushed Eva's backpack aside and read the medical book.

Another squall line slapped rain against the front windows.

With the lights flickering, Barbara lit the hurricane lamp. "Fritz, you have a point about her backpack. Eva has only enough clothes and money for two or three days, like she's taking a short trip from home to home. Although in her condition, it could be a lost journey. Poor thing. Eva may not remember where she came from or where she's going."

"Organic psychosis?" Mark looked up at his mother. "I didn't know any illness could make someone psychotic. ... Are you saying Eva may have lost contact with reality?"

"You said she refuses to believe she was shot. Then there's her believing she lives at the West Indies, a place that doesn't seem to exist anymore."

"Now, Barbara. Hotels and motels change their names as often as banks. The West Indies place could have a different name."

"Good idea, Dad. I'll check the courthouse in Deland. Motel names are registered there." Mark looked at the storm outside, whipping palm branches. "This viral encephalitis is worse than Doctor Williams explained at the hospital. This book makes it sound devastating. Psychotic, confused, delusional are strong words for any disease. And it says this illness can leave its victims permanently damaged and it can be fatal."

Barbara reached across the table and patted her son's hand. "Fortunately, most patients recover over time. Only a few need rehabilitation. Eva's in her twenties; her chances for recovery are good. She just needs a little help."

Mark closed the book. "I plan to take care of her."

"Son, you can't keep her. She's not like a stray beach creature. We have to give her back to her family."

"Not without knowing what happened to her, for two reasons. First, she told me she had no family. And second, I have to be careful who gets near Eva. Both of you keep forgetting someone shot her. That person meant her harm. And, Mom, you said there were old bruises on her body."

"I won't let anyone hurt her." Swiveling his chair around, Fritz looked at the photo of his daughter. "Eva can stay with us as long as she wants. She's safe here."

"Don't worry, I'll take care of her." Mark closed the medical book. *We've only known Eva for a few hours*, Mark pondered. *Yet she has brought back memories we have all tried to bury. If we're not careful we'll overreact and swamp her with our problems. God knows Eva has enough problems of her own.*

Overhead, the dining room lights flickered. Outside on the nearby telephone pole there was a crackling as electricity arched across a transformer.

"I better take a lamp to Eva. She'll be confused if she wakes in a strange, dark place." Barbara picked up a hurricane lamp. "Oh, Eva asked me to bring the notebook from her backpack. She's been keeping track of when she takes her medicine."

Mark looked up. "There wasn't any book in the backpack."

"Here it is." Fritz pulled a book from the end table beside the window. "I laid it in the sun to dry out. It fell on the wet sand when she tumbled off her bike."

Barbara took it. "Dear, this is a novel, not a notebook."

Fritz shrugged his shoulders. "That's the only book I found."

"What kind of a novel is it?" Mark reached for the book.

"I just laid it out to dry. I didn't read it. It's probably one of those romance novels." Fritz slid the book down the table. "I can tell you it's no western. Not with the title *Alligator Baby.*"

Barbara watched the book slide past. "That's not a cover of a romance novel. Looks more like a murder mystery."

"Murder?" Mark grabbed the novel. "A murder mystery and a CD of relaxing music is a strange combination."

"Well, what does the inside cover say?"

"Give me a minute, Mom. I can't read upside down." Marked flipped the book over. "It says: A woman attorney returns to Florida to find her biological parents. The heroine discovers her mother was murdered and dumped in a swamp. Beside the body was an infant and an alligator curled beside her. With the aid of three local police officials, the heroine tries to unravel her past, not knowing one of the men murdered her mother. Feeling he is about to be caught, the killer tries to destroy the only evidence against him, the alligator baby. He must kill – Oh my God."

"What's wrong?"

"Our Eva may be a Jane Doe after all." Mark dropped the book on the table. "In this novel Eva is reading, the heroine's name is … Eva Johnson."

~ 16 ~

Daytona Beach, Florida – Dawn, August 20th

An animal's jaws slid across Eva Johnson's throat. Dark beady eyes stared at her soft skin. Nostrils sniffed.

Opening her eyes, Eva saw teeth. Rough, wet skin slapped her cheek. "Good doggie. I'll wake up if you stop licking my face."

After a few gentle pats on his head, the German shepherd backed up. Rex studied the stranger lying in the bed and glanced at the floor nearby where two kittens curled in a basket. Their eyes wouldn't open even when he licked them.

Eva focused on the flame in a hurricane lamp sitting on the nightstand. Soft light washed across the room with warm tones, making the strange surroundings appear friendly. *Is this another one of my weird dreams?* Eva wondered. *If so, it must be a new one, I don't remember any of this – dog and lamp – story. Maybe this is a new version of Goldilocks with one big dog instead of three bears. And this place is too warm to be my dream of the Siberian tundra and the Ice Palace.*

Beyond the flickering light the images were too blurry to recognize, and her mind was too fuzzy to try to make sense of the surroundings. It was nothing she remembered. It looked like a home, someone's home, but not her home.

"Say dog. Where are we?" There was no answer. "This isn't a good dream. A woman shouldn't wake up not knowing where she is. Even worse, I don't remember getting here. Wherever here is." Eva looked into the dog's beady eyes. "Well dog. Is this real?"

The dog nudged her arm.

"Don't rush me. I need some time to think. And believe me, that's not an easy thing for me to do these days." Eva pulled the covers tight to her chin. Across the blanket's satin binding, an IV tube dangled. "The last thing I remember is a hospital."

Sitting up, she scanned the room. A long desk across the far wall was anchored with a sewing machine on one end and a desk lamp made of driftwood at the other. On the wall hung a rack displaying spools of thread, forming a colorful collage.

Eva glanced at the needle in her arm and the plastic IV tubing threading its way up to a bag, almost empty of liquid. "This doesn't look like a hospital room and that dog doesn't look like a medical technician, he's too friendly."

At the sound of her voice, Rex's chin plopped on the edge of the bed. The kittens meowed from their basket.

"Oh, my precious little kitties. Did I forget to feed you?" Whispering, Eva retrieved the kittens from their basket and hugged them. "Poor babies. If I knew where I left my backpack, I'd get that can of milk for you. If only I could remember more of what I want to and forget what I don't. Maybe I'm losing my mind. My memories are fading almost before the day is over. I don't even know how yesterday ended."

Soft footsteps swished in the hall. Rex backed away and watched the doorway with his tail wagging. A slender woman with short, curly hair and a broad smile stepped into the bedroom.

"Good morning, Eva. I'm Barbara, Mark's mother. I surprised you're awake so early. It's barely six." Barbara walked across the room and raised the blind. "The hospital ER staff gave you a sedative last night and you were much too drowsy to be on your own. So we brought you to our home. I hope you don't mind."

"It was very nice of you to look after me." Eva squinted at Mark's mother, silhouetted against the window. Bright morning sunlight streamed around the slim figure, almost consuming it. "Do you know where my backpack is? I need to feed the kittens."

"Fritz, my husband, brought it up from the beach. I put your things on the chair, over here. And Mark fed your kittens last night." Barbara stepped beside Eva. "Before you get up, let me remove the IV from your arm."

Eva studied Barbara's face as it moved closer. A few gray hairs swirled among the warm brown curls. A smooth complexion was accented by fine, smile wrinkles around her eyes, soft blue like Mark's. Eva glanced down at the faded writing on her hand: Feed kittens, Mark Reining, Find Home. *At least,* she thought, *I have a record of part of yesterday. Six words are better than nothing.*

"There you go, Eva. The IV is out. The doctor said it would make you feel better and lower your fever. When you want to freshen up, the powder room is down the hall to the left. The kitchen is beyond that, to the right, when you're ready for breakfast." Barbara rolled up the tubing. "I hope Rex didn't bother you. Your kittens fascinate him."

"He probably hasn't seen creatures too young to open their eyes." Eva looked at Rex licking the kittens' furry little heads. "They're well washed. Now I should do the same."

Glancing down, Eva wondered how she had gotten into her pajamas. She was shy but not overly modest. When she was a little girl, her aunt told her that a body was nothing to get embarrassed about or to show off. Eva fastened the top button of her pajamas and the thought of a warm shower washed away her concerns.

After stepping out of the shower and wiping steam off the vanity mirror, Eva combed her hair. "What happened to it?" Eva whispered. "Looks like someone chopped it with a scalpel. Maybe beach tar got stuck in it and they had to cut it out. One thing for sure, that doctor would never make it as a hairdresser, unless it was for a punk-rock band." Her laugh faded into a frown as the comb suddenly caught in a tangle, a painful reminder.

"Or did Jim? He grabbed my ponytail and my garden clippers. He was furious I wouldn't sign ... sign something." Eva looked at the mirror, steamed over again, fogging her image like her mind had blurred that memory. "Better put some makeup over the bump on my forehead. I want to look good for Mark."

Smiling, she looked down at her pale skin and the purple blotches where her body had bounded against her Blazer. The smile faded like her memory had. "How did I get so many bruises from my little accident? ... I just fell off my bike at the beach."

Eva could not remember her auto accident. The concussion from her head hitting the steering wheel had erased that fragment of her memory: a common condition in blunt head trauma. More critical was the fever from the viral encephalitis raging in her brain. Her short-term memories faded fast in the growing fog of the illness clouding her mind.

With light streaming through the curtains, water droplets sparkled on the mirror and she drew a happy face in the steam. "Who cares what happened. The sun is shining. I'm ready to ride down the beach. Today I'm going to find the West Indies."

Eva slipped on a long-sleeved, white blouse and long white slacks to cover the bruises. "It's time to go. If I stay, Mark and his parents will ask too many questions. I only have a few answers and I don't want to tell them I don't remember. They might think I'm sick or something. Besides, I'll be better off on my own. I can take care of myself."

Ready to leave, Eva zipped closed her backpack. "Now, how am I going to make a graceful exit from this place?"

~ 17 ~

"You look rough around the edges this morning." Mark slid pages from his laser printer across the breakfast table. "Dad, check out these articles on viral encephalitis."

"No. I'm tired of checking things."

"What are you talking about?" Mark pulled up a chair.

Fritz refilled his coffee mug. "I spent all night checking things. Checking on your mom who was checking Eva. Checking on Rex, checking out those little kittens. Checking on the electric company crews replacing the blown transformer. Checked on the storm. And of course, I checked on you. Your lights were on all night. How did you have electric?"

"I bought my own emergency generator. It's hurricane season and your generator is still broken. My computer requires electricity to work. And what kind of professor would tell his students he didn't get their test made because the power was off?"

"You shouldn't wait until the last minute to make their tests."

"They were done, but I threw them out. I got a new angle. Instead of just a test, I'm going to give them a challenge. They've been begging for one. This should spark their interest. It's a real case study. I want to know how they would handle an investigation if they were on the other end of a missing person's case."

Mark glanced out the back window at his garage apartment, separated from his parent's home by a screened breezeway. "Want me to run an extension cord over to your house?"

"No. I'm going to fix my generator. Tomorrow." Fritz sipped coffee. "So, what's your excuse for looking whipped?"

"After I finished with the case study, I searched the Internet. There are a number of web sites about viral encephalitis. I checked most of them. Guess I lost track of time."

"No damn computer would keep me up all night. I need my sleep." Fritz yawned. "Where's your mom?"

"Checking on Eva." Mark nudged a pile of documents towards his father. "This is just some of the information I found on the Internet. I didn't realize viral encephalitis was such a serious disease. There are more than one hundred viruses that can cause it. Look at this list. Now I understand why the doctors have trouble diagnosing which virus any one patient has."

Fritz scanned down the list Mark was tapping. "Did the doctor say which one of these Eva had?"

"Since it's summer, Doctor Williams suspected an arbovirus. There are four of them. Well, five now." As if lecturing to students, Mark turned a page and read. "La Crosse, St. Louis, Western equine, Eastern equine, and now West Nile encephalitis. The chances of getting viral encephalitis are 1 in 200,000 and –"

"Mark. ... Skip the probabilities. How did she get it?"

"Probably a mosquito bite."

"Mosquitoes. Sounds like I better patch the screen door before I fix the generator." Fritz watched his son flipping though the pages of printouts. "What's eating you?"

"I read some of the personal stories of those who had viral encephalitis. They were chilling. One man couldn't remember his wife of 15 years. Others lost memories of other relatives and friends. Some couldn't recall what happened during their illness and most had serious problems with their short-term memories."

Mark fanned the inch-thick stack of computer papers. "I keep thinking of Eva. You should have seen her sitting in the hospital, telling the doctor she didn't have a bullet in her arm. Dad, she doesn't even remember being shot. She thinks it's May not August, and she doesn't know what year it is. Then she told them her home was at the West Indies. It doesn't exist. And after finding that novel last night, I'm not even sure Eva Johnson is her real name. She may have assumed the heroine's name from that novel because she can't remember her own. How do I ask her who she is?"

"You don't." Barbara stepped in the kitchen and put her hands on her son's shoulder. "I've been reading my nursing book on caring for viral encephalitis patients. Among other things, it says it's important to provide emotional support. Asking a lot of prying questions that Eva probably can't answer will be threatening."

"But it's important to know who she is."

"At least give her a few days to get her strength back." Barbara glanced down the hall. "If you give her the third degree with all your questions, she's going to leave. She doesn't have to stay here. And I afraid Eva doesn't realize how ill she is."

"Mom, relax. I'm going to be discreet."

To check into Eva's past, Mark had prepared an agenda for his investigation: check missing persons reports, search for a county record for a motel named the West Indies, and, more importantly, get Eva's fingerprints. *I have to consider the danger to my parents,* Mark thought. *They've been through enough with my sister's death. I can see it in their eyes; Eva reminds them of Susan.*

Mark glanced at his mom's nurse's uniform. *Eva's body shows signs of violence. I can't ignore that. Violence she can't even remember. How can you forget being shot?* Mark added a note to his agenda. "Mom, did you ask her about her past?"

"No. I don't pry. My concern is for her health and how she feels. Think of what it would be like if you suddenly lost part of your past. Having only fragments of memories, past and present swirling around in the fog of a fever." Barbara patted Mark's shoulder. "Think of how Eva must feel."

Mark watched his mother turn away. *It must be hard on Mom. Looking at a woman lying in my sister's bed with a bruised body. I wonder what Mom's thinking.* "How do you think Eva feels?"

At the cupboard, Barbara pulled out a box of pancake mix. "I've been thinking about that all night. Patients that lose part of themselves, say a leg, go through a grief phase similar to losing a loved one. They experience shock, denial, anger, and recovery."

"Well, last night, Eva denied she'd been shot." Mark watched his mom whip batter and pour it onto a hot griddle. When troubled, his mother always fixed a big, hot, stick-to-the-ribs breakfast. "In her condition, Eva can't take care of herself. She needs help."

Fritz poured more coffee. "Fear may be involved in Eva's case. With a failing memory, she could be afraid to put her life in strangers' hands. She doesn't know anything about us. After whatever she's been through, she may not want to trust anyone."

"And having that doctor tell Eva she'd been shot didn't help." Mark looked across the kitchen table where his sister used to sit. *If sis hadn't been so trusting she would be alive today.*

While Fritz leafed through the pages of medical information on viral encephalitis, he watched his son.

"Mark. ... Mark." Barbara put syrup next to his plate. "Better eat your pancake. You'll need it to get you through the day."

Eating, Mark's eyes remained fixed on the pancake but his thoughts focused on what to do. *Since my students want to be detectives, I'll put them to work helping me track down Eva's past. They can use their local police connections to get the basic facts. I'll use my federal contacts to get the sensitive information: fingerprint identification and background check.*

Mark sliced into his pancake while his mind raced. *I need to know who Eva Johnson really is and why someone shot her. Does she have relatives and do any of them have a motive for killing her? And does she know anything about that "Aunt Killer" murder? Eva was shot about the same time that woman was murdered on the north section of the beach. Was Eva wandering the beach the night the murderer dumped the body and did he shoot Eva hoping to silence a witness? And why did Eva have that newspaper article about the aunt being killed tucked in her novel?*

Mark put his fork down as his thoughts continued. *And what's the probability she has the same name as the heroine in that novel? Who is our Eva Johnson?*

"Here's another pancake. You need energy for your lecture."

"Mom, is Doctor Williams a virologist?"

"No. He's a plastic surgeon."

"Well then, what does he know about viral encephalitis?"

"A lot now." Barbara took a deep breath. "His son, John, got viral encephalitis during the 1997 outbreak. He was one of the first to get it: a bad case. ... That incident almost devastated Doctor Williams. He felt guilty for not recognizing his son's symptoms. John didn't come home one weekend because he thought he had a bad case of the flu. Later, some friends found John in his off-campus apartment, having a seizure. The university doctors put him in a medically induced coma, trying to prevent complications. They ran a series of tests, but they take time. The doctors didn't know there was an outbreak of viral encephalitis sweeping the state. When Doctor Williams got to the university hospital, he was shocked by his son's unresponsive condition. John had lost forty pounds. There was nothing more they could do for his son except wait for the virus to run it course and hope its wouldn't destroy too much of his son's brain. But John got worse. ... A week later, Doctor Williams had to order them to remove his son's life support. ... Doctor Williams' son died in his arms."

Mark watched his mother dab her eyes. "How old was he?"

"John was twenty-five. About Eva's age."

Stillness settled in the kitchen. Only the griddle hissed.

~ 18 ~

Weak footsteps and the tap of four paws clicked down the hall. With his tail wagging, Rex rounded the corner first and headed to his water dish. Eva stepped into the quiet kitchen and put the basket with the kittens near Rex.

"Good morning, Eva." Mark got up and pulled out the empty chair, his sister's chair. *Eva is smaller than my sister,* Mark observed. *But Eva has blond hair and it's cut strangely, like it has been chopped off.* He wanted to ask what happened but changed his mind. "What would you like for breakfast?"

"Just some coffee." Eva smiled, sliding into the chair.

Barbara filled a china cup. "Would you like cream in it?"

"Skim milk, if you have some."

"Sugar?" Mark asked. "Or would you prefer sweetener?"

"No sweetener. I'm allergic to aspartame."

"Do you have PKU?" Barbara touched her nursing pin.

"No. I'm just allergic to artificial sweetener. That's all."

Mark poured coffee in his mug. "What's PKU?"

"It's a tongue twister. Phenylketonuria." Barbara took a sip of tea. "PKU for short. It's a metabolic disorder that makes the normally harmless chemicals in aspartame toxic in some individuals. It affects mostly children so hospitals check all babies at birth for PKU. If it goes undetected, a child can suffer brain damage. Those with PKU can't digest the phenylalanine in aspartame or any product containing that chemical."

Eva pointed at the diet pop beside the refrigerator. "That's why soda cans carry a warning label. It's dangerous for children with PKU to drink diet pop."

Mark gave his mother a skeptical look. "I've seen warning labels on cigarette packs but not on pop cans. Surely they wouldn't put a chemical dangerous to anyone in soda pop." After retrieving a can of diet pop and turning it sideways, Mark read the warning. "Never noticed that before. You'd have to be a chemist to know what that meant. What's this phenylalanine do to you?"

"Gives me splitting headaches." Eva cringed. "That's one thing I don't need right now."

Barbara put a small pitcher of milk next to Eva. "Do you have any other allergies?"

"No." With milk, Eva lightened her coffee to the shade of milk chocolate. "Fortunately, aspartame is my only allergy."

Standing next to the stove, Barbara flipped on a burner. "Since you didn't have dinner last night, you should have a big breakfast. Would you like pancakes, bacon and eggs, or some hot oatmeal?"

"I'm afraid I don't have much appetite these days." Eva glanced at Barbara pulling out a saucepan and a round box. "A small bowl of oatmeal would be fine."

"Good. That's just what I was going to have. Nothing like oatmeal to get you through a busy morning." Barbara adjusted the apron over her nurse's uniform. "One thing about oatmeal, it sticks to your ribs. Mark, Fritz, do you want a bowl?"

"No, Mom."

Fritz grimaced behind his wife's back. "I'm still working on my stack of pancakes."

"Well, then, it's oatmeal for two." Oat flakes poured into the boiling water. Stirring, Barbara glanced over the stove at the stranger sitting in her daughter's chair.

At arm's length, Fritz held one of the Internet articles, focusing on it and then on Eva at the other end of the table. In the corner, Rex stretched out on the floor beside the kittens in their basket.

"Mark, you better finish that pancake."

"Yes, Mom." Mark glanced at Eva, hoping no one noticed.

Barbara slid a bowl in front of Eva. "Now eat your oatmeal."

"Yes, Ma'am." Eva's spoon slipped into the steaming oatmeal.

"Good girl." Barbara patted Eva's shoulder and turned away.

Hearing his mother's voice crack, Mark glanced at her retrieving a Kleenex and wiping her eyes as she stared out the kitchen window. As his stomach tightened, Mark considered his parents' feelings. *Does having Eva here remind Mom of Susan? Maybe it wasn't such a good idea having Eva stay with us. She brings back too many memories of my sister. But our memories aren't Eva's problems and where else would she have gone in her condition? Wander the streets? Slept on the beach? Just where would Eva have been during last night's big storm?*

"You need another cup of coffee." Fritz filled his son's cup. "Don't want you to fall asleep during your morning lecture."

"No lecture today. We're starting a case study." Mark poured more syrup on the last of his pancake and watched his father looking deep into his coffee mug. *What about Dad? He's been unusually quiet. How does he feel about having Eva here? Hard telling. Dad clammed up after Susan's death. Hung a "For Sale" sign on the business and walked away. Now he spends most of his time fishing and reading western novels.*

A clank distracted Mark. He glanced at Eva, retrieving her spoon. It had slipped from her hand and was sinking into the oatmeal. *Look at her*, Mark thought. *She hardly has enough strength to hold a spoon. How could she defend herself from whomever shot her? Weak and confused, she's easy prey. She can't take care of herself. She needs someone to protect her.* Mark filled his lungs with determined air. *I'll protect her. Eva will not end up like my sister.*

Quietness settled in the kitchen. Mark swirled the last piece of pancake through the syrup. With a cup of tea, Barbara returned to the table. Fritz cut his second pancake into smaller pieces.

"Do you want another pancake?" Barbara glanced at her son.

"No, Mom." Mark saw his parents taking short glances at the woman sitting in their daughter's place at the breakfast table. For two years that chair had remained empty and now a stranger sat there. A young woman that was an eerie reminder of what they had lost. Although their looks were quite different, Eva resembled Susan in her mannerisms: a cheerful smile, graceful movements, and the same shy silence that had cost Mark's sister her life.

Although he tried not to, Mark glanced back at Eva. *It must be hard for her to eat with the three of us staring at her. She has no way of knowing how much she reminds us of my sister. I wonder if Eva can feel the emotional tension at this table; it's like the crackling charges just before a transformer blows. ... I wonder what Eva is thinking.*

~ 19 ~

My last memories of Mom are in a kitchen like this at the West Indies. Eva's thoughts of earlier years surfaced. *We did so many things that year. It's strange how my childhood memories are so vivid and the rest of my mind is so foggy. Maybe happy thoughts last longer.* Eva stared at the light streaming in the east window like it did long ago at the West Indies motel.

The walls looked like fresh lemonade in the morning sun and the glasses on the counter sparkled like ice cubes. Crisp white curtains flanked the window over the sink and seashells sat on the sill. It was a cheerful kitchen.

A clank of silver hitting china startled Eva. Her eyes blinked and she picked up her spoon before it sank into the hot cereal. *Oatmeal,* Eva mused. *Mom always gave it to me when I was sick. Said it would stick to my ribs and make me well. Mom knew I would eat some if I got to put on lots and lots of sugar. With enough sugar, it almost tastes like candy.* Eva smiled. *Of course, you have to have a good imagination and bad eyesight to think oatmeal is candy. Maybe cookies but not candy.*

The teakettle whistled on the stove.

"You haven't touched your coffee. Would you like some tea instead?" Barbara touched Eva's shoulder. "Eva?"

"Oh. Yes, tea with sugar would be nice." Lost in old thoughts, Eva had forgotten about the cup of coffee sitting there.

Eva watched Mark's mother walk across the kitchen, wipe her hands on her yellow apron, and carefully pick up the kettle with a hot pad. *Potholders,* Eva's mind flashed. *Mom taught me how to weave potholders and I sold them to the neighbors. Forget the lemonade stand, Dad said, there's more profits in potholders. Indeed,* Eva recalled, *I always had spending money for Popsicles and craft supplies.*

"Would you like some more sugar?" Mark passed the bowl.

"Thanks." Glancing at her palm, Eva read his name, Mark. Although the writing was fading, the memory of their meeting was strong, etched there by a strange attraction. Finding herself gazing into Mark's soft blue eyes, she blushed. He was watching her.

Why is he staring at me so intensely? Eva wondered. *Just what kind of man is Mark, rescuing a woman from the beach and taking her home? Does he have ulterior motives? I want to trust him but can I? My emotions are as scrambled as my thoughts. And I don't understand this strange attraction I feel for Mark.* Eva closed her hand. "Mark, thanks for saving my kittens."

"You're welcome. Did you –"

"Mark." Barbara interrupted. "Why don't you get Eva a glass of water? It's time for her to take her medication."

"Oh, I almost forgot." Eva pulled a bag of white capsules from her pocket. "It's time for my antibiotics. I have to take them till they're all gone, doctor's orders."

"Antibiotics won't kill a virus." Mark handed her a glass of water. "Doctor Williams said you had viral encephalitis."

Eva shook her head. "No, my doctor said I have a sinus infection. He gave me antibiotics to take."

"Do you have the prescription bottle for those?" Mark asked.

"Bags are better. I don't like those childproof bottles. They're too hard to open and they're always falling over. You don't want to take an antibiotic after it has fallen on the floor." Eva removed one capsule and zipped the plastic bag closed. "This is waterproof. If it falls in the sink, the pills won't get wet."

Mark picked up the bag. "But the prescription bottle has your doctor's name and the refill information."

"There are no refills left, so I threw the bottle away."

"Mark!" Fritz tapped his son's plate. "Finish your pancake."

"No more questions." Barbara slipped off her apron. "Eva needs to eat her breakfast and take her medicine."

Enjoying the silence, Eva inhaled the spicy fragrance rising from the teacup. Old memories rose with the steam. "This smells like pumpkin pie and Thanksgiving at the West Indies."

"Tell us about the West Indies." Mark sipped coffee.

Eva stirred more sugar in her tea. "Mom had only a small oven at the West Indies, just enough room for a big turkey. So we used the ovens in the empty efficient-units to cook Thanksgiving dinner. We had a pumpkin pie in the first oven, sweet potatoes in the second, a green bean casserole in the next, and homemade dinner rolls in the last one. I ran back and forth, checking on each oven. I thought it was a neat way to cook."

Stirring her oatmeal, Eva smiled. *I haven't thought about that Thanksgiving in a long time. At least a part of my memories are still intact. My happy childhood is still there.*

Barbara added more water to the teapot. "A woman never has enough oven space for Thanksgiving. But I hadn't thought about using more than one oven. I'll have to try that."

Grabbing a pencil, Mark leaned forward. "Do you remember the address of the West Indies?"

Eva watched her spoon sink into the thick oatmeal. *Be careful*, her mind warned. *You don't want to get others involved. How could I ever tell them about Jim? I don't know what makes Jim tick. How could I expect Mark and his parents to understand?*

Her spoon scooped out more hot oatmeal. *Hopefully, Jim will leave me alone after they serve the restraining order. When he gets served, Jim will be furious. I don't want to be near him then.*

"Eva." Mark touched her hand. "Eva!"

"What?" She pulled back.

"Are you okay? Your hands are shaking."

"I'm okay. Really, I'm –" The quivering spoon dropped into the oatmeal. Her chair scooted back. "I afraid I've imposed on you long enough. I should be moving on. The West Indies is –"

"Why don't you stay with us?" Mark glanced at his parents. "We have plenty of room and you need to rest a few days."

"Mark's right." Fritz looked up. "We'd love to have you. And that'll give me time to fix your bike. A piece fell off when you fell on the beach. It'll take a couple days to get a new one."

"You've done so much for me already. I don't want to impose any longer." Longing to leave, Eva listened to the sound of the surf pounding and seagulls calling. Behind Mark, the door was open.

"Stay with us. We have plenty of room." Barbara poured more tea into Eva's cup. "And I'd enjoy having a woman around. It'll be nice to talk about something besides fishing tackle and computers."

Fritz leaned over and pushed back the calico kitten trying to climb out of the basket. "Your little kitties had quite a tumble from the bike. A few days rest will do them good."

Trying to think of a way out, Eva sprinkled more sugar on her oatmeal. Steam from the spicy tea rose. Sunlight twinkled on her water glass. But no good excuses for leaving came to her. "I'll rent a room for a day or two. Just until the kittens have rested."

Outside, seagulls called.

"Good. That's settled. You can stay with us as long as you want." Glancing at the clock, Mark pushed his chair back and then carried his plate to the sink. "I need to leave; I have a few things to do before class." Picking up Eva's water glass by the rim, he replaced it with a fresh one.

With his back turned, Mark carefully slid Eva's empty water glass into a plastic bag and hid it in his briefcase.

~ 20 ~

"Be careful! No telling what's under there." Fritz warned.

"That's why I want to look." Eva turned over a long chain of seaweed, looking like dark-green garland. It divided the dry and moist beach sand at the high-water line. The fuzzy green line of seaweed meandered in both directions and then disappeared in the morning fog. "Some neat stuff washes up after a storm."

After breakfast, both Mark and his mother had gone to work, and the kittens were napping. Eva and Fritz walked up the beach, checking on storm damage.

"That smells like dead fish." Flipping over a piece of seaweed with his walking stick, Fritz pointed. "See. Looks like a mullet. It's too far gone for bait so I'll leave it for the seagulls."

"I'm sorry I missed the storm. I would have checked the beach for sea-foam. Strange to see the ocean whipped into yellowish suds. Odd stuff, sea-foam." She picked up a cluster of bubbles stuck to a clump of seaweed. "I don't know how I slept through the northeaster. It must have rolled through like an Alberta clipper."

Dropping the seaweed, Eva glanced back at Mark's home. A sailing ship's mast, used as a flagpole, rose out of a sand dune looking like an old beached treasure ship buried in the sand. *Treasure chest,* she mused. *Odd, I remember we buried a treasure chest in the sand.*

"Eva, something wrong?" Fritz walked back.

"I'm fine. Just thinking." Walking on, Eva flipped over seaweed looking for treasures of the sea: shells, driftwood, and sea creatures like small, clear jellyfish shimmering like polished glass.

After sniffing at a fishy corpse, Rex backed away and kicked sand at it. Spotting a gull walking towards them, he gave chase. The seagull took to wing, squawking its protest.

"Rex, leave those poor seagulls alone."

"He's just having fun." Eva pulled back a clump of seaweed. "Look. A sea-bean. This one's shaped something like a heart. Isn't it cute?" In her hand, it was slightly larger than a silver dollar. She stroked its smooth dark skin. "They remind me of little pancakes."

"Looks like the ones I cook. Well done on both sides. Mark used to calls them charred cakes." Fritz picked up another sea-bean and skipped it across the sand towards Rex.

Eva watched the dog snatch it and head back. "Mr. Reining –"

"Please, no Mr. Reining. Call me Fritz or Dad."

Eva inhaled the intoxicating ocean air, tinged with fermenting seaweed. "That's an odd name. Fritz Or-dad Reining." She smiled at her offbeat humor.

Fritz grinned. "Yeah. 'Or-dad' is a bit stuffy. Just plain Dad or Fritz is more appropriate."

As he strolled on down the beach, Eva studied Mark's father. Fritz was similar to her father. He had the same rugged build, good nature, but was a bit quieter. *Perhaps,* she thought, *that's why I feel relaxed around Fritz. He reminds me of my dad. Mark is lucky to live next to his parents' home.*

"Fritz." She caught up with him. "What does Mark teach?"

"He teaches law enforcement courses."

Eva stopped suddenly. "Is he a police officer?"

"No. He's a professor."

"A professor." Eva flipped over more seaweed, searching. "Don't you have to be some kind of a police officer or a retired one to teach law enforcement?"

"Mark ... well he ... used to be with the Secret Service."

Even with the ocean waves pounding on shore, Eva could hear an undercurrent in Fritz's voice. That was the way her father sounded when he wanted to hedge on an issue.

"Secret Service. Now, that must be an interesting job. They get to meet lots of important people and travel. So –" Her foot hit something that slithered over her toes.

Eva froze. That's what she had done as a child. Playing at a friend's house on the mainland, her little sandal had stirred up dry leaves. Something slithered from them and across her toes. It had colorful rings around its small body. But even beauty could not disguise a snake. And it was no ordinary snake. Eva knew it was poisonous. It was a coral snake. Its slippery body was the size of her big toe, an easy target, as it slid past. A slight movement would have startled the snake into a defensive strike. She didn't move. When the coral snake slithered north, Eva ran south.

"Eva. Eva what is it?"

Her heart raced as fast as she had run from that snake years ago. She blinked and pulled her foot back from a long green thing. "Seaweed, just seaweed. A long, stringy vine of seaweed."

"No, it's a rope. A slimy rope." Fritz flipped it away with his stick. "You look a little pale. Maybe we should go back. Barbara said you're supposed to rest and not overdo it. You need to get your strength back."

"I've been sleeping all night. I don't need a nap. I need exercise. Besides, I have to burn up all that sugar I poured on my oatmeal. If I don't, it will be sticking to my ribs." She patted her small waistline and walked on.

"Those look like spare ribs to me."

Eva stepped away from the row of seaweed and onto the still wet sand. "Look. Air pockets."

The high storm tide had overrun the normally dry sand. In their rush back to the sea, the waves had left air pockets trapped under the wet sand. They looked like flat soap bubbles: small ones and some larger than a man's foot. One step on them and they flattened with a soft pop.

Beneath her bare feet, the sand was soft like leather. As she stepped on them, the air pockets collapsed with a pop. "I never understood what made them."

Fritz pointed with his stick. "Well, you see, the waves –"

"No. Don't tell me," Eva insisted. "Knowing the truth would destroy the magic. Sometimes, not knowing is more fun."

"You're right." Grinning, Fritz squashed a big one. "Haven't done that in a while. When Mark was a little tyke, he stomped them down to flatten the beach. He said the grown-ups would stumble over the air pockets because they didn't look down. After every storm, he'd run up and down the beach flatting it out. Said it was his job to make the beach safe."

Eva watched Fritz stepping from bubble to bubble, seeming to enjoy himself. She followed him, flattening the smaller bubbles. Rex raced between them to a flock of sandpipers pecking in the seaweed. The soft lapping of the morning waves mingled with the call of seagulls.

Inhaling the salt air, she studied the shoreline. *Where is the West Indies?* Eva pondered. *My childhood home should be around here somewhere. This feels like the right place. So where is it?*

"Looking for something?" Fritz stopped popping air pockets.

"The West Indies motel. It's up this way, isn't it?"

"Mark couldn't find it listed in the phone book. Maybe a new owner changed its name."

"But the West Indies was such a good name. My mother picked it out and Dad had to go to Deland to register that name. They have to approve all motel names. It's sort of like a trademark." Eva squinted north at the distant motels along the beach. Nothing seemed familiar in the morning fog.

Have I forgotten what it looks like? Or has it changed so much that I can't even recognize it? I just wanted to go back to where I would feel safe and hide until my personal storm blows over. Some place to recover from this illness. ... But the doctors must be wrong. I can't have viral encephalitis. You get that in the south. We don't have a mosquito problem in Ohio. And I live on one of the highest spots in the state. So, this can't be viral encephalitis. Eva rubbed her forehead, hot from the fever burning deep inside her brain, frying short-term memory circuits.

"Eva." Fritz touched her shoulder. "It's time we go back. You need to get some rest."

She took a deep breath, but the salt air no longer blocked her headache. Fur brushed her leg, it bent, and she dropped to a sitting position. Eva hugged the dog, watching her intently. "Rex. Poor doggie, you look a little tired. ... Fritz, we should rest a minute until Rex gets his wind back."

"Good idea." Frits sat down beside her. "Chasing seagulls takes the wind out of Rex. And his bum leg tends to give out when he overdoes it. All he'll needs is something to eat when we get back and then a long nap beside those kitties."

"Remind me to feed the kittens when we get back. They need their strength; they're about to open their eyes. I wonder what they'll think when they look up at Rex licking their faces. Will they —" Eva rubbed her forehead. The complex question she wanted to ask vanished, dissolving like the morning fog under the rising sun. When she tired, compound sentences slipped away and trying to retrieve those thoughts was futile.

"Eva." Fritz watched her. "Are you okay?"

"Just a little sinus headache. That's all." She patted Rex, who looked back at her with big brown eyes as his chin rested on her knee. "Has Mark had Rex since he was a puppy?"

"No, he got Rex a couple of years ago. Rex was a police dog that got hurt in … in a raid of sorts. His injuries prevented him from continuing as a police dog, so Mark brought him home."

"That was kindhearted of him. You have a good son."

"Yep, Mark's the best." Fritz rubbed Rex's fur. "Couldn't have asked for a finer son."

Other morning walkers strolled the beach, waiting for the sun to dry off the storm-drenched sand. The light fog was fading and blue sky sparkled above it. In a few hours, there would be little trace of the northeaster except what washed ashore.

"I think Rex is ready to head back. Time to check my kittens." Standing up, Eva brushed off sand and picked up the piece of driftwood she'd found earlier.

"Eva, what are you going to do with that?"

"Don't know yet." She pulled off a barnacle. "It looks really, really old. Could be from an Old Spanish galleon or a pirate ship."

"You've got a good imagination." Taking the driftwood, Fritz shook it hard and gave it back. "No gold doubloon in it and no treasure map."

"Darn." She shook her head. "I had my heart set on a treasure hunt. Well, then I have to use it for a still life."

"Still life?"

"An arrangement. See, I'll sit it on its side and put shells in front of it. Then I can make a drawing of it." Turning the driftwood, Eva felt its texture and studied the light playing on its weathered surface. "It has a lot of character. From this direction, those contours and crevices look like my brain. And these holes are where my memories were stored. They're just empty holes now."

~ 21 ~

Maybe this is wrong. Mark pondered, stopping outside his classroom door. *My investigation of Eva is one thing, but getting my students involved could be an invasion of her privacy.*

In the early morning hours, giving his students a real case study – Eva's case – seemed like a brilliant idea. After all, they were studying missing persons procedures. Giving them the reverse side of such a case would be more challenge than a test. His students had asked, even begged, for a real case study.

After shifting his stack of case-study handouts to his left hand, Mark reached for the doorknob. His grip tightened on the cold steel knob. He hesitated.

This could be dangerous. What if? Mark deliberated. *What if a killer is stalking Eva? I could be putting my students' lives in danger. What if Eva knows something about that "Aunt Killer" murder two days ago? She could wind up in jail, unable to defend herself with no memory, no alibi, no friends, and no money. No, Eva isn't the kind of woman who would be in trouble with the law. She's too much like my sister. A victim. I can't let her down.*

His classroom door opened. "Professor Reining. Did we lock you out?" A student held the door.

"No." Mark's moist hand slipped from the knob. "You can't lock a professor out on test day. We carry keys."

The student yawned. "We were beginning to worry about you. Thought you overslept because the electric was off last night."

Another student chimed in. "And if you weren't able to make up our test, that's okay. Believe me, we know the power was out."

"Professors don't wait until the night before to write exams." Mark felt the heat from the fresh copies in his hands. "If we did, we'd have emergency generators for our computers."

Strolling to the front, Mark studied his sleepy students, surmising what their night had been like. A bone weary, ragged lot they were. He assumed those in crumpled uniforms worked late in traffic control. The ones employed by security companies spent the night checking out false alarms triggered by power outages. Those with wrinkled skin worked on the highway patrol and had been out in the pounding rain, pulling stranded motorists off I-95.

"Good morning." Mark heaved the thick stack of paper on his desk, sipped more coffee, and glanced at the back row. Bob was missing, but in his chair sat a big, brown teddy bear with a pink bow. "Looks like Bob shrank last night."

Chuckles rumbled just as the door opened and Bob tried to slip in unnoticed. All eyes were on him and the teddy bear.

"What the –" Bob's hands snapped to his hips and he eyed the room for the prankster. His cold stare stopped at a grinning face and giggles from the front. "Dixie, this isn't funny."

"Sorry, it wasn't my idea. The chief said it was a souvenir from your drug bust of the firecracker kids."

Whipping the teddy bear out of his chair, Bob defiantly gave it a big hug. "Hope the exam answers are in his secret compartment."

"Careful, I hear that was one loaded bear." Dixie chuckled. "And he was packing quite a pistol."

Mark let the kidding and laughter play out. He knew what it was like to be exhausted to the point of silliness and a bit of humor would rejuvenate them. It was even refreshing for him.

Not wanting to look too amused, Mark turned and erased the blackboard. A grim outline of murder was chalked on the board;

common causes of death in homicide cases: shootings, knifings, beatings, and poisonings.

With the class quieting, Mark walked in front of his desk and separated the copies into a tall, thick pile and a small one. "Today, I'm giving you a choice. You can take either this exam." He tapped the thick stack of paper and then held up a single sheet. "Or you can take this case study."

Students shifted in their chairs, mumbling among themselves.

"Professor Reining, we get to choose?"

"Right. Either the test or the case study." Mark held up a copy of each. "The test will take about two hours if you studied hard for it last night. The case study will be a joint project and I'll give you a week to complete it."

In the first row Dixie leaned forward, looking at the two choices. "That test is thicker than the handout on missing persons."

"Is that an old case study?" Bob asked from the back.

"No. This is a current … Jane Doe case."

"What's the catch?" Another student asked.

"You might not be able to find out who she is in a week and there is an element of risk involved."

"Danger?" Bob grinned. "How much?"

With reservations about giving Eva's case to his class, Mark put down the papers and wiped sweat from his hands. "The hospital found a bullet in her arm and she doesn't remember the shooting."

"Amnesia?" Dixie asked.

"Not exactly. She has early memories of Daytona but her short-term memory is fuzzy at best with gaps in between. She has viral encephalitis which often causes memory problems."

"Yep." Dixie nodded. "My cousin had that a few years ago. He had to drop out of school for a year. Couldn't remember the last paragraph he read, let alone take a test."

"Speaking of test, those of you who want to take the quick, two hour exam need to get it now and go across the hall."

Chairs shifted and students eyed one another. Weary, they looked indecisive.

After strolling forward, Bob picked up an exam, scanned the top page, and dropped it. "The case study sounds interesting. We should be able to find out who she is in a day." Shaking his head, Bob plopped into the seat next to Dixie.

"No takers on the written exam?" Mark doubted if there would be any after Bob rolled his eyes to the class while skimming the first page of test questions. Bob and Dixie were the class ringleaders; he was the prankster and she was the serious one, and both were outstanding students.

"If there's no takers for the exam, here's a one page summary of the case study." Walking across the room, handing out papers, Mark studied the resources now available to him. His students were from various agencies: local police, county sheriff's office, highway patrol, and local security agencies. Although they were all young and new to law enforcement, they were an eager bunch.

After reviewing the fact sheet for the case – Eva's case – the students started discussing the possibilities. Chairs moved as they clustered together in two groups: Dixie and the more serious students, and Bob and his gang.

At his desk, Mark made notes on his students' comments. Their ideas would be fresh and more objective. Brainstorming was always helpful and working in teams on a real case would be a good experience for his students.

Hank, an auxiliary sheriff's deputy, muscled forward. "We should get her fingerprints and see if we can find a match."

"Hank!" Dixie whipped around. "She's a victim. You can't haul her to the police station and fingerprint her like a common criminal. She's gone through enough without being treated like she did something wrong. Being sick is no crime."

"But it says she was shot. Could have been during a robbery."

"Not the type." Bob leaned back. "She reminds me of my Aunt Flora. She wouldn't kill an ant. No pun intended. Besides, most women aren't violent criminals."

"Guys, lets not waste time." Dixie made notes. "Y'all check the missing persons filings and I'll check the domestic violence records. Someone can contact the phone companies for a listing for Eva Johnson."

"No local listings." Bob said. "And I've already called the other phone companies in the state. There were a few listings for Eva Johnson in Florida but those ladies are accounted for."

"We just got this. What do you mean, you already checked?"

Bob glanced at Professor Reining. "Eva was found on my beach. The firecracker kids just about ran her down and the rescue squad took her to the hospital. When the doctors found a bullet in her arm, I had to go in to get the report. ... The rest of the facts are on this sheet."

Hank whispered to Bob. "You mean this isn't from Professor Reining's old clipping file? It is a real case?"

"Yep. Eva is very real." Turning, Bob whispered, "A certain professor has taken a special interest in her. Need I say more?"

Mark missed the last part of Bob's comment when the crime lab instructor opened the door. "Excuse me, class."

In the hall, Mark looked at the fingerprint sheet of Eva's prints. "Thanks, Dave. I owe you one."

"Don't mention it. It gave my morning class a chance to practice pulling prints from a water glass. They got a good set of lady's prints. Want me to see if there's a criminal record?"

"That won't be necessary. I'm going to check with the FBI." Mark knew that wasn't his real plan, but it was close enough. "This is for a case study I've assigned my class."

"A case study. That's something I haven't give my class for a while." Hank looked into Mark's classroom. "Your students seemed enthused. It's not easy to motivate them during summer quarter. Let me know if there's anything else you need."

"Will do."

"Oh, here's this." Hank handed back a water glass with the initial "R" engraved on it. "Looks like it belongs to a set."

"We use them only for company." Mark took the glass.

"When you get a break, I'd like to hear about this case study."

Back inside his classroom, Mark stashed his mother's water glass in his briefcase. Copies of Eva's fingerprints were slipped into a folder for safekeeping. When he got back to his place, Mark planned to fax her fingerprints to his friend, Bruce, at the Secret Service who could run a background check through the FBI without questions being asked.

"Professor Reining." Bob walked up as the other students left. "Should we call you when we find out about Eva Johnson?"

"Yes." Mark's briefcase closed. "Call anytime."

"Oh. Would you give this to Rex." Bob put the teddy bear on the desk. "Your dog took a liking to the bear. In fact, it took us fifteen minutes to get it away from him. He kept shaking it and dragging it down the beach. Poor bear must have whiplash."

"Was there really a gun inside this?"

"Yep, right here. If Rex hadn't ripped it open, we wouldn't have found the gun. It had been fired; Rex must have smelt the gunpowder." Bob flipped it over and unzipped it. "That kid had a .22 pistol in here. We're both damn lucky he passed out. As stoned as that kid was, he could have shot us both while we were saving him from drowning."

~ 22 ~

"Where's Eva?" Mark rushed into his parent's kitchen. "She's not in her room."

"Relax." Fritz put groceries sacks on the counter. "Eva is sleeping on the front deck. She wanted to watch the sand dunes while she listened to her CD of ocean sounds. It's been playing over and over. Says it helps her headache."

Following the music, Mark found Eva on the front deck, sleeping on the doublewide lounge chair. Beside her a haunting melody of lonely piano notes mixed with sounds of the surf.

Poor Eva. Mark's mind tugged at his heart. *I wonder if that is how she feels. Searching. Looking for a home that no longer exists. Does she even know where she came from? I wonder. If she doesn't remember being shot, there may be a lot she has forgotten.*

Across from Eva, Mark sank into the lounge chair and put up his tired feet. After his morning class, he had checked with the major airlines flying into Daytona Beach International Airport. None of them had any records of a passenger by the name of Eva Johnson arriving in the last two weeks.

After nudging the calico kitten back in its basket, Rex trotted over and put his head on his master's arm.

"Don't worry," Mark whispered to Rex. "She'll be okay. Mom will nurse her back to health. You and I have the job of protecting her from whomever hurt her."

Leaving Eva sleeping, Mark returned to the kitchen. "Dad, you went to the grocery and left Eva alone?"

Unpacking groceries, Fritz put milk in the refrigerator. "She's not a child. If you haven't noticed that, you need glasses."

"My eyesight is fine. I just don't want her wandering the beach alone. She's too weak and could get lost."

"It's hard for an adult to get lost on the beach. You can only go up or down it. Anyway, she seems to knows her way around." Fritz glanced out the window at the dunes. "We went for a short walk up the beach after you left this morning. I think she was looking for that West Indies place. Did you find its new name?"

"My students are checking at the county courthouse records."

"Mark! You got your students involved?"

"They're just doing some basic research. Most of them work for the county and can access the confidential records. I can find out who Eva is faster with help." Mark flipped open his briefcase.

"What's you mother's water glass doing in your briefcase?"

Mark looked around, making sure they were alone. "Since we don't know if Eva Johnson is her real name, I needed Eva's fingerprints. I'm going to have them checked with the FBI files."

"Damn it! You can't get the FBI involved. Eva's no criminal."

"Relax, Dad." Mark wiped his sweaty hands before pulling out her fingerprint card. "Many employers require fingerprinting as part of a background check. Teachers, childcare providers, and banks, just to name a few. Eva may have worked someplace that requires her fingerprints be filed with the FBI."

"Still, I don't like you taking her fingerprints without her permission. We have no business prying into her private life. And for heaven's sake don't tell your mother. You know how she feels about snooping."

"Believe me, I didn't like doing it that way. But I thought this way wouldn't upset Eva." Mark glanced at his sister's empty chair. "And I have to protect you and Mom. I don't want anything to happen to you because I brought Eva into this house. After all, we really don't know much about her. That's why I'm faxing Eva's fingerprints to Bruce. You know how tightlipped Secret Service agents are and he can run a confidential check through the FBI without telling them a thing."

"Eva is a good person." Smiling, Fritz pulled a box of oatmeal from the sack and looked out the window at the ocean. "This morning we popped air pockets on the beach. I haven't done that since you were a kid. … You know, Eva reminds me of Susan."

Mark watched his father hug the box of oatmeal, a favorite breakfast of his sister. *Dad misses Susan more that he lets on,* Mark thought. *He'll be crushed if Eva has a criminal record or a troubled past. I'll have to be careful what I tell Dad. I don't want him hurt again; he's just starting to come out of his shell. How will Dad take losing someone he is making into a surrogate daughter?*

"Mark, are you all right?" Barbara felt her son's forehead. "You look a little pale."

"Mom, what are you doing home early?"

"Lunch. I took a long lunch hour so I could check up on my patient." She laid down a hypodermic. "Doctor Williams wants to run another blood test."

"Did they identify which type of viral encephalitis she has?"

"Not yet. Doctor Williams said the first test results looked atypical." Barbara took off her nurse's cap. "He wants to check for a secondary infection. That's always a possible complication with such a serious illness. Her immune system is weak. That's another reason she's better off in a home environment."

"Eva can stay with us as long as she likes." Fritz put the oatmeal box in the cupboard.

"You bought more oatmeal?" Barbara asked.

"Used up the last of the other box. Between naps, Eva made Cocoa No-Bake cookies. Her dad always liked them so she made a batch for me." Fritz munched one. "Here, try one."

Reaching for a cookie, Barbara knocked Mark's file folder off the table onto the floor. "Mark Reining! What's this?"

"Fingerprints." Mark cringed.

"Yes, I know what fingerprints look like." Barbara tapped the sheet. "Why is Eva's name on this?"

"I had the lab pull her prints off the glass from this morning. I need them to check her identity." Mark took a deep breath. "Since that novel she's reading has a heroine with the same name as hers, I thought it would be wise to see if Eva Johnson is her real name. She may have forgotten her name. ... I mean what's the probability of Eva having the same name as a novel's heroine?"

"Probability is your field." Backing up, Fritz grabbed another cookie. "I'm going to take Rex out for some fresh air."

Mark watched his father retreating. Rex was a step ahead.

Barbara waited until her husband left. "You know how I feel about snooping into other people's private lives. So I don't need to lecture you. But promise me you won't tell Eva about this. I don't want her to think we're prying. Taking your guest's fingerprints isn't my idea of southern hospitality."

"I hope you understand I have to find out who Eva is for her sake." Mark bit deep into a chocolate cookie.

"Be careful how you treat her. She's very vulnerable. Don't take advantage of Eva."

"Mom! What kind of a man do you think I am?"

"You're a good son. I didn't mean it that way." Barbara toyed with a cookie. "I watched how she looks at you. Eva is very attracted to you."

"How can you tell that from just watching her at breakfast?" Mark stared at Eva's fingerprint card.

Barbara patted her son's hand. "Women's intuition. Trust me."

"And trust me. I would never take advantage of Eva."

~ 23 ~

"Don't touch that." Mark pulled Eva's hand back. "Trust me, it's poisonous. That's a Portuguese man-of-war."

"I know better than to touch one. It's just I haven't seen one that big for a long time." Eva knelt on beach sand at the water's edge. As a child, she had seen them after storms, blown in from the warm Gulf Stream. *Another of nature's deadly creatures,* Eva considered. *A Portuguese man-of-war is poisonous like the coral snake. Do they wear colorful skins to tempt an unsuspecting prey or to warn the wise? Or both?*

As she studied it, Mark watched her. Nearby children played in the surf. The water was warm and the afternoon heat had cooled. Low tide had passed and the ocean struggled to return.

Mark knelt and flicked open his fishing knife, using it like a lecture pointer. "Normally, we don't see man-of-wars this time of year, but last night's storm must have washed it in. Its poison is in these long tentacles that hang deep in the water. Unsuspecting fish swim into them like they were seaweed, thinking there is plankton to eat. But it's a trap. The fish brush the tentacles and poison is released. The more the fish struggles to get free, the more it gets tangled in the strings of poison. Soon the fish dies."

Eva studied the almost transparent Portuguese man-of-war with veins of purple fingering up its sides. *Purple is poison;* she remembered her mother's waning. Its body looked like a half inflated balloon, shaped like a small, squashed football with long hairy strings of purple hanging beneath it. "I know how it kills. But how does it eat if it has no mouth?"

"Good question." Mark flicked his knife closed.

"We can't just leave it." Eva pulled Rex back from sniffing it.

"I'll bury it. Even dead, it still has poison. The tourists, especially children, don't know how dangerous they are. You wait here, I'll get the scoop." Turning, Mark walked towards his bait bucket. His father was already wading into the surf to fish.

Growling, Rex kicked sand at the dangerous sea creature.

"Purple is poison," Eva whispered to Rex. "Too bad humans don't have your ability to smell danger. It would save us from …" The thought of Jim flashed in her mind and vanished.

Three children walked past dragging their floats as they waded into the beach waves and then headed into deeper water. Seagulls chattered as they fled the sandbar, disappearing under the wash of returning surf. Beyond them the breakers pounded.

"This should do it." Kneeling, Mark dug a hole in the sand and carefully slid in the man-of-war. The shovel firmly packed the sand, sealing the deadly sea creature in a sandy grave. "Now the beach will be safer."

"Look, you dug up an olive shell." Eva turned it over. "It's alive. The little creature is still inside. Poor thing, we probably scared it." After digging a shallow hole, she carefully laid the shell inside and covered it with a little sand.

"Didn't you want to keep it for your shell collection?"

"Oh no. It would be wrong to kill a little creature just to take its pretty shell." Eva looked up into Mark's eyes. She could see his approval and the character of a kind man. *Indeed,* she thought, *Mark reminds me of my father. I can see it in his eyes: a strong man with great respect for nature. And Mark is a nice specimen.*

Mark reached down to help her up. "We better be getting back. Dad is already out in the surf. I don't like him fishing alone after a storm. Don't want him to step into any potholes."

"Potholes?" Eva took his hand, letting him pull her up. A little faint from standing suddenly, she held onto him as they walked.

Rex tugged at his leash, eyeing a ball rolling down the beach.

Mark pointed south. "Normally, the ocean current flows in from the southeast, moving along with the Gulf Stream. Last night's storm was a northeaster. They slice in from the opposite direction, chopping into the beach and ripping sand out. The normal current fights against the storm surge. In some places they swirl around like small underwater tornadoes, sucking sand out of small areas, making holes on the bottom." Mark stopped to get his fishing pole. "Dad calls them potholes. Says some of them feel like they could swallow a car."

"Tell him to step sideways. The bottom's generally nearby."

"Sounds like you know the beach." He tucked bait into his pocket and walked into the ocean. "I'll give Dad your advice."

With her white pant legs rolled up, Eva waded knee deep into the surf and splashed water on her forehead. It cooled the heat radiating from deep inside her skull. *That's better,* she thought. *If I stand in the ocean long enough, my brain might just cool off.*

"No." Mark stepped in front of her. "Mom said you weren't to go swimming. With your fever you shouldn't overdo it."

"I'm not going to swim, just some bodysurfing."

Mark looked down her body. "Maybe we'll go bodysurfing later. Right now you're still to weak for that sport." Smiling, he backed into the surf.

"Okay. We'll save the swimming for tomorrow." She watched Mark wading out to his father, already fishing. Her legs wobbled at the impact of a knee-high wave. *Mark's right. I'm too weak for swimming.* She sighed, rolling up her long sleeves. *How can I be tired after all those naps today? Maybe I'm weak because I sleep too much. What I need is ... is –"* Her thoughts washed away with the throb pounding in her head.

Barking, Rex tugged at his leash, pulling her towards shore.

"Okay, Rex. We'll play in the sand. Let's make an old-fashioned sandcastle." Above the wave line, Eva sat down to rest.

After a short time on the beach, she was already growing weary. Any prolonged conversations took effort and concentration. The viral battle inside her mind was leaving potholes in her memories, as unseen as storm holes on the ocean's floor. The brain's electrical currents were swirling, washing away the minor thoughts of the day.

Sitting on the sand above the water line, Rex licked her face.

"I'm okay, Rex." Eva pulled a sack from her pocket. "A cookie will help. No, you can't have any. Dogs can't eat chocolate. Don't give me that look. I don't remember why." She munched one cookie and saved the other for her next boost of energy.

"Come on, help me dig a hole. Down to the water line."

Paws and hands dug into the soft sand creating a cereal bowl size hole with water pooling in the bottom.

"Perfect. Now sit, Rex. I'm going to show you how to build a real old-fashioned sandcastle." She glanced at Rex, who was stretched out on the sand, his head on his paws as he watched. "First, I take out a handful of wet sand. Then I'll drip it on my castle. As the sand slips off my fingers, it creates small stone shapes where it falls." Silent and trance like, Eva continued to scoop out more wet sand and dribbled it on the sandcastle, creating walls and fancy towers.

A paper-thin wave slipped across the sand, touching her toes.

Startled, she glanced at the ocean, surprised to see it had moved so close. "See that, Rex? It must have been the seventh wave. They always wash in farther than the others. Mom always said the seventh wave of an incoming tide was always bigger and stronger than the others. The tide is coming in fast."

Farther out, Mark and Fritz stood in chest high water, fishing. Not as deep as she saw them the night before but much safer considering the condition of the ocean floor. In front of her, she saw the deep holes created by the storm in the shallow slue. A little further north, the slue turned abruptly and emptied directly into the ocean with a channel of rushing water, strong and swift.

"See that, Rex. It's a run-out. You don't swim near those." Eva glanced back at Mark. He was well clear of the run-out. "Mark is a cautious man. And he's ... oh, what's the word?" Eva blushed.

Rex's head popped up and he looked out to his master, baiting a hook, then casting out into the calm water beyond the breakers.

Splashing, a little girl ran past and retrieved her yellow float, washing into the shallow slue by the shore. She stepped in a hole, tripped, and splashed into the water. Laughing, the little girl grabbed her yellow float and ran back to a boy riding in on a wave.

"That looks like her brother." Talking to Rex, Eva watched the boy and girl playing. "I wonder what it would be like to have a real brother? One who would play with you and care about you. Not like my half-brother. Dennis and I had only our mother in common, nothing else. I haven't seen him since I was twelve."

Eva tossed sand at an incoming wave, remembering the violence of her last meeting with Dennis. "At our mom's funeral, Dennis shoved my father into a table of flower arrangements," Eva told Rex. "Dad fell. I screamed. Dennis ran towards me. I tried to stop him. I was stupid; a twelve year old can't stop a grown man. Denis knocked me down and shouted, 'You're no sister of mine.' I sat on the floor and cried."

Sitting in the sand, Eva pulled her legs to her chest. "I wish I could forget that memory. Just wash it out of my mind forever."

~ 24 ~

"What's wrong?" Startled, Eva looked up.

Barking, Rex yanked his leash trying to get to the ocean.

"What is it Rex?" Eva glanced across the waves. Mark was reeling in his fishing line and Fritz was casting his out. "They're okay. Looks like Mark and his dad are catching some fish."

Facing up the beach, Rex barked louder.

Eva saw a flash of navy blue pop into the air and then the float fell back into the surf. Closer to shore, a small child screamed as he ran through the knee-high wave breaking on the sandbar. A little green float washed ahead of him. Chasing it, he stumbled in a hole and sank into the slue, now too deep for him.

Seeing the child panic, Eva ran to help him. His high-pitched screams could barely be heard over the pounding surf and a nearby blaring radio. Almost stumbling in the uneven slue, Eva scooped the frightened child from the water.

"You're okay. I've got you."

Stopping beside the child, Rex barked at the surf beyond.

A dark blue float washed ashore, beside Eva.

"Rex. Stay." Putting the little boy on the shallow side, Eva spoke softly as she slipped his hand around Rex's collar. "Hold on to the doggie. Stay with the doggie until mommy comes. Stay."

Reaching over, Eva grabbed the blue float and headed back into the surf. Her eyes searched the waves and her mind focused. *Where are the other two? The brother and sister. A few minutes ago, they were riding their floats in.*

Farther out, she saw heads bobbing beside a yellow float. Eva waded faster through the knee-deep waves. A sudden rush of water jerked her legs, toppling her. The float pulled free and swished past, heading out to sea.

It's a run-out. Oh my God! They're caught in a run-out.

Stepping faster through the deepening surf, she grabbed the float's rope and headed towards the two children dead ahead, floating out towards the last breaker.

I have to get to them before they're swept out. They'll panic in the deep water. Panic can kill even a good swimmer.

To minimize the impact, Eva turned sideways in the now waist high surf as a breaker smashed against her. Waves after a storm carry an angry punch, capable of knocking a strong man to his knees. She had seen her father smashed under their force.

Eva focused on the bobbing heads as she pushed against the current, yanking at her rolled up slacks and drenching her long sleeved blouse. Not being dressed for swimming slowed her progress but she knew a faster way. Eva stepped into the run-out, letting it pull her towards the children beyond. She knew it was a dangerous place to be. The current was strong and fast, ripping eddies of water out as the tide fought to roll in.

Use it. Don't fight it. It's a waste of energy. You know what to do. Get the children and swim parallel with the beach until you're free of the run-out. They aren't wide, just strong and frightening.

Her body turned sideways as a wave smashed against her ribs. The sound of the breakers grew louder and their size increased. She watched the small heads bobbing beside the yellow float near the last breaker.

Just focus on what to do. Remember they may be terrified. A panicked swimmer will grab for you. Even children can pull you under. If they do, drop under the water, they'll let go.

Screaming, the two children clung to the side of the small yellow float.

Eva dove under a face-high breaker. It was too high to jump. Diving under a breaker was safer, easier, and faster. Under the wave, Eva felt a sudden jerk. The float's rope tightened around her wrist. Above, the wave had smacked the blue float, yanking it back as the undercurrent dragged her out. Her head popped up and she swam towards the screams.

They're too exhausted to get on top of the float. And it's too small for two. I have to get there before they lose their grip.

Eva stopped swimming and let her feet drop. If she could touch bottom, she could easily pull them in safely. Her legs sank. Her toes reached, searching for the sand. There was a cold, swift current. There was no bottom. Her heart skipped a beat, then raced.

No bottom! ... Don't panic. Don't panic. It's just a hole that's all. A pothole. Take a deep breath. Focus. ... Get the children. I can swim. I have a float. Let the current do the work. Just don't let go of the float.

She wrapped the float's rope tighter around her wrist. With a crippled sidestroke, Eva swam on out to the two children. Their screams increased and the boy frantically reached for her.

"Hang on to your float. Hold on with both hands." Staying out of their reach, Eva spoke calmly to the children. "You're going to be okay. Just keep both hands on your float. Both hands."

"Help us!" The boy gasped. "It's sucking us out."

"You're okay. I'm going to take you in. Just hold on to your float." Eva watched the little girl clawing at the sides, barely able to keep her face above the water.

I have to get the girl on the float, she's too weak. Her lips are trembling. She can't hold on much longer.

"I'm going to put your sister on my float. I want you to hold onto both floats. Can you do that?"

"Yes. Hurry ... Hurry. My sister is slipping."

Eva scooted her float towards the boy and waited until he had one hand on each float. Turning, Eva grabbed around the little girl's chest. "Okay. Don't worry. I have you. I'm going to put you on the blue float. Then your brother."

Sobbing, the little girl let go. The child was too exhausted to scream anymore. Her little arms went limp.

"There you go." Eva pushed the girl onto the float. "Lie down and hold onto the rope. Both hands. ... Good girl. Okay, be ready for your brother. He's going to help you hold on. You're okay."

"I'm ready." With his lips quivering, the boy nodded. "Hang on, sis. I'm coming." As soon as he let go of the yellow float, the current sucked it out into the ocean.

Eva pushed the boy on top. With both children on the blue float, Eva swam parallel to the beach, heading north towards the lifeguard tower and north with the normal current. Eva hoped the lifeguard had spotted them by now. They didn't like swimmers beyond the breakers, especially after a storm. Eva prayed the lifeguard would have blown his whistle, dropped the tower flag, and be hightailing it through the water towards them.

I have to buy us some time. Eva concentrated. *Swim parallel with the beach, free of the run-out. Then head in towards shore. By then some handsome lifeguard will be there to meet me.*

After a few strokes, they were free of the run-out. Now ocean swells scooted them in towards the beach, towards the breakers.

"Look, Sis, we're going in." The boy's head rose.

"No, no," cried the little girl, grabbing her brother. "I scared."

"You'll be okay." Eva spoke softly, keeping them calm, hoping to keep their minds off the breakers forming in front of them. "I watched you riding the waves in. You're good at it."

"But we never make it all the way. Sis keeps falling off."

"Your sister can hold on to your neck and you can hold on to the rope on both sides." Eva watched the swell grow large as it approached the breaking point. "I'll tell you the secret of surfing."

"A secret?"

"Yes. Surfing is all a matter of location. You want to stay on the front edge of the wave. The front is where the pushing power is. Stay in front."

"Not the middle?"

"No. For floats, the push is in the front edge. Stay in front." Swimming slower, Eva scanned the beach trying to focus her thoughts. *Where are the lifeguards? What's taking them so long? We're getting too close to the breakers. ... Three on this float is too many. I can't ride in with them. My weight on the side will flip the float. ... I'll have to let go.*

"I scared," the little girl cried. "Waves too big."

"They're just right." Although tired, Eva kicked hard, moving the float forward between swells. It was important to be in the right location. The breaking crest was too dangerous for a float. After the wave curled in on itself, its wall of water would fall like a ton of bricks. The float would have to be beyond that danger zone.

Eva swam faster seeing the swell rising behind her, peaking, preparing to crest. This would have to be the wave. Behind it loomed the seventh wave, taller and more powerful: too powerful for children.

"Hang on to your brother's neck. Don't let go until you get to the beach. Young man, hang on to the rope on both sides of the float. And keep the float in the front of the wave. On the edge. In front. Understand?"

"In front," he repeated.

"Good. Ride this wave all the way to the beach." Exhausted, her heart pounded, feeling like it was smashing into her ribs. Her wet clothes hung heavy on her body.

Eva let her legs sink, feeling for the bottom.

A rush of cold water swept past her feet. There was no bottom.

"I scared," the little girl cried.

"You're going to be okay. Just hang on to your brother's neck." Eva swam towards the beach, pulling the float into position.

A roar behind her warned that the wave was crashing down.

Eva unwrapped her hand from the rope. The children would have to ride in alone, without her. Turning, Eva aligned the float. "Remember, keep the float in front of the wave."

"I can do that," the boy replied. "In front."

"Hang on." Eva shoved the float into the front of the breaker.

The children screamed.

The wave caught the float, pushing it towards the beach.

Eva ducked under the wave, avoiding its smashing force.

Water churned above, muffling the roar.

When her head popped up, Eva glanced at the children on the float halfway in. Quickly she looked back. Behind her the approaching wave loomed high.

It was not just a seventh wave, but a double one; two waves rolling in together. The crest was forming fast, curling in, and turning white with foam like a mad dog.

There was no time to swim from its fury.

Eva took a deep breath.

Her body sank into the cold, deep water.

~ 25 ~

"Eva!" Mark shouted before her head sank. With full force, a wave slammed his chest. His heart pounded, adrenaline washed through his muscles, and his mind raced. *I have to get to her fast. She's too weak. The surf is too strong. Where is she?*

A blue float with two children zipped in on the passing wave, riding the front edge. The boy was holding the rope with the little girl clinging to his neck.

Mark glanced at them. *The children are safe. The lifeguard will get them. I'm closer to Eva. I'll get her.*

A large wave roared in front of Mark. In shoulder high water, it was too high to jump. Diving under the breaker, he avoided the impact. Popping up on the other side, Mark scanned the water line.

Her head popped up, but Eva was still in the breaker zone.

Mark swam faster, trying to get there before the next wave smashed over her. "Eva! Behind you!"

She turned around. A ridge of water was cresting.

There was no time to shout. He watched her head sink beneath the breaker. *I have to get her before the next one,* Mark thought. *She's struggling to stay afloat. She doesn't have the energy to swim in. The next wave will be too much for her. She'll drown.*

He dove under the wave and surfaced, looking for her.

Eva was nowhere to be seen.

The next swell began to compress, forming another ridge, peaking, preparing to crest above where Eva went under.

Eva surfaced. Facing the wave, she backstroked away from it.

With his powerful muscles straining, Mark swam faster, racing the cresting wave. *I have to grab her before it breaks on top of her. It'll knock her out and the current will pull her beyond my reach.*

Above Eva, a curved wall of water rose. Along its thin edge, sunlight flashed like off a razor blade with foam falling from it.

"Eva!" Mark reached out. His hand caught hers. He saw her take a deep breath; he did the same. With a tug, Mark pulled her under, down deep. His arms slid around her waist as they sank.

Even below the surface, the horrible rumble of water smashing against water echoed. The churning surf whipped air bubbles with sand, clouding his visibility. Mark knew if he left go, the current would suck her into the murkiness and she would disappear. His grip tightened around her and he pulled her against his chest.

Her body was cold and limp in his arms.

He had to get her up fast. His lungs ached.

Time was running out.

Holding her tight, he kicked with powerful legs.

Popping out of the surf, Mark gasped for air.

She coughed.

"Eva." He held her body close. "Are you all right?"

"Okay."

"I'll take you in. Hold on." His arms chopped into the water. Mark glanced at the swell behind them, preparing to crest. It was time to get out of the way. With powerful strokes, Mark swam in, keeping Eva close. He could feel her legs kicking, but there was no power in them. She had no strength left.

"Just relax. I'll swim for both of us."

"Okay."

"We'll be there soon. Hold on, a breaker is behind us."

"Let's bodysurf in."

"Never tried that with two." Mark slid his arm around Eva, pulling her against his body. Her wet skin slipped against his.

"Let's try." She wiggled closer.

"I'm game." His muscles responded to her touch and firmed up for the ride.

The wave's forward thrust caught them, propelling them in on its leading edge. Their bodies skimmed the foaming water like a surfboard. The churning surf bubbled around them like warm champagne, swishing through their clothes and tingling their skin.

Eva giggled. Her hands slid up his back, drawing him closer.

"Don't do that." He laughed. Sinking in the bubbles, their lips bonded. Salty was their first kiss.

Mark pulled her up in the waist-high water. "We'll have to try that again, but another day. I've had enough excitement for now."

"You're a strong swimmer." Her hands slid down his chest. "Your body makes a good surfboard. I enjoyed the ride."

Scooping her in his arms, Mark carried her towards shore.

A lifeguard ran through the surf. "Is she all right?"

"She's okay."

"Anyone on the yellow float out there?" The lifeguard asked.

"No." Eva rested her head on Mark's chest.

On the beach, a crowd gathered around the emergency squad as the paramedics examined the little boy and his sister. Squirming under the attention, the boy refused to let go of his blue float. Nearby, their parents were talking to the lifeguard. Mark's father waited with Rex at the water's edge.

"Here we are." Mark stepped out of the water and walked to the rescue squad. "The paramedics have to examine you."

"No need. I'm fine." She coughed. "Really, I'm okay."

"Now, Eva, you know the routine. They have to make sure you didn't get water in your lungs. It's their job." Setting her on a stretcher, Mark motioned for the paramedic to follow.

"Is there a problem?" The paramedic asked.

"Eva has viral encephalitis. She has been sick for some time." Mark watched her.

"She shouldn't be swimming," the paramedic scolded.

"She wasn't, but she must have seen the children in trouble. I don't think she realized the danger of going out there. She forgets how easily she tires."

The medic looked at Eva. "We'll double check your wife."

"She's not my —"

"Mark." Fritz pulled his son out of the way. "How's Eva?"

"She's exhausted and cold. Eva should have let a lifeguard get the children."

"Might have been too late." Fritz nodded towards the lifeguard talking to the children. "From what I overheard, the lifeguard was already on the beach breaking up a fight. By the time he would have gotten there, it could have been too late. The little boy said they were being pulled out fast and his sister was losing her grip on her float. The boy said the lady rescued them and told him the secret of surfing the waves."

Rex yanked at his leash.

"Oh, I almost forgot. Their baby brother said Rex pulled him out of the slue. Said the big doggie saved him. He didn't want to leave go of Rex's collar and he wanted to keep the big doggie." Fritz patted Rex. "And how was your save?"

"I thought I was going to lose Eva. Every time she went under a wave, my heart stopped. She is too weak to fight the surf." Mark studied Eva talking to the children. "I must admit, she knows how to handle herself in the ocean. Dove under those waves like a pro. She's just too weak to be swimming."

Fritz tugged Rex's leash. "You've got a big enough crowd here. I'm going to take Rex and the fishing gear up to the house. Call me if you want me to pick the two of you up in the Jeep."

Mark took the cell phone. "I'll let you know."

The spectators wandered away and the children begged their parents to let them go back out into the surf. A lifeguard waded in from the ocean, towing the lost yellow float, returning it to the little girl before heading to his tower. The backup rescue squad pulled away, leaving the paramedics and their van.

A dune buggy, with two surfboards mounted on top, pulled up. "Professor Reining." Bob hopped out. "Dispatch said there was a problem on your patch of the beach. Figured you'd be checking it out. Didn't expect you to be in the middle of it."

Mark watched one medic put a blanket over Eva as the other one checked her blood pressure again. "Did your team finish checking out the private air carriers?"

"Yes. None of them flew in anyone by the name of Eva Johnson. We also checked all the rental car companies and at the train station. No luck there either." Bob pulled a small notepad from his pocket. "Nothing under boat rentals and none of the yachts docked here are registered under her name."

Mark saw Eva hugging the little boy before he ran back to the surf, tugging his blue float with his father and the girl tagging along with her yellow float. "Did you check with Greyhound?"

"Done that, no luck. Most bus tickets are for short hops with cash payments. Unless the ticket was purchased with a credit card, they don't have a record." Bob flipped a page. "Since Eva was found on my beach, I checked with all the concession owners. Got one hit up the beach at Joe's bike rental. Said a blond matching her description bought a bike there the day they found that aunt's body up the beach. He remembered Eva looked like someone hit her."

"Did Eva pay by check or use a credit card?"

"Nope. Cash he thinks. He's not a man for keeping records."

"By chance, did she talk about where she was from?"

"Nope. He only remembered her saying something about going home." Bob sighed. "We haven't found any record of her living here or coming in. It's as if she washed ashore like that Cuban kid awhile back. Maybe she's an illegal alien."

Mark looked at the sunlight sparkling on Eva's wet hair. "Not many Cubans with fine blond hair and fair skinned. Besides, she speaks perfect English. A slight northern accent though."

"Maybe she's from Canada. A lot of them winter down here."

"Bob, it sounds like you're grabbing at straws."

"This missing person's stuff is tougher than I thought. I was sure we'd have identified her by now. So far, we don't have a clue as to who Eva Johnson is. I'm beginning to wonder if that is her real name." Bob closed his notebook.

"Excuse me." The paramedic interrupted. "She refuses to go to the hospital. I explained it would only be a quick checkup but she kept mumbling something about doctors finding bullets that didn't belong. Do you know what your wife is talking about?"

"Wife?" Bob asked.

Mark shrugged his shoulders. "They just assumed that since I carried her out of the water, she belonged to me."

"Sure, Professor. Perhaps I should check the missing mermaid reports." Bob rolled his eyes. "I'll stick around and give you and your ... wife a lift home."

"Let me see how she is first." Walking over to Eva, Mark grew concerned. *She looks exhausted,* he thought. *A few minutes out there took its toll on her. Eva needs to rest.*

Mark stepped beside her. "They want a doctor to look at you."

"You don't like the way I look?" She grinned.

"You look fine. But they want to make sure you're okay."

"I'm fine." Dropping the blanket, Eva stood. Her wet clothes clung to her like sheer white skin. "Mark, will you take me home?"

~ 26 ~

"Oh, you poor thing. Are you all right?" Barbara held the door open. "You look exhausted."

"I'm fine, Mom." Mark carried Eva inside his parents' home. Still wet from her ocean rescue, she was limp and looked pale like a china doll. *Eva doesn't even have the strength to hold her head up. I don't know how she managed to swim as long as she did. She's exhausted and her body feels like an ice cube.*

It was a warm August day but the deeper ocean water was seventy-eight degrees. Warm for air temperature but water twenty degrees below body temperature drains heat from an individual. In time, it can sap the strength of a healthy swimmer.

"Mark, I know you're fine. I was talking about Eva." Barbara felt Eva's forehead. "With her fever, she shouldn't be swimming. She could get a relapse. Take her in the bedroom."

"Should we take her to the emergency room?" Mark asked.

"No! I'm fine." Eva's cold hands slipped from Mark's neck. "You can put me down. I rested in the dune buggy on the way back. Really, I can walk."

Reluctantly, Mark put her down, but held onto her just in case. "You need a hot shower. You're chilled and white as a sheet."

"Mark's right. A warm shower, something to eat, and rest are what the doctor ordered." Barbara took Eva's arm. "Mark, you need to put on some dry clothes before you catch cold. Can't have Eva exposed to any germs."

Mark watched his mother guide Eva down the hall. Behind them, sunlight streamed in from the west window illuminating Eva's white outfit. Still wet, the fabric clung to her curves and shimmered as she moved down the darker hall, giving the illusion of an angelic figure beside his mother.

"Are you okay?" Fritz tossed a towel to his son.

"I just looked away and she was gone."

"That's what the mother said about her children." Fritz dried off Rex. "The mother turned to listen to a song on the radio, and when she looked up her two oldest children were gone and the youngest was holding onto a big dog. The mother said her heart stopped. She ran to the little tike, babbling about the doggie saving his life. She yelled to her husband who was buying ice cream from a vendor. And he ran up the beach to the lifeguard station."

Although Mark nodded, his mind was on the figure walking towards what had been his sister's bedroom. Old memories of his sister mingled with the image of Eva. Both haunted him.

Eva glanced back, smiled, and disappeared into the bedroom.

"Mark, are you listening?"

"Yeah."

"You look like you could use a good, hot cup of coffee."

Inside, Mark felt the smoldering of desire sparked by Eva's body clinging to him as they rode through the bubbling surf. It was an intoxicating sensation. "No, I need a cold shower."

"You already look a little blue around the gills."

"Dad, did you and Mom ever go bodysurfing? Together?"

"Yep. But that was after we were married." Fritz grinned. "You and Eva were bodysurfing together?"

"Well, I had to bring her in and she was too weak, so I held her tight and we bodysurfed in together."

"In that case, you better take a long, cold shower. I'll make you a big pitcher of ice tea."

As the screen door closed behind him, Mark could hear his father chuckling. Walking through the breezeway, Mark inhaled the warm afternoon air, calming his adrenaline rush. His apartment was over his parents' wide double car garage and had once been a self-sufficient rental cottage. Detached from the main house it afforded him privacy and a feeling of independence. Yet he was there for his parents if they needed him and his presence filled the void in their lives left from the death of his sister.

Inside, Mark checked his fax machine and then headed to the shower. Standing in the cold water, he tried not to think. *I need to keep some distance. After all, Eva could be someone's girlfriend or wife. Surely there has to be a man in her life.* Cold water streamed down his face but he could feel the heat inside him, yearning.

The phone rang. Mark listened to the fax machine pick up. That's probably about the next faculty meeting. *Bruce couldn't have gotten an answer this fast. He's a hotshot Secret Service agent with lots of pull, but it'll take time for the FBI to search all their fingerprint records for her real identity. Unless Eva is on their hot list.*

Flicking off the cold water, Mark grabbed a towel. Stepping beside the fax machine, he watched a small section of a picture beginning to form as he slipped into dry clothes.

"What on earth is that?"

After the fax machine finished, Mark slipped the copies in a file folder and walked back to his parents' home. The information he received from Bruce at the Secret Service raised more questions than it answered. Mark knew it would disturb his parents.

"What's wrong, Mark?" Fritz sat in his captain's chair.

Mark dropped a file folder on his parents' dining room table and fumbled for his cordless phone tucked in his shirt pocket. Its ringing was quickly silenced and the formalities were short. "Bruce. ... Right, I got the fax. What's the scoop?"

Mark grabbed a tablet. "Give that to me again. ... Kidnapping. Is the FBI involved? I understand their reluctance to give all their details to you. ... The local authorities are considering it a homicide. What's his name? Detective Paul Galloway. Yeah. I know how the FBI is. But I could use two days. Can you buy me that much time? ... Thanks Bruce. I owe you one."

A click ended the call but Mark held onto the phone. His thoughts swirled faster than his mind could grasp.

"Well?" Fritz scooted a glass of iced tea in front of his son.

Turning from the table, Mark walked to the open living room door, closed it, and flicked the lock. He needed a moment to think. *It's worse than I thought. Bruce could only get the basic facts from the FBI and the local police. How much more is there? What should I do now? It's my duty to protect my parents and my students, but what about Eva? How can I protect her unless I know the rest of the facts?*

Mark heard his father's footsteps fade away. *How should I tell Dad? He was against my sending in Eva's fingerprints. He's not going to like this.*

A few minutes later, Fritz returned and sank into his captain's chair. "Mark, I locked the back door. Sounded like Bruce found something. I have to know. How bad is it?"

Returning to the dining room table, Mark pulled the fax photo from the folder and slid it to his father. "Eva Johnson is her real name. Her teaching position required a fingerprint check. The FBI had her file active but it wasn't for a missing person's report. They think Eva is dead. ... The police are looking for her body."

Fritz studied the fax photo. "Is this her car?"

"Yes. Actually it's her Blazer."

"Doesn't look like much now. If she walked away from this, it's no wonder her memory is fuzzy. And that would explain all those bruises. Looks like it was quite an accident."

"It was no accident." Mark took a sip of tea. "Bruce couldn't get all the details, but by the time the local police located the car, they already suspected foul play. At the scene, the crime lab found a bullet hole in a piece of glass. Later they reconstructed the driver's side window and found two 9mm bullet holes."

"Hardly a hunting accident."

"Exactly. And yesterday the doctor here removed a 9mm slug from Eva's arm. But she doesn't remember being shot." Mark glanced down the hall. "I thought it was just a memory problem from her viral encephalitis. But that's only part of it."

Fritz studied the photo of a crumpled Blazer resting on its side in a creek. "Do the police suspect a drive-by shooting?"

"No. Bruce said the FBI had already been called in because they suspected a kidnapping. But no ransom request was made and they assumed it was either a botched kidnapping or a homicide. The local police are continuing the investigation."

"Local police? Was she shot by that nephew who killed his aunt here in Daytona?"

"No. Eva is from Ohio." Mark walked over to the bookcase and pulled out a road atlas. "Here it is. Mansfield, Ohio. It's about halfway between Cleveland and Columbus."

Fritz glanced at his son. "Are you going to call the Mansfield police and let them know Eva is alive?"

"No. ... I don't know anything about that police department or this Detective Galloway. There are too many holes in their story. For all I know they could be covering up something. Why did the FBI back out? Why are they holding out on the feds? The police report seems a bit fishy to me. So I'm going to Mansfield to find some answers before I tell them about Eva."

"What are you going to tell Eva?"

"Nothing for the moment. I don't think Eva has the energy to cope with the trauma of knowing someone tried to kill her."

~ 27 ~

"Aren't they precious?" Smiling, Eva ambled into the dining room carrying her two kittens. "They've finally opened their little eyes. It's their first look at the world. I wonder what they think."

After a warm shower and blow-drying her hair, Eva felt refreshed. Two cookies and a cup of hot tea gave her an energy boost. Her muscles, however, were still a little wobbly from her swim in the strong ocean current.

"Let's go sit on the sofa." Holding her arm, Barbara guided Eva through the dining area into the living room. "You'll be more comfortable here until dinner is ready."

Sitting at the dining room table nearby, Mark glanced at Eva hugging her kittens, then at the fax photo in his hand.

With assistance, Eva sat on the edge of the sofa cuddling the kittens. In her hands, their little furry bodies felt as weak as she did. *They seem so helpless,* she thought. *But with a little love and good food, my kitties will be strong in no time.*

"Is it okay for the kittens to be on your good sofa?"

"Yes, dear. Now you should rest for a bit. You must be exhausted from rescuing those two."

"No, I found the kittens yesterday under the dumpster." Eva set them on her lap. "The trash man did the heavy work getting them out for me. I couldn't leave the little creatures starve."

Barbara smiled. "I was talking about your pulling the two children from the ocean. They could have drowned."

"The children had a float. Getting caught in the run-out just frightened them. All I did was pull them back. Actually it was Rex who saved them. He must have heard their shouts and started barking. I didn't notice they were being pulled out but Rex did. He's the hero. I just took the float out to the children."

Eva glanced out the front window at the ocean. *That swim did cool my hot little brain.* Eva's thoughts slipped inward. *This viral encephalitis is the strangest illness I've ever had. Even though my short-term memory is failing, thoughts are flashing through my mind at light speed, almost nonstop. Strange thoughts and feelings, all so real, so vivid, so ... what's the word ... I don't think there's one to describe this feeling. It's the weirdest experience of my life.*

After the silence caught Eva's attention, she glanced at Mark and his parents looking at her. Even Rex sat in front of her, staring up with big brown eyes.

The kittens meowed. "Mark, what should I name them?"

"What would you like to call them?" Mark closed his folder.

"Let's call the tan one Sandy. I don't know if it's a boy or a girl, so Sandy will suit either. Calico kittens are always females so I'll call her Princess after my cat."

"You have a cat?"

"Yes, but she was killed. The vet said it was ant poison. Be careful what you eat, my little darlings." Stroking the calico kitten, Eva's thoughts rambled. *I don't understand how it happened. I don't use insecticides on the garden or keep poisons in the house. And surely no ant poison. So what killed Princess or who?*

"Are you all right?" Mark touched Eva's arm as he sat down.

"I'm fine."

"I'll get you another cup of hot tea." Barbara turned.

"Barbara. Lets go for a walk." Fritz got up. "We need to talk."

"Well in that case you can help me in the kitchen. While I fix Eva some tea, you can make the salad and we can talk."

As the sound of their footsteps faded, silence returned to the living room. The ocean lay muffled far beyond the wall of windows and closed doors.

As Mark fluffed two pillows and slid them behind Eva's back, his lips tightened but he remained silent.

"Mark, is something wrong?"

"No. Why do you ask?"

"You look worried."

"I was worried about you being out in the surf today. You aren't strong enough to go swimming."

"But I'm a good swimmer. I just don't like being in over my head. As long as I can touch bottom, I feel safe."

"If you can touch bottom, you don't need to swim."

"True. But it's good exercise. I have –" She paused to consider. *No don't talk about that. He'll ask questions that I might not want to answer. I don't want to get Mark involved with my problems. With my fuzzy thinking, I'm not sure what my problem is, let alone know how to explain it to a stranger. And what would Mark think of me? Nice women don't get involved with ... with men like Jim.*

"What do you have?"

"I forgot what I was going to say." Smiling, Eva looked out the window at the sea oats blowing in the evening breeze. Sunlight glistened on their seedpods, golden like ripening wheat fields in Ohio. "I have imposed on your hospitality long enough. I should be going home to the West Indies."

"But yesterday you agreed to stay with us." Mark picked up the tan kitten. "You and your kittens need to get your strength back. And I don't want you to leave."

Staying appealed to Eva but going home tugged at her like the ocean's run-out current. It was swift and strong.

Looking away from the door, Eva spotted the cordless phone on the dining room table. *The phone book,* she thought. *That's how I can find the address.* "Do you have a phone book handy? I have to look up the West Indies. I've forgotten the phone number."

"You know motels often change their names." Mark walked over to the bookcase and paused. "I want you to stay with us for a while. You're much too weak to be alone. Besides, they may be full. It's getting close to Labor Day weekend."

"Don't you mean Memorial Day? Labor Day is in September. This is the beginning of summer, that means it has to be Memorial Day." Eva took the phone book from him and flipped through the yellow pages. Slowly scanning the list of motels, their names brought back memories. As a child, the bright neon signs in creative shapes had fascinated her. They were all so different and had clever names with a tropical flair. But now the list included big national chain hotels. Stack of concrete boxes, her dad had said. There was nothing homey about them. Eva sighed.

Mark watched her finger skim over the last section, again. "A new owner probably changed its name. Do you know the address?"

"No, I'm afraid I don't remember. I swear I'd lose my head if it weren't attached." Rubbing her forehead, Eva watched the kittens pawing the pages. "Oh, well. If I can't find the West Indies, maybe I can find Ocean Dunes."

The kittens crawled up the sofa arm and began to explore the mountain of pillows behind Eva.

"I'll look it up for you." He reached for the phone book.

Eva closed it. "No need. I can find it. ... Mark?"

"What?"

"Did you ever get lost as a child? Like in a big crowd in a strange airport. Suddenly you turn around and there are no familiar faces." Feeling lost, Eva put her head on his shoulder for comfort.

"Yes." Mark slipped his arm over her shoulder. "When I was seven, I got lost at the raceway. Dad always took me to the Daytona 500. It was a cold February day and I ran ahead looking for a short cut. When I stopped, I didn't know where I was."

Eva snuggled closer, feeling Mark's strong arms pull her closer like when he pulled her from the surf. "What happened?"

"At first I thought Dad would be there soon. But he didn't come. So I pushed through the crowd looking for him. I couldn't find him anywhere. Then suddenly Dad grabbed me from behind and hoisted me into his arms. I gave him the strongest chokehold he ever had." Mark's voice was soothing and reassuring.

"How did you feel, being lost?" Eva cuddled closer.

"Strange. The race didn't interest me anymore. I just wanted to go home." Mark stroked her hair. "After watching a few laps, we left. Dad said he was afraid I would catch a cold, but I think he was just as upset about the incident as I was. After we got home, we watched TV and I curled up beside him on the sofa."

"Childhood memories are always so vivid." Feeling safe, Eva closed her eyes, hoping to ease the throbbing in her head. "Mark, I need to tell you something."

"I'm listening." He leaned closer as her voice grew softer.

"I'm sorry, Mark. I've forgotten what I was going to say."

He stroked her hair. "Don't worry. You're just tired. We'll have plenty of time to talk later."

"My thoughts keep slipping away," she whispered.

Her craving for sleep returned. It was the only thing that freed her from the headaches and thoughts racing through her mind: too many, too fast, all swirling together. They wore her out. As her body went limp, her eyes closed. Eva could no longer fight it. The deep sleep crashed over her like a breaking wave.

~ 28 ~

"Where am I?" Eva rolled over in the bed. In the dim light, the bedroom looked familiar but it took the nudging of a German shepherd's nose to put the pieces together. "Well, is this another dog and lamp dream?"

Rex's soft whine seemed to disagree.

At one-fifteen in the morning, the house was quiet and dark except for the shell lamp on the nightstand. Conchs, scallops, and auger shells fanned out from its plaster base with white coral standing tall like a castle tower. Hidden behind a tall scallop was a nightlight. It illuminated the pearly interior of the abalone shell, shimmering with turquoise, hot pink, and warm cream.

Reaching over, Eva touched the rough spire of coral. Rex nudged her hand away and she petted his soft, furry head.

"Okay, Rex, I was just kidding about the dog and lamp dream. You're real and I know where I am, although I'm not sure how I got here. The last thing I remember was sitting on the sofa with Mark's arms around me. ... He has such a nice body, so cuddly, like a teddy bear. A big, strong teddy bear."

Rex dashed to the corner of the room and returned with a big brown teddy bear with a pink bow. He offered it to Eva.

"Good, boy. You like teddy bears too." Patting Rex's head, she studied the collage of colorful spools of thread mounted on the wall. "Mark's mother must like to sew. If you squint, it almost looks like an Amish quilt. That's about the last thing I remember before I left Ohio. I think I drove into Amish country."

Rex put his head on his teddy bear and listened to Eva.

"But I don't remember getting home or where I left my Blazer. It wasn't in the garage and it wasn't in Kroger's parking lot. Maybe it's at the repair shop for service." She glanced back at the light. "Doesn't matter. I wasn't up to driving all the way to Florida. The bus was better. I got to nap on the way down."

After swallowing another antibiotic, Eva recorded taking it and put the wet cloth on her forehead. It felt cool, but not as refreshing as her dip in the ocean. Inside, her brain felt like smoldering charcoal. With her immune system weak from the swim, the viral encephalitis increased its attack. More brain cells would die in the battle, destroying more of the neuronal-network.

Whining, Rex nudged her arm.

"You know I'm sick, don't you?" Eva patted him. "The only time Princess slept on my bed was when I was sick. When she got worried, she come over and licked my face to wake me. Pets know when people are sick. They can smell it. At least you can smell the antibiotics oozing through my pours. Rex, did you know that some dogs are trained to alert people to seizures? ... Don't look at me like that. I saw that on TV, I swear."

Rex sniffed her arm and rested his head on the bed.

Curled on her side, Eva pulled her legs closer to her chest. The back of the neck, where it joined the skull, ached and her stomach felt like a boulder when she laid on her back. Remaining curled and motionless on her side brought comfort.

The kittens cuddled together, sleeping in their basket.

Rex stretched out on the floor.

"Sorry, Rex, I have to rest." Swiftly, the craving for sleep returned. Her eyes closed and the heavy sleep took hold. Each time its grip got tighter, pulling her deeper into a coma-like sleep. It brought dreams more real than life. An altered reality few ever experience, generated from the psychotic state of a brain fever.

For a time, Eva remained almost motionless, curled on her side. Her breathing slowed and her eyes darted beneath her eyelids. Her subconscious returned to a familiar vision.

I'm glad I came back to this place. It cools my brain. It feels so good to lie here on the Siberian tundra. The snow is so cold it's frozen into small hard pellets like grains of sand. It's a pretty sight. I love the way sunlight makes the snow sparkle like diamond glitter sprinkled on a cold white blanket.

There's the Ice Palace in the distance. Maybe I can get to it this time. The pale winter sun is on the horizon. I can feel the Arctic wind slapping my back and its cold is seeping into my bones. When my form shatters, its crystals will be blown towards the Ice Palace. Then I'll be home. There is no one left here, just me, and I will soon be gone.

What's that black figure on the horizon? It doesn't belong here. This is a cold land of white. Why is that figure walking from the Ice Palace towards me? Doesn't he know it's too late? My body is already frozen. I will soon be gone, blown like the other ice crystals into the cold light of the Ice Palace. It's waiting for me.

With a jerk, Eva sat up. Suddenly wide awake, her mind was focused on distress signals reaching it.

I'm not breathing.

Her mind was aware of its pending doom.

I can't feel my heart beating.

She waited for a response.

Breathe, breathe!

Adrenaline rushed through her body, somehow reaching her heart, kicking it into sporadic beats. Finally, she inhaled. Her mind was awash with chemicals and her thoughts were crystal clear. The dangerous seconds had passed.

Frantically, Rex pawed at her arm.

"What's wrong, Rex? Did I frighten you? Did you smell death on my breath?" She gave him a big hug. "I'm okay. See I'm breathing now. Calm down. I'm okay, really I am."

Her words calmed him but he tugged at the sheet.

"You're right. I should get up and get my blood moving."

Slipping out of bed, Eva grabbed the tablet from the nightstand. Her little spiral notebook had been lost but Mark had given her a legal tablet. Its bright yellow pages had plenty of room to list what she had done that day, notes of things to do, and one page listing the time she took her medication. She had given up on trying to remember the little things and relied on notes.

"Come on Rex, I need to find a dictionary. I want to write a new will." She slipped out of bed. "After reading that article, the 'Aunt Killer', I've changed my mind about leaving my worldly possessions to my niece. Not that she'd do any anything that drastic to get money, but –"

Maggie sounded frantic on the phone recording. The thought troubled Eva. *Maggie said she needed help, but I know that means she needs money. How much does she want this time? And how desperate is she? Would Maggie kill her Aunt Eva for her money like that nephew killed his elderly aunt for hers?*

Walking down the hall, Eva stepped into the dining area and searched through the bookcase. After finding a dictionary, she followed Rex to the kitchen. There the light wouldn't wake anyone and it was cheerful enough for a somber task.

"Let me think." Talking to Rex, Eva sat down and flipped to a new page. "I want this to look official. How do lawyers start? Something like, 'this is my last will and testament.' Then they throw in, 'being of sound mind and body.' No." Eva erased that line. "Better scrap that. Neither my mind nor body is sound. But good enough for deciding who gets my stuff."

Under the overhead kitchen light, the shiny yellow walls looked like lemon pie with meringue curtains at the window. It was a friendly room except outside the darkness seemed menacing.

After closing the curtains, Eva returned to writing. "Rex, I have to keep this simple with small words. God knows I've lost my ability to spell. This viral encephalitis zapped it for sure."

Rex watched the dictionary pages flip and pencil tap.

After writing the basics, her pencil stopped. "So who gets my stuff? Not many choices left. There's my older half-brother, Dennis. I think he still lives in Denver but I haven't seen since I was twelve. I wouldn't recognize him if I passed him on the street. We may have a few genes in common, but that's all."

Eva toyed with the pencil. "Then there is Dennis' daughter. Maggie is about my age and we used to be close. And we had some good times when she first moved to Columbus but then she changed. She doesn't have much time for her Aunt Eva anymore. Unless she needs money, then she shows up on my doorstep."

Rex put his chin on Eva's leg.

"I can see why people leave their money to their pets. At least they are faithful and loving." She hugged Rex. "I know. I'm getting too tired to think and should go back to bed. But just in case I don't wake up from one of those dreams, I have to finish my will. The question is: To whom should I leave my worldly possessions?"

~ 29 ~

Daytona Beach, Florida – 7:00 am – August 21st

"My Delta Airlines flight to Ohio leaves shortly after my morning class." Mark walked across the kitchen of his parents' home and poured a cup of coffee. "After I land in Columbus, I'll rent a car and drive up to Mansfield. My appointment with Detective Galloway is just before noon."

Barbara pulled open the white drapes over her kitchen sink. "Take him to lunch. He'll be more talkative after a good meal. Mark, do you want one or two pancakes this morning?"

"Just one. I'll get a snack on the flight." Staring out the window, Mark watched the ocean rolling in under the bright morning sun. *It's a good day for flying,* Mark thought. *One stop in Atlanta, then a direct flight to Ohio. Haven't been to Columbus since I was a Secret Service agent working the Presidential campaign. It's the bellwether of America, a campaign staff aid told us. Columbus represents Middle American values and if you can't carry Ohio, you're not going to make it to the White House.*

"I'll make you two." Barbara flipped on the stove burner.

"Fine." On the far sand dune, Mark studied the sea oats on their tall thin stalks. They were almost motionless in the calm morning air and silhouetted against the rising sun they looked almost black. Dark thoughts surfaced. *It's hard to picture someone with Midwest values trying to kill Eva. She's kindhearted and trusting. Not the kind of person to have enemies who would want her dead. So what was the motive? Money? But with little more than two hundred dollars in her pocket and a secondhand bike, it seems unlikely that money would be the motive.*

"Mark. Your pancake is ready." Barbara slid the syrup beside his plate. "You look worried. Anything wrong?"

"I just thought of some more questions for that Mansfield detective. Hand me that tablet."

"That's Eva's tablet."

"I only need one sheet." Mark reached across the table and pulled the tablet from under the dictionary.

Barbara put the teakettle on the stove. "When I went to check on Eva about three this morning, I found her in here. She was writing something. Must have been important, she was looking up every word. I made her eat some toast and sent her back to bed."

Looking at Eva's handwriting on the tablet, Mark sank into his chair. His chest tightened as his eyes scanned the title: "Last Will and Testament of Eva Johnson."

Clearly printed on the legal tablet were Eva's last wishes. In it, she gave everything she had to Mark Reining for the kindness he had shown her during her last days. The only request was for him to see that her two kittens got a good home.

"Mark? Are you okay?"

Slowly, he slid the tablet back under the dictionary. "Mom, is Eva getting worse?"

With a cup of tea, Barbara sat down beside her son. "I'm worried about her. In the short time Eva has been here, she's gotten weaker. Swimming out to save those children yesterday didn't help. And she's barely eaten enough to keep an ant alive."

"Mom. Promise me: if Eva gets worse while I'm gone, you'll take her to the hospital. Tell them not to worry about her not having insurance, I'll pay her expenses." Mark sliced into his pancake. "I want her to get well, whatever it costs."

"Yes, I know how you feel about Eva." Barbara patted his arm. "Don't worry, Mark. I talked with Doctor Williams last night and he's coming over to see Eva before his morning surgery. Since his son died, he's taken a special interest in anyone with viral encephalitis. And I'm taking a few days off. I'll take care of her."

Thinking about Eva's last will, Mark glanced back at the yellow legal tablet. *If Eva has relatives, she would have named them in her will, unless there is some conflict there. That could be a motive. Women are more likely to be harmed by someone close: family, friend, ex-boyfriends, or a husband. Most often they are crimes of passion ... or greed, like that nephew who murdered his aunt a few days ago. And even if Eva doesn't have money, someone may have taken out a large insurance policy on her.*

"Here's your second pancake." Barbara slipped another one on his plate. "Where's your dad?"

"He took Rex for a walk on the beach."

"No. We're back." Walking in, Fritz hung up the leash. "Rex needed to get out. He spent the night sleeping beside Eva's bed. I think he's worried about her. As soon as he got in, he made a beeline for her room."

A few minutes later, there was the clicking of paws and feeble footsteps in the hall. Eva turned the corner with Rex by her side.

"Good morning." Glancing at Mark, Eva smiled, then put the kittens in the corner box and stared out the kitchen window. The sunlight sparkled on her golden hair. "Looks like a beautiful day."

"You're up early." Mark pulled out her chair. As her hair swished forward, he noticed an old bruise on the back of her neck, the purple now turning yellow. The photo of her crumpled Blazer flashed in his mind. *Is that bruise from the accident or did someone hit her? How could anyone do that? She isn't strong enough to defend herself. When I get my hands on him, I'll –"*

"Mark, what's today's date?" Eva pulled the yellow tablet out from under the dictionary.

"It the 21st."

"May or June?" Her pencil hesitated on the page.

"August."

"August?" Eva gave him a questing look. "Are you sure?"

Mark retrieved the newspaper from the counter and gave it to her. He recalled in the hospital Eva couldn't remember either the date or year. "Last night's paper is dated the 20th, so that makes today the 21st of August."

Eva studied the newspaper date before printing it on her document. "Do you have an envelope?"

Mark watched her carefully tear the page off the tablet and neatly fold it in thirds. "Do you want me to mail that to a friend?"

"I want to put this in my safe deposit box." After laying the paper on top of the dictionary, Eva spooned sugar into her tea. "All I have to do is find the key for my safe deposit box. I sure hope I didn't lose it. Banks charge a lot to replace those keys."

"Where do you bank?"

"I don't remember the bank's name. But I wrote it down, in my small notebook. Wherever that is."

"Eva. You need a good breakfast." Barbara reached into the cupboard. "Do you want pancakes or oatmeal?"

"Oatmeal. Just a small bowl."

The teakettle whistled and the saucepan clanged against the stove burner. Barbara poured oatmeal into the water and Fritz concentrated on his stack of pancakes. Stretched out beside the kittens' box, Rex kept a careful eye on them, nudging them back in as they tried to climb out.

On a paper napkin, Mark jotted down the questions that flooded his mind. *I have to ask that Detective Galloway who would profit from Eva's death. Were there any insurance policies on her?*

In what bank does she have a safe deposit box? What about relatives? Old boyfriends? ... There has to be a motive.

Ripping a page from her tablet, Eva smiled at Mark, busy writing on a paper napkin. "Here, why don't you use a piece of paper? I've never used a napkin for my lesson plans."

Startled, Mark looked up and took the paper. "Your lesson plans? Are you a teacher?"

"I am, part-time. Or at least I was."

"What do you teach, where?" He watched her rub her forehead and bite her lip. This was the first time he had gotten her to talk about her past. Now he was concerned he had blown it by snapping back such a pointed question that obviously upset her.

Eva glanced at the doorway. "Do you have class today?"

"A morning class. I was just making some last minute notes. You know how teaching is." He baited her for a response. "Don't you sometimes have last minute topics to cover in your class?"

The kitchen became quiet. Even the teakettle hushed.

"Art is a little different." Eva glanced out the kitchen window. "This would be a good place to bring my art class. They could sit on the sand dunes and paint. It would give them a change of pace. Generally, I find interesting locations on drives through the countryside. ... I remember driving."

Her voice faded and her spoon shook. Eva stared into her tea.

I've upset Eva, Mark thought. *Her hand is shaking and she looks like her thoughts are a million miles away. Perhaps more like a thousand miles away, in Mansfield, trying to recall that last drive. From the looks of her Blazer, she's better off not remembering that accident. No, that's wrong. The 9mm bullet in her arm was no accident.*

Mark glanced at her left arm; a long white sleeve camouflaged all signs of violence. *Who would want to hurt Eva?*

~ 30 ~

"You're leaving?" Eva's words hung in the calm morning air as they stood on the front deck. In the sunlight, her hair was as golden as the salt glazed sea oats on the sand dune behind her. Beyond her, the low breakers lapped on the shore with a lazy beat.

Still holding her arm to keep her steady, Mark stepped closer. "I'll only be gone for a day. It's a … business trip."

"I guess our bodysurfing will have to wait until you get back." She felt his strong arms draw her closer. *He's so kind,* she thought. *Kind is not the right word. He's much more than that. It's like a strong current is pulling me towards him. I feel all warm and bubbly when he holds me like this.*

"No swimming today." Mark brushed a strand of hair from her face. "You need to rest after overdoing it yesterday. And the weather report says it's going to be a scorcher today, even here at the beach. A quiet day inside with the air conditioning is what you need. Just stretch out on the sofa and read your novel."

"It's a special novel. The heroine's name is Eva Johnson. I've never read a story where a character had my name. It's a strange feeling." Eva glanced at him.

"What's your novel about?"

"It's a murder mystery."

"Who did it?"

Eva tied to recall the story but parts had already faded. Only the dramatic scenes stuck in her memory. "A woman returns to Florida and someone tries to kill her."

"Why does someone want to kill her?" Mark asked.

"I haven't read that part yet."

"We better go in. It's already getting hot and you need to be in where it's cool." Mark's hands slid down her arm.

Looking into his eyes, her heartbeat grew stronger. "Mark, I wrote something for you. I think I left it in the kitchen by the dictionary. It's important." With her voice fading, Eva gave him a gentle hug. Her strength ebbed and flowed like the tides, and now it was slipping away. Soon the rush from the sugar and breakfast coffee would give way to a need for rest, but being close to Mark gave her an exhilarating feeling. "You have been so kind to me. I want you to have it. It's –"

"Hush." He kissed her. "I'll be back soon. We can talk then. Now, I must be going. Professors shouldn't be late to their class and you need to rest."

Inside, Mark closed the living room door and locked it. "I'll give you a call this afternoon if I have a break in my … meeting."

"Drive carefully and fasten your seatbelt." After straightening his flag-red tie, she pulled him closer. His warm lips tasted like maple syrup.

"Now, I want you to curl up on the sofa and read your book." He handed it to her and left quickly.

Sinking into the sofa, she hugged the book and listened to his footsteps echo down the hall.

After Rex barked, there was silence.

Alone except for the kittens napping nearby, Eva flipped open the novel. Seeing her name, Eva Johnson, in print as the heroine was fascinating and her eyes scanned through a paragraph. The words were all familiar but the images they created vanished before the sentences ended. Inside her skull, she could feel her mind growing hotter, frantically trying to concentrate, trying to connect the images of words with their meanings, trying to hold onto complex sentences. It was futile. The thoughts disappeared.

Weariness was crashing in on her like a giant seventh wave. Leaning back, she tucked a pillow around her stiffening neck, making it firm like a cast. Quickly, she sank into a deep sleep.

Time slipped by and her almost motionless body finally uncurled. Voices began to sift into her consciousness.

"Eva. Eva. It's time to wake up."

Something wet and cold rubbed her arm. A needle pricked her skin. Fighting the heavy sleep, Eva tried to make sense of the voices and sensation. *Is this some sort of* Sleeping Beauty *type of dream? A needle pricked the princess and sent her into a deep sleep. Only a handsome prince could wake her with a magic kiss.* Rudely, the smell of rubbing alcohol cut into the fairytale thoughts.

"Eva wake up."

Her eyes opened, but it was a stranger leaning over her, not a prince, not Mark. The man had a friendly face with chocolate brown eyes peeking over gold-framed glasses.

"Eva, I'm Doctor Williams. You need to sit up so I can listen to your lungs."

"Doctor?" Eva looked around. "Am I in the hospital again?"

"No. You're still at home. Now take a deep breath. I want to make sure your lungs are still clear." Doctor Williams put a cold stethoscope to her back. "Good. Take another deep breath."

Waiting for his next order, she glanced around the living room. With the drapes drawn, the light was soft and easy on her tired eyes. Barbara was standing behind the doctor, holding two bags of liquid. At the foot of the sofa, Rex sat tensely, watching the doctor's every move. Beside him the kittens peeked over the edge of their box. They were strong enough to climb the sides but too weak to make it over the top to freedom. Eva knew how they felt.

"Is it still ticking?"

"Sounds like you could use some hot tea and a good meal." Doctor Williams nodded at Barbara and took one bag of liquid from her. "And I have just the thing for a quick pick-up. It's like a liquid power bar." He slid an IV needle into her arm.

"That stuff looks old. It's yellow. I've never seen a yellow IV." Eva tried to pull back but his grip was firm.

"They toss in a little carrot juice for color. This is just what the doctor ordered." His voice lost its joking tone and grew serious. "It has the vitamins and nutrition you need, young lady. You have to start eating better. Try small frequent meals to start. Barbara is going to make sure you eat something every couple of hours. Viral encephalitis is nothing to take lightly. If you don't start eating, you'll wind up in the hospital. Understand?"

"Yes, sir."

Barbara handed him the other IV bag. "I'll make you a cup of tea to start. Would you like some coffee, Doctor Williams?"

He slipped the second IV bag on the metal pole beside Eva.

"No, thanks. I don't drink caffeine before surgery. It makes my hands shake."

"Are you going to perform surgery?" Eva sat up and glanced down at her body. There didn't seem to be anything wrong. But she was still too sleepy to comprehend why he was there.

"Relax, Eva." He patted her shoulder. "Didn't mean to startle you. I have a nine thirty surgery at the hospital. You're safe. I'm here to check on your viral encephalitis. How are you feeling?"

"Fine. Just fine. Really, I'm all right. But –"

"What is it?"

"Since this is a virus, I can stop taking those antibiotics?"

"No. Your white blood count is up. Keep taking those antibiotics. You may have picked up a secondary infection and your immune system is too weak to fight off anything else."

"But they give me a headache."

"That's not uncommon. Try taking them after you eat. Just avoid drinking milk when you take them." Doctor Williams wrote out a prescription. "Barbara can get you these tablets for your headaches. I'll have the lab check for secondary infections."

Eva looked around the room, making sure Barbara wasn't there. *Should I ask the doctor or not? I don't want him to think I'm crazy, but I want to know.* She watched him extract a blood sample from her arm. "Am I going to live?"

Startled, he looked over his glasses. "Yes, if you take care of yourself and follow doctor's orders. Why do you ask?"

Eva watched the drops of liquid slide down the IV tube and into her arm. Her thoughts were troubled. *No. I better not tell him about my dream. He won't understand the Ice Palace. He'll think I'm crazy. I don't want to end up in the psycho ward. I read that comment last night in Barbara's nursing book. Organic psychosis. I've taken psychology courses, I know what a psychosis is.* Eva pulled the cover around her shoulders.

Doctor Williams kept his hand on her wrist, feeling her pulse. "You haven't answered my question."

"Sorry. I keep forgetting things." She looked around for something else to talk about. Nothing came to mind.

"Are you having trouble with your memory?"

"I remember the past just fine. It's my short-term memory that's fried."

"Tell me about it." He sat back.

"Sometimes it's okay, but when I'm tired my thoughts just seem to dissolve like a lump of sugar in a glass of water. And I have trouble keeping track of time and days." She shook her head. "Everyone keeps saying this is August. For me its like May or June. How could I lose track of that much time?"

Doctor Williams leaned forward. "You have been very sick for a long time. Viral encephalitis is a serious illness and it has sapped your strength. Your body has had more important things to do than keep track of time and the little things in you life. So don't worry about your short-term memory loss. It will recover as you get stronger."

"How soon will I get well?"

"This is not like a cold or the flu. It'll take time to get your strength back. And you'll have to work at it." He adjusted the IV flow. "Are you worried about something?"

Eva leaned back into the pile of pillows behind her. "No. Nothing much worries me these days. I feel very mellow. I've never felt like that before. It's like a long continuous high. Weird but nice. Really tranquil."

"The mind produces it's own intoxicating chemicals. There are Valium type receptors in the brain and it produces its own opium-like chemicals." Doctor Williams slipped off his glasses. "Perhaps your mind wants to keep you very tranquil while it's busy fighting that virus in there."

Eva rubbed her forehead. "Or maybe that's the way the brain kills viral encephalitis. It tranquilizes the virus, and then it can sneak up and destroy the enemy virus. Some sort of strange chemical warfare."

"Never thought of that." Doctor Williams laid a cold compress on her forehead.

"Whatever the reason, it's a very pleasant sensation." Eva sighed as her eyes closed. "I don't have a care in the world."

~ 31 ~

Mansfield, Ohio – Noon, August 21st

Sirens wailed outside. Telephones rang and keyboards clicked. Police officers walked down the hall, escorting a shaggy man in handcuffs. It was a typical day at the Mansfield Police Department, except for two detectives studying the stranger from Florida, sitting on the other side of the room.

Mark had taken the early flight to Ohio. After landing in Columbus, he rented a car and drove up to Mansfield. The hour drive north gave him time to mull over his concerns one more time. There were more questions than answers. And he hoped his students back in Daytona were using their day off to find the answers to Eva's childhood down there.

A Mansfield police officer strolled past Mark and nodded.

Sitting beside a desk in the far corner, Mark studied the items on it for clues about the detective who worked there. Besides the usual items were two fishing photos flanking a family picture and a paperweight encasing a Hollywood actor's guild card for Paul Galloway. *That's a twist*, Mark thought. *Actors play detectives but not many detectives are actors.*

Mark was wearing his Secret Service uniform, as his mother called it. The black suit was cut to fit well and yet discreetly conceal a weapon; however, he carried no gun these days as a college professor. Over a crisp white shirt, a flag-red tie was anchored with a discreet gold tie tack, an award for meritorious government service.

Casually scanning the office, Mark studied those at work, determining what kind of police department this was. *It's well equipped*, he observed. *But it's the quality of the police officers that counts. I want to know how they are handling Eva's case. Who are the suspects? Have they made any arrests?*

On the detective's desk the phone rang.

Which one of them is Detective Galloway? Listening to the phone recording, Mark glanced at the empty desk chair, where a tan suit coat waited, and then at the two men huddled on the other side of the room. *They both have on tan slacks but the one with thinning gray hair and glasses looks like the captain type. The wiry one must be my detective. Politely listening to his boss but determined to handle me his way.*

"Galloway, your Florida man is waiting," a passerby shouted.

Mark watched the wiry one raise his arm in acknowledgement but couldn't hear his comment. *I'm right. It's the one with Hollywood features. It will be interesting to see how he plays this.*

Wearing a blue shirt and tan slacks, the detective strolled towards Mark. "Professor Reining. Sorry to keep you waiting."

"Just call me Mark." He stood to shake hands. "Detective Galloway, I appreciate your taking time to see me."

"It's the least I could do for someone who flies all the way from Florida to discuss a case. And my friends call me Paul." Detective Galloway pushed the play button and listened to the phone message as he made a note.

Mark watched the detective's lips tighten as he wrote.

After taping the note to his phone, Detective Galloway pulled a file folder from his desk and laid it beside his fishing photo. The folder remained closed. "Before we get to the Eva Johnson case, I have a few questions."

Studying at file folder, Mark could see the detective sizing him up and the silence gave him time to think. *Detective Galloway is fishing for my real reason for being here. Can't blame him, I'd be just as suspicious if I was on his side of the desk. He'll dangle bait in front of me until he gets what he wants.* Mark put his black leather briefcase on the desk, pulled out a file folder, and laid it on top. "Paul, let's cut bait and put our cards on the table."

"I'm game." Paul leaned forward. "When you phoned me, you said you were doing a research paper. Is it in the capacity of a professor or as a consultant for the Secret Service?"

Mark straightened his tie. "It's a case of publish or perish."

"Professor, with an answer that evasive, I assume you aren't free to comment." Picking up Eva's case file, Paul gripped it firmly. "Of course I did some checking on your background, Professor Reining. Rather impressive. We don't get many Secret Service agents interested in our cases."

"Ex-Secret Service."

"But you still do consulting work for them and you still look like a fed." Paul glanced back at his captain's office. "What interests you so much about this case that you'd take the time to fly up from Florida?"

"It's just a couple of hours by air." Mark put his file folder back into his briefcase and snapped it shut. "Paul, why don't I buy you lunch? Someplace quiet where we can talk in private."

"I know just the place. I got the captain's permission to take you in my car, being you're an ex-fed. It'll be faster. Unless you're a townie, you'd get lost in our maze of one-way streets."

After wandering through the halls, Paul opened a side door.

A wall of heat rolled in as they stepped out. The dark asphalt parking lot was soaking up the August sunlight and giving off the fumes of hot tar. The souls of Mark's shoes stuck to the tacky surface that sloped dramatically. "It's rather hilly around here. I was expecting Mansfield to look more like Columbus. Flatter."

"Nope. This is the high country. Highest city in the state. We're right smack dab on the continental divide." With theatrics, Paul pointed. "From here, the rainwater either runs north into Lake Erie or south into the Ohio river, then down to the Gulf of Mexico. The pioneers who founded Mansfield built their stockade on top of this big hill for protection from the Indians. But I suppose you aren't interested in a history lesson."

"Actually, I find history important in understanding a complex case. The past often sets the stage for today's events." Mark slid into the passenger's seat of an unmarked police car.

"Spoken like a true professor. Buckle up. It's a state law." Pulling the police car into the traffic, Paul headed south through a series of one-way streets, up and down hills. Older buildings hung onto the slopes and numerous churches occupied prime corner lots. Veering right at the top of a long upgrade with another church splitting the traffic, the road leveled a bit and widened.

After a considerable drive in silence, the right blinker clicked noisily. Beyond was a shopping mall with a Kroger store. A turn took them into the drive-through lane of a McDonald's restaurant.

"I figure if a Big Mac is good enough for an ex-President, it's good enough for me. It's the only way I get to cheat on my wife's low cholesterol diet." Without asking, Paul ordered for both of them and moved to the last window for the pickup.

As Mark pulled a twenty from his wallet, he could feel his grip tightening with impatience. *What's his game? Silence? Not even small talk. Paul's the most tight-lipped detective I've ever met. Is he acting the part of a tough detective or was he told to keep me in the dark? Are the locals covering up something? Paul is playing this close to the vest. He's trying to get me to reveal what I know first. But he's out of his league. Feds talk when they're darn ready and professors are worse. I'll wait.*

The money disappeared from Mark's hand and was replaced with a large Coke. A sack of sandwiches was stashed on the dashboard and the smell of fries filled the air-conditioned car.

Paul pulled the police cruiser into traffic and turned again at an intersection where two more churches sat on corner lots.

Where is he taking us? Mark thought, sipping Coke. With each turn, he studied the affluent residential area they were winding through. Tree lined streets and stately homes on large, well-manicured lots.

Suddenly, Detective Galloway turned sharply, pulled into an oval driveway lined by towering Oak trees, and stopped. Grabbing the lunch sack, Paul opened his door. "We'll eat inside. We can talk in private here."

Stepping out into the afternoon heat, Mark studied the white-brick two-story Georgian colonial home. On each side of the main house were two wings with classical pane-windows flanked by black shutters. Beside the massive center doorway, two giant Magnolia trees stood sentry duty and were sadly joined together by a yellow crime scene tape.

"Mark, if you're squeamish about eating inside, you can stay out here. I'm eating in the dining room, its cooler." Paul ducked under the yellow tape and unlocked the front door. Opening it, cool air rushed out into the muggy August afternoon.

Stepping inside, Mark felt a wave of apprehension roll over him. "Whose house is this?"

"This is Eva Johnson's home." Detective Galloway closed the door and locked it. "We think this is where Eva was murdered."

~ 32 ~

"Murdered here? But, your report said Eva was shot in her Blazer." Mark followed Paul through the house, Eva's home. It was cool and quiet, but on the floor were numbered tags where evidence had been found. There was a conch shell on the kitchen windowsill and nearby fingerprint dust remained on the yellow countertop. A pile of notes was stacked near the coffee pot. They were Eva's reminder notes.

Mark's stomach tightened as he read the message on a big yellow note stuck to the refrigerator with a shell magnet. *Was that her last note?* Mark wondered. *What does it mean: 2:00 C.H. – get papers – check with Paul? ... Does the reference to Paul mean Detective Paul Galloway? I need to know more about Paul before I tell him that Eva is alive.* On the kitchen desk, Mark noticed a set of car keys lying in an old cigar box.

Paul stepped into the dining room and sat at the long table covered with an aquamarine tablecloth. "We believe the auto accident was just a cover up. In this house is where Eva Johnson must have been murdered. We found traces of blood in the upstairs shower and more stains on a towel in the washer. From the preliminary DNA from the hair samples we took from her comb, the blood stains match her blood type." Ketchup dripping from Paul's Big Mac splashed on the white paper napkin below.

Munching a fry, Mark studied the dining room, wondering how many meals Eva had eaten here. Over the table, the crystal teardrops of the chandelier sparkled with a rainbow of colors as light streamed in from the bay window. A large cherry breakfront stretched across the opposite wall. Behind its beveled glass doors, china figurines shared the shelves with a collection of sand dollars.

"Eva's home is lovely." Mark glanced into the living room beyond. "Bigger than I expected for a school teacher."

"I don't remember my report saying Eva was a school teacher." Paul poked a fry into the ketchup. "But she did teach watercolor painting at the local branch campus. In fact, that's how I met Eva."

"You took an art course from her?"

"Nope. I helped her set up a field trip. I'm on the preservation board of the old Ohio State Reformatory north of town. It was built in the late 1800s and the prison looks like an old stone castle. You've probably seen it in movies. It was the setting for a large part of 'The Shawshank Redemption.' But I like the movie 'Walter and Harry Go to New York' the best. I'm one of the prison guards in that one; even got a line in the movie." Paul grinned. "Had to join the actor's guild."

"What does the old prison have to do with Eva?"

"She used it for the setting of one of her watercolor classes. Wanted her college students to get a different view of life. They came up with some strange paintings." Paul shook his head. "Never thought one subject could be seen so many different ways. There was one painting of cellblock doors with wild-eyed inmates clawing to get out. But most of her students stuck to the basics of capturing the gray stone wall from various views."

"Did Eva do a painting of the old prison?" Mark pushed his fries over to Paul.

"Yes and no. Her painting made it look like a massive Gothic home with a lady walking towards it wearing a turn of the century fancy dress. Reminded me of the cover of one of my wife's romance novels. Eva thought the old stone prison resembled a Russian princess' home."

Paul flipped a fry for accent. "Mind you, it was a hot spring day. Eva sat in the sun and painted snowdrifts and made the prison into a Russian castle dripping with icicles. Eva called it an Ice Palace." Paul stirred his icy Coke. "It's a shame she was murdered. Eva had talent."

Mark got up to study the paintings on the wall. *These are Eva's paintings.* His thoughts were somber. *Yes, I can see part of her in them, a soft gentle touch. The three oil paintings behind Paul are mammoth bleeding hearts, yet they look so real. And the watercolor painting on the other side shows daisies and summer fruits, good enough to eat. They are all bright and happy paintings. So how did violence enter her life? Why?*

Mark slid back into his chair. "Besides the blood stains, did you find any other evidence of a crime here?"

"In one of the bedrooms, we found two .38 caliber bullets under the dresser. No fingerprints on them. And on the floor in the front hall, there was a thousand dollars in hundred-dollar bills, so at first we thought it was a botched robbery."

Mark studied the detective. "Maybe Eva just left."

"No way." Paul shook his head. "We found her car keys in the kitchen and the spare set was in the bedroom. Yet we found her Blazer two miles from here at the bottom of a creek. No keys in it. And no woman would leave home without her credit cards."

Mark gave his untouched Big Mac to Paul. "What's your theory about the crime?"

"Several theories, actually." After munching the sandwich, Paul continued. "Since there were hundred-dollar bills on the floor, the captain thinks it was extortion that turned into murder. But I don't buy that. I know Eva. She's not the kind of woman who would do anything shady that an extortionist could use for blackmail. Eva's what you feds would call squeaky clean. Not even a speeding ticket. So I've ruled out the captain's theory."

"What's your theory?"

"Murder for profit. And I'll see him fry when I get enough evidence." Paul twisted a French fry until it ripped in two.

Mark saw the anger in the detective's eyes, but it wasn't as intense as the fire burning in Mark's stomach. "He who?"

"James Hellmann. He claims to be Eva's husband. I don't buy that either. She'd have to be out of her mind to marry that weasel. And surely Eva would have told her friends. We checked with all of them and with her church group, but none of them knew about the marriage. Her closest friend said she hadn't dated anyone since her father passed away."

"What does that have to do with her dating?"

"Something about a promise Eva made to her father. No one knew exactly what that was about, but they doubted she would go against her father's wishes. But Jim claims they were married secretly in Las Vegas. Said they planned a big public wedding later. That makes no sense." After pausing, Paul continued. "I sent the wedding certificate to the FBI lab to check the handwriting and for her fingerprints. It's got to be a forgery."

Keep your cool, Mark thought. *I have to hear it all before I tell Paul what I know.* Pushing his Coke aside, Mark probed for more information. "What was Jim's motive?"

"Look around. ... Money. He wants to inherit all this. And that wasn't enough; he'd taken out a million dollar insurance policy on her. Of course he's the sole beneficiary." Paul wadded up the ketchup stained paper napkin and tossed it back into the sack. "I'll make sure he won't get a penny of her inheritance."

"Eva's inheritance. Is she wealthy?"

"Around here, the pursuit of wealth is not how we measure our lives. If it were, we'd move to one of the three big C's: Cleveland, Columbus, or Cincinnati. But Eva is financially independent. Her father, Adam Johnson, was a prosperous building contractor and when he died last year he left everything to her. She was his only child. His wife died when Eva was about twelve."

"Is Jim the only one who would inherit her wealth?"

"No. Eva has a half-brother. Dennis is her mother's son by an earlier marriage. I've checked him out. Although he lives in Denver, on the 17th he was in Columbus visiting his daughter. Now the niece, Maggie, is my second choice for the murderer. That gal definitely has her eyes on her Aunt Eva's money. And Maggie is knee deep in debt: credit cards charged to the limit, a heap of college loans, and she's behind on her car payments."

"A half-brother, a niece, and a possible husband." Mark bit his lip. "Anyone else to profit from her death?"

"In her will, Eva left part of her estate to her cat." Paul looked up. "Don't laugh, folks around here are partial to their pets. But we haven't been able to find it. Her cat must have been frightened the night of the murder and run away. I keep coming back here, looking for the cat. She must have meant a lot to Eva." Paul's voice trembled. "I'll find her cat. It's the least I can do for Eva."

"Eva's cat was killed by ant poison. Princess is dead." Mark blurted out and cringed.

"How do you know the cat's name was Princess?" Paul leaned forward, his eyes piercing and his voice sharp. "And what makes you think the cat was poisoned?"

Knowing the game was up, Mark flipped open his brief case and reached for his file folder on Eva. It contained the Daytona Beach police photos taken in the Halifax Hospital of her bruised body and the gunshot wound to Eva's arm.

Reluctantly, Mark handed the folder to Paul. "I apologize for withholding this information, but I needed to know more about the investigation. I didn't want to risk her life. – Eva Johnson is alive."

"What?" Paul grabbed the folder. "Eva is alive?"

"On August 19th, I found Eva sleeping on the sand dunes in front of my parents' home. It's in the report there. When a car almost ran her down on the beach, she was taken to the hospital and they found a bullet in her arm."

"A 9mm." Paul shook his head reading the report. "We found two 9mm bullet holes in the driver's window of her Blazer but we only recovered one slug from the headrest."

"In there is the ballistics photo of the 9mm slug they removed from her arm. It looked like it had passed through something before it hit her."

Paul glanced over the folder. "It doesn't say who shot her. Who did she name as the shooter?"

"Eva doesn't remember being shot or the accident."

"Amnesia?"

"No. Eva has viral encephalitis. It causes short-term memory problems. There's much about this summer she doesn't remember. For her, most of the time, she thinks its June, not August." Mark glanced at the oil painting of two bleeding hearts. "I haven't told her about her auto accident. The doctors said she lost that memory in the concussion."

"You mean Eva doesn't know someone tried to kill her?"

~ 33 ~

"I haven't told Eva about the attempt on her life." Mark leaned back, waiting for Paul's response.

Detective Galloway closed the file folder. "Why not?"

"Many reasons. For one thing, she's been too ill and I want her to concentrate on getting well, not worrying. For another, until yesterday, I didn't know where she was from and I wasn't even sure her real name was Eva Johnson."

"She's too sick to even remember her name?"

"No." Mark stood up. "She told us her name was Eva Johnson. But when I found her novel with a heroine by the same name, well, I assumed she just took her name from the book."

Strolling into the living room, Mark continued. "Finding out she's from Ohio was a surprise. We thought she lived in the Daytona Beach area and we were looking for the West Indies motel where Eva said she lived as a child. We haven't found it yet; some of the old county records were destroyed in a fire. But we did find her name in the old Lenox school records."

"You've found out a lot in a few days." Paul glanced at the desk in the corner. "You'd make a good detective."

"I haven't done it all alone. My students have helped tracking down the leads. I teach various law enforcement courses so I've used Eva's case as part of their summer studies." Mark looked around the living room for clues about Eva's life.

There were photos of the beach near a glass lamp base, filled with seashells. The room's colors were sandy colors with coral accents and sea-blue carpet. Sunlight flooded in from three massive windows.

"I can see Eva's father was a builder. He put a lot of nice details in this home." Mark's hand slid across the massive fireplace centered the long wall. Above its mantel was an oil painting of the beach and below the fireplace was a thick slab of marble. Across the rest of the wall was expensive cherry paneling with crown molding. It was a builder's home.

"Did Eva live here with her father?"

"Yes, and a maiden aunt lived with them for a while, but she died some years back." Pausing beside a writing desk, Paul gently laid his hand on the CD player and took a deep breath. "They say every detective has one case that really gets to him. This one has haunted me. I keep hearing that song in my head. Over and over."

"Song? What do you mean?"

"I haven't figured out why it was playing." Paul pushed the play button and skipped the music ahead. "It's called 'The Boxer' and it was playing when I got here the night of the crime. The player was set to repeat."

Guitar music and the voices of Simon and Garfunkel from their record "Bridge Over Troubled Water" filled the room, and the song "The Boxer" played.

"Why this song? I just don't understand how it fits in." Paul closed his eyes as his head nodded to the song.

Listening, Mark understood the meaning. "Home. The songs about wanting to go home." Mark glanced at the ocean painting above the mantel. "It must have been what Eva was thinking. Planning to go back to her childhood home at the beach, back to a happier time, perhaps running away from someone."

"Hadn't thought about that angle. This song has been haunting me since I heard it that night." Paul stared at the front hallway. "The house alarm system was triggered at eleven forty-eight.

When the security company arrived, they found the front door ajar and blood on the doorknob. They backed away and called us. I entered with the patrol officers and this song was playing. It was eerie, just the music pounding in the darkness."

Mark watched Paul's grim face.

"When we stepped into the hall, we saw the money scattered on the floor and assumed it was a burglary. There was no one inside but one of the back windows had been broken by either a fallen branch or by someone. We had a big storm that night."

Mark glanced at the floor; ten numbered tags marked where evidence had been found. *Someone frightened her and she dropped her money as she ran away,* Mark considered. *That's why she had only two hundred dollars when I found her.*

After a pause, Paul continued. "Of course we pulled our patrol cars away, thinking the burglar would return for the rest of the money. I waited inside with two officers. We didn't want to tip our hand by turning off the music, so we waited in the dark, listening to this song play over and over, for hours."

"Did anyone show up?" Mark asked.

"Yes." Paul's head was nodding to the music. "At two ten in morning, a car pulled in the drive. ... By then our nerves were hot-wired and our guns sticking to our sweaty hands. ... A car door slammed and we could see it was a man, not Eva. So we flattened ourselves against the wall and waited. As soon as he stepped in, we flipped the lights on. The sucker froze with three gun barrels pointing at his head."

"Who was it?"

"Jim Hellmann." Paul turned off the record player but his head continued to nod to the song's beat. "Jim was bringing in a box of his belongings. We had no idea who he was. That was the only time Jim has been at a loss for words. But it didn't take long for him to demand a phone call to his lawyer."

"That doesn't make sense." Mark walked into the hall. "If he claimed to be Eva's husband, why was he moving in at that hour?"

"Precisely what we asked him. There was nothing else of his in this house, except for some fingerprints in the kitchen. We found a few things of Eva's father but nothing belonging to Jim. With his lawyer butting in, we haven't gotten a straight answer yet. ... And you have to ask yourself, why would Jim be sneaking into Eva's house unless he knew she wouldn't be here."

"Do you have any proof he shot her?"

"Not enough for an arrest warrant. I need something concrete to nail him." Paul turned at a sound in the drive.

Outside, a red sports car pulled in and stopped. Sunlight glanced off the Pontiac Firebird, looking like a red candy apple.

"Then there's the niece. Suspect number two, Maggie." Paul opened the front door. "This should be interesting."

Mark followed Paul outside. The afternoon heat was stifling, feeling like an oven. The magnolia trees stood motionless; there was no ocean breeze to cool them.

The dark window of the red sports car slid down. "Detective Galloway, have you found my aunt's body yet?"

Paul walked to the edge of the brick walk and stood in the shade. His hands slipped around his belt and stopped at his gun.

Maggie peered over her big sunglasses at Mark, checking out his body. "See you got the FBI back on the case. Good, at least they have some brains. So did you find my Aunt Eva's body yet?"

Stepping forward, Mark ran his hand along Maggie's car door, across the red paint, remembering. *Eva mentioned she thought she saw a gun pointing out of a red car. But the one on the beach was maroon, not red. Did she confuse it with what happened to her up here? ... Did Eva see a gun in her niece's red car?*

~ 34 ~

"How'd you get that dent in the right front fender?" Mark nodded to the front of Maggie's red Firebird.

"Some idiot scraped it in the mall parking lot. Didn't even leave me their name." Maggie touched Mark's hand.

Mark pulled back. "When was that?"

"No need to make a federal case of it." She pushed up her sunglasses. "I didn't come here to talk about fender benders. I want to know if you found my aunt's body? A yes or no would suffice."

"No." Paul walked from the front of her car. "Do you know where Eva's cat is?"

"Her cat? Don't tell me you hick cops can't even find a dumb cat." Maggie shook her head. "How would I know where Aunt Eva buried her cat?"

"What makes you think the cat is dead?" Paul asked.

"Uh, I came up for the Mid-Ohio races and stopped by to show my new boyfriend my aunt's house. He's going to be an architect. Thought he'd be interested in my aunt's Georgian colonial home." Maggie's grin faded. "Aunt Eva was crying because her cat had died. It was embarrassing the way she fussed over her cat like it was human."

"What do you mean?" Mark felt the sun baking through his black suit coat. It was getting hot, like his insides.

"Of all things, she was making a coffin for her cat." With a longing look, Maggie scanned at her aunt's house. "Lets go inside. I have to find her bank papers. Aunt Eva would want me to take care of things for her now that she's gone. And I want to pick up some of her jewelry. I have a date tonight."

As the car door swung out, Paul stopped it. "Can't let you inside, it's a crime scene. And you definitely can't take anything."

With a tempting smile on her face, Maggie's voice turned sweet. "Why not? I'm going to inherit it all anyway; I'm her only niece. Besides, Aunt Eva would want me to have her jewelry."

"We don't know that and –" Mark straightened his flag-red tie, deliberately pausing, waiting to toss out some bait. "And Jim would have to give his approval."

"That scumbag. He's just after my aunt's money. If you ask me, he's the one who killed Aunt Eva. Who does he think he is, muscling into my aunt's life?" Maggie slammed the car door closed. "When I stopped up last time, Aunt Eva didn't say anything about being married to that jerk. She would have told me. And I know she would've had a proper church wedding."

Mark put his hand back on the car door. "Did Eva say anything about Jim or anyone else she was dating?"

"No. I already told the local cops that. In this hick town there aren't many eligible bachelors. Anyway, as straight-laced as Aunt Eva was, I doubt if she was sleeping with anyone and surely not that scumbag, Jim." Maggie moved her side mirror and fluffed her hair. "But I know she was having some sort of problem with someone. When I used her phone in the kitchen, I saw a copy of a legal document. I wasn't snooping. It was just lying there."

"What kind of document?" Mark leaned closer.

"You FBI agents are good." Maggie gave him an inviting smile. "Now that I think of it, it looked like a restraining order. I've seen them before. And there was a note clipped to it, to check with someone named Paul. I remember the Paul part because that was my last boyfriend's name."

Mark glanced at Paul who was looking ill as he turned away. *Paul again?* Mark contemplated. *First the note on the refrigerator and now another note on a missing restraining order. Paul is holding back information. Why? Is he protecting Eva or himself? Does Detective Paul Galloway have a motive?*

Maggie touched Mark's hand again. "Say, handsome, I didn't get your name."

"Reining." Mark gave only his last name, hoping to continue the impression he was a federal agent so he could ask more questions. "Did Eva tell you how she met Jim Hellmann?"

"Well, Agent Reining, now that you ask, I think it was in church. I stopped to see Aunt Eva after the races and she was hosting a Christian Women's church group. That Jim character was there, explaining some sort of investments scheme. Aunt Eva dragged me in to listen." Maggie put the car in gear. "Jim acted like a fox in the hen house. Those church ladies politely listened to him like he was a preacher. But when he started quoting the ten commandments of good investing, I got disgusted and left."

Mark stepped back as the car slowly rolled forward.

"If you ask me, Jim is the one who killed my aunt." Maggie leaned out. "Call me when you find Aunt Eva's body?"

As the red Firebird peeled from the drive, Paul walked back. "Maggie is quite a contrast from her aunt."

"Why would Eva have two notes with your name on them?"

Paul walked towards the side gate in the picket fence. "I've been asking myself the same question. And I don't like the answer I keep coming back to. If I hadn't been at Lake Erie on the 17th fishing with my captain, I'd be a suspect in this case. When I got back to headquarters, there was a phone message from Eva. But it was late and I went on home. I assumed she wanted to set up another outing to the old reformatory for her summer watercolor class. It never crossed my mind that Eva could be in trouble."

Mark stopped beside Paul, who looked as pale as the white picket fence. The anguish was written in Detective Galloway's furrowed brows. Mark knew the torment "what ifs" could play on a mind. They had run through Mark's head after his sister's death. He had asked himself numerous "what ifs" and agonized over the answers, but none of them could bring back Mark's sister.

Paul opened the gate and continued. "As that song played over and over, I kept asking myself, What if I'd returned her call? Could I have saved Eva? Her house is on my way home. What if I would have stopped by that night? She could have asked me about the restraining order. Then I could have warned her, helped her." The gate slammed behind them. "No. I didn't do any of those things. I went home and cleaned fish instead. Had a beer and watched TV until … until I got the call about a break-in at her house. My heart sank when I pulled in her driveway that night."

Mark kept silent, waiting for Paul to get it off his chest. This was a time to listen, not to talk.

"They're right about a thousand deaths." Paul stopped in front of a little waterfall trickling into an outside pond. "God, I died a thousand times every time that song played. Just standing in the dark, listening and waiting for someone to return, waiting to find out what happened to Eva. It was only a couple of hours but it was the longest stakeout of my life. Surely the most tormenting."

Mark knew that feeling. He remembered the long grueling hours of waiting to find out what happened to his sister. It had been two years ago, but the "what ifs" still ran through Mark's head. But for Mark there were no answers and his sister perished.

"Paul." Mark touched the detective's back. "Eva is alive. We can't undo what happened to her but we can find out who did it."

"One way or another, I'll make it up to Eva." Paul grabbed a small shovel leaning against the nearby garden shed. "The crime lab is on their way. Maybe we can find it before they get here. Where do you think Eva would burry her cat?"

"Someplace special." Mark walked though the garden. White daisies, like in her dining room painting, seemed wilted in the heat but the earth there hadn't been disturbed. Eva's flowerbeds looked like she had just stepped away and would soon be home. Garden tools lay beside flowers like they had been forgotten. From the trees, a redbird called for its mate: singing, pretty, pretty.

A crime lab team arrived and began to dig in an empty flowerbed by the fence. A squad car stopped and the officers were searching the raspberry patch where vines had been knocked down.

Mark and Paul returned to the waterfalls. Near it sat a statue of a cat, curled up, gazing towards the birdbath. Catnip and miniature daisies had been planted beside it.

"This looks like a fresh concrete slab." Mark carefully moved the cat statue aside. "It has Princess inscribed on it."

With the shovel, Paul removed the dirt. A clang stopped it.

"Sounds like wood. This must be it." Mark pulled out a box tightly wrapped in clear plastic. Inside was a little wooden coffin of polished cherry wood. Prying open the lid, he found Eva's cat.

On a blue satin pillow, the body of Princess was curled up like the statue. Toys surrounded her and a can of expensive cat food was tucked in the corner of the coffin. A note decorated with hand-painted daisies was pinned to the cat's blue satin pillow.

Mark pulled out the note and read Eva's message.

> *Princess,*
> *My beloved cat and faithful companion,*
> *I will always remember you.*
>
> *Eva*

~ 35 ~

Daytona Beach, Florida – Afternoon, August 21st

"Princess! Don't eat that. Those could poison you." Eva pulled her new calico kitten away from her prescription medication. "That medicine would surely give you a splitting headache. Take my word for it. That stuff has quite a punch."

Eva had spent the morning resting on the sofa in the living room of Mark's parents. Before Doctor Williams left, he had inserted an IV and left two bags of fluids dripping antiviral medication, liquids, and vitamins into her arm. Tethered to them like an astronaut tied to a spacecraft, Eva had limited mobility. But that didn't matter; her strength was about flat-line, as she had kidded Barbara, who didn't seem amused at the analogy.

"Here kitty, kitty." Eva pulled a satin ribbon across the sheet. A flurry of calico and tan fur pounced on the ribbon and then pulled it into their pillow cave.

The two kittens that Eva had rescued days earlier continued to explore their world. Their afternoon's adventure was climbing the stack of pillows on the sofa. They napped as much as Eva but they had more energy in between. Keeping track of two balls of curious fur was even beginning to tire Rex, determined to keep the kittens rounded up like a sheep dog.

"Rest time. The two of you are wearing Rex out." After Eva deposited the kittens in their tall cardboard box, she sank back into the pile of pillows, thinking about Mark. *Why is his faculty meeting taking so long?* Eva wondered. *Why was he dressed so formally? In Ohio, faculty meetings are casual. Maybe it's an old southern custom. Not a bad idea. He looks strikingly handsome in that black suit. But he should have worn an ocean blue suit; it would have accented his beautiful eyes and of course it would be cooler. If he's out in the sun long, he'll bake in that black suit.*

Eva rolled over and glanced out the living room window. The sand dunes glistened like snow in the afternoon sun and were too bright for her. The cold compress slid back over her eyes and across her forehead to cool the heat radiating inside.

Watching, Barbara put down her sewing. "I better close those drapes. That sand gets mighty bright in the afternoon. Mark says you almost have to wear sunglasses in here." Turning, she looked back at her patient. "Eva, if your headache is worse, I'll get one of those prescription tablets Doctor Williams gave you."

"I'm fine, Barbara. All I need is a short nap." Eva rolled over, but her mind wouldn't rest. It was in another spin cycle. *No use fighting it,* she mused. *It takes too much energy to stop it. I wonder where we're going now. I hope it's someplace cold.*

In a few minutes, her mind journeyed to a world of its own making, leaving her body behind. It was a virtual reality with pleasing sensations and a relief from the headaches.

Pulling the phone closer, Barbara watched Eva curl up again into a tight fetal position as her breathing slowed.

Rex deserted the sleeping kittens and moved next to Eva.

As the room quieted, Eva's mind focused on inner thoughts. Lying motionless, only her eyes fluttered beneath their lids.

Oh my, this is not what I expected. The images plying inside her head surprised Eva. *I thought we were going someplace cold. This ... this is a hot sticky jungle. At least the dark, tropical forest is easy on my eyes, and I can hear the trickling of a little waterfall. It's interesting here but it looks too much like Vietnam. This is a man's place. A place of violence. I need to escape, but how?*

That sounds like a jet. As she turned in her dream, a runway came into view with a pilot waving for her to join him. In a black flight suit, he stood beside a shimmering white jet. *That's better; I always wanted to fly a fighter jet. In that I can get to Siberia fast. It's just a couple of blinks away.*

Eva's eyes blinked. *That's better, there's the Ice Palace waiting for me. Everyone's gone again. It's so quiet and cold here. I can sleep in peace on the frozen tundra. I'll just let my head sink into the icy snow. That's better. Only the cold of Siberia can cool my brain and quench the fire raging inside. But I don't understand why the snow turns red every time I lay down. ... I know it's blood, my blood. Strange, I don't remember being shot. Who shot me?*

"Eva!" Barbara called. "Eva, you have to wake up! Now!"

Rex nudged Eva's arm and pulled the covers off the sofa.

"Rex, don't do that. Her hands are like ice." Barbara put the covers back over her. "Come on, Eve, I'm going to sit you up. Then I'll make us some hot tea and I'll turn down the air conditioner. Eva? Are you awake."

Finding herself in a sitting position, Eva opened her eyes. "But, my dream wasn't over. I have to get to the Ice Palace."

"That'll have to wait. You need to eat something and take your medication."

"I need a nap." Eva sighed. "Traveling makes me tired."

Barbara took her patient's pulse. "Traveling? Were you dreaming about traveling?"

"It was a long trip from a tropical jungle to Siberia."

"That's probably Fritz's fault. He's outside tinkering with the air conditioning system. He says it has only two settings, too hot and too cold." Barbara nodded at her husband outside, swinging a wrench and having an animated conversation with the compressor unit. "When he gets done telling it off, he'll go to the repair shop and get a new thermostat relay or whatever it's called. Along the ocean they corrode fast in the salt air."

"At the West Indies and the Ocean Dunes, we didn't have air conditioning. Strange I don't remember it ever being too hot."

"Speaking of hot, I'll fix us some tea. It's time for your medication." Barbara stood, pulling her patient up. "Now, you need to walk around some to get your blood circulating."

"I could stroll down to the beach." Eva eyed the sand dunes, which looked inviting in the early evening light.

"You can't pull that IV stand through the sand. I'm afraid you're confined to the house and hard floors."

Having been helped to her feet, Eva wandered into the dining area adjoining the living room. Picking up her novel from the breakfront, she scanned the books on the shelf above it. An old scrapbook labeled "The Lenox Days" caught her eye.

"I went to school at Lenox," Eva whispered to Rex. "It was a grand old stucco building with a big playground. They had the best food there, as good as Morrison's cafeteria. Yummy brownies with thick chocolate icing."

Listening, Rex followed her to the dining table.

Spreading the scrapbook out, Eva flipped through the pages. Looking at the photos, old memories surfaced. "I remember the little first grade building had just two rooms and was isolated from the main building. It was nestled among tall palm trees with Oleander bushes by the front door." Eva inhaled the memory of her first school days, sweet and spicy.

"Here's your tea." Barbara sat a tray on the table. "Fritz went over to the bakery and got some of those sweet roll you like."

"That was sweet of him." Eva smiled and reached for one.

"It doesn't take much to persuade him to get these rolls. They're his favorite." Suddenly, Barbara noticed the album open on the table. "I didn't know that was still on the bookshelf."

While her tea was cooling, Eva flipped through the pages. "I remember the old Lenox School. I had so much fun there."

"Not many people equate school with fun."

"Oh, but I loved going to school. It was the only place I got to be with children my age. We lived way out on South Atlantic Avenue and there were no children in the neighborhood." After biting into a sweet roll, Eva wiped her fingers and flipped the page. "I remember the big box of toys our first grade teacher had in the back of the room. If we were good, we got first choice at the toy box. I was always good. My favorite was an old-fashioned doll with a china head. It was so beautiful and fragile. I carried it very carefully so I wouldn't break its porcelain head." Eva rubbed her forehead, feeling more fragile than a china doll.

"It's time to take you medicine." Barbara handed her a tablet.

"Those things give me a headache. I think I'll skip it for now. Surely all this IV stuff is enough."

"You have to take antibiotics until they're all gone."

Picking up the pill, Eva turned a page in the scrapbook, hoping to distract Barbara long enough to slip the pill out of sight and avoid the fuzzy feeling it gave her. "Look!"

Leaning over, Barbara stared at the page. "That's a sixth grade class. Do you recognize anyone?"

"Yes. Right there in the back row. The grinning girl with blond hair and butterfly barrettes; that's me." Eva's grin matched the one in the old photo. It had been a long time since she had seen that sixth grade class picture. Her childhood was vivid and filled the void left by her foggy short-term memory.

A feeling of nostalgia rolled over her, happy times and sad moments. *I never got to finish that year at Lenox*, she recalled. *We had to go back to Ohio. Back to a cold, snowy winter and the long gloomy days that followed. My heart was broken.*

The room was strangely silent for a moment.

Aunt Killer

Looking closer, Eva recalled the others in her class. "This is Nancy and Donna. We played hopscotch on the south walk. And that's Leslie." Eva blushed remembering Leslie, the first boy she ever kissed. It was an innocent first grade kiss in the back of the school bus. *Now that's an odd memory,* she mused. *I wonder if Leslie became an architect like his father?"*

Barbara's voice trembled. "Do you remember this girl?"

Eva studied the photo of a girl in the front row with curly, dark hair like Barbara's. "That's Susan with blue eyes. I always thought all Susan's had black eyes."

"No. ... My Susan had big blue eyes. Ocean eyes. Mark used to tease his sister about them."

"I didn't know Mark had a sister."

"Susan died two summers ago."

"I'm sorry." Eva closed the album and returned it to the bookcase. It obviously upset Barbara to look at that photo of her daughter. Eva understood the sorrow of losing a family member: first her mother at twelve then her father a year ago. "When is Mark coming home from school?"

"Mark's meeting is out of town." Barbara moved Eva's teacup and tapped the table. "Eva. What's this? You didn't take your pill. No fair hiding it under your plate."

"Gee, how did it get there?" Eva sheepishly picked up the capsule. "I guess I forgot to take it. My memory must still be asleep." It was easier to swallow the pill than argue.

Barbara watched. "Good. You need some exercise."

"Surfing or jogging down the beach would be good exercise. Perhaps I'll try dreaming about surfing in my next nap." Eva tugged her IV stand back into the living room, towards the sofa. The thought of surfing with Mark warmed her more than the tea. "Mark and I are going bodysurfing when he gets back."

~ 36 ~

Mansfield, Ohio – Late afternoon, August 21st

"Mom, you sound upset. Is Eva alright?" Holding his cell phone closer, Mark stepped away from Detective Paul Galloway's police car and continued talking to his mother in Florida. "Good. She needs the rest. What did Doctor Williams have to say? ... Another blood test? Does she have a secondary infection? No. That's good. Make sure she takes her medicine. ... Yes, I know. But I'm worried about her."

Nearby, Paul sat inside the car talking to his captain on the police phone. Parked in the shade of a weeping willow tree near a row of town houses, they were waiting for Jim Hellmann to return.

"If Eva is getting better, what are you upset about?" Mark recognized the uneasy tremor in his mother's voice. "Eva was looking through the old Lenox school scrapbook. So? ... What! Eva was in the sixth grade with Susan."

The unexpected connection of Eva with his sister startled Mark. *I should have considered that,* he thought. *My students did find a record of her attending Lenox. It's just that Eva seems younger, frailer than my sister. I hadn't considered they might have known each other. It's no wonder Mom was upset seeing Eva's picture in Susan's sixth grade class. It's a reminder of my sister. I wonder if Eva was ever at our house for one of Susan's many slumber parties. Did I meet her then? Is that why I'm drawn to Eva?*

A gray station wagon pulled into the driveway and disappeared behind Jim's town house complex.

With his cell phone, Mark walked down the drive and continued to talking his mother. "No. Don't tell Eva about Susan. Not yet. I don't want her to be upset. I'll explain when I get home. ... I'm taking the late flight back tonight. Detective Galloway will be coming with me. He knows Eva and has to ask her some questions. ... No, Mom. It'll be late and we'll get something to eat on the plane. I have to go now. Yes, I'll call you before we leave."

Clicking off the phone, Mark considered the similarities of what Eva was going through and what had happened to his sister. A restraining order couldn't protect either of them. For his sister, it had given her a false sense of security that led to Susan's death.

Standing on the freshly coated asphalt drive, the tar stuck to Mark's shoes and his black suit soaked up the late afternoon sun. After hours of standing in Eva's garden, he was roasting. The Midwest heat wave was scorching and the humidity, stifling. There was no cooling ocean breeze here. The air was dead still.

"Mark." Paul slipped out of his unmarked police cruiser. "Just talked to the crime lab. The clumps of blond hair they found in the raspberry patch matched Eva's. And they found fingerprints on the bloodstained garden clippers. A man's prints. The preliminary report says they could be Jim Hellmann's." Paul flicked his tan suit coat back and rested his hand on his gun clipped to his belt.

Mark boiled inside remembering Eva's strangely chopped off hair and the cut on the back of her neck. "Jim assaulted Eva."

"We don't know if it's her blood on the clippers. The lab is working on the blood test but it will take time to get the results." Paul walked to the front door. "Let me do the talking."

Mark slipped his cell phone into its leather case clipped to his belt. Under a suit coat it resembled a gun and that is where he kept his weapon when he had been a Secret Service agent. It felt comforting to have something clipped there, even if it was just a cell phone. His hand slowly slipped from it. "Don't worry, Paul, I won't get in the way of your investigation. Did the crime lab determine what killed Eva's cat?"

"They're checking the clippers first." Paul rang the doorbell.

The drape at the window moved but no one came to the door.

After knocking, Paul rang the bell again.

Mark straightened his tie. He wanted to look as federal as he could, hoping Jim would assume he was either a cop or an FBI agent. It would add a little pressure on Jim. Mark knew nervous people often talked too much, attempting to hide their guilt.

The door opened a crack and a grumpy voice responded. "Well, Detective Galloway, did you find my wife's body?"

"May we come in?" Paul pulled the storm door open.

"Sounds like you have some bad news." After wheezing, Jim sneezed. "Well, don't just stand there, you're letting in the pollen and all that damn heat."

Mark scanned Jim Hellmann, the prime suspect, the man who claimed to be Eva's husband, and the man who tried to move into her home the night she disappeared.

Jim backed away. His stature was short for a man and oddly proportioned. A stained T-shirt stretched over a bulging waist that looked like a tire was hidden beneath it. Ragged cutoffs exposed stubby legs and knobby knees. One broken sandal strap flapped as he backed behind the coffee table.

With his first cold glance, Mark knew that Jim was not Eva's type. On her desk, Mark had seen the photos of her father and grandfather. Both were well-dressed, tall muscular men. Each of them had relaxed smiles in their wedding photos with their arms around their dainty wives. Having studied federal profiling, Mark knew women were likely to be attracted to men who resembled the positive male role models in their lives. Jim looked nothing like the important men in Eva's past.

"Well, did you find Eva's body?" Jim staggered around the coffee table, strewn with pamphlets and investment portfolios, and flopped into the sofa.

"No." Paul pulled a small notebook from his suit coat. "We have a few more questions."

"I've already told you everything I know. If you have more questions call my lawyer." Jim slipped on his thick glasses and plopped his feet on the coffee table. "It's been days since you found my wife's Blazer. You should've found her body by now. How hard can it be to find a woman's body?"

Mark picked up a church directory that had fallen off the coffee table. The photos of several women about Eva's age were circled. "How did you meet Ms. Johnson?"

"Well, I see the FBI is helping out again. You feds shouldn't have let the local cops run with this case. They're clueless. It'll wind up as another one of their unsolved murder cases, mark my words." After blowing his nose, Jim grabbed two ice cubes from the ice bucket and splashed them in his drink.

Mark was glad Jim had assumed he was an FBI agent. Now he could ask questions and, unless asked, there was no need to correct Jim's assumptions about him being a federal agent.

"We can use all the help we can get in this case." Paul glanced at Mark. "The FBI read our reports but you know they like to ask their own questions."

"If you ask me, Eva's niece did it. Hired a hit man to knock off her Aunt Eva. Thought she'd get all her aunt's money. But she didn't count on a husband showing up. Well, that just shows you what a dingbat Maggie is, just like her aunt." Jim slurped his drink and continued. "Eva would forget her head if it weren't screwed on. She definitely needed someone like me to look after her affairs. It's a good thing I came along."

"How did you meet Ms. Johnson?" Mark repeated as he laid down the church directory.

Putting his head back on the sofa, Jim put drops in his eyes.

Paul stepped to the other side of the coffee table and looked down at a stack of booklets on the floor beside the sofa. "You don't remember how you met your wife?"

"What kind of a dumb question is that? Of course, I remember." Jim sat up. "We've already gone over that. It was at one of those income tax agencies. I went in to get some Schedule D's, you know, for capital gains. I was short a few for an investment seminar. Eva waited on me. She was a cute chick and I've always been partial to dumb blonds, so I let her prepare my taxes for me. Just for fun, of course."

That seems strange, Mark thought. *Paying to have Eva do his taxes just for fun. More likely it was a way to get to know her and her vulnerabilities.* Mark glanced down at a church directory with the picture of a woman circled like a target. "Eva Johnson filed your income tax return for you?"

"No way. My return was too complicated. I have a lot of investments so I do my own tax return. Like I said, I just had her do one for me for the fun of it. I wanted to ask her out." Jim put his glass on the coffee table. "All that stuff's in the police report. You feds can read it on your own time. What you need to do is get some of those dogs that find bodies and search that creek bed. That big storm must have washed it way down stream or buried it in a pile of rubble. Her body has to be there, somewhere."

Paul flipped closed an investment pamphlet he had been reading. "Her body may not be there."

"What!" Jim's feet hit the floor. "It's got to be there. That's where you found her Blazer with bullet holes in it. A hunting accident or some sort of road rage."

"We don't know if Eva was driving. Her Blazer could have been stolen." Paul watched Jim for his response.

"That's the lamest excuse I've heard of for giving up the search." Wheezing, Jim grabbed an asthma inhaler.

"I could use something to drink." Mark glanced down the dark hallway. "Mind if I get a glass of water?"

"Make it quick. I'm done talking."

Paul turned a page in his notebook. "Do you know what happened to Eva's cat?"

Mark looked at the beads of sweat below Jim's crew cut.

"I have no idea. I keep my distance from cats. I'm allergic to them." Jim sank back into the sofa and sneezed. "Eva spoiled that little furry monster. Treated it like it was a child. Silly woman."

While Paul continued his questioning, Mark wandered down the hall towards the kitchen in the back, looking into the rooms as he passed. The bathroom was cluttered with shaving supplies and prescription medication in brown containers. On the counter was a woman's curling iron. *A strange item for a man with short hair,* Mark thought. *I wonder what woman has been here?*

The next door was closed, but Mark assumed it was a bedroom; there were no other doors in the hall. From the street Jim's townhouse looked impressive, but inside it was small and sparsely furnished.

Stepping into the kitchen, Mark found more clutter. Empty pizza boxes stuffed in the trash with paper plates and cans. Newspapers and magazines cluttered the table. More prescription bottles for antihistamines and decongestants were on the counter. Truly a man with allergies, Mark noted.

Pulling a glass from the cupboard, Mark spotted a can of cat food hidden in the back. It was the same gourmet brand that had been tucked into the corner of Princess's little coffin. Mark reached for the can of cat food, but stopped short of touching it. If the police needed it for evidence, he couldn't tamper with it.

Why would a man who was allergic to cats have cat food in his cupboard? Mark pondered. *He's not the type to feed a stray cat gourmet food. Would he kill Eva's cat just because he was allergic to it? Or did he know Princess was in her will and didn't want to share his inheritance with a cat?*

Hearing Jim's voice grow louder, Mark headed back down the dim hall. The bedroom door was now open a crack, but it was too dark to see inside. A whiff of perfume seeped into the hallway, smelling like gardenias that had baked too long in the hot sun.

Stepping into the living room, Mark found Paul and Jim glaring at each other.

"I'm not going to answer that without my lawyer." Jim stomped to the door. "Now get the hell out of here."

"We'll be back." Paul stepped outside.

Mark handed the glass of water to Jim and followed Paul, making a beeline to his cruiser. Slipping into the passenger's side, Mark studied Paul's red face. "What happened?"

"I asked if he knew about Eva's restraining order." After smashing the key into the ignition, Paul started the car. "Must have hit a hot spot. He blew his stack."

"You didn't tell me you found the restraining order."

"We didn't. I didn't know about it until Maggie mentioned it to you. But it sure touched a nerve when I mentioned it to Jim. He knows something about it." Paul stopped at the traffic light. "Strange, Eva's attorney didn't tell us about her asking him to file a restraining order. Surely she would have consulted him."

"Perhaps not. She may have planned to ask a friend first. A detective." Mark watched Paul's hands strangle the steering wheel. "Sorry, that was a low blow."

"No. You're right. I've been thinking about that since Maggie told us. And that may be why Eva phoned me the day before it happened. To ask me how effective a restraining order would be. We both know the answer to that." Paul pulled onto a country road.

Mark recalled how happy his sister was when she got a restraining order, preventing her ex-boyfriend from seeing her. But he ignored it and took out his anger on Mark's sister. *No,* Mark thought. *Sometimes a restraining order is useless.*

On the country road, Paul pulled his police car over to pass an Amish buggy. "That could be why Eva was so interested in the old reformatory. That field trip for her students could have been more about Eva's interest in the criminal mind than for an interesting art location. When I took her students through the old jail section, she asked a lot of questions about prison life. And now that I think of it, there was more to those questions than I realized."

Mark studied the Ohio valley tucked between rolling hills. The high country as Paul called it. It was rich in vegetation, with lush towering trees, wide fertile fields, and trickling brooks. "What kind of questions did Eva ask?"

"How the justice system works, the sentencing structure for white collar crimes versus capital crimes, and what incarceration does to men." Slowing, Paul pulled near a bridge where yellow crime scene tape shimmered in the afternoon sun. "There was one question I didn't answer. Eva wanted to know what happened to the victims of crime."

~ 37 ~

"Is this where you found Eva's Blazer? This creek area looks deeper than the accident photos you sent." Mark walked down the steep bank to where Eva's mangled Blazer had been found. The weeds were trampled flat in the search for evidence. Yellow crime scene tape flapped from stakes, looking like storm warning flags.

"Actually, two Amish boys found the Blazer about six thirty in the morning. They were exploring the creek after the night's storm. If they hadn't spotted it, it could have been days before it was found." Paul stopped short of the trickling water. "Right now this stream looks peaceful but in a gully washer, it runs deep in this narrowing in front of the bridge. Those tree branches, over there, had washed against her Blazer. You couldn't see it from the road."

Mark stepped on the stony creek bed. A chipmunk scurried away, chattering. "The pavement up there is straight and level. She must have been run off the road. Did you find any evidence of her Blazer being struck by another vehicle?"

Paul shook his head. "The sides of the Blazer were too smashed to determine that. The only real evidence we found were the two bullet holes in the driver's side window. Our crime lab technician has sharp eyes and she found a small piece of glass with one hole in it. I remember her telling me it was a 9mm. She insisted we needed to find all the glass and reconstruct the window. I was a little skeptical of her call until we found a slug in the headrest. A 9mm. But we didn't find the second slug. Of course, we now know that it was in Eva's arm."

"Your crime lab staff was very thorough." Bending over, Mark couldn't find any glass or metallic parts. "They must have picked up every scrap. There's nothing left."

"The glass was up there, on the bank, above the high water line. The side window must have busted out on the first roll. Down here, there wasn't much left after the storm, except the hull of the Blazer. A fender was caught on that bridge abutment, over yonder, and one tire was found downstream."

"Sounded like it was a big storm." Mark remembered the massive weather system several days earlier. There had been numerous severe storm warnings in the Midwest. He and his father had planned to go deep-sea fishing. But after watching the weather reports showing the front roll through the Ohio valley then whip southward, they changed their minds. His father had said it would kick up a northeaster for sure. Only a fool would go out to sea in one of those. Killer storms, the old timers call them. The ocean got so angry during them it frothed with salty foam.

Mark glanced up at Paul, staring at a gouge in the creek bed, seemingly lost in thought. *Looks like he's reliving how he felt when he found Eva's Blazer.* Mark knew that sick feeling. *Paul must have been racked with guilt for not being able to help a friend. It's even worse when it's your sister that you let down.*

"Which way does Eva live from here?"

"What?"

"Where is Eva's home from here?"

"Back that way. Upstream. Her home is beyond that high point." Paul looked at a line of clouds building in the west. "If I'd just returned her phone call, I could have spared Eva all this."

"You don't know that, Paul. We can never know what would have happened if we would have intervened. ... Just remember, Eva is alive and you'll see her tonight." Mark wandered upstream. "Tell me what you did after you found the Blazer."

Paul trudged through some weeds and followed. "Like I said, the Amish boys found Eva's Blazer shortly after daybreak. They ran home and told their parents. Their father took his buggy down to a farm where there was a phone and had them notify the police. By the time we got here, a group of Amish men had gathered to help with the search. With some of our officers, they searched the fields on foot and horseback."

"They didn't find anything?"

"No. It was slow going by foot. The ground had been pounded by heavy rain and they had to slouch through knee-deep mud along the creek bed. We called in the Civil Air Patrol to assist us. With their little airplanes, they can fly low and slow. Mud and flooded fields doesn't slow them. Also, they are trained to search for the missing. One of their planes covered the area upstream and another one did the downstream section. They only spotted some car debris downstream. No body was found."

A pickup truck slowed and stopped on the bridge. An arm reached out the window, pointing to the accident site.

Mark watched it. "If I had been shot at and run off the road by a passing vehicle, I would avoid the road. Eva could have been afraid the car would return. And from here, she could have walked home. Or Eva could have gotten a ride back."

"No. We ruled that out. The story made the front page. Anyone who would have given her a lift would have called the *News Journal* or us." Paul stepped over a turtle, sunning itself.

"Did your police dogs find her trail back?"

"Like I said, it was a hard rain. Most of the scent trail was washed away and when the dogs grew too exhausted wading through the mud, their handlers pulled them out. They looked pretty pitiful, drenched in mud." Paul pointed towards the high point. "The dog that came upstream headed towards the ridge. We send a patrol car up the road to get him. He wouldn't stop."

"He must have found her scent. I know Rex is pretty good at tracking, even after a rain."

"You have a police dog?"

"Rex is retired. He was injured in the line of duty." Mark walked on, not wanting to explain it was during the search for his sister. It almost cost Rex his life. Mark didn't discuss that with anyone. Only he and Rex shared that grim experience.

"If Eva walked home, it must have been before the storm."

Mark looked back at the creek. "When did the storm hit?"

"A little after one in morning. We watched the hot lightning to the west. Then suddenly a gust of wind smacked the big oak trees in front of Eva's house and the sky let loose. Beating rain and sizzling lightning bolts." Paul shuddered.

"If Eva triggered the house alarm a little before midnight, where was she during the storm?" Mark asked.

"Beats me." Paul shook his head. "We'll have to ask her."

"She may not remember." Mark turned and headed back downstream. "She doesn't recall being shot or the accident. Between her illness and a possible concussion, I doubt she'll know where she was. Or anything that happened that night."

Paul stopped. "What's that over there, sticking in the mud?"

Both of them stepped across the rocks to a sand bar. A piece of metal glittered in the late afternoon sunlight. A small brush stuck up beside a boulder. Only a small portion of its black handle protruded from the dirt. A red band circled beneath the shining metal strip holding sable hair like a torch, bent downstream.

"It's a watercolor brush." Mark yanked it out and rinsed it off. "Eva must have rested on this rock before heading home."

"It's amazing it didn't get washed away in the current."

"The boulder must have protected it from the rushing water." Mark tucked it into his pocket. "What did you find in her Blazer?"

"Not much. A Coke can under the seat, her proof of insurance, and a map." Paul smiled. "An old map of Florida."

Above them, two cars raced down the road, playing tag, covering Paul's unmarked police cruiser with dust.

"What's that rumbling?" Mark turned south.

Detective Galloway listened to the distant rumble of high-powered engines. "That noise is from the racetrack. There're practicing for the weekend races at Mid-Ohio. It's over yonder, behind that hill. It's not exactly the Daytona 500 but sports car fans enjoy it. It even draws some big name racers like Paul Newman."

"More Hollywood connections?"

"For Hollywood, the Ohio high country is like the other end of the world. When the film crews were in making the last movie, they said the local people were weird. Of course we think the Hollywood folks are the strange ones." Paul chuckled. "I guess it's just a matter of perspective. You have to admit, Ohio is much greener than 'shake-and-bake' California."

"Speaking of baking, lets get back in your cruiser and turn on the air conditioning." Mark started up the bank. "It's hotter here than Florida. I need to get back to the ocean."

"I'm right behind you." Inside the car, Paul flicked the air conditioner to high. "What time does our flight get to Daytona?"

"About eleven thirty." Mark glanced back at the creek bed. A deer was sipping water. And near the police cruiser, a red-winged blackbird sat on a tall reed, defending its territory.

It looks so peaceful down there, Mark thought as he pulled the watercolor brush from his pocket. *And yet it was almost a tragic end for Eva. She's as fragile as this little brush caught in the torrent of storm water. If it hadn't been for the rock shielding it, this brush would have perished. What protected Eva? How did she manage to survive?*

Aunt Killer

~ *38* ~

Daytona Beach, Florida – Early evening, August 21st

Am I going to survive? Eva wondered as she watched another drop of liquid slip down the IV tube and into her arm. *No, survive is not the right word. Recover is more exact. How do you recover from viral encephalitis? After I've taken all the medicine and the fever in my brain is gone, then what do I do? From the outside, I appear normal and I manage to function. But I know inside, I'm not the same person. Who am I?*

Pulling her IV stand along, Eva strolled to the glass living room door of Mark's parents' home. She stopped, but her mind rambled on. *In summer, this is my favorite time of day. Early evening. The world has quieted and the daylight is soft. That's when I do my gardening.*

Eva put her hand on the glass, separating her from the cool evening air she loved. *Early evening is a perfect time to be out, except for an occasional mosquito. Mosquitoes. ... No one worries about mosquitoes in Ohio. We just swat them and forget it. We don't think our mosquitoes carry diseases. Surely nothing deadly like viral encephalitis. ... Will my life ever be the same?*

"I glad to see you up and walking around. It'll help you get your strength back." Barbara slid a big box on the dining room table. "I've been collecting this stuff for the church bazaar. Thought you might want to rummage through it. You might find something to occupy your time while you're recovering."

"Thanks." Although her mind was still swirling, Eva walked to the box. "I need something to do beside nap."

Barbara held the television guide. "You could watch TV."

"No. All that flickering hurts my eyes. The commercials make me feel sick with all their flashing images. Once I counted twenty-five in sixty seconds. Too many." Eva rummaged through the box.

"You're right, if you have a fever, you shouldn't watch too much TV." Barbara tossed the television guide on an end table.

"Oh, look at this. It's precious." Eva pulled out an old-fashioned doll. "Its like the one I played with in first grade. Our teacher kept one in the toy box in the back of the room. I loved that doll. Its china head fascinated me. So smooth and fragile."

"Too bad this one has a broken head." Barbara pointed.

"I know how that feels. Are the rest of the pieces in there? I could put her head back together." Eva touched the forehead of the china doll. "Poor baby, you must have a splitting headache."

"Do you want something for your headache?" Barbara asked.

"No. I'm tired of taking pills."

"Maybe we should have a little snack. Some tea and a few of those cocoa cookies we made will make you feel better."

"Just one for me. I made them for Mark. When's he getting home?" Eva glanced down the hall, hoping to see him.

"When he called this afternoon, he said it would be late." Barbara left for the kitchen. "I'll bring back some food for those hungry kittens. We all could use a pre-dinner snack."

Searching the box for other treasures, Eva pulled out a yellow ribbon for the kittens to play with and tossed Rex an old tennis ball. An assortment of children's books, stuffed toys, and old video games covered some picture boxes on the bottom.

"What's this?" Eva dug deeper. "Puzzles. Picture puzzles. I haven't put one of them together since I was a kid. I wonder if I can still do that?'

"Do what?" Barbara returned with iced tea, crackers, milk for the kittens, and a dog biscuit for Rex on a tray.

"Put a picture puzzle together. I used to enjoy the challenge."

"Give it a try. I'll have Fritz get the card table and set it up by the window. You seem to enjoy watching the ocean."

"I haven't seen Fritz since lunch. Where is he?"

"He got that part for your bike. He's in the garage working on it. Tinkering on bikes is his specialty. Mark's always seemed to need repairs. Mark and his friends used to race them on the beach, pretending they were motorcycles. They never seemed to learn bikes couldn't jump sand dunes without crashing."

"Falling in the sand isn't as bad as tumbling into a creek." Eva grabbed a box; its picture intrigued her. "Cool. A snow scene. It looks like Siberia. I'll do this puzzle. Concentrating on this icy landscape will cool my thoughts."

"But the lid on that says some of the pieces are missing."

"That's okay, so are mine. I wonder if I can put it back together." After slipping into the chair, Eva pulled the lid off and retrieved one piece. It was pale blue, the color of Mark's eyes. "This is exactly what I need. I can concentrate on this."

Fritz strolled in, wiping his hands on an old rag. "I could use a tall glass of iced tea. It's a scorcher out there. Eva, your bike is almost ready. After I remove a few dents from the fender and give it a fresh coat of paint, it will be better than new."

"Better than new." Eva smiled. "I hadn't thought about that. Take what you have and make it better than new." She stared out the window at the ocean beyond the sand dunes. *Can I do that with my mind?* Eva somberly considered. *Make it better than new, at least better than it used to be? How much have I forgotten? Can I fill in the missing pieces of my memory?*

Barbara and Fritz watched Eva toying with a piece of the puzzle. It was solid white like blank paper.

In the kitchen, Eva heard a sound. "The phone is ringing."

Fritz reached for the cordless phone beside the table. Its ringer was turned off, but the light was flashing. "Hello. ... Mark, where are you?"

A wave of excitement swept through Eva. She had been asleep when Mark called earlier and was hoping he would call again.

"Yes, she's awake. Do you want to speak to her?" Fritz asked.

"Mark." Eva tried to control her voice and slow her mind. "Yes, I'm feeling much better. Almost good as new."

Even with the background noise, Mark's voice was clear. "I'm glad you're much better. Make sure you keep taking your medicine and get lots of rest. We can have a long talk tomorrow."

"Tomorrow?"

"I won't be getting home until very late," Mark said. "You'll be asleep by then, so we can talk tomorrow."

"With all the naps I've had today, I'll wait up." Eva toyed with a strand of her hair. "So tell me about your faculty meeting."

"Well," Mark hesitated. "That'll take too long on the phone. I'd rather tell you about it when we get home."

"We?" Eva asked. "Are you bringing a friend?"

"Yes, he'll be staying for a few days."

"He." Eva sighed in relief. "Well then I'll have to make another batch of cookies. Is he another professor?"

"We'll talk when I get home. I need to speak to Dad."

"Fritz, Mark wants to talk to you." Reluctantly, she handed over the phone. Hearing Mark's voice excited her, like a call for the prom date. Silly, she thought as a swirl of emotions rushed through her. Strong feelings she had almost forgotten.

With the cordless phone, Fritz walked down the hall.

Barbara returned from the hall with a card table. "Here we go. You can take the chair and I'll put the table up. It'll give you plenty of room to work. By the window will be a good spot."

"Do you know Mark's friend?"

"I don't believe we've met." Barbara flipped out the legs of the table. "Are you sure you want to put that winter picture puzzle together? It looks like a hard one."

Keeping her eye on the hall, Eva dumped the pieces on the card table. "If it was easy, it wouldn't be a challenge. Most anything can be done if you do it in steps. First you flip all the pieces right side up and hunt for the four corners. Next you put all the flat sidepieces together to make sort of a picture frame."

"But then how on earth do you get all the rest back together?"

Eva started picking up one piece at a time and laid them in different areas. "First I sort them by color. Then the fun begins."

Fritz returned and put the phone back on its base. "Mark will be home after eleven thirty. He ... uh ... got tied up and couldn't make the earlier connections."

"Barbara, remind me to make another batch of cookies. Mark and his friend will want a snack if they're coming in late."

"We can make another batch after dinner."

Eva stared at the clock. *Why so late?* Eva wondered. *That's over five hours. Where on earth was his faculty meeting? Silly, this is Florida not Ohio. It takes eight hours to drive from Miami to Jacksonville. It must have been a statewide meeting in Tallahassee.*

Later at dinner, Eva nibbled some fish and mashed potatoes. Her appetite had faded again, not from the illness but from excitement. The room seemed filled with expectation. Even Rex seemed excited when Barbara and Fritz talked about Mark and some of his childhood antics on the beach.

Listening to the stories of Mark's adventures sent Eva's heart spinning. *Strange, I miss Mark. Well, miss isn't exactly right, but I don't know him well enough for the other four-letter word. Love. You have to know someone before you use that word, love. And we've just met. Love takes time. Doesn't it? ... These strange feelings I have for Mark must be from my fever. I've surely never felt this way before. I'm not sure I understand how I feel.*

After helping Barbara clear the table, Eva took a short nap, hoping it would be her last before Mark returned. She was anxious to hear about his meeting. If it were like any of the faculty meetings she had attended, there would be some amusing stories to tell. A room full of professors created tension with conflicting views, witty remarks, sharp puns, assorted inside jokes, and of course a smattering of tales about student antics.

"There you go, my little kitties." Eva put them back in their box as Rex watched. "If you eat any more you won't be able to walk. It's time for your nap."

Scooting the box under the card table, Eva returned to putting the picture puzzle together. She wanted the time to pass quickly and to stay awake. As she sipped more iced tea, she studied the liquid. *Amber is an interesting color. It feels rich and relaxing.* She smiled, amused by her mind. *My synapses are crackling with crazy thoughts today. Now, crazy is when all the colors swirl together, competing for attention, chaos, no color scheme.*

Eva picked up another piece of the picture puzzle. *White is the presence of all color. Strange most people don't consider it a color. But an artist knows the importance of white and all the hues of the rainbow. Color connects our thoughts.* Eva chuckled. *Don't laugh. It's true. Even the telephone company knows that. That's why they color code all those little wires. The blue wire connects to the blue wire and the white wire to its mate. Send and receive, a pair. Connect the wrong colors together and you'll fry the system.*

"Color counts," Eva mumbled.

"What did you say?" Barbara glanced up from her sewing.

"Color is important in putting a puzzle back together."

"Just remember some of the pieces are missing."

"That's okay. I'm missing some pieces myself."

"Is your headache back? Do you want me to get you something for it?" Putting down her sewing, Barbara walked over to check Eva's pulse. "Your heart is racing a bit. I think you've had enough ice tea. I'll get you some orange juice."

Nodding, Eva returned to sorting the puzzle pieces. A big pile of snow white, a small stack of pale yellow, and her attention was now focused on finding all the pieces with her favorite color.

Blue, she thought, holding one piece. *Blue is such a happy color. It's not at all sad. Sad is dreary winter gray. Blue feels good. It's the sky on a sunny day, sparkling and cheerful. It's the color of Lake Erie on a hot August afternoon and the color of the clear water at the Ponce Inlet. Blue make me feel good inside.*

Adding that piece to the sky blue stack, Eva continued her search. A piece was pulled from the bottom of the pile. Eva frowned. *Purple. I don't understand how anyone could like purple. It makes me feel sick. For an artist to make purple, you have to mix equal parts of loyal blue and blood red. Purple is the color of war, purple hearts, Vietnam, and violence.*

Turning on the CD player, Eva listened to the sounds of ocean music. In disgust, she tossed the purple piece in the wastebasket. Eva wanted no violent purple around her.

Nosing through the trash, Rex tried to retrieve the piece.

"Rex, don't touch that. Purple is poison. Go in the kitchen and get a dog biscuit from Barbara."

Eva tapped the replay button on the CD player. *That's better. The ocean will wash away the purple with soothing blue sounds. Music connects the emotions like color connects the thoughts.*

The mound of blue puzzle pieces grew. A glass of orange juice slid next to her along with a white capsule.

Barbara tapped the table. "It's time to take your medicine."

"Really, I'm feeling fine. I don't need that."

"Take your antibiotic." Barbara turned away.

Eva picked up the capsule. "What are you sewing?"

"A special pillow to support your neck." Retrieving it, Barbara slipped the small crescent pillow around Eva's neck. "I have a lot of fabric pieces. What color do you want for the cover?"

"Any color but purple." Eva cringed, sliding the capsule under her plate as soon as Barbara turned her back. "You can't sleep on a purple pillow."

Barbara chuckled. "What color is good for sleeping?"

"Blue. Sky blue. ... The color of Mark's eyes." Eva blushed.

"Well I have the perfect piece, a sky blue satin. I used that kind of fabric on Mark's crib. You always make a fuss over the first child. I have a whole closet shelf of blue fabric."

"Oh, I don't want to use a keepsake on my pillow."

"I have plenty." Barbara disappeared down the hall and returned with a stack of blue satin in varying tints. "See, I have a wide selection. Which one do you want?"

Eva's fingers slid across the satin fabrics, feeling the soothing, soft blues. "This one."

Barbara pulled it out. "That's exactly the color of Mark's eyes. It will make a lovely pillow cover for you to rest your head on."

"It will be interesting to hear about Mark's faculty meeting."

"Did he say anything about it on the phone?" Barbara asked.

"He said ... we'd talk when he got home." Eva felt strange not being able to remember what Mark had said. Although she had listened intently to his words, she couldn't remember them, just the sound of his voice and the knowledge he was coming home. "What time will he be back?"

"He told Fritz it would be about eleven thirty." Barbara flipped the fabric across the dining room table. "I should get busy with this pillow cover. It will give you sweet dreams tonight."

Eva slipped the CD player's headphone back on and returned to sorting sky blue and listening to the soft tinkling of piano notes blending with silky violins; they made a nice sounding pair, connecting romantically. It was like a blue sky caressing the deep sea in seven smooth waves of melody.

Goose bumps rippled up her arm. Watching the sea oats sway in the evening breeze, thoughts of Mark floated in her mind.

"Take your medicine." Barbara's voice cut into the music.

Nodding to the tune, Eva pulled one capsule from the plastic bag she had and reluctantly took it. *This medicine knocks me out,* she considered. *It's too strong. I don't know why the doctor wants me to finish these antibiotics when I have viral encephalitis. This stuff makes my mind go fuzzy and it leaves a bitter taste in my mouth like poison. It makes me feel purple.*

After taking the capsule, she returned to sorting colors.

"Eva." Barbara turned off the music and tapped the table. "What this? You can't hide your pill under the plate. You have to take one every twelve hours."

With her mind already a little fuzzy, Eva swallowed a second capsule. "But I could have sworn I already took one."

~ 39 ~

Daytona Beach, Florida – Midnight, August 21st

"You shouldn't have done that." Mark put his briefcase beside the kitchen table. Two places were set with a midnight dinner waiting. It warmed his heart to be home, to see his parents, and to have his favorite meal waiting; but, as a grown son, he didn't want to admit it. He kissed his mother's cheek and smiled. "Looks good, Mom. I see Dad went fishing today. It's a good catch, and we could use some home-cooked food."

"I'll second that." Paul pulled out a chair. "I know your son needs some fuel. He only nibbled a couple of fries in Ohio and a few peanuts on the flight down. He must have known he was coming home to a good, Southern home-cooked meal."

Barbara and Fritz joined their son and Detective Paul Galloway at the kitchen table. With the introductions made, they sipped decaffeinated coffee. Barbara added more fried fish to the center plate and slipped another pan of corn bread into the oven. Amused, Fritz watched Paul eat piece after piece of fresh ocean fish. Fritz chatted about Mark's childhood bike escapades for Paul's amusement.

Mark glanced at the hall. Two doors down, Eva was safe and sleeping. He had looked in on her as soon as he got home. The only reminder of her frail condition was the IV fluid dripping into her arm. But he knew that five days ago she was lying at the bottom of a rocky creek bed surrounded by her crumpled Blazer.

Somehow she had crawled out and made it home. What happened to her from then until Mark found her sleeping on the sand dune, neither he nor Paul had any clues. On their flight to Daytona, they had speculated on those missing hours.

After handing Paul a piece of Key-lime pie, Barbara sliced another piece for her son. "Do you want some pie?"

"Just a small piece." Mark glanced at the platter in the middle of the table. The pile of fish was gone, along with the dish of black-eye peas and a major portion of the corn bead. Beside the pie was a plate of cocoa cookies that Eva had made, and they were being nibbled as everyone finished their coffee.

"Mom, how did Eva feel today?"

"She has her ups and downs." Barbara glanced at her son, then at Paul cutting into his pie. "After her naps, her strength returns for awhile. As long as she doesn't overdo it, she seems fine. Except –"

"What?"

"Well, I've been watching. After she takes one of her capsules, she seems to get more forgetful, almost confused, like tonight. After she took her antibiotic, she could hardly separate the puzzle pieces. Some medication can fog your thinking."

Fritz put his coffee down. "We barely got her to the bedroom before she fell asleep. I think she should stop taking them."

"Can't do that," Barbara insisted. "You can't just stop taking antibiotics. But in her condition, they may be too strong. I'm going to call Doctor Williams tomorrow and check with him."

"Excuse me," Paul interrupted. "I'm confused. I thought she has viral encephalitis. I'm no doctor, but I know antibiotics can't cure a viral infection."

"True," Barbara continued. "But not all encephalitis is caused by a virus. Sometimes a bacteria can cause it or another illness. So far Doctor Williams hasn't been able to pin that down. He is almost certain it is viral but her blood tests haven't proved that.

Knowing she caught it in Ohio may help him pinpoint or at least narrow down which virus may have been involved."

"Sounds like the doc's playing detective." Paul sipped coffee. "I'll have my staff find out her doctor's name and then your doctor can talk to hers."

"Good idea." Barbara watched her son, with a familiar faraway look in his eyes, then turned to her guest. "Tell me, Paul, how do you know Eva?"

"Excuse me." Mark headed to the hallway, wanting to see if Eva was awake. There was no need to hear Paul repeat his story; Mark wanted to hear Eva's story.

As Mark turned into her room, Rex trotted over to his master with his tail wagging. He had greeted Mark at the front door but quickly returned to Eva's room to watch her sleep and keep track of the overly curious kittens.

"That's okay, Rex," Mark whispered. "I understand; you have to guard her." Quietly, Mark stepped beside Eva's bed, hoping not to wake her and yet hoping she would be awake.

Under a sheet, Eva lay curled up with her neck supported by a blue satin pillow. An IV tube dangled from a bag of liquid, dripping more Acyclovir antiviral medication into her arm. The night-light cast a warm glow across her face.

Crouching beside her bed, Mark studied her sleeping. *She looks so peaceful,* he thought. *Like she doesn't have a worry in the world. Her life seemed so secure and protected, so how did she become a victim? Does Eva remember who tried to kill her? Can she provide the evidence Paul needs to capture the guilty person?*

Brushing her hair back, Mark studied the chopped off clump at the back of her neck. The other ends of those strands had been found in her raspberry patch. Under the broken branches, the crime lab recovered garden clippers with Eva's hair and bloodstains, and Jim's fingerprints on the handle.

"Don't worry, darling," Mark whispered. "Eva, I promise, I'll protect you. I won't let anyone hurt you."

Rex growled.

A shadow in the door caught Mark's attention. Turning, he caught only a glimpse of Paul walking away. "Good boy. Don't trust any strangers. Not even if he carries a badge."

Watching Eva, Mark hoped she was having pleasant dreams with no nightmares of what happened or what was to come. *How will she cope with Paul's presence,* he wondered.

"Mark." Barbara put a hand on her son's shoulder. "Why don't you take Rex out for some exercise. He's hardly left her side. I'll watch Eva. And it's not polite to ignore your guest. Paul went out to check the ocean. Strange thing about tourists, they always want to check the ocean. Like they think it's going somewhere."

"Come on, Rex. Let's check on Paul, checking the ocean."

Outside, beyond the last sand dune where the old wooden sidewalk ended, Paul leaned against the flagpole, staring at the ocean. The first quarter moon hung in the eastern sky, tipped like it was pouring water back into the ocean. Beneath it, the waves pounded in measured beats.

"The surf sounds different at night." Mark stopped while Rex dashed out to the ocean. "It's a restful pounding. Almost like it's happy to be alone. Free of the swimmers cutting into its waves."

"My wife likes to listen to it at night." Paul slipped his shoes off and buried his feet in the cool sand. "We stay at one of the older motels where you can actually leave the windows open at night. My wife thinks the waves have a romantic sound." Paul chuckled. "It seems to work. Both our children were born nine months after our annual vacations here."

"Nature has a strong rhythm and the ocean is teeming with life. Men have always been drawn to wherever the ocean and land meets. Perhaps that is why Eva came back here." Mark scooped up a handful of sand. "If you've been raised along the beach, it's always part of your life, drawing you back to the ocean. ...Even the sea turtles return every year."

Rex dashed back, dripping wet and carrying a stick.

Mark tossed the stick high. "When we talk to Eva tomorrow, how do you want to play it?"

"I had it all planned out on the flight down. The usual straightforward approach." Paul sat down on the sand. "But after seeing Eva tonight with that IV, I've changed my mind."

"I'm worried about Eva being upset by your presence." Mark joined Paul on the sand. "You may consider her a friend, but you're also a detective. I know you have to get the facts but I –"

"I know." Paul interrupted. "You're in love with Eva."

"What?" Mark turned.

"It's obvious, you're in love with Eva." Paul's feet slid deep into the sand. "I suspected that the moment you walked into her house. So I watched you walk through Eva's home like it was a shrine and you touched her possessions like they were sacred. There was contempt in your eyes when you questioned Jim. And when you found her art brush in the creek, you tucked it in your pocket like it was a precious gem."

"That's just being considerate and thoughtful."

"It's more than that. It's a personal involvement. Lets face it Mark, Secret Service agents, even ex-ones, are hardly the frivolous types. No, you guys play it close to your bulletproof vests. Really serious types, people who can be trusted to protect the life of a President and his family. You don't get involved in an ongoing criminal investigation on a whim."

Tossing his stick down, Rex stretched out beside Mark.

"Good boy." Mark was interested to hear the rest of Paul's assumptions. So far Paul had been basically correct.

"Take your dog for example. Not many people have a police

dog as a pet. Not even a detective. I have a pound pup, a stray cat, several goldfish, and whatever the kids brought home today." Paul reached over to pet Rex, but pulled away seeing teeth. "Okay, Rex, you want to see my badge." He laid it on the sand.

After sniffing the badge, Rex nudged it back to Paul.

"Detectives can tell a lot about a person by their pets. Eva's cat was a pedigreed Himalayan, well cared for and loved as a faithful companion. That reflects Eva herself. Refined, independent like a cat, and yet vulnerable." Paul paused. "So it's not hard to imagine you falling in love with her. I've noticed the serious types fall hard when it comes to matters of the heart."

"I want to make sure you don't upset Eva." Mark glanced back at the house. A warm light streamed across the front deck, cutting into the darkness. "She's still very weak and her memory is a little fuzzy at times. You'll have to take that into consideration when you talk with her. I don't want you to use any hard-nosed detective questioning. Remember, she's not a criminal to be interrogated, she's a victim."

"Believe me, I have no intention of upsetting Eva."

"Good, because I won't permit it. If she gets too tired, I'll cut you off." Mark listened to the ocean pounding, like his heart.

"I understand. But there are some questions that I need to ask her in private." Paul wiped sand off his feet.

"No! I have to hear all of her story."

"Mark, there may be things she would rather you not know."

"Why?"

"Because Eva may be in love with you."

~ 40 ~

Early Morning – August 22nd

I have to know what happened to Eva. I hope she's up to answering our questions. Mark stood beside the living room screen door, watching Eva sitting outside at the deck table. Her back was to Mark and her head eclipsed the early morning sun. As the rays of light streaked through her blond hair, it glowed like a halo around her. *How could anyone want to harm her?*

Up before dawn and free of her IV, Eva had taken her breakfast to the front deck to watch the sunrise. The kittens were in their box playing with a ping-pong ball and Rex lay near them, watching to make sure they didn't climb out. Fritz sat in the doublewide lounge chair, reading a western novel while he kept an eye on everyone.

"Morning, Mark." Sipping coffee, Paul strolled to the screen door. "Don't worry, I'll be as tactful as possible when I question Eva. If she needs time to rest during the questioning, that's no problem. I'm in no hurry to get back to Ohio. It's too hot up there. This ocean breeze is refreshing."

"Did you check with the crime lab about Eva's cat?" Mark continued to watch Eva, who was outside nibbling her breakfast.

"The autopsy showed Princess died from poison, like Eva said. But it wasn't ant poison." Pulling a paper out of his pocket, Paul reviewed his notes. "They identified it as an alkaloid, Datura. Jimsonweed is its more common name. It comes from a plant native to North America and the alkaloid poison is in most parts of the plant and especially strong in its dark seeds. The crime lab is going back out to Eva's house to search for any jimsonweed plants. If they find any they'll have to destroy them."

"Surely you aren't accusing Eva of growing a deadly plant in her flower bed." Mark glared at Paul.

"I didn't say that. It grows wild and a bird could've brought in a seed. She may not have known what it was. Her cat could've eaten some of it."

Mark shook his head. "Princess ate gourmet cat food. I doubt she'd have nibbled a poisonous plant."

"But cats sometimes munch grass."

"Has the crime lab checked Princess's stomach content to see what part of the plant was ingested?"

"Not yet. They'll be doing that today." Paul sipped coffee.

"Until they do, we don't know if it was murder or accidental."

"You're right." Paul nodded. "And I don't buy the accidental theory, either. Even my stray cat is finicky about what she eats. Surely Princess wouldn't eat a nasty plant like jimsonweed."

Mark opened the screen door. "Let's avoid talking about Eva's cat. I don't want to upset her."

As Mark and Paul approached, Fritz put down his book. "Morning, Mark. It's good you slept in a bit. You looked pretty ragged last night."

Smiling, Eva turned; her eyes were locked on Mark. "I'm glad you're home. I want to hear all about your faculty meeting."

As Mark walked to the glass-top deck table, he studied Eva. She looked rested and her IV was gone. *Eva seems ready for some questions*, he thought. *But will she want to answer them. Before I went to Mansfield, Eva avoided any questions about her past. I assumed it was a memory problem. Now I'm not sure she'll want to remember. But, for her safety, Paul and I have to know what happened.* Mark pulled out a chair. "Mind if we join you?"

"Please. Have you had breakfast? I can get you something."

"We already ate, but we'll join you for coffee."

With her eyes still focused on Mark, she moved the doll with the broken china head aside. "It was a beautiful sunrise this morning. There was a light haze over the ocean and the sun looked like a bright yellow ball slipping over the horizon. It was a pale lemon color, a crisp clean yellow."

He watched her eyes sparkle and a shy smile curl her lips. *She seems happy this morning.* Mark hesitated. *I hate to ruin it with questions. So far she hasn't even noticed Paul. How will she respond to his presence?*

Paul sat beside her. "Good morning, Eva."

"Good morning." Eva gave Paul only a quick glance.

No response to Paul. Does she even remember him? Mark's coffee cup clanged on the glass top. His nerves tingled. The cool morning air seemed to fill with tension. His father had already left and Rex, looking nervous, moved next to Eva like a guard dog. "What are you working on?"

Eva picked up the doll with blond hair. "I'm repairing her china head. Putting all the pieces back together." Eva smiled, touching the smooth china face. "She's a beautiful doll. It would be a shame to throw her away. She just needs a little tender loving care. I'm going to fill her head with this gray fabric. I thought that was appropriate for brains. And then I'll reinforce the inside of her porcelain skull with fabric strips and glue. When I'm done, she'll be better than new."

"Will the paste hold the parts together?" Paul asked.

"Barbara gave me some of that special craft glue. That stuff will hold anything, but you have to be careful with it. It contains acetone and you need good ventilation. That's why I brought it out here. Didn't want the toxic fumes in the house." Eva frowned. "They can cause headaches and I don't need any more of those."

"How are you feeling today?" Mark studied her. *I hope she's up to this. Paul will have to tell the district attorney what kind of witness Eva will make. How will she hold up under intense cross-examination? Can she tell them enough to make a case they can prosecute? Does she remember who did it?*

"I'm feeling fine." She gazed into Mark's eyes. "Now, tell me about your faculty meeting."

Mark cringed, wishing he didn't have to begin. "I wasn't at a faculty meeting. I was —"

"He was helping me out with a case." Paul interrupted, then took a deep breath. "I needed Mark's expert help. ... In fact, we could also use your help."

Eva glanced at Paul, then Mark, and back to Paul. Looking perplexed, she turned back to Mark. "I'd be glad to help you, Mark. What do you want me to do?"

Mark's grip tightened around his coffee. "We'd like you to look at some photos and tell us if you recognize them."

"Sure." Eva studied the photos that Paul slid in front of her. "Looks like an auto accident."

"Do you recognize it?" Paul asked.

"No. Can't tell what kind of car it is."

Mark leaned forward. "You don't remember the accident?"

"What accident?"

"Your accident." Mark paused, watching her look puzzled at the photo. "That's your Blazer."

Eva picked up one photo, stared at it, and shook her head. "That's can't be my Blazer. Mine is sea-blue, this one is brown."

"That's mud," Paul added. "That's your Blazer. We tracked it through the registration number." He slipped an enlargement showing the license plate number on the crumpled back end.

"So that's why I couldn't find it. Someone stole my Blazer." Eva stared out towards the horizon.

Paul and Mark watched her and waited in silence.

Finally, Eva picked up the photo again. "I would have never recognized my Blazer. ... It's all wrecked. Who stole it?"

"Did you drive out towards Amish country?" Paul prodded.

"I drive out there often. It's so peaceful and relaxing. In fact, I had planned to take my art students there. It would be good for them to slow down a bit. They're always racing around, like my niece in her sports car. It's a beautiful candy-apple red."

Mark watched Eva rubbing her arm. "Do you remember the last time you drove your Blazer?"

"The last time I drove it. Let's see. I remember pulling around a bend and an Amish buggy was in the road. I swerved to miss it. That frightened me. I was going too fast and I almost hit the buggy. There were two cute children and a mother inside."

"Then what happened?" Paul asked.

"I think my headache got worse and I took a shortcut home. I remember being upset because I was lost. I didn't recognize the bridge." She picked up the doll and hugged it. "Silly, how could I get lost in Richland County? I know all the side roads."

Mark watched her rocking the doll, wishing he didn't have to continue. His mind churned. *She's getting upset. If she doesn't recall the accident, maybe she'll know what happened after it.* "Do you remember getting home from the bridge?"

"No." Her head shook.

Mark swallowed. "When you were driving, do you remember someone shooting at you?"

"Shooting?" Eva rubbed her left arm where the doctors had removed a 9mm slug. "How could I forget being shot?"

~ 41 ~

Why does everyone keep saying I've been shot? Eva thought. Her head was throbbing, not so much from pain but from a swirl of confusing thoughts and unpleasant feelings. She avoided looking left, at the man sitting there. Although he was with Mark, the man next to her resembled someone she knew back in Mansfield. *They even have the same name*, her mind churned. *It can't be the Paul I know. My Paul's a detective and lives in Ohio. He wouldn't know Mark. Would he?*

Paul put the photos of her crumbled Blazer back in the folder.

"Eva, are you feeling okay?" Mark rubbed her hand. "Maybe you should take your medication? Do you need to lay down?"

"I'm ... I'm confused."

"About the accident?" Mark asked.

"I don't remember any accident. That's not it. I'm confused about ... Paul." Turning, she glanced at his familiar face, truly out of place in Florida.

Slowly, Paul leaned forward. "Eva, do you know who I am?"

"You're –" She studied Paul's features: the same rich brown eyes and a movie star smile. "You're Paul Galloway, or at least you could be his twin brother."

Paul put his police identification on the table. "I'm sorry I kept you in the dark. I needed to know if you would remember me."

Her stomach tightened, still queasy about the pictures of her wrecked Blazer and confused about Paul. "Of course I remember you. So, Paul, why are you in Florida?"

"I've been worried about you. We found your Blazer in a creek bed and I was afraid you were ... were lost."

"I'm not lost." Eva sat back. "I know exactly where I am. This is Daytona Beach and that, out there, is the Atlantic Ocean."

"I'm glad you're not lost." Paul flipped open a little notebook. "Just how did you get here without your Blazer?"

Picking up the doll, Eva brushed its blond hair over the missing pieces of its china head. "I took the bus. It was a long ride, but I slept most of the way. I would have flown down, but I didn't think my head could take it. You shouldn't fly with a sinus infection. At least that's what I thought I had until the doctors down here told me it was viral encephalitis. But I'm better now."

"After you left your house and before you got on the bus to Florida, where were you?" Mark poured her some water from the pitcher beside her sack of medication.

"Let me think a minute." She closed her eyes. *Have I forgotten something else?* Eva wondered. *First they tell me I was in an accident, and then they say I was shot, or was it the other way around? So, what do I remember? Where was I?*

Next to her medication, the alarm clock rang. Mark silenced it. "Eva, it's time for your medication."

"If I take one of those, I might not be able to answer your questions." She pushed the clear plastic sack away. "That's the kind of medication you don't take and then drive. Its worse than those cold pills that disconnect your brain."

"Now the doctor said you can't stop taking your antibiotics." Mark put one white capsule on the plate. "So take your medicine."

Eva ignored the plate. As soon as they were distracted, she'd planned to hide the capsule. With Mark home, she wanted to avoid foggy thoughts at all cost. "I forgot what the question was."

"Before getting on the bus to Florida, where were you?" Paul flipped a page in his notebook.

"Let's see. I walked to the store. I remember that. I was upset because I couldn't remember where I left my Blazer. I was hoping it was in front of Kroger's again. Sometimes I walk over to the little shopping center, sometimes I drive, and recently I sometimes forget my Blazer and walk home. But the night I left, I don't remember finding it in the parking lot." Eva glanced at Mark, looking nervous. "I saw lightning above the hill behind Kroger's, so I went inside before the storm hit."

Mark poured water in her glass. "What did you do then?"

"Shopped, I suppose. I remember the terrible lightning and wind sounded like it was going to rip the roof off."

Paul jotted a note. "How long did you stay in Kroger's?"

"After I took my medication, I must have fallen asleep at the deli table. Someone woke me and when I went outside it was morning. Then I saw the city bus, so I took it downtown. Thought I should fill out a missing car report at the police station."

Surprised, Paul leaned forward. "You were coming to see me at the police station?"

"I was going to ask you what to do, but it was too early and it started raining again. So I sat in the bus station reading their schedule." While Mark and Paul exchanged looks, Eva slipped her capsule under the doll. *That pill will make me sleepy*, she thought. *I want to stay awake today and talk to Mark. He hasn't told me how he knows Paul. And did Paul tell me why he came here? Things are already getting foggy and I haven't even taken my pill.*

"Where did you go after the bus station?" Mark asked.

"Bus stations. There were so many of them on the way down."

"You got on the bus to Florida?" Paul questioned.

"I guess so. I remember getting off here. It was morning."

"When did you get the backpack?" Mark asked.

"I had my backpack with me when I want to Kroger's. As soon as I found my Blazer, I was going to leave for Florida. Just hop on I-71 and head south. It's a simple trip, I know the way by heart." Eva rubbed her forehead. "Maybe it was better I took the bus and let them do the driving. With my memory these days, I'd probably have missed the connection with I-75 and gotten lost."

"Eva, here take your pill." Mark held one in his hand. "You didn't take your antibiotic yet."

Reluctantly, she swallowed the capsule. *Too many questions,* she thought. *Everything is beginning to swirl around in my brain. I'm losing my train of thought. What are we talking about? Why?*

"Eva, maybe you should take a nap." Mark pushed the new photos back. "Paul. Lets wait. She's getting tired. It's time for her to rest. No more questions."

"No. I'm fine." Eva reached for the photos. "What are these?"

Ignoring Mark, Paul laid out the three photos. "Do you know any of these people?"

"Why, did one of them steal my Blazer?" Eva looked at the photos, beginning to blur slightly. "This is my niece. But she wouldn't take my car, says it looks like a big blue tank. A Blazer isn't sporty enough for Maggie."

"What about this man?" Mark slid a photo in front of her.

Her finger slid across the man's face as she picked it up. He was a nice looking man, older than Mark. "I don't recognize him. But he doesn't look like a thief; men his age don't take cars on joy rides." She touched the photo again. It disturbed her. *He has my mother's eyes,* she analyzed. *Strange, he looks sort of familiar but I don't recognize him. He makes me feel sad inside.*

"Do you recognize this man?" Paul moved a photo closer.

"That's Jim." Pulling back, Eva folded her arms across her chest and looked away. Fear mixed with anger. She had definitely planned to forget him, to escape his presence, to be rid of him once and for all. But Jim still seemed to be stalking her.

Mark pushed the photo away. "Jim who?"

"Jim Hellmann. ... Actually it's James Hellmann IV."

"How do you know Jim?" Paul continued to take notes.

"He came to my friends tax office. I remember it was between the February rapid refund rush and the April filing deadline. I help Linda during tax season, doing basic tax returns. Anyway, Jim came in to get a stack of forms for a seminar. He even asked me to help him with his tax return, which I thought it was odd."

"Did you date Jim?" Mark probed.

"Of course not. He's married."

Paul coughed. "Married?"

"Yes. Well –" Looking up, her eyes scanned the empty sky as she tried to recall what his tax form had looked like. "Jim checked the wrong block for filing status. He checked, married filing joint. I told him he couldn't use that."

Eva took a deep breath. *See, some of my brain is still there. I remember tax season and Paul helping me plan the outing at the old reformatory in May. But after that there are just bits and pieces.* Toying with the broken pieces of the china doll's head, Eva wondered if she could put her own memory back together.

"If he was married why couldn't he file joint?" Paul asked.

"His wife died just before Christmas. That means on December 31, Jim was single. By IRS rules he couldn't claim the extra tax exemption." Eva pulled back, recalling that embarrassing scene. "Jim was furious when I told him that. Ripped the papers out of my hands and stormed out of the office."

Mark took a deep breath. "When did you see him again?"

She shook her head. "Church, of all places. He came to our women's group meeting. Jim was giving a series of lectures on investments. After the meeting he took several of us out to lunch, trying to impress the ladies. I knew he was wasting his time."

Paul and Mark exchanged glances, waiting for her to continue.

"Why?" Mark watched her.

"Jim was pushing investment in the commodity market, or was it the futures market. Anyway, his investment scheme was too risky. He was talking to the wrong people. Lutherans are conservatives. We invest in the widow and orphan type stocks."

"What do you mean?" Paul asked.

"Utilities, like telephone company stock. Ones that pay steady reliable dividends: slow growth but good returns. Low risk stocks."

Mark sat back. "I'm impressed."

Eva blushed. *I should keep quiet. I'm beginning to ramble. Jim said men don't want financial advice from a woman.*

"Did Jim say how his wife died?" Paul asked.

"In an auto accident."

Paul's pencil slipped. "In Ohio?"

"No. Jim is from back east. One of those New England states: New York, New Jersey, or New Hampshire. I remember his social security number started with 00. Most of ours in Ohio start with 200's. So when I saw his, I thought it was fake until I looked it up. It was from back east. His was 007 to be exact. He joked about being James 007. Jim is a weird character and nothing at all like the fictitious James Bond."

Paul put down his pencil. "From that, I take it you wouldn't be interested in marrying Jim Hellmann."

"Heavens, no." Eva stared at Paul like he was crazy. "Me marry Jim? Never, never, never." She shuddered.

"Then why were you a getting a re –"

"Paul!" Mark snapped. "Eva needs to rest."

"Just a few more questions."

"No." Mark glared at Paul.

"I need some answers. The faster the better."

"No." Standing, Mark shoved his chair back. "Paul, we need to talk. Inside. ... Now!"

"You're right." Paul flung the folder of photos on the table.

In the morning warmth, Eva shivered at the tension of their crackling voices. "Rex, you better go. You may have to mediate. And close the door, I don't want to hear the argument."

After checking the napping kittens, Eva flicked on the CD player. Ocean music rolled from the speakers. A breeze fluttered through her blond hair.

With each gust, the photo of Jim slid closer to the doll's head.

"Don't get near him, Dolly. He's a bad man. He'll follow you everywhere. He's crazy, or is the word psychotic?"

Pulling the doll away, Eva found a white capsule under it. "Oh my, did I forget to take my medication. Can't let Mark find it, he's already upset with Paul." A quick sip of water washed the medication down. "You know, Dolly, I could have sworn I already took one. My brain feels fuzzy enough."

Brushing back the doll's blond hair, Eva's thoughts slipped back to more pleasant memories. *First grade was such fun. Dolls. Crayons and paper. Other children to play with. Happy time. I remember the beautiful yellow canary that sat by the window and the smell of the Oleander bushes out front.*

With the doll carefully cradled in her arms, Eva stepped into the sand. Walking over the sand dunes, she headed north.

"Come on, Dolly. I'll show you where my first grade school used to be. It's gone, along with the West Indies and the other things I cherished. Like in my Siberian dream, there is no one left and I, too, will be gone soon."

~ 42 ~

"I told you not to use strong arm tactics on Eva." Mark's voice rumbled with anger. "You're pushing too fast."

"No. You're dragging your feet. Overprotecting her isn't going to help." Paul's hands clenched his waist. "We have to move faster before she forgets more."

"No!" Mark snapped. "Eva needs to rest."

With the crackle of anger between Paul and her son, Barbara slipped a tempting Key-lime pie on the table and left the room.

"Eva's memory is fine," Mark argued. "She remembers Jim's tax problem and even part of his social security number."

"That's not enough," Paul snapped back. "Her story will never hold up under cross-examination, too many contradictions. First she says Jim is married, then a widower on December 31."

"Well, check it out!"

"I plan to," Paul snarled. "But on the witness stand, testimony like that will be destroyed by a shrewd defense attorney. We've all watched them demolish witnesses on those high profile TV cases. They'll slice the word – is – in half just to get their man off."

"I won't have you upsetting Eva." Mark grabbed the pie knife.

"I'm trying not to." Paul yanked a chair out and sat down. "If she can't hold up to my mild questioning, she'll crumble in the witness stand."

"When she's rested, she'll do okay," Mark insisted. "Anyway, what's your rush? You aren't even close to arresting anyone. You have a lot of work to do before you have a good case."

"Don't tell me my job. Believe me, I know this is going to be a tricky case to prosecute. A witness with a memory problem." Paul took a deep breath. "And Jim Hellmann has already hired a big Cleveland law firm. His attorney is so slick he could make a camel dance through the eye of a needle. Can you imagine what he'll do to Eva if we put her on the witness stand?"

"Then don't put her on the witness stand." With the kitchen knife, Mark sliced two pieces of Key-lime pie. "If you get enough evidence, you can prosecute Jim without Eva's testimony."

"That's why I need to question her. I have to dig for all the facts, regardless of how unpleasant they are. We have no valid case without good hard evidence." With a fork, Paul whacked off a piece of his pie. "Don't forget, Jim isn't our only suspect. We haven't ruled out her niece. Maggie has the knowledge and motive. Then there's Dennis. She didn't even recognize his photo."

"That may have been a bad photo of Dennis, and if he lives out West, Eva probably doesn't see him very often. Not all brothers and sisters are close." Mark glanced at the end of the table where his sister had sat when she was alive. They had been as close as brothers and sisters could be.

Mark heard the phone ring in the living room and his father answer it. Footsteps echoed in the hall.

"Paul, your captain would like to speak to you." Fritz handed over the cordless phone, glanced at Mark, and left.

"Captain. Yes, I've been questioning her." Paul sat straighter, talking to his boss. "Eva says Jim's first wife died in an auto accident. …Exactly. Have them check for an insurance policy on his former wife and last year's IRS files. Something is fishy there."

Mark watched Paul nodding like his captain was sitting across the table from him. From the tone and pace of the conversation, Mark could fill in the captain's conversation.

"They what!" Paul flipped open his notebook.

Mark watched Paul grow tense listening to his captain.

"No jimsonweed in the garden. Then where … in the cat's stomach? What was in the capsule? An alkaloid poison."

"What kind?" Mark asked.

"Jimsonweed. What else was in it?" Paul jotted notes as he listened. "The crime lab found another capsule under a dish in Eva's kitchen. It had been tampered with."

Standing, Mark, knocked the chair over. "What color was it?"

"What color was the capsule?" Paul repeated into the phone. "White. A white prescription capsule. Damn!"

The phone bounced on the table.

Mark dashed through the living room and out the screen door.

He stared in disbelief.

Eva was gone.

Only the bag of white prescription capsules sat on the table.

A gust of wind sent the photos tumbling to the deck.

"Dad." Mark scanned the dunes. "Did Eva go in to lay down?"

"No. I thought she was with you. … I'll go check."

Stepping to the table, Paul snatched the plastic sack of white capsules. "If these have been tampered with, we'll need them for evidence. They may have fingerprints on them."

"Eva!" Mark shouted. "Eva!"

There was no response.

"Rex." Mark held Rex's nose to her chair. "Find Eva."

Sniffing the deck, Rex headed towards the wooden walk.

"Would she go to the beach?" Paul followed.

"God, I hope not. She doesn't have the strength to swim."

At the end of the wooden walk, Rex abruptly stopped and doubled back, following a scent, sniffing across the dunes.

"Let's split up. Paul, search the ocean side of the dunes. She may have cut over towards the beach." Mark ran behind Rex. "Shout as soon as you see her."

"Right. She couldn't have gone far."

"Eva!" Mark rushed to the top of the dune. There was only sand and tracks: a woman's footprints in the sand. As his chest muscles constricted, his emotions coiled tight. "Eva!"

Rex raced ahead. His barks sank into mournful bays.

The chilling howl froze Mark's heart. It was how Rex sounded when he had located Susan's body. "Oh God, no! Please." Mark headed for the high dune. "Eva!"

At the top of the dune, Mark stopped breathing.

Below, a body lay curled in the sand. Clasped in her hand was a china doll. Blond hair fluttered in the breeze, tangling in a morning glory bloom.

Eva lay motionless.

"Eva!" Mark raced down the dune. "Eva."

Rex nudged her arm but she didn't move.

"Paul! I've found her." Mark dropped to his knees. Brushing her hair back, his hand slipped across the cold skin of her throat, feeling for a pulse. Slow heartbeats pulsed.

"Eva. Wake up. Please wake up. Eva."

She did not respond.

"Mark." Paul popped over the dune. "Is she … how is she? Does she need an ambulance? … I'll get help."

Snatching the doll, Rex raced ahead. Bits of gray fabric fell from the doll's china head.

"Call 911." Mark scooped Eva from the sand. "Have Mom call the hospital. Tell them about the poison. Hurry."

~ 43 ~

"Let's hurry!" Mark cringed as the doors slammed shut. For a moment, the inside of the rescue squad was dark like a tomb. He held Eva's hand, strangely cold for a summer day. But that was the way his sister's hand had felt before she slipped out of Mark's life.

With siren blaring, the rescue squad rumbled north, up South Atlantic Avenue, towards the bridge and the mainland. The Halifax hospital staff would be waiting for their arrival.

Stomach acid slouched inside Mark and the fire of guilt burned in his brain. *Why didn't I know there was something wrong with her medication? She told me they gave her headaches and I saw how they affected her. Why didn't I suspect they had been tampered with? After all, someone already tried to kill her once. I should have protected her. What kind of man am I?*

The paramedics' voices were drowned out by his churning thoughts. *Eva looks so frail and helpless lying there. She trusted me and I let her down. I can't lose Eva like I lost my sister.*

"Eva, we'll be there soon. Hang on, darling." Mark tenderly warmed her hand. "I'm right here. I'll take care of you."

"Sir, is she your wife?" The medic adjusted her IV line.

Mark took a deep breath. "I have her power of attorney. Eva is my responsibility. Whatever medical treatment she needs, I'll sign for it." He didn't want them to waste time calling her next of kin, especially under the circumstances. And having her power of attorney was only a slight exaggeration of the truth. In Eva's will, besides leaving her possessions to him, she had given Mark her last wishes for her medical treatment. Although it was not the most legal of documents, it was all Mark needed.

"Sir, does she have a 'do not resuscitate order?'"

"No. Do whatever is needed to keep her alive." Mark lurched forward as they stopped. "Eva, we're here, hang on."

The back doors jerked open. Sunlight and heat rolled in. With a swish, the stretcher slipped out, its legs popping down, forming a gurney. Mark kept a firm grim on Eva's limp hand as they rolled her down the hall of the Halifax emergency room.

"Sir." A technician stopped Mark. "You have to wait here."

"No, I'm staying with Eva."

"You have to wait here. We need to empty her stomach." The technician firmly nudged Mark back. "We'll let you know when you can come in."

"Professor Reining?" A beach patrol officer stepped forward.

"Bob. Who called you?"

"Duty. Had to bring in a moped biker. He wanted to cut across the soft sand; the bike didn't. Flipped him off like a pesky flea. Unfortunately, the bike landed on top of him. Mostly cuts, bruises, and dented pride." Bob glanced at the next treatment area. "Professor, is that who I think it is?"

Mark nodded. "Yes, that's Eva."

"Is her viral encephalitis getting worse?" Bob stepped closer.

"Mark." His mother hurried down the hall, her hospital ID flapping. "I'll go in and see how she is."

"I'll come with you."

"No." She held him back. "We need to take care of her first. Eva wouldn't want you there right now. You can come in later."

"But –" Mark felt helpless and waiting made it worse.

"Professor, give the doctors room to work." Bob moved aside for a technician, wielding a tray of blood samples. "I read up on that illness. Hope I never get that virus. Did Eva have a seizure?"

"Mark. How is Eva?" Detective Paul Galloway rushed down the hall. "Did they take care of the poison?"

"Poison?" Bob turned to Paul.

"Paul, this is Officer Bob White, one of my law enforcement students." Mark glanced at the two of them. "Bob, this is Detective Paul Galloway from Mansfield."

"Eva's home town?" With a questioning look, Bob shook hands with Paul. "So what brings an Ohio detective to Florida? And what's happened to Eva?"

Another gurney rumbled down the hall, wheeling in a patient.

"I'll explain, but let's get out of the way." Paul pulled Bob back out of the way. "On the flight down, Mark told me about your help tracking down Eva's past."

The rest of Paul's conversation faded as Mark stepped closer to the curtain. A few of the technicians were leaving. *Is that good?* Mark worried. *Does it mean she's going to be okay?*

"Mark. You can see Eva now," his mother said. "Don't wake her yet. She needs a little time for the medication to wear off."

Medical instruments clanked as a nurse cleared the area and a cart screeched down the hall.

Lying on the exam table, Eva looked pale. An IV line joined two bags of fluid and trailed down to her arm. A blanket covered her, warming her body in the air-conditioned emergency room.

"Eva." Mark took her hand, rubbing it for warmth. "I'm right here. Don't worry, I'm going to take care of you." That promise taunted his thoughts. *That's what I told her before. So far I have done a miserable job of protecting her. All my training hasn't helped me. There's no excuse. Can she forgive me?*

"Eva is going to be okay." Barbara patted her son's back. "All the way in, I kept asking myself, why didn't I notice her medication was tampered with? After all, I'm a nurse. How could I have missed the signs of poisoning?"

"Mom, don't blame yourself. You couldn't have noticed. None of us did." Mark put his arm around his mother. "And we don't know for sure if there was poison in those capsules."

"Yes, we do." Doctor Williams stepped beside Barbara. "But let's talk in the hallway. Eva needs to rest."

In the hall, Mark suddenly stopped. "What did you find?"

"Our lab checked the capsule you brought in ..." Doctor Williams flipped open Eva's chart. "And based on that, there was the equivalent of two doses in her blood stream. The report says it wasn't enough of the alkaloid poison in those capsules to be fatal to an adult. It was only a small amount of the jimsonweed."

"What are the effects of jimsonweed?" Mark questioned.

Doctor Williams reviewed the lab printout. "It can cause headaches, confusion, and short-term amnesia until it wears off. Some of the other general side effects can be dilated pupils, high temperature, and a fast heartbeat." The doctor shook his head. "I remember several years ago a number of teens in New Jersey were hospitalized after experimenting with jimsonweed. Fool kids could have killed themselves."

"New Jersey?" Mark turned to Paul, already taking notes.

"Right." Doctor Williams read on. "Jimsonweed grows wild in the northern states."

"Loco Weed is what my grandfather call it," Paul chimed in. "He found some in his fields one year. Farmers have to be careful it doesn't get into their feed grain. It made the cows act crazy."

Mark took the lab report from Doctor Williams. "What's this other chemical they found in the capsule?"

Doctor Williams glanced at it. "All the antibiotics had been removed and repacked with the jimsonweed and a harmless sweetener called Aspartame."

"Aspartame?" Mark asked. "But –"

"Oh, no," Barbara interrupted. "Eva is allergic to Aspartame."

Doctor Williams flipped through her chart. "I don't see that here. Did she have PKU?"

"No." Barbara said. "She's just allergic to that sweetener."

"Maybe that's why some of her blood tests seemed strange." Doctor Williams looked over his glasses. "I thought the abnormal readings were from virus encephalitis or a secondary infection. But now it make sense."

"What? I don't understand." Mark moved closer.

"Basically, children born with PKU can't metabolize phenylalanine, part of the sweetener, and it builds up in the blood. It can cause mental retardation in developing children. Most hospitals screen all babies at birth and shortly thereafter for PKU. Early treatment can prevent brain damage. Come to think of it, Eva has a typical profile for a PKU patient, fair skinned and light eyes, generally blue." Doctor Williams glanced at Mark's eyes.

"That sweetener sounds dangerous." Paul jotted more notes.

"Most people are unaffected by it, only a few are sensitive to it. About one baby in twelve thousand will test positive for PKU. While their brains are developing, they have to avoid anything with phenylalanine in it. That's why manufacturers put those warning labels on any food product that contains that chemical."

"You'd have to be a chemist to understand that warning label." Mark voice was sharp.

"Damn." Paul flipped back several pages in his notebook. "Jim's undergraduate degree was in chemistry. If he knew Eva was allergic to Aspartame –"

"He could use it to kill her." Turning, Mark looked at Eva, lying on the exam table. "Chemically designed to kill without causing suspicion. Who would consider a sweetener poisonous?"

"There's one other thing to consider." Doctor Williams slipped his glasses off. "Aspartame breaks down over time and under heat. Letting those contaminated tablets sit in the sun would start the process. And Eva's been running a fever. I'm ordering more blood test to check her for phenylalanine. We'll get to the bottom of this." Doctor Williams walked to Eva's treatment area.

Mark watched the curtain close. "Paul, that should help to prove Jim is the guilty party."

"Not necessarily. Eva's niece works part time in a medical lab. Maggie could easily alter a prescription antibiotic in a capsule and she had access to Eva's home. And it seems to me that a niece would know if her aunt was allergic to Aspartame."

Acid burned in Mark's stomach, fueled by anger and guilt. He had promised he would keep Eva safe. But by insisting she take her medication, he, unknowingly, had pushed her closer to death.

"Eva didn't want to take her medication because they gave her headaches." Mark looked down. "But I insisted she take them."

"Mark, you didn't know." Paul flipped his notebook closed. "I'm a detective and I didn't suspect anything. Those pills sat in front of me all morning. There was no way to know that Eva was carrying her would-be killer's poison with her. What a sinister plan someone has devised. But I promise I'll get the guilty party."

"We still have two suspects." Mark turned away. "Jim and Maggie. Both have the knowledge and a motive for killing Eva."

~ 44 ~

"Where am I?" As her eyes opened, Eva stared up at the white ceiling tile. A vanishing dream swirled in her mind. *It's cold like my Siberian dream, but I smell alcohol. I wonder if the tundra ferments in the summer heat. What's that? Sounds like trampling feet. Maybe a herd of reindeer is coming my way. Do they have reindeer in Siberia?*

"Eva." Mark stepped closer and rubbed her cold hand. "Eva, you're all right now. The doctors took care of … of you."

Still woozier, Eva focused on Mark's face, recalling his walk through her dream. "You look good in that long black coat. It makes a nice contrast to the snow."

"Snow?"

She stared up at him and the cold, white ceiling lights. "Next time you come to Siberia, you better wear one of those fur hats."

"Siberia?" Leaning over, Mark kissed her hot forehead. "Darling, we're in Daytona Beach, not Siberia."

"We were. I saw you there. You were walking towards me." Eva saw a nurse approach. "What am I doing in the hospital?"

"You took too many of your capsules," Mark said.

"Excuse me, sir. I have to take another blood sample."

Eva glanced at him. "Mark, are you sick?"

"Ma'am, we need another blood test." A needle pierced Eva's arm and a vial filled with red liquid.

"Another blood test. It's no wonder I'm tired all the time."

"What did you say?" Mark returned to her side.

"I said I want to go home. I don't like hospitals."

"We have to wait for a bit."

Eva took a deep breath, clearing her head. "Why?"

"There was poison in your antibiotics." His voice trembled.

"Poison! You must be kidding." Her eyes closed in disbelief and her mind rambled on. *Poison? Surely that can't be true. Barbara's medical book said my illness could cause organic psychosis. But I think they're the crazy ones. First my doctor says my headaches are from a sinus infection, then the doctors say it's viral encephalitis. And someone finds a bullet in my arm even though I don't remember being shot. Next thing I know, Detective Galloway shows up, telling me I've been in an auto accident. And now Mark brings me back to the emergency room, afraid the medication I'm taking is poisoned. ... Really, they're the crazy ones, not me. ... I just have a splitting headache, that's all.*

More footsteps rumbled across the hard hospital floor. Detective Paul Galloway stepped next to Mark. Even their whispering seemed noisy, like the volume of the world had been turned up. Ever since her fever began, noise had bothered her. Only the soft sounds of her ocean CD soothed her.

"Eva, where did you get that prescription antibiotic filled?" Paul's voice sounded concerned and too loud.

Confused, Eva sat up. "What prescription?"

"The white capsules you've been taking." Mark steadied her.

"You mean my prescription antibiotics?"

"Where did you get them?" Paul asked, taking notes.

"From the drug store. I don't remember which one."

"Did anyone else handle those capsules besides you and the drug store?" Paul flipped a page in his notebook.

"I got the first batch sometime in May, I think, and the last refill Maggie picked up for me. I was rushing to get ready for the lady's church meeting and didn't have time to go for them."

Mark frowned. "Did anyone else besides your niece have access to them?"

"Could have. I keep them on my kitchen counter. I put two pills on the dish each morning to remind me."

"Who has been in your home recently?"

From the serious expression on Mark's face, she knew something was wrong. "Maggie sometimes stops in during race weekends. The art club was in for a meeting. And I think the repairman serviced my air conditioner."

Mark stepped closer. "Was Jim in your home?"

Eva slid her legs over the exam table. *Why can't I get away from Jim?* Eva pondered. *I left town to forget him. But he haunts me even down here. Why would he want my pills?*

"When was Jim at your house?" Mark repeated.

"He was the speaker for my church's ladies group."

"Did Jim have access to your prescription medication?" Paul walked around the exam table.

Pulling the blanket tight around her shoulders, her thoughts were colder than the room. "He could have. Jim stayed inside while I showed the ladies through my garden. Said his allergies were bothering him. When we came back in, Jim was stacking all our coffee cups in the sink. That made a big hit with the ladies. They all wanted to take him home. I was praying they would."

Quickly, Paul jotted a note. "Did you see him tamper with your medication?"

"Why would he do that?"

"Did Jim ever propose marriage to you?" Mark blurted out.

"I wouldn't marry Jim." Eva cringed. "Besides, he's married."

Paul looked up. "But you said Jim's wife was killed in an auto accident around Christmas and he was single for tax filing."

"Right." Eva sighed. "His wife had died before December 31st, but he didn't marry again until early January. So according to IRS rules he had to file as a single taxpayer. A January marriage doesn't count for a prior year tax filing."

Mark moved closer. "Did you ever meet his second wife?"

"No. I'm not sure she was real."

"What?"

"I think it was a paper marriage. It was a comment he made, or was it some paper I saw. I don't quite remember what it was, just that I doubted it was a real marriage. I think they were just living together." Eva looked around for her shoes and considered how she could escape the emergency room.

"Paper marriage?" Paul shook his head.

"Don't look at me like that, guys. You see some weird things preparing taxes. I filled out one rapid refund for a man on his lunch break only to have him return with another social security card for a son he somehow forgot he had an hour earlier. He wanted a bigger earned income credit. Anyway, I had Linda finish that one. I didn't want my signature on that return."

Mark and Paul looked at each other and retreated to the hall.

"Good," Eva mumbled to herself. "Now's my chance to get my shoes. I wonder if I can sneak out of this place. Maybe I should go west to that little town in Texas. No one would ever look for me there. Its name was Kyle … Kyle, Texas. I bet the President doesn't even know where that is."

"When I was there, it wasn't much more than a crossroad with a gas station, and Ace and Ann's diner." Turning her shoes upside down, Eva shook them vigorously to make sure nothing was hiding inside. "I vividly remember being stung in Kyle. If that scorpion had been the fatally poisonous kind, I'd be dead."

~ 45 ~

"What happened to the sun?" Eva looked at the early evening sky. "It seems like the sun was just rising, now it's just about sunset. What happened to the day?"

"It's been one of those days you might as well forget." Slowly, Mark walked Eva across the front deck to the doublewide lounge chair, big enough for two. *Eva could use some fresh air,* he thought. *And she loves to watch the ocean. It'll help her feel better.*

After leaving the hospital, Mark had brought Eva back to the safety of his parents' home. After several naps the effects of the Jimsonweed was wearing off. The dose wasn't enough to kill a healthy adult, but as Eva had grown weaker from the viral encephalitis, the poison had become more powerful.

Eva looked around. "Did everyone disappear with the sun?"

"Mom and Dad went shopping. Paul is with Bob to … uh, to see how the Daytona Beach police department operates."

Eva stretched out on the lounge chair. "Bob?"

"Bob is one of my students who is a beach patrol officer. You met him when you pulled those children out of the surf." Sitting down next to Eva, Mark studied her glassy eyes that were fixed on the sand dunes. *I'm not sure what she remembers,* he thought. *Doctor Williams said the effects of the capsules would wear off in a few hours. It's the viral encephalitis he's still worried about. She has to regain her strength to kill the virus.*

"Mark, is something wrong? You're so quiet."

"I'm enjoying the evening and the lovely company." Mark hesitated. *Should I tell her how I feel? Is it too soon to tell her I love her?* Sitting on the lounge chair, Mark slid his arm around her, gently pulling her closer. "Would you rather go inside?"

"No. I love the evenings. It's such a gentle time of the day. Soft and fuzzy." Smiling, Eva leaned against Mark's shoulder. "This is the blue time of day."

Mark felt her head, a little warm but no more so than usual. "Are you feeling all right?"

"Yes." She smiled up at him. "You worry too much, Mark."

Pulling her hair back, he studied her greenish eyes staring into his. "I guess we all worry too much."

"You know, since I've had this viral encephalitis, I haven't worried much. A lot of thoughts swish through my brain, but they don't trouble me. I don't know how I can explain it. I've never felt this kind of peace before. It's like ... I can't think of the right words. It's just a good feeling flowing through my brain."

Although her voice sounded sincere, Mark questioned her choice of words. *Perhaps she's confused from the Jimsonweed,* he considered. *How can a person feel good when they are sick? When she's been shot and poisoned, how can she not worry?*

"Really, Mark. I'm not worried about anything." Her hand slid across his chest as Eva cuddled him. "I'm home and you make me feel good. That's not quite the right word, but I feel wonderful."

"So do I." He kissed her forehead. With her chest pressing tightly against his, Mark's heart raced. *Careful,* he cautioned his feelings. *Eva needs more time. I want her to be ready for my love.*

"Mark, is it time for me to take my medication?"

"No more antibiotics. Doctor's orders." He took her hand. *This is not the time to explain to her about the prescription capsules being tampered with. I want Eva to enjoy this moment and not to worry about who might be trying to kill her or why.*

As the shadows grew longer, the ocean breeze shifted. Mark heard a siren in the distance. "In the hospital you said you saw me in your dream. Tell me about it."

Looking up at Mark, her smile grew more inviting. "You're in my Siberian dream. Everything is so white there and from the horizon you come walking across the snow. Your long black coat flaps in the wind and the snow crunches under your leather boots."

"Crunch? Most snow I've walked through has been soft."

"You haven't lived in Ohio during the dead of winter when the Arctic fronts lash across Lake Erie and howl up the slopes to Mansfield. When it gets below zero, snow freezes and it has a spine-chilling crunch when you walk on it." Eva shivered. "When the temperature drops to twenty-three below zero, the water in the air freezes into ice crystals. It's beautiful. The low winter sun makes the frozen air shimmer like glitter suspended in the sky."

"That's a flowery description. Sounds like you like winter."

"The snow is beautiful on sunny winter days."

"Paul said you have ski resorts near Mansfield. Do you ski?"

Abruptly, Eva pulled away. "No. I don't ski."

"I thought if you like snow, you would be a skier."

"No. My father wouldn't allow me to ski." Her arms wrapped round her body as Eva sat up. "My mother was killed in a skiing accident. She went to Denver to visit my half-brother, Dennis. It was a February ski trip in the Rocky Mountains sponsored by his insurance company and he invited Mom. She was a good skier on our local slopes, but they're hardly the Rockies. Dennis slept late and Mom went skiing alone and –" her voice froze.

Mark draped the summer blanket over Eva's shoulders. *So, Mark considered, that's why Eva doesn't talk about her half-brother. Dennis reminds Eva of her mother's death. It's no wonder she didn't recognize his photo. She probably hasn't seen him since the accident. Was it an accident? Why did I bring up skiing?*

Mark rubbed her arms. "What am I doing in your dream?"

"In my dream, you walk out of the pale winter sun that hangs on the horizon." Relaxing, Eva leaned against his chest. "And you keep walking towards me, right past the Ice Palace."

"And what do you do in the dream."

"I just watch you while I'm lying in the red snow."

"Red snow?" Mark hesitated, not sure if he should continue. "What makes snow red in your dream?"

"Blood. The snow around me is red from my blood." Eva snuggled closer to him. "Someone shot me."

His arms wrapped around her. *So part of her does remember being shot,* he considered. *Her subconscious knows what happened to her, she just doesn't remember.*

"Mark, it's just a dream. And I only remember the pretty part: the rising sun, the sparkling snow, the glittering Ice Palace, and you." Her cool hand slid across his face. "Next time you walk across the frozen tundra, wear one of the fur hats. You know, like the Russians do. I don't want you getting hypothermia."

"I promise I'll wear a hat next time." He kissed her lips, feeling strangely cool. "Do you have other dreams?"

"Is it time to take my antibiotic?"

"No, those capsules are all gone." True, Mark thought; Paul and Bob took them to the local crime lab for more testing and to look for the fingerprints of the person who tampered with them.

"Good. Those capsules give me a splitting headache like that sweetener."

"Aspartame?"

"Yes, it takes days for those headaches to go away."

Brushing her blond hair back, the whacked off clump was still noticeable. *Perhaps it was a result from the confrontation with Jim in her raspberry patch,* Mark considered. *The Mansfield crime lab found some of her hair near the garden clippers. Jim Hellmann's fingerprints were on its handle.*

"You have a large patch of raspberries in your garden. It must take a lot of work to grow them." Mark probed, hoping to find out what happened.

"Red raspberries are quite productive and easy to grow. You just have to keep their long shoots tied up so the wind doesn't break them." Although there was plenty of room on the lounge chair, she rolled towards him and her leg slid across his. "This is about the time of the day I like to work in my raspberry patch."

"That's a big raspberry patch. Does someone help you tie them up?" Mark took a deep breath, partly wishing he hadn't asked but knowing Paul would be asking her tomorrow.

Eva's hand slipped through her hair, stopping at the chopped off section. "No. I do it all myself. You have to be careful you don't break the canes."

"Some of them got broken. What happened?"

Sitting up again, Eva pulled the sheet blanket tight around her shoulders. "How do you know about that?"

"You can tell me. It's important that I know."

Eva reached into the box beside the lounge chair and pulled the calico kitten out. "Poor Princess. Are you lonesome?"

"Eva?"

After she pulled out the other kitten, she hugged it. "There's this guy, Jim, who ... what's the right word. Well, he's sort of been stalking me. He keeps coming around. Showing up wherever I go. I told him to go away but he won't. He wants something."

"Is that Jim Hellmann that you talked about this morning?"

She turned to Mark. "Did I already tell you about him?"

"Just that you did his taxes and he gave an investment seminar for your church group." Mark watched her scanning the sand dunes as if she was reading them and trying to remember. "So tell me what Jim did near the raspberry patch."

"He sneaked into my garden and startled me. Then he began ranting about something and demanded I sign the papers he was waving at me. I had no idea what he was talking about. He wasn't making any sense. I just ignored him and kept on tying up my berries. When he shouted at me, I grabbed my cordless phone and told him I would call the police if he didn't leave."

"Did you?"

"No. They'd make me fill out a police report. And I didn't want my name in the newspaper." She looked into Mark's eyes. "What would the women's church group think? Besides, it'd be my word against his. James Hellmann IV is the kind of man who could ruin a woman's reputation."

"Did he threaten you?"

"I don't recall what he said. His rambling just made no sense to me. But I remember he frightened me."

Mark's chest tightened with anger. "Did he hurt you?"

She rubbed the back of her neck where a cut was healing. "I turned away from Jim and continued to tie up my raspberries. And … and he yanked my ponytail. All of it happened so fast. I just remember the clippers chopping at my hair. I tried to pull away. He laughed at me because I was crying. That made me mad and I grabbed at him. Something ripped. He swore at me and … and the next thing I remember is lying in my raspberry patch."

After waiting for her to relax, Mark continued. "What happened after you fell?"

"Jim threw the clippers at me. I grabbed the phone and told him to get out of my life or else."

"Then?"

"I could hear him laughing all the way to his car." She sighed. "That's when I decided to leave, just pack a few things and run away, right then and there."

"Did you leave the next day?"

"No. I had a class to teach the next day and I was waiting for Paul to return my call. I wanted his opinion on ... something."

"A restraining order?" Mark waited as Eva reached over for the doll with the china head, sitting on the nearby table. He wished he hadn't asked about the raspberry patch incident, but it was too late now. *It's a beautiful evening,* he scolded himself, *and you're ruining it for Eva with all these questions she obviously doesn't want to answer. She was feeling good until you mentioned Jim.*

"Here, Rex." Eva patted the chair and moved closer to Mark. "There's room for you up here. Bring your teddy bear."

Eagerly, Rex hopped up. With Mark, Eva, the china doll, the two kittens, Rex, and the big, brown teddy bear with a pink bow; the doublewide lounge chair was filled to capacity.

Settling in, Rex's dog tags clanked.

"Mark, why don't you get me one of those?"

"Dog tags?"

"Yes. You can put my name on them and your phone number. That way if I get lost, whoever finds me can call you to come fetch me. And metal tags would be better than your card. It doesn't have my name on it."

"What?"

From her pocket she pulled out a chain with two keys and Mark's waterproof business card. "Don't you remember, you gave it to me when we first met?"

"Of course." He was surprised she still had it and he hadn't seen it since she fell off her bike when the car almost hit her. "I thought it got lost on the beach."

"No. I left it at the hospital on my first visit. They gave it back to me today when I left." She handed it to him.

"A safe deposit box key. Where is your bank?"

"It's south of the burger stand. The bank has a nice, cool lobby." Her cool lips drew closer and planted a tender kiss on his.

"You need to rest, darling." Mark ran his fingers through her soft hair. *I need to be careful,* he thought. *I don't want to go too far, too soon. She's not ready yet. She's too vulnerable.*

"Mark." Eva whispered. "Did I take my medicine?"

"No more pills." Mark watched her drifting into a peaceful sleep. Having his arms around her sent a wave of feeling though him. It was so natural, like she'd always been part of his life. He wanted to hold onto the moment, enjoy it, and not think about what happened or what was to come. His thoughts rolled like the ocean and his heart pounded like the distant breakers.

She's such a loving little thing, he considered. *And when she's up to it, I'll tell her I love her.*

As Eva snuggled next to him like a wife cuddling her husband, Mark stroked her hair. He could feel Eva's body inviting more and his temptation to respond. *This is not the right time for either of us*, Mark considered. *We'll have to wait for that special moment. I want Eva to remember our first time. I know I will.*

A distant siren disturbed Mark's thoughts. *We need a little time to catch the person who hurt her. Paul is right; a good defense attorney will cut her testimony to shreds. With her fuzzy memory, Eva can never take the witness stand.*

~ 46 ~

"I need a cold shower." Mark took a deep breath and slipped away from Eva. Standing beside the lounge chair, he stretched his arms like he was casting a fishing line into the sea.

With Mark gone, a wave of emptiness rushed through Eva. Sleeping in his arms gave her lovely dreams filled with sunshine and visions of the warm water of the Ponce Inlet, teeming with young life. There was no dream of the cold, lonely, Siberian tundra this time. "Mark, the blanket was probably too warm for you."

"Something like that." Chuckling, he walked to the door.

Curled up next to Mark's body, she felt part of him and longed for more. *It's a shame he has to go in,* Eva thought. *I wanted to tell him how much I like him. ... No, that isn't the right word. Is this really love I feel burning inside me or just the fever of viral encephalitis? It's strong, like a rushing riptide.*

Eva watched him hesitate at the door. "Mark, I've had a nice nap. We could go bodysurfing if you want to cool off."

"Don't think that would do it." He pulled the screen door open. "I've had enough excitement for one day."

As Mark stepped in, Fritz came out, seeming to tease his son about something. Although Eva couldn't hear them, she noticed Fritz's hardy pat on his son's back. But Mark didn't seem amused.

Rex barked at Fritz's words, then slipped between them, dashing in through the living room door towards the rustling sounds of Barbara, unpacking groceries.

In the box beside the lounge chair, the kittens were napping. Beside them, shadows slipped across the deck as a formation of pelicans headed south towards the inlet for an early fish dinner.

Fritz propped open the wide screen door. "Eva, do you want me to bring the card table with your puzzle out here?"

"That would be nice. I'll help."

"No need. It's a one-person job. Just wait. Right there."

They act like I'm going to wander away again, she mused. *I only do that when I'm tired and my mind is all fuzzy. I'm rested now. In fact, I'm feeling good, very good. Sleeping in Mark's arms was ... what's the word. Oh, well, tantalizing is close enough.*

Glancing towards the dunes, Eva noticed a gate on the deck railing, closing off the steps to the beach. "I don't remember that."

"What?" Fritz carried out the card table.

"That gate on the deck railing."

"Oh, that." Fritz put the table down. "Thought I better put the gate back up for safety. Last night Paul didn't see the steps. Almost tripped. Wouldn't want a detective falling off my deck and breaking his leg."

His story seemed a little fishy and she figured it was probably put there to keep her from wandering away again. *How foolish,* she mused. *Why would I want to wander away from Mark and his strong, comforting arms? Besides, I'm not running away anymore. I'm home.* Studying the dunes, Eva watched the rays of sunlight sparkle on the tips of the sea oats.

"A penny for your thoughts." Fritz pulled up a chair.

"A penny is too much for my thoughts."

"You seem drawn to those sand dunes."

She remembered her childhood home. "Ocean Dunes."

"Oceans have waves, dunes have sand." Fritz looked puzzled.

"But they both move and yet remain in about the same place." Her feet slid off the lounge chair as she turned to the card table.

Sitting in a nearby chair, Fritz slowly turned the pages of his western novel as his eyes darted from them to her and back.

While her CD was playing ocean music, a nice quiet settled around Eva. Pieces of the puzzle occasionally fitted together and she studied the sand dunes. *I hope these feeling lasts forever,* she reflected. *If it's from the viral encephalitis, I'm not sure I want to get well. It's such an incredibly peaceful feeling. Maybe this is what they call organic psychosis. If it is, being crazy isn't so bad.*

"Eva." Mark lightly touched her shoulder. "Do you want me to get you something for your headache?"

"No. I'm fine, really." Startled, she stopped rubbing her forehead. "I was just massaging my brain. It helps me think."

"What's that music you're playing?" Paul asked.

Turning, Eva saw Paul had replaced Fritz in the big chair. A shiver of uneasiness rippled through her. She hadn't noticed the changing of the guard and Detective Galloway looked serious.

Rex laid his head on her leg. She hadn't felt him climbing back on the lounge chair and he was stretched out like he had been there for a while. Next to Eva, the kittens romped in their box, batting around a ping-pong ball.

The question slipped from her mind. "What?"

"What's the name of that music?" Paul repeated.

"Oh, that music is 'The Mystic Sea.' It's one of my favorites because it reminds me of the beach and my Florida home."

Mark sat down. "It's a long piece. Doesn't it ever end?"

"It goes on forever if you hit the repeat button." Eva turned down the CD player. "I like the sound of certain songs rolling around in my head. It helps me concentrate. If I listen to the music long enough, it keeps playing even when I turn off the CD."

"I know that feeling." From his pocket, Paul pulled out a CD, and put it into the CD player. "Recently, one song has haunted me. Haven't been able to turn it off."

From the CD player, voices harmonized to guitar strings.

"Paul." Mark reached for the off button. "I don't think this is the time –"

"I know that," Eva interrupted. "That's 'Bridge over Trouble Water', Simon and Garfunkel. Right?"

"Does it have special meaning for you?"

"Paul," Mark snapped.

"It's a classic." Eva reached over and pushed the skip button, stopping on the sixth song, hitting repeat as soon as it started playing. "This one, 'The Boxer,' is my favorite on this album."

Paul and Mark watched Eva turn towards the ocean, her head nodding and her lips moving to the song.

"Going home," she whispered. "Those are lovely words."

"What do you mean?" Mark moved closer, reaching for her but not touching her.

"Listen to the song again, not so much the words, but the music." The CD music repeated. "Hear the restless rolling movement, its a melody traveling through time. The sharp crashes of suddenness. A sad twang of guitar strings. The mournful voice, longing for something he desperately wants but can't have. Obsessed by a past he can no longer get back to. It's all gone and he will soon be gone too."

With her head nodding to the music, Eva turned up the music. "Now listen! Towards the end, that's how this virus makes me feel. Hear the booming, heavy background roll in over top of the soft foreground, crashing down like a seventh wave, drowning out the main beat. Both scores churn together, then separate again, and the music plays on."

As the song repeated, Eva toyed with several puzzle pieces as she took short glances at the two of them.

Both of them looked like they were lost in their own thoughts. Detective Galloway's head continued to nod as his hand slipped to his gun. Mark's eyes were fixed on the ocean.

I must have said something wrong, she worried. *I hope they don't think I've completely lost my mind. If Mark has seen his mother's medical book, he knows this viral encephalitis can cause organic psychosis. Does he think I've lost contact with the world? Oh, why don't I keep my mouth shut?* She trembled.

"You're shivering. Are you cold?" Mark touched her.

"I'm fine." Looking into his warm blue eyes, she smiled. "It must be this snow scene. Reminds me of chilly winter in Ohio."

"Not may people come to Florida and put together a winter picture puzzle." Mark smiled.

"True, but I like the colors in this one."

Paul turned off the CD player. "Now that you've got the puzzle border put together, what's your next step?"

"Now it's a matter of matching the patterns and colors, then looking for the shapes that go together." Eva picked up two pieces. "The patterns are easy. It's the sea of solid colors that present the challenge. You have to find the right one."

"I promise we'll get the right one." Paul glanced at Mark.

"Soon." Mark nodded.

What are they talking about? Eva wondered. *I must have missed something.*

She picked up three puzzle pieces, each a different colors. "Six is pale blue, seven is white, and eight is purple. Artsy people think of numbers a little different. They're shapes and color to us."

There was total silence, again.

"All right guys. I know what you're thinking." Sheepishly, Eva looked up. "I'm not crazy. It's really true; some people see colors in words. And I think the shape of some numbers fit together, like seven and six." She moved the white and blue pieces together, and then tapped the purple piece. "But eight is jealous of seven's slender beauty. And there is a lot of conflict when the three of them are in a number series together."

Rex watched her hands intently.

Mark and Paul exchanged questioning looks.

Like a card trick, Eva moved the colored pieces again, white, purple, blue. "His numbers were wrong. It shouldn't have been seven, eight, six."

"Who's number is wrong?" Mark probed.

"Jim's Social Security number. I filled out a form 1040X correcting his filing status so he could send it to the IRS. Jim was angry that I did it without asking him. But I told him he would be audited if he didn't correct his original 1040 form. As soon as the IRS computers interfaced with the Social Security files, they'd know his wife was deceased. It's like they say: you can't escape death and taxes. The IRS knows both."

Mark watched her rub her arm. "Did Jim hurt you?"

"After he wrote in his Social Security number on the form, he grabbed my arm. Hard. Told me keep my mouth shut about his finances. Said he didn't want any dumb blond telling him about tax law." Eva shook her head. "I may be blond but I know the IRS would catch that mistake."

Leaning forward, Paul pulled out his little notebook. "Do you remember what Social Security number Jim wrote down?"

"The first part was zero, zero, seven – 007. Jim Hellmann is no 007, James Bond." Pausing, she rubbed her forehead. "I don't remember what the middle digits were but the last three numbers were a violent combination: seven, eight, six – 786. It's bad when eight comes between seven and six. Those weren't right."

Scribbling down the numbers, Paul shook his head.

Mark watched her. "Was that different than the first time you saw his Social Security number?"

"Yes. When Jim first came in, the first three digits caught my eye because we don't see many Social Security numbers starting with zero, zero in the Midwest. So I watched him write the rest of it." Eva cringed. "There was no purple in his number. No eight."

"It's hard enough to remember my own Social Security number, let alone someone else's." Paul leaned back.

"You should try thinking in color. I wouldn't forget purple." Eva picked up the offending puzzle piece and held it over the card table for Rex to sniff. "Purple!"

Rex growled.

"Good boy."

After gently pulling the purple piece from her hand, Rex trotted off the deck and into the sand. Pawing at the ground, he dug a little hole, dropped in the piece and buried it like a bone. Following one last sniff, Rex lifted his leg.

"Rex." Mark snapped his fingers. "You don't need to water it. It won't grow."

Shaking his head, Paul chuckled. "I think he's aiming to dissolve it with that liquid."

Nonchalantly, Rex returned to Eva's side, watching her play with colored pieces in odd shapes.

Eva patted Rex. "No purple in our lives. Purple is poison."

The screen door slammed and Barbara walked across the deck with a tray. "Eva, how about some peaches for a snack?"

Eva grinned. "See ... food is color. A peach, an orange, and don't forget to eat your greens."

"We give in." Laughing, Mark threw up his hands. "Paul, we better go fishing. It's getting deep around here."

Paul hopped to his feet. "I think we aught to catch a red snapper for Eva, or at least get her a blue crab."

"I think I missed something here." Barbara set the tray down.

"Mom, you'll have to let Eva explain. I'm not sure I remember her theory." Mark grabbed his fishing pole. "Come on, Rex."

"Go, Rex." Eva coaxed him. "You should get some exercise. Barbara and I will watch the kittens."

Barbara dished out some peaches into bright blue bowls. "What on earth was Mark talking about?"

Eva smiled. "I was driving them crazy with my color theory. They must think I'm a bit touched."

"Men." Barbara smirked. "Most of them think the world is black and white. And the rest are colorblind."

"Yes. But I shouldn't have rambled on so. I don't know what got into me." Eva watched Mark boldly walking towards the ocean like he had walked through her dreams.

"I'm sure they understand that color is important to an art teacher." Barbara poured some cream over her peaches.

"Still, I shouldn't rattle on about colors and numbers." Eva pushed aside six blue puzzle pieces. "Barbara, I read your nurse's book on viral encephalitis. It mentions some patients can suffer from organic psychosis. ... Do you think I'm crazy?"

~ 47 ~

"If Eva gets on the witness stand and starts talking about the color of numbers, the jury will think she's crazy." Standing chest deep in the Atlantic Ocean, Paul cast his fishing line into the surf.

"We'll have to make the case strong enough so Eva won't have to testify." After baiting his hook, Mark glanced back at his parents' house. On the deck, he could see his mom and Eva.

Poor Eva. Mark's thoughts were like lead weights. *What's it like for her? Being able to remember some things so clearly and yet forgetting much of what's happened to her. How could she explain that to a jury? ... Things tied to strong emotions she recalls, like the encounters with Jim, the hospital, and the mother cat being killed. And she remembers vivid details of her childhood. But recent day-to-day events just don't get recorded. Her short-term memory is full of holes.*

"You can't catch anything holding the line in your hands." Detective Galloway chided.

"Paul, it's important to have just the right weights." Mark cast into the quiet water of a slue just beyond the low breaking wave. "Tell your prosecuting attorney not to call Eva as a witness."

"I doubt if he will, but if Jim's defense attorney finds out she had viral encephalitis and what it did to her memory, they may call her as a witness just to destroy her credibility and the case."

Mark watched his line bob on the water. "Don't worry, I'll coach her on how to answer questions under cross-examination. After Eva has had time to regain her strength, she'll do okay." The words rolled off his tongue but his mind questioned them. *How long will it take her to recover? The medical books skip over that phase. They leave recovery up to the patient and their families. But Eva has no one, except me. I'll see she gets the help she needs.*

Paul tugged his fishing line. "I have mixed feelings about what Eva just told us. I want to believe it, but she told us Jim's wife had died. This afternoon, when I checked in with my captain, he said they couldn't find any record of Jim Hellmann's wife, living or dead. Now Eva tells us about a different Social Security number."

In chest high water, Mark stepped sideways, feeling the ocean floor for a better footing. "Maybe there is more than one Social Security number for Jim Hellmann or maybe he's using another person's number. Could be a form of stolen identity."

Paul shook his head. "Not likely. People who steal identities don't bother paying taxes. It's more likely she is merely confused about what she thinks she saw."

"I believe Eva." Mark watched a ripple near his fishing line. "When we get back, I'll call my contact at the Secret Service. Identity theft falls under their jurisdiction. I'll give them the first three and last three numbers Eva gave us. It shouldn't take long for them to run a check against the Social Security files."

"That could be a long list of names."

"We'll see." Mark felt a slight tug on his line. "They can narrow it down by checking how many of them had wives who died last year. Especially wives killed in auto accidents."

Paul pulled his line up. The hook was empty. "Good, I'd feel better if I had some facts before I report back to my captain. Don't want to give him any more reason to doubt our only witness."

"He has no reason to doubt Eva. You have her smashed Blazer, her poisoned cat, the slug taken from her arm, and the bloodstained clippers with Jim's prints." Mark's voice grew sharp. "What more does he want? ... A body?"

"Of course not. That's not what I meant."

A low wave slapped their chests. Silence settled in.

Above them pelicans broke formation. The first one folded its wings back, dropped fast, sank deep into the ocean, and then popped up with a nice size fish dangling from its beak. Nearby, other pelicans dove in and all found a tasty dinner.

"Think we could hire one of them as a fish spotter?" Paul reeled in his empty line. "An aerial view is what we need."

"You right, we're too close." Mark watched his line, not far from where the last pelican caught a fish. "What if the attempt on Eva's life wasn't a case of trying to get her inheritance? What if she was the only witness to a scheme of deception, like investment fraud or identifying theft?"

Paul cast his fishing line out. "That would put a different spin on things. When you were with the Secret Service, did you study how those guys operate?"

"It's not always guys. But in this case we're talking about Jim Hellmann. It's unlikely Maggie would steal her aunt's identity."

"I disagree. Eva's niece is more likely to steal her aunt's identity or at least her credit. Maggie would have more access to Eva's social security number than Jim. And remember, Maggie was anxious to get in Eva's house to get her aunt's bank papers. Have your Secret Service contact check on Maggie's background."

"They will but my gut tells me it's Jim we're after."

"Gut feelings won't hold up in court." Paul baited his hook.

"Papers. If we could find some documents that proved his guilt, that might be enough to convict Jim." Mark jerked his line, but the hook came up empty. "The incident in the raspberry patch was about Jim wanting some papers from Eva."

"We don't know that for a fact." Paul stepped back. "We can't rely on Eva's memory. But I agree, Jim is working a scheme. You saw those church directories with photos circled."

Aunt Killer

Mark cast his fishing line into the surf. "Jim's victims are unmarried churchwomen with money to invest. They're trusting and that makes them vulnerable targets for a swindler."

"I suppose a church-going woman wouldn't want the world to know she gave her money to a scoundrel to invest. I wonder if anyone has ever pressed charges against Jim?"

Mark shook his head. "Probably not, unless he got too greedy. But when you're checking on that, also find out what kind of investments he's pushing: futures, commodities, day trading or some kind of pyramid scheme. Remember, Eva said she thought it was too risky for her women's church group."

"When we get back, give me that list again. I didn't bring my notebook, just bait."

With a jerk, Mark set the hook and began reeling in his catch. "At last, some dinner."

"Glad the pelicans left a few for us." Paul jerked his line. "I can have another fresh fish dinner before I go back to Ohio. And I promised my captain I'd bring him the catch of the day."

"When are you going back to Mansfield?"

"I have the morning flight to Columbus."

"If you get up early, we can fish before you leave. But to be safe, cast your line right over there. That's the spot the pelican above us is circling. He's got his eye on something there." Mark plunked his line into the surf nearby.

The water rippled around their fishing lines. Something moved just below the water. One line was snagged.

Grinning, Paul reeled in his catch. "Check the size of that!"

"Just pan size." Mark teased, pulling in his line. "Try again."

With wings folded, three pelicans dropped from the sky and snatched their choice from the sea.

"Man this is living!" Proudly, Paul held up an even bigger fish and stepped back.

"Don't move!" Mark watched an object skimming across the water. "Stay absolutely still until I tell you which direction to go."

"Mark! ... Don't go pulling my leg." Paul stood motionless. "And for God's sake don't tell me you see a ... a shark's fin."

A breaking wave temporarily hid the dark form.

"I won't." Standing on his toes, Mark spotted the object again. "Slowly, take one step back towards me."

"Next time. I'm bringing my gun." Paul's voice shook.

"Don't think that would do any good." Mark pulled Paul aside. "You're safe. ... See."

"What's that?" Paul took another stepped back.

"It's a Portuguese man-of-war. That last northeaster blew some of them in from the Gulf Stream."

The puffy little sea creature floated by on a wave. Its fat, translucent sail was shaped like a distorted balloon and oddly colored veins fingered up its body.

Mark touched it with his fishing pole. "The man-of-war's tentacles are poisonous. They hang deep into the water. Didn't want you to get tangled up in them."

"Poison. That figures." Paul shook his head.

"Why?"

"It's purple." Paul chuckled. "Eva is right."

"Or maybe that's how she got the idea that purple is poison. When she was young, her parents probably showed her a Portuguese man-of-war and told her not to touch them because they were poisonous." Mark used his fishing pole to turn the man-of-war back out to sea. "She equates purple with poison."

Paul waded towards shore. "Kids come up with the craziest associations. At dinner one night, my youngest told us cauliflower looked like a brain. It does, sort of, if you think about it. Anyway, after that remark, it took me a long time before I could eat cauliflower. Still have to cover it with lots of cheese."

Mark and Paul waded ashore.

A young sandpiper followed it parents as they pecked at the water's edge for their dinner. A flock of seagulls landed nearby, eyeing the string of tempting fish dangling from Mark's hand.

"Nice catch, Professor Reining." Bob walked from his beach patrol car, parked a safe distance from the water's edge. "Your folks said I could find you down here. I see you showed your Yankee detective friend how to fish."

Proudly, Paul held up his fish. "Not quite as big as a string of Lake Erie walleye, but it'll do for a start."

Mark stepped past the last baby wave, flattening out on the sand, hesitating for a second, and then slipping back to the big ocean. "Bob, we ran across a Portuguese man-of-war. You need to notify the lifeguards."

"They have the warnings posted, but I'll call it in." Bob pulled a clipboard from his beach patrol cruiser and made a note.

Mark leaned on the cruiser. "Tomorrow, could you check the local branch banks to find out where Eva has a safe deposit box?"

"A safe deposit box?" Paul interrupted. "You didn't tell me about that."

"I'll explain later. Bob, can you find the bank?"

"Sure. Shouldn't be a problem. Do you have a general idea where her bank is?"

"South Atlantic Avenue." Mark hesitated. "It's south of a burger stand with the big dumpster."

"That's not much of a description." Bob glanced at Mark.

"That's more than most detectives get." Paul chided.

"Speaking of detective work, we've found out more about Eva's earlier years in Daytona. Dixie's team located some old construction records on the West Indies. Adam Johnson, her father, financed the motel's construction with a loan from a bank in Ohio. But we already know she's from Mansfield."

"What was the address of the West Indies?" Mark asked.

"It was a post office box. We're checking for other records but some of them were destroyed in a fire. Dixie found school records showing Eva left the Lenox School when she was twelve."

"Twelve," Paul repeated. "That's when her mother died."

"Killed. Eva's mother was killed in a skiing accident while visiting her son in Denver."

"Whoa." Paul's line of fish dropped. "You didn't tell me Eva's half-brother was involved with her mother's death."

Glancing back at the house, Mark saw his father sitting guard duty near Eva. She was at the card table. "Paul, when you get back to Mansfield, check on Dennis. Maybe her half-brother has a grudge against his sister. Eva's attorney might know what was in her mother's will. Maybe we're missing something."

"Another suspect." Officer Bob White pulled out a note. "A half-brother, a niece, and an impostor husband."

"What?" Paul and Mark's voices merged.

"Yeah. That's what I came out to tell you. Paul, the chief got a fax from your captain. The FBI determined Eva's signature on the wedding certificate was a forgery. Jim is no husband of Eva's."

"That's what Eva told us." Mark took a deep breath. *I knew she wouldn't marry anyone like Jim. She couldn't even look at his photo. When he finds out we know the wedding certificate is a forgery, Jim will leave Eva alone.*

Mark's mind grew cold. *But what if Jim thinks Eva knows some deadly secret about him? Would he still want to silence her? Jim doesn't know she can't remember much of this summer. Does Eva have something that incriminates Jim? What's in Eva's safe deposit box?*

~ 48 ~

Keep your mouth shut, Eva's mind warned her lips as she carried a tray of vegetables to the dining room table. *No more talk about numbers and colors. Just sit and listen. Understand?*

"Eva." Mark got her attention. "Would you bring the butter?"

"Butter. Of course." She sat a bowl of cauliflower beside Paul.

In the dining room, Fritz sat at the head of the table in his big captain's chair. Next to him, Mark and Detective Paul Galloway were swapping fishing stories. It was a family style meal with the men munching their salads while they waited for the main course, their catch of the day fresh from the ocean. Refreshed from a nap, Eva was helping Barbara.

"Cauliflower." Paul frowned at the white vegetable shaped like a brain, stem and all. "Ever since my son made that remark. I keep thinking it looks like a —"

"Paul." Mark reached for the bowl. "Keep it to yourself."

Halfway to the kitchen, Eva stopped and turned back. "What?"

"Butter," Mark said. "Paul wants butter for his veggies."

"Butter." *That's a mellow yellow.* Her mind meandered into creamy thoughts as Eva glanced out the front window. In the late evening sun, the sand dunes were turning golden like dinner rolls, piping hot from the oven. Turning into the kitchen, an odd feeling swept through her. "What did I come in here for?"

"What?" Barbara looked up, pancake turner in hand. In her skillet, fresh fish were frying in the crackling hot oil.

"Nothing." Eva scanned the room, hoping something would remind her of why she was there. The yellow walls looked warm like muffins. "Cornbread. They want the cornbread."

"Tell them to start eating while I finish this last batch of fish."

"They've already started." Eva carried the hot bread into the dining room and put it next to Mark. "Here's your cornbread."

"Thanks." Mark took a slice. "Uh, we'll need some butter."

"Butter. Right." Backing away, Eva mused at the color yellow. *It's so warm and happy; like a smiley face. Now, don't get started with colors,* her mind chided. *Concentrate on what you're doing.*

Back in the kitchen, Barbara wiped corn meal crumbs off the yellow counter top. "Eva, why don't you start eating?"

"I just came in to get –" Eva thought for a moment, looking at an orange box. "Cheese for the cauliflower."

"I just put it on the tray, over there." Barbara pointed.

On the tray beside the cheese sauce, Eva put a dish of black-eyed peas. *They really don't look like eyes,* she mused. *Maybe polka dots or ... now, what am I thinking about? Oh, nothing.* She wandered back to the dining room table.

"Thanks." Fritz took the bowls. "Here, Paul. Have some black-eyed peas to go with that cauliflower. And do you want some cheese sauce to bury those brains?"

"That's the only way I can eat cauliflower." Paul grinned, dribbling a thick layer of sauce over the white mass. "Have to cover all the evidence."

"Eva," Mark smiled. "Would you get me some butter?"

"Butter. Sure thing." Eva put the empty salad plates on her tray and headed to the kitchen. *What are they talking about? Covering the evidence, brains, and eyes. They sound like boys at summer camp. At least my thoughts are colorful, not grim.*

Barbara pulled out a chair. "Eva, sit down for a minute. You look white as a ghost."

"I'm okay. Really, I am." But her mind was fuzzy, feeling like electric pulses were hopping across the wrong wires, overloading them. "I just forgot what I came in here for."

"That's nothing to worry about. We all have those moments." Barbara slid a cup of tea on the table. "You just need something to perk you up."

Sipping the amber tea, Eva studied the yellow kitchen. *What did I forget?* She pondered in vain. *It was a yellow thought.*

"Eva. Come. Let's go join the men." Barbara pulled off her apron and grabbed the last platter of tender ocean fish with a crispy crust. "If we don't get there soon, there won't be anything left."

Retuning to the dining room table, Eva carried her tea. *Look at them.* She could feel her smile. *They're so engrossed with their fish stories. You can hear the happiness in their voices. A man's deep voice is so soothing, especially his.* Eva focused on Mark's lips, grinning at some joke.

After getting up, Mark pulled a chair out for his mother and then Eva. "Do you need anything?"

Looking up into his warm smile, touched with cheese sauce, Eva smiled. "While you're up, would you get the butter?"

Mark headed to the kitchen. "Butter, coming right up."

After retuning, Mark joined his father and Paul in a lengthy conversation on fishing lures and the best method to catch the really big ones. Barbara and Eva exchanged bits and pieces of conversation, but they mainly listened to the men and their adventures. Paul gave an animated narrative of his short career as a bit actor in a film shot at the old Mansfield Reformatory.

Keeping quiet, Eva watched Mark's every movement and his glances at her. Although the conversation was entertaining, she was interested only in the sound of their words. They rolled through her with comforting warmth. *It's good to hear laughter,* Eva thought. *It would be nice if this would go on forever. It's so homey. Mark is so lucky to live near his parents and be part of their lives.*

"Eva." Barbara's voice cut in. "You look a little tired. You should lay down for a bit after dinner."

"I'm okay." Eva picked up her fork, hoping no one noticed it had slipped from her hand again. This time it cut into the mashed potato dike holding in a pool of warm yellow butter, now trickling across her plate towards the fish. Not much had been eaten. The fish was excellent, but her appetite wasn't. And eating with so many interesting people was exciting after a year of dinners alone.

"We'll clean up." Paul reached for her plate. "Sorry we didn't get a red snapper for you."

"This fish is fine. I'm saving the rest for a midnight snack." Eva felt her chair move back.

Mark helped her up. "I think our stories wore you out. Why don't you rest a bit while we clean up?"

"But I need to feed the kittens."

"I'll bring them to your room." Mark walked her down the hall. "Your kitten could use a few quiet moments, too."

After feeding the kittens, Eva laid down on the bed. *Just a short nap,* she promised herself. *It'll give the men time to finish their fish tales. And Mark should spend some time with his guest. Paul and he will be swapping police stories soon.*

Curling up like a kitten, Eva's muscles froze. Her energy seemed to drain from her fingertips like a sack of sugar with a hole in the bottom. Time slipped by and the house grew quiet.

Beneath Eva's eyelids, a vision formed.

A pale yellow winter sun hung on a white horizon. The sound of wind howled across the lonely Siberian landscape. Her body lay in the snow. Coldness seeped into her bones.

Around her a pool of red oozed into the snow, now frozen into sparkling crystals. The whiteness was blinding.

Her vision focused on the glistening towers reaching into the light blue sky and the shimmering Ice Palace. From it, a man walked towards her. Beneath his feet, the snow crunched with chilling coldness. As he marched towards her, his black coat flapped in the Arctic wind. Black fur rimmed his hat and the sun hung behind his head like a crown. Without seeing his face, Eva knew it was Mark. It was his walk, the way his body moved, and she could feel his blue eyes on her.

Behind her, there was the sound of crunching, like heavy footsteps, awkward and uneven. An unseen stranger moved closer. His shadow snaked across her frozen body.

In front of her, Mark shouted. But his words were consumed by the raging wind. Running, he reached for her.

Beside her only a hand was visible. A glint of light reflected off cold steel. A barrel slipped next to her head, pointing at Mark.

It's a ... gun!

Eva tried to scream but her lips were frozen shut. Only her mind screamed. ... Mark!

Hot red light flashed beside her head.

A blast of gunpowder exploded, deafening her.

Her vision was frozen on Mark. ... Mark grabbing his chest, Mark crumpling to the ground, Mark's last glance at her, Mark's head sinking into the snow. ... Mark was gone.

Eva heard a blood-curdling scream.

The blue sky melted into the blood red snow.

Everything turned purple.

~ 49 ~

"Eva! ... Eva!"

She felt her body being lifted. Suspended by something. *What's happening?* Eva tried to comprehend her dream. *Whose arms are those? Why is someone picking me up?*

"Eva! Wake up!" Mark pulled her cold body close to his chest.

The familiar voice was deep and comforting. His body was warm. Slowly, Eva opened her eyes. "Mark?"

"It was just a dream, darling." He brushed her hair back. "I'm right here. You're safe. You were having a dream."

"Purple," Eva mumbled. Still disorientated, her thoughts were swirling in muddy colors and her vision was blurry.

"What?"

"Mark?" Eva touched his face. "Are you okay?"

"Yes. Of course." Mark held her trembling body.

"But ... but I saw someone shoot you."

"It was just a nightmare." He glanced at the doorway.

"But it seemed so real." Eva peered over Mark's shoulder at the figures in the hallway. Fritz hung onto Rex's collar, holding him back. Barbara had the cordless phone, ready to dial. Beside them, Detective Paul Galloway stood with his hand on his gun. Their faces looked worried.

"I'll fix her some hot cocoa. It'll soothe her nerves." Barbara tugged her husband's sleeve. "Fritz, you can give me a hand."

"Mark." Paul stepped forward. "Maybe some fresh air would make her feel better. The air conditioning is a little cool in here."

Mark propped her up. "Eva, would you like to sit on the deck? We can watch the moon rising."

"Some fresh air sounds good." Confused, Eva didn't know if her heart was racing from the dream or because Mark was holding her. "It was my favorite dream, but it turned violent this time."

With Mark's help, she slipped out of bed. *I'm glad I was napping in my clothes,* Eva thought, as Mark and Paul helped her up. *My pajamas are too sheer to have two men pulling me out of bed. They both look upset. I hope that scream was just in my dream. It was blood curdling.* Goosebumps ran down her arms.

Slowly, Mark and Paul walked her down the hall, through the dining area, across the living room, and out onto the front deck.

"Let me know if you need anything." Paul tactfully retreated.

Just as swiftly, Barbara delivered two cups of cocoa and left.

The night air was moist and inviting. The fragrance of night-blooming jasmine floated in the warm evening breeze. Above, the stars twinkled and a ribbon of light shimmered across the ocean from the new moon, just clearing the horizon.

Holding a cup of cocoa, Eva inhaling its rich aroma. "The ocean sounds different at night, booming like the background in that song. It's strong enough to drown out a bad dream."

"Eva." With his arm around her, Mark steadied her. "Did we say something at dinner that upset you?"

"No. It was just a dream." Putting the cup down, she hoped he wouldn't ask her about it. It was too real.

"If you're not upset, why are you trembling?"

The soft porch light added a glow to Mark's face and Eva saw the shimmer of desire in his eyes. Her cheeks flushed with warmth. "Being near you makes me quiver. Maybe that's not the right word. But, anyway, you make me feel delightful."

His hand gently tilted her chin up and he gazed into her eyes. Slowly his lips approached hers, caressing them with warmth.

Mark's touch was tantalizing.

Eva wanted more.

Her hands slipped around him and felt his strong muscles rippling beneath his shirt. Her fingers interlocked behind him and pulled him closer. Mark's body heat melted the chill of her dream and his touch sent a delightful tingle through her.

Slowly, their lips parted but the sweet taste lingered.

"Eva, I bought you something." He pulled a box from his pocket. "I want you to wear this."

She heard the odd tremble in his voice, amused by the shyness of it. *Mark's a university professor and an ex-Secret Service agent,* she mused. *Yet his voice echoes with the awkwardness of a teenager on his first date. How sweet.* Her heart skipped with similar youth. Taking the little white box, she paused before opening it. "For me?"

"I want you to wear it."

Opening it, she gazed at the heart-shaped pendant on a gold chain. Under the porch light, its metallic surface glistened a soft blue like Mark's eyes. Her name was engraved above his name, address, and phone number. "Oh, Mark. It's sweet. An aquamarine heart. Would you put it on for me?"

His hands shook as he slid the chain around her neck. "I want to make sure I don't lose you."

"It's lovely. I've never had a man give me his heart." Gazing at their name together, her smile beamed. "Does this mean we're going steady?"

Mark grinned. "Something like that. Unless you –"

Her lips smothered his words.

He pulled her closer.

Together their bodies sank into the lounge chair and the summer blanket slid over them.

In a steady rhythm, the surf rolled ashore, paused, and returned to the ocean to repeat its cadence. The seventh wave punctuated the eternal beat of the sea.

A distant boom echoed up the beach.

Startled, Eva rolled over. "What was that?"

"Just fireworks." Mark pointed south over the ocean. A stream of lights briefly flickered in the sky and then vanished with a boom. "Someone is celebrating Labor Day early."

"Much too early. I haven't even celebrated Memorial Day." Eva rubbed his chest. "Mark, are you sure you want a girlfriend who doesn't have it all together?"

"From what I've felt, you're all there and in the right places." His hand slid down her body. "What more could a man ask for?"

His touch felt tantalizing and Eva cuddled closer. "You know that's not what I mean. What about up here." She put his hands on her forehead. "Can't you feel those little missing places?"

"Give me a minute to give it a good feel." His fingers massaged every inch of her scalp, slid across her forehead, and touched each feature. "Nothing's missing, darling."

With his hands cupped around her head, he drew her closer. A long moist kiss sealed his investigation and they snuggled under the summer blanket.

The evening breeze rolled over the dunes and across the deck. The distant waves lapped the shore.

"Mark." Eva interrupted the gentle silence. "I love you."

"And I love you, darling."

"Mark." She laid her head on his shoulder. "I should tell you."

Mark pulled her chin up. "Tell me what?"

"I'm not sure how to tell you this." Eva paused to think. *Perhaps I shouldn't tell him. He may think I'm crazy. Maybe I am.*

"I've always found just saying it, is best. So tell me what on your mind. After all, we are going together, right?"

"Yes, but ... but I may not be the person you think I am. I know it sounds a bit crazy, but viral encephalitis is a strange illness. It's almost something you have to live through to understand."

"Darling, don't worry, you can tell me anything."

Eva took a deep breath. *I have to be honest with him,* she considered. *You shouldn't keep secrets from the man you love. Love: it's a strange feeling, like this virus.*

"Eva. You're trembling." He pulled the blanket up around her shoulders. "Do you want to go inside?"

"No. I need to tell you, but it may not make any sense." Her voice trembled with uncertainty. "I fell like Humpty Dumpy. I can't be put back together again, at least, not the way I was. I'm not the same person I once was. Deep inside, I'm different. I'm not sure who I am now ... or who I'll become."

"Does that frighten you?"

"No. But it's an odd feeling. It's like having a second life. It's exciting in a way. It's like I get to rediscover who I am."

"Well, since I'm not the same person I was before we met, we can explore who we are together." His hand slid down her side.

She studied the tempting twinkle in his eyes. "It could be a strange journey. I have no idea what's going to happen to me."

"I have some thoughts on that." Mark kissed the heart shaped pendent dangling around her neck. "You need a partner for your journey. Someone to show you the way."

"I'd love to have you." Inside her mind, Eva felt a glowing like hot sparklers blazing in the darkness and a wave of enchantment crested, waiting for him. "Just remember, I've never been down this road before. My fate is in your hands."

~ 50 ~

5:00 am – August 23rd

"I've never seen one that large." Her hand ran down it, stopping at its head. "I didn't know they grew that big."

"It's a real handful, that's for sure." He grinned. "The guys will envy it."

Barbara dumped more ice into the cooler, covering the large fish. Her kitchen counter was covered with average size fish, but the trophy size one was going home with Detective Galloway. "Paul, you're quite a fisherman, even for an Ohioan."

"Yes, ma'am. That's the biggest fish I've ever caught. No stories about the one that got away. Not this time, anyway." Paul leaned against the counter, watching his magnificent catch being packed in ice for his flight back to Mansfield. Ohio was only a three-hour flight north. Paul's sunrise finishing adventure with Mark had been exciting.

"Mom, that's an almost-got-away fish." Looking up from his breakfast, Mark flipped his fork out like a fishing pole. "Paul got so excited reeling in that big one; he forgot he was in the ocean. Stepped into a deep slue and darn near drowned. If I hadn't held on to him, that fish would have dragged him all the way to the Gulf Stream. Paul wouldn't have let go, even to save his fool neck."

"No way was I going to leave go of that baby. It was a battle to the end: fish, man, and the surf." Grinning, Paul patted more ice around his prize fish. "Thanks for loaning me your cooler. When I send it back, I'll pack it with real maple syrup from Ohio. I have a case of jugs from the Malabar Farm spring maple festival."

At the breakfast table, Fritz smacked his lips. "Real maple syrup sounds good. Haven't had any of that for a long spell. It sure beats this manmade stuff." Fritz tapped the side of the syrup bottle, getting the last drops onto his pancake. "Mark, are you just making out the final exam for your class today?"

"No. They're in my briefcase. This is a list of things to do." Sipping coffee, Mark tapped his pencil on the tablet. After talking with Eva until the wee hours of the morning, he was filled with ideas on how to help her recover and his plans for her future with him. "Let Eva sleep in today. She was up late and needs a little more rest. Make sure she eats a good breakfast. Also, don't let her wander down to the beach. And definitely no swimming."

Barbara tapped her icy hand on her son's shoulder. "I'm a nurse, remember. I can take care of Eva."

"I know." Mark tossed his tablet in the briefcase and snapped it shut. He planed to finish his list while his students took their final exam. "Don't let her sit in the sun too long. And tell her I'll be home about noon."

With her bowl of oatmeal, Barbara slid into her chair. "Your dad and I will look after Eva. Now you better get off to school." Her voice was motherly. "And drive carefully."

Mark slipped on his suit coat and grabbed his keys. "Come on, Paul, we better get a move on it. You don't want to miss your flight home."

"Right." Paul taped the ice chest closed. "Think they'll accept this as carry on baggage?"

"Looks more like a little casket," Fritz said. "If you have any problems, flash your police badge and tell them you're taking a body home as evidence."

Paul nodded. "That's no lie. It's a very fishy body and it's evidence I've been here."

"Sounds like a tall tale to me." Mark grabbed his briefcase. "Now lets get moving before that carcass starts smelling fishy."

Paul thanked Barbara and Fritz for their hospitality and then scurried down the steps with Mark to the Jeep. Buckling up, Paul held the cooler on his lap with a tight grip. "Mark, you were up most of the night and you've hardly said a word when we were fishing this morning. What's on your mind?"

Heading north on South Atlantic Avenue, Mark pulled around a slow moving linen-delivery truck. There was a lot on his mind, but not much he wanted to share. "Are you going to get an arrest warrant for Jim?"

"First, we'll get a search warrant for his townhouse. I want to make sure we get all the evidence we can. Don't forget, this isn't going to be an easy case to prosecute. I want to get Jim off the streets as much as you." Paul held onto the cooler, as they turned left, heading towards the bridge. "Eva's scream last night made my blood run cold. She sounded terrified. Hearing a victim's agony after a crime really gets to me. For them the violence lingers. Did she tell you what the nightmare was about?"

"She dreamt someone fired a gun beside her head. Although she doesn't remember being shot, in her subconscious, there's a fragment of that fear." Pulling his Jeep onto the bridge, Mark hoped Paul would let the subject drop. *What Eva told me*, he reflected, *were her private thoughts, and I won't break her trust.*

"But Mark, she screamed your name."

"What flight are you on?"

Paul pulled the ticket from his pocket. "Delta's 1599 flight. It leaves at six. So what about Eva's dream?"

"Six." Mark glanced at his watch. "We'll get to the airport in plenty of time for you to stop at the gift shop. Better pick up something for your wife and kids. Somehow, I don't think the fish is what they are expecting. Even if it's a big one."

"Got a point there. Besides, the fish goes to my captain. Told me not to come back empty-handed. He was kidding, of course, but this baby beats the walleye he pulled out of Lake Erie last week." Glancing out the window, Paul gawked at the cabin cruiser heading down the Halifax River towards the inlet. "Man, look at that beauty. I could use one of those on the lake."

Mark glanced left. "That's built for the Atlantic Ocean. It's too big for a lake."

"Obviously you've never been on Lake Erie during a storm. It's a shallow lake and the wind whips it into some monstrous waves." Paul gripped his cooler. "The Great Lakes have sunk many ocean freighters in a matter of minutes. Just swallows them like a hungry fish snatching a fly off the water's surface."

As Mark's Jeep rolled onto the mainland side of the bridge, silence settled in. The streets were almost vacant and the parking lot of the Daytona Beach International Airport was mostly empty. After watching Paul's flight leave the runway, Mark strolled to his Jeep for the short drive to the university library to do research before class.

Five hours later, Mark sat at his desk in his classroom while his students took their final exam for the summer quarter. After Mark finished reviewing the articles on viral encephalitis he had pulled from the Internet, he jotted more notes on his tablet.

So much information, he pondered. *Yet little of it deals with helping the patient recover. Supportive care doesn't tell me much. I want to know how to help Eva put her memory back together and to rebuild her life. It must be strange to be twenty-seven and suddenly not be the person you used to be. To know who you were, but not know who you are. ... What would it be like to lose your sense of identity? I find that hard to fathom. And what else does Eva feel that she hasn't told me yet?*

Sitting in his classroom while his students took their final test gave Mark the quiet he needed. Everyone had finished before the allotted time except one student in the back. Mark studied Bob toying with his pencil, looking into space as if lost in thought.

"Bob, you have five minutes to finish your final exam."

"Oh." Bob slid out of his chair. "Sorry to keep you waiting, Professor Reining. I finished fifteen minutes ago. I wanted to wait until everyone else left."

"Why?"

"I found Eva's bank." Bob put his test on top of the stack.

"Fast work. I'm impressed."

"Well, I know most of the tellers that work in the branch banks along South Atlantic Avenue. It's all in the line of duty, of course." Bob grinned. "The Beach Patrol provides the back-up for any trouble the banks report. We're generally the closest patrol cars, so we can get there quick if there's trouble."

"But the banks were already closed yesterday when I asked you to check on Eva's safe deposit box and you were here before they opened." Mark slipped the class exams into his briefcase.

Bob grinned. "I take my job seriously and collect the phone numbers of all the single bank tellers. So, after making a few calls last night, I found one who remembered Eva.'

"The teller remembered Eva?"

"Yep. Remembering names and faces is part of their job. Do you want to head over to the bank now?"

"No need to take up your time. Just give me the bank's name."

"It's no bother. It's an order. The chief wants me there when Eva opens her safe deposit box. If there's any evidence in it about who tried to kill Eva, the chief doesn't want you touching it.

You're too involved and it will hold up better in court if only the police have handled the evidence."

Walking out the classroom door, Mark knew his student was right. *But what will Eva think,* Mark considered. *She could have personal items in there that she wouldn't want others to see. Not even me, let alone the police. What if there's something in there that could destroy her credibility if misinterpreted?*

"Don't worry, Professor, I won't look at her stuff unless you think I should see it." Bob tagged along down the hall. "I wouldn't want strangers snooping through my safe deposit box, if I had one. I'll trust your judgment on what's important to her case."

"Let me to talk to Eva first." Mark stopped at the entrance. "I want to make sure she's up to going to the bank. I'll call you."

"I'm going on duty at noon, so call dispatch. They'll give me your message." Outside, Bob headed to the students' parking area.

Slowly, Mark walked to the faculty parking lot. His mind churned. *Why did I ask Bob to find Eva's bank? I should have done that myself. Now the police will be there when she opens her safe deposit box. What was I thinking? What will Eva think when I tell her? She may not want to show anyone what's inside that box. But Bob is right. If there's evidence in there that will help put Jim behind bars, it's better if the police secure it.*

So what am I worried about? Mark slid into his jeep. *Even if I ask her, will Eva remember what she put in her safe deposit box?*

~ 51 ~

"Maybe the bank has been robbed. There are two police officers inside." Eva stopped in the bank's doorway, feeling uneasy. Cool air rushed out as Mark held the door for her. "I don't want to get in the middle of a shootout."

"It's okay," Mark said. "They're two of my students. Dixie works in police dispatch and Bob is a Beach Patrol Officer. You met Bob when you pulled those children out of the surf."

"I don't remember his uniform and gun." Looking around, Eva stepped into the chilly air-conditioned lobby. It was after one thirty and there were few customers in the bank. "This feels like the right bank. Cool. Really cool."

"Good afternoon, Ms. Johnson." A familiar looking teller walked over. "Did you bring your safe deposit box key?"

"Yes." Eva handed over the long slender key and followed the teller into the vault. Something seemed wrong, but she couldn't pinpoint it. *I feel like everyone's watching me.* Her mind clicked like the key in the lock. *Is that right? I thought my box was on the left not on the right. ... And something seems strange. Even Mark acts nervous. Or am I just imagining it?*

"There you go, Ms. Johnson." The teller opened the safe deposit box's little door, removed the bank key, and left Eva's key dangling in the second lock. "Since you've been ill, you can use the manager's desk in the lobby so you can sit down."

"Thank you." Eva pulled out the long safe deposit box. "What did I put in here? It seems heavy."

"I'll take that." Mark carried Eva's safe deposit box to the manager's desk. "Do you want to be alone when you open it?"

"No need. This will be quick. I only need to get a little spending money out. I want to go to the craft store. I need more glue to finish repairing the doll's head." Eva sank into the manager's big chair, her feet stretching to touch the floor.

Dixie and Bob stood several feet behind her, chatting while they watched. Both in uniform and armed, they got the attention of customers entering the bank.

Across from Eva, Mark sat in one of the smaller chairs used by customers. "Why didn't you open a checking account?"

"I didn't have the address for the West Indies." Flipping open the long thin lid, she found it. "So that's what happened to it."

"What?" Mark sat up.

Eva blushed, pulling out a little bag. "I was wondering where I left my French fries. ... Want one?"

"No thanks. They look a bit stale."

Setting the fries on the desk, Eva reached into the box and pulled out a fast-food burger bag with its top neatly folded over. *I hope I didn't leave my fish sandwich in here.* Her thoughts turned sad. *No, I gave it to the momma cat. Poor thing got killed.*

"Eva, is there something wrong?" Reaching across the table, Mark touched her hand. "You're trembling."

"After I left the bank, I saw the momma cat get killed. Poor thing, a car hit her. She was a calico like my cat." Eva sighed and set the sack aside. "Now they're both dead."

Reaching back in, Eva pulled out a blue box, looked at Mark, then at Dixie and Bob. "I better be careful with this. Wouldn't want them to get the wrong idea."

"What's that?"

"It's a gun." Eva slid the box to him.

Mark pulled the top off. Inside was a .38 caliber Smith and Wesson revolver with a four inch barrel. It was an expensive gun in excellent condition. A bag of spare bullets were tucked in the corner. "Did you bring this for protection against –"

"Be careful," Eva interrupted. "It's loaded."

After nodding to Bob, Mark opened the cylinder and removed the bullets. "Now it's safe. Why did you bring your revolver?"

"It's really not mine. It was my father's. I didn't want anyone to steal it." Eva paused, touching the barrel. Strangely, the gun brought back fond memories of her father and the afternoons he had taken her to a friend's farm to teach her how to shoot. "My father said every woman should know how to handle a gun. Said a revolver like this is just a matter of point-and-shoot. No need to worry about the safety or to pull back that slide gizmo. That's too much for a frightened person to remember. … Anyway, Dad gave me his favorite .38 revolver when I was twenty-one."

"Without a safety they can be dangerous." Mark glanced up at Bob, eying the gun.

"I know. But I keep it in a safe place and there are no children in my house. In fact, there's no one at home anymore. They're all gone and now, so am I." Eva picked up the gun and slid the six bullets back into the chambers.

"Maybe you should leave them out." Mark said.

"What good is a gun without bullets?"

Mark glanced at the gun barrel. "Got a point there. So why did you bring a gun with you?"

"I wanted to do some target practicing. There used to be a public firing range over on the mainland. But maybe it's gone too, like the West Indies." Carefully, she laid her gun back in its box.

"A gun is no protection if you keep it in the bank."

"I don't want to shoot anyone." Eva rubbed her arm where the doctors had removed a 9mm slug. "No one knows I'm here. So I'm safe and the gun will be safer in my safe deposit box. I wouldn't want to lose Dad's favorite gun."

"What's in the burger sack?" Mark asked. "More fries?"

"My greens are in there." Unrolling the top of the brown bag, Eva peeked inside. Twenty-four clear plastic zipped bags with hundred-dollar bills in each. She pulled out only the top one. "I'll need a hundred ... no, two hundred for art stuff."

"Must be expensive glue." Mark chuckled.

"Not just glue. Art supplies. The craft store is having a pre-holiday sale and I want to pick up their class schedule. Sometimes I teach watercolor painting there. Well, not here, in Ohio."

Eva studied the Spanish bayonet outside the window. *That's a lush dark green,* Eva analyzed. *Its leaves are Hooks' green with a touch of ivory black and china white on the tips.* On the ends of each bayonet leaf were needle-sharp points that caught the sunlight. A chameleon rested near one tip, blending in, waiting for a meal. "I could teach art here. ... When I'm feeling better."

Mark scooted his chair back. "Anything else in there?"

"There's my driver's license. I thought I lost it." Eva pulled it and a stack of papers out. Her hand trembled. "What's this? I forgot to mail it!"

A thick envelope fell on the desk.

Reaching for it, Mark nodded to Bob. "This is addressed to Jim Hellmann. What's in it?"

With her hands crossed tightly across her chest, Eva sank in the chair. "Jim dropped those in my raspberry patch."

"Is that when he chopped your hair?"

"They fell out when I ripped his pocket. I found that hanging in my broken raspberry plants."

"Professor." Bob walked forward. "What's in the envelope?"

Eva sank deeper into the chair, glancing at Bob's uniform and gun as he stood next to her. "It's one of those plastic things you keep your identification cards in. Not a wallet, just the ... well, I'll show you what I mean."

"No." Mark stopped her hand. "Let Bob open it. The police may want to keep them."

Slipping on latex gloves, Bob slit the envelope with a letter opener and nudged the contents out. An accordion style plastic credit card folder fell on the desk.

"Interesting." Bob nodded to Dixie. "Call the chief. Tell him we may have something for him."

Eva felt her body tremble, her hands got cold and her brain seemed to fry. *How can I explain that I was too tired to go to the post office?* Eva wondered. *Do they really need to call the police chief? I just forgot to mail them. Surely that's not a crime. Now Mark is upset. He looks nervous.*

Eva watched Mark's eyes as he intently read the contents. "I know I should have mailed them back sooner. But I didn't know how much postage to put on the envelope. Am I in trouble?"

"Eva. Don't worry. It's okay." Mark's voice was comforting.

"Check this out, Professor." Bob flipped over the accordion cardholder. "Multiple Social Security cards."

"That's not unusual," Eva said. "During tax season, parents often carry the Social Security cards for all their children."

Leaning close, Mark examined the cards. "Eva, do you know who Jimmy Lee Hicks, Junior is?"

"No."

"What about the Social Security number that begins with zero, zero, seven and ends with seven, eight, six?"

"That's Jim's. He wrote it on his 1040X tax form. That's one thing he was shouting about in the raspberry patch. He wanted my draft copy back for some reason." Eva leaned forward. "See, I told you there was purple in that number; white, purple, blue. That's seven, eight, six."

"What?" Bob asked. "I don't see any colored numbers."

"I'll explain later." Mark studied the Social Security cards. "Eva, was Jim's deceased wife's name Mary Jo Hicks?"

"No. Jim's wife's name would have been Hellmann." Rubbing her forehead, Eva tried to comfort her memory. A fragment of what Jim had told her was now disturbing. "I remember Jim saying his wife had been killed in a one-car auto accident."

~ 52 ~

"Did you get the arrest warrant?" Mark stomped to the edge of the front deck, talking to Detective Paul Galloway on the phone.

Not wanting to disturb Eva napping in his parents' living room, Mark dragged the regular phone and its satin-line cord onto the deck. The conversation with Paul, now back in Ohio, was too private to be discussed over a cordless phone. Mark wanted no one to eavesdrop on his conversation.

"Have you served the arrest warrant yet?" Mark continued. "No. Well, you may need to revise it. The Secret Service will be calling you from their Orlando office. They'll want to add additional charges to include identity theft. James Hellmann IV is really Jimmy Lee Hicks, Junior."

Mark listened to Detective Galloway's surprised remarks.

"Jim dropped his Social Security cards in Eva's raspberry patch. Yes, that's plural. There were several. The one that ended with seven, eight, six was for Jimmy Lee Hicks, Junior. That's his real name." Mark turned away from the house. "And there was one card for a Mary Jo Hicks. ... Right, that could be the late Mary Jo. Yeah. Let me know what you find out about the missing wife."

Reaching the end of the phone cord, Mark stopped. "What's all that noise in the background? ... You're at Jim's townhouse with the search team. What have they found?"

Beneath his feet, Mark felt the afternoon heat rising off the front deck. Even the gun clipped to his belt absorbed the sun, warming its black surface. After returning from the bank with Eva,

Mark slipped on his old service pistol, hoping to steady his nerves. So far it hadn't helped.

"Paul, how much jimsonweed did they find? ... Enough. Are they the same white capsules that Eva was taking? ... Yes, I understand Jim could have a prescription for the same medication. You'll have to check with his doctor."

Mark flipped the phone line across the deck.

Nearby, a light tan chameleon dashed across the hot sand and into the shade. Its body turned darker, blending with the new background, changing its identity to hunt a new prey.

"You'll have to add Jim's alias to the arrest warrant. No, I'm not telling you your job. But I don't want him getting out on any technicality. ... I know. You have your own reasons for nabbing Jim. But I want to make sure he stays locked up. Eva needs time to recover before the trial."

The thought of Eva taking the witness stand unsettled Mark. Glancing back into the living room, he saw her sleeping on the sofa. *The trip to the bank tired her,* Mark thought. *When Eva saw the envelope addressed to Jim, she turned white. She was upset because she had forgotten to mail it. Having the police chief show up with his crime lab technicians didn't help.*

Mark looked back at the hot sand dunes. He needed to concentrate on what Paul was telling him.

"Have your men picked up Jim? ... Mansfield isn't that big. Yes, I know. It's only been a matter of hours. ... Paul, what's all the commotion?"

A confusion of voices drowned out Paul's conversation.

"Paul. What's going on?" Mark waited. There was no response. No words were audible, only the tone of the voices. A mixture of excitement, anger, and disgust. Even over the phone, the sounds of a search were familiar. Footsteps faded and a door banged shut. "Paul, what did they find? A receipt for a storage locker. That was a lot of commotion for finding a piece of paper. What else did they find?"

On the Ohio side of the conversation, Paul evaded the answer.

"Paul. I need to know what you found."

Slowly, Paul explained.

Mark leaned on the deck railing. "Blond hair and blood. Where? ... In the bedroom. Did you find a body? ... No. ... Let me know what the crime lab finds at the storage locker."

Straightening up, Mark's hand slid to his back, touching his gun. "Call me the minute you arrest Jim. Whatever his name is."

With a click, the phone connection dropped, but Mark's troubled thoughts hung on, chilling him in the afternoon heat. He visualized what he had seen when he and Paul visited Jim at his townhouse days earlier.

Blond hair and blood. The words churned in Mark's mind. *Was there a woman in Jim's bedroom when I walked passed? I smelt perfume and saw a curling iron in the bathroom. Surely a woman had been there. Did Jim fight with her? Did she get away like Eva? Or did she wind up like my sister: brutally murdered. If Susan had run away like Eva, she might still be alive. This time I won't wait for the police to move in, I'll –*

"Mark." His mother's cool hand slid across his back. "Is anything wrong?"

"I was thinking. Mom, since you have a few days off, why don't you and Dad take a little vacation?" Mark avoided looking at her, but hoped she'd take the bait. It would be safer for his parents if they weren't around if things got worse than they already were. "Why don't you go visit with your friends Marcy and Dick for a few days? You know how Dad enjoys deep-sea fishing and you could do some shopping at those fabric store outlets."

"I know exactly what you're thinking. But your dad and I have already discussed it. Only a hurricane will get us to leave."

Mark studied the horizon. A crystal-clear blue sky hung above the ocean. "Mom, a hurricane of sorts could be brewing."

"Fritz and I have weathered many storms. Home is the best place to ride them out. Besides, I have a patient to look after and your dad is busy fixing things. Now that he's in the repair mood, I'm surely not going to drag him away. I've been waiting two years for that mood to strike him. So we're staying." Barbara tugged her son's arm. "Let's go inside. I'll make you a tall glass of iced tea. You'll need it to stay awake while you grade your students' final exams. You have other responsibilities besides Eva."

"I'll be there in a minute." Mark handed her the phone. "I need to collect my thoughts."

"Don't be long. It's roasting out here." Barbara went inside.

Standing in the hot sun, Mark's thoughts sizzled. *This is all my fault. If I hadn't been in such a hurry to help Eva and find out her past, she wouldn't be in danger right now. I should have waited until she recovered. She was safe as long as no one knew where she was. Now a Mansfield detective has been here, the Daytona police are involved, and the Secret Service is investigating. I hope no one else finds out Eva is here.*

Turning, Mark looked inside at the figure peacefully sleeping on the sofa, curled up like one of her kittens. *Eva doesn't have the strength to defend herself.* His mind was tormented. *Now I've put her in real danger. Revealed her hiding place. Made her open her safe deposit box for the police. She may have to testify. And –*

"Mark!" His mother called. Alarm rang in her voice. "There's some strange man walking up the drive."

~ 53 ~

Dashing down the hall, Mark got to the door before the bell rang. One hand reached for the knob, the other for his gun.

"Don't shoot." Maggie peeked from behind her father. "Agent Reining, you remember who I am, don't you?"

"Maggie, how did you find us?" Mark snapped. Standing in the doorway, cool air rushed out and hot air rolled inside.

"I'm Dennis." His hand extended. "I'm Eva's brother."

Mark studied Eva's half-brother waiting for a handshake. Dennis was average height, middle-aged, with graying light-brown hair. The only resemblance to Eva was his shy smile.

"I need to see my sister." His hand pulled away. "I'm sorry if we caught you at a bad time, but I need to see Eva."

"Aunt Eva." Maggie called through the screen door before looking up at Mark, barring the doorway. "Is this an FBI safe house or something? Why didn't you tell me my aunt was alive?"

"Because –" Wanting to keep his conversation private, Mark stepped onto the back porch. "Because you are a suspect."

"Me? A suspect?" Maggie pulled back in contempt. "Really. Do I look like someone who would kill her aunt?"

"You have both motive and opportunity." Mark was blunt.

Maggie flipped off her sunglasses. "Motive. What motive?"

"Money."

"Money? Get serious." Maggie flipped on her glasses. "You cops think everything revolves around money as a motive. I may not be the world's best niece, but Aunt Eva has always been there for me. And I wouldn't kill my aunt. If you ask me, it was that jerk, Jim, that tried to kill Aunt Eva."

"Agent Reining, I demand to see my sister."

"Name's Mark." He stepped away from the door. "Let's go down to the north end. We need to talk. There are a few things you need to know before I let either of you see Eva."

"Why can't we go inside?" Maggie fanned herself.

"I don't want to disturb Eva. She's resting." With the others following, Mark strolled to the shady north porch. "You have to understand, Eva has been ill with –"

"Viral encephalitis," Dennis cut in. "I know. I got a copy of the hospital records."

"How did you get access to them?" Mark interrogated.

"It was simple. I'm an insurance agent." Dennis handed over one of his business cards. "I told the hospital accounting office we carried the health insurance policy for Eva Johnson and we needed a copy of the records before paying her hospital bill. ... So you're right, money motivates people. The hospital was glad to find her insurance company and gave me her records and your address."

Mark stopped. "How did you know Eva was in Daytona?"

"I know she loves it here. When they didn't find her body, I thought she might have come here. We may not have been close, but I know my sister well enough to know where she'd hide. And Eva loves this beach." An undercurrent of sadness ripped through Dennis' voice. "I knew if Eva was alive, she'd be here, along the beach somewhere. This was always her favorite home."

Listening, Mark studied Dennis' face, wrinkled with lines of worry. *Or was it guilt?* Mark wondered. *What is his motive? He hasn't seen his sister in years. Why does he want to see her now?*

"Where's Aunt Eva?" Maggie looked around.

"How is she?" Dennis sat on the porch railing.

"If you read the hospital records, you know Eva has been ill for some time and her memory is a bit fuzzy." Mark avoided the mention of jimsonweed poisoning in Eva's capsules, knowing Maggie worked in a medical lab and was still considered a suspect. "At the hospital, the doctors found a 9mm slug in her arm."

"Someone shot Aunt Eva?" Maggie looked away. "I thought she was injured in the car accident."

"Both. But Eva doesn't remember either the accident or being shot." Mark found it hard to talk about Eva's condition. It seemed too personal.

Sweating, Dennis rolled up his shirtsleeves. "I understand. I've read enough accident reports as an insurance agent to know that's not uncommon. Many times a driver will walk away from an accident but not be able to explain what happened. So how is Eva's memory? How much has she forgotten?"

The hopeful tone in Dennis' last question made Mark suspicious. *Is that his motive? He's come to see if Eva has ... forgotten something he wants forgotten. What does Eva know about her brother that he doesn't want others to know? Is there a skeleton in Dennis' closet?*

Mark studied Dennis' tight lips. "You have to judge that for yourselves. But one thing I do know." Mark paused to watch their reaction. "When Detective Galloway gave Eva the photos of the two of you, she identified Maggie but not you, Dennis."

Looking down, Dennis closed his eyes.

"Dad, don't worry." Maggie slipped her arm around her father. "It must have been a bad photograph. And she probably didn't recognize you because of your new mustache."

Dennis turned away and leaned on the railing. "You can't blame Eva for not remembering a brother who was never around. She was about six when I left for good. I was eighteen, married, and Maggie was on the way. After I moved to Denver to work for my father, I only visited our mom a couple of times." Dennis sighed. "The last time I saw Eva was at our mother's funeral."

Again Mark detected an undercurrent of emotion in Dennis' voice. "Why have you come to see Eva now?"

"I want to make sure my sister is all right. If she wants, I'll take her back to Denver so she won't be alone. I should have gone to see her after her father died but … well her father and I didn't get along. The usual stepson-stepfather conflict." Suddenly, Dennis turned. "If Jim tries to hurt Eva again, I'll kill him. I mean it."

"You shouldn't make threats."

"That's a promise, not a threat."

"Strong feelings for a brother who hasn't shown much interest in his sister's life." Mark pushed the issue, searching for a motive.

"Maggie, go down to the car and get the gift you got for Eva."

Reluctantly, Maggie headed down the hot west porch, towards the steps and down to the driveway below.

"Maggie seems closer to Eva's age," Mark commented.

"True, Maggie was born when Eva was about seven. Age wise, they're more like sisters than niece and aunt." Dennis stepped closer. "Let me be frank. I have personal reasons for staying out of Eva's life and it's none of your business."

"Protecting Eva is my business."

"She doesn't need protection from my daughter or me."

"I don't know that."

"Take my word for it. We have no reason to harm Eva."

"What about her inheritance?" Mark probed.

"I doubt if I would be in Eva's will. You said yourself; she didn't even recognize my photo. As for Maggie, well, money is not something she values. Believe me. If it was, she wouldn't have taken off from work just to find her aunt."

"Still, Maggie is Eva's only niece."

"Maggie wouldn't kill her Aunt Eva." Dennis looked over the porch railing at his daughter pulling a box from the trunk of a red sports car. "You should be concentrating on Jim Hellmann. He's your man."

"His real name is Jimmy Lee Hicks, Junior."

"Anyone who uses an alias is hiding something." Dennis jotted the name on his business card. "Maybe I can help. Insurance agents have access to a lot of information."

Mark considered the offer. The more he knew about Jim the easier it would be to protect Eva. It would also help him prepare Eva for being a witness. As soon as Paul arrested Jim, Mark reminded himself. "We think Jim Hicks' wife was killed in an auto accident and Jim had a life insurance policy on her."

"The answer to that is only a phone call away." Dennis stepped into the shade. "What was his wife's name and do you know Jim's social security number?"

Mark headed back down the west porch towards the back door. "The wife's name was Mary Jo Hicks. And Jim has several social security numbers. I have them inside."

"Multiple identities. Sounds suspicious. Our insurance fraud investigators may already have a file on this Jim, at least on one of his aliases." Dennis stopped at the door, waiting for his daughter jogging up the steps. "If Jim is the type of person I think he is, he'll want to silence anyone who knows too much about him. Eva could be in real danger."

"Like I said, Eva's memory of this summer is fuzzy." Opening the door, Mark glanced down the dark hall towards the living room where Eva was napping. "So what she remembers couldn't put Jim in jail. Unfortunately, he doesn't know she has a memory problem. All Jim knows is that Eva has his social security cards and that alone makes her a target."

~ 54 ~

Running across the front deck, tears streamed down her face. "Aunt Eva, Aunt Eva. You're alive."

"Maggie?" Startled, Eva dropped the tube of glue on the deck. She barely had time to stand before her niece's arms wrapped around her in a powerful hug. "Of course I'm alive."

With sobs mumbling her words, Maggie held onto her aunt.

"Take it easy, Maggie. I'm all right. Really, I'm fine." Eva patted her niece's back. *How'd she find me?* Eva pondered. *First Detective Galloway shows up. Now Maggie. Does everyone in the world know where I am? ... Does Jim know?*

"Aunt Eva, maybe you should sit down. You're shaking."

"I'm surprised to see you." As Eva pulled back from her niece, a man's figure caught her eye. Fear flashed through her. *Is that Jim? Did Maggie bring Jim?*

"Eva," a man called.

It wasn't Mark, but the voice was familiar. Holding her breath, Eva turned and glanced at the two figures. The bright afternoon sun was behind them. Almost blinding her. Eva watched a figure move slowly towards her. It wasn't Mark's walk.

The man strolled forward. "Eva. It's me, Dennis."

"Dennis?" Slowly, Eva walked to him, not sure how to greet her half-brother after so many years. "Dennis, I hardly recognize you. What brings you here?"

With a shy smile, he reached out for her. "I knew if you were alive, you'd be here. I've been worried sick about you."

Her arm wrapped around him with a little sister hug. "I was thinking about you today."

"Oh! How so."

"I was remembering how you taught me to make fort walls around my sandcastles to keep the ocean out. I always built my castles too close to the water and the incoming waves would wash them away before I had finished them."

"I'd forgotten about that." Dennis walked her to a deck chair. "You better sit down, Eva. You look a little pale."

"Dennis, I'm surprised to see you here." Eva studied his face. It was so different from the young man she last saw at their mother's funeral. But Dennis was only twenty-four then and she was just twelve. That was fifteen years ago and they both had changed a lot. And their parting had been filled with trauma.

Does he remember? Eva wondered. *How could he forget? He was so angry with my father. I heard them shouting in the back room of the funeral parlor. As I ran in, Dennis shoved my father into a pile of flower arrangements. I screamed and Dennis shoved me aside. I'll never forget him saying I was no sister of his.*

"Sis, are you okay?" Dennis touched her trembling arm.

"I'm okay. Really I am." Sitting at the table, Eva moved the china doll and the tray of porcelain head fragments aside. "I'm surprised you and Maggie are vacationing at the beach. You never liked the ocean. I don't remember why."

With his back to the surf, Dennis sank into a chair. "The ocean terrifies me. Don't you remember? I almost drowned out there. I'll never forget that day. Mom told me to stay close to shore. Naturally, I had put on my life vest and went way beyond the breakers. Everything was fine until a husky kid swam out. He stopped next to me, thinking I was standing on a sand bar, and then he panicked when he couldn't touch bottom. He grabbed me and we both sank like a rock."

Dennis shuddered. "I didn't think we'd ever hit bottom. I was never so terrified in my life. That kid had a choke hold around my neck and I couldn't get free. I tried to surface but my life vest wasn't enough to float two of us. ... And if that lifeguard hadn't pulled us up, well, we'd have been fish food."

Maggie grabbed Dennis's arm. "Dad, you never told me that."

"I try not to remember it." Dennis picked up the doll. "Eva, you're still collecting dolls. As I recall, you could hardly find your bed at night for all the dolls and furry animals. Mom called it your zoo. Lions, tigers, and teddy bears with an Easter rabbit or two."

Eva glanced back into the sun, looking for Mark. He was still talking on the phone. Dragging it and the satin-line cord as he paced like a caged zoo animal.

"I hear you had viral encephalitis," Dennis continued. "Have the doctors cured it?"

"There's no cure." Eva picked up her doll. "It's one of those you either live-or-die illnesses. It's the strangest thing I've ever had. The virus sneaks into your brain and fries all the circuits. Really zaps your short-term memory, and, well, I feel like this doll. Both of our heads are a bit cracked. A little glue will fix hers but I don't think it will help me."

"Aunt Eva. Don't say that. You'll be fine."

Eva patted her niece's hand. "I didn't mean to sound morbid. Really, I'm okay. I just needed a place to recuperate."

"You can come home with me." Dennis toyed with a broken piece of the doll's china head. "Now that Maggie is on her own, my wife and I have extra room. You can recover in Denver."

"No, Dennis." Goosebumps covered Eva's arm. The thought of going anywhere near the mountains that killed her mother chilled her. "No. I'm staying here at the beach."

"But the mountains are beautiful," Maggie piped in. "If you go way up in Estes Park, you might find snow on one of the peaks."

"Maggie!" Dennis turned to his daughter. "Go inside and get us some ice water."

As soon as Maggie left, Dennis continued. "Sorry about that. Didn't mean to bring back bad memories."

"Memories." She took her brother's hand. "Fortunately the bad ones burned up fast; for me at least." Glancing at the sea oats swaying, Eva considered what she had just said.

That's not exactly true, she thought. *I remember how hurt I felt when Dennis told me he didn't consider me his sister. But at twelve, I didn't understand grief.*

"Eva, with your hair cut like that, you look like Mom."

Does that make him nervous? Watching her brother fidget, Eva considered. *Does looking like our mother touch a cord of guilt in him about her death? It was an accident. He should let go of his guilt. I don't hold him responsible. Even if Dennis would have gotten up early that morning and gone skiing with Mom, he couldn't have prevented the accident.*

"Eva, I want to … to explain what I said to you when I pushed you aside at Mom's funeral. I should have told you sooner."

"Dennis, that was a long time ago."

"I know, but I didn't mean what I said. I only said it to hurt you because … well, I was angry." Dennis stared at the deck floor. "I was angry at the whole world. I lashed out at everyone. Your dad tried to reason with me but I decked him. If your scream hadn't startled me, I would have hit him again. When you tried to stop me, I told you –"

"Dennis." Eva patted his hand. "That was fifteen years ago and if I don't remember, is there any reason to tell me now?"

"But I need to explain. To apologize."

"Whatever it was, I accept your apology." Eva saw the relief on her brother's face. "I only want to remember the good times. Like those funny little volcanoes you used to make in the sand."

"My sand volcanoes?" Dennis chuckled. "I used most of my chemistry set trying to make them look like real volcanoes with lot's of smoke and flames. With all the chemicals I poured on the sand, I'm surprised there aren't holes in the beach."

"Holes in the beach?" Maggie set a tray of refreshments on the table. "Did I miss another one of Dad's wild adventures?"

"Fathers don't do wild things." Dennis broke into laughter.

"Aunt Eva?"

"Don't ask me. My memory is on the fritz."

"Sure." From under the table, Maggie pulled up a gift box. "I bought you something."

Taking the box, Eva studied the flowered wrapping paper. "It's beautiful paper. The roses are as red as your sports car. But my birthday isn't until next month. This is only May."

Maggie gave her father a perplexed look. "This is August."

"I need one of these." Eva pulled out a straw hat trimmed with berries and small flowers around the hatband. "I lost my last one on the beach when Mark pulled me in from the surf."

"Did you almost drown?" Dennis glanced at the ocean.

"Of course not. I know how to swim. I just got out a little too far. And I don't quite remember the rest. Except bodysurfing in." Eva shyly glanced at Mark, strutting back and forth across the deck, flipping the phone cord like a fishing line.

"Aunt Eva, try it on. I know you love straw hats and that one reminded me of your berry patch"

"It does." After slipping the hat on, Eva tied its strings under her chin. The tightness around her neck sparked a memory. *I wonder if I left my garden hat in the raspberry patch? Jim knocked it off when he grabbed me. He was so angry about something. It made no sense and ... and I don't remember what he wanted.*

~ 55 ~

"What about the blood and blond hair in Jim's bedroom?" Mark asked Detective Paul Galloway, now back at the Mansfield police department. The question of who had been in Jim's bedroom was nagging Mark. The answer was important to him. Mark had to know, one way or the other.

He turned away from Eva, sitting on the other side of the front deck talking to Maggie and Dennis. Mark held his breath, waiting for Detective Galloway's reply.

"No. ... It doesn't match Eva's hair sample and it's not her blood type," Mark repeated. Turning, he smiled at Eva, shyly glancing at him. "No, Paul, I didn't think Eva was ever in Jim's bedroom. So do you know who the blond hair belongs to?"

On the other end of the phone, Paul listed the possibilities.

"Well by now, Jim could have transported a body anywhere. Have you checked with the surrounding counties? ... No, I'm not telling you how to do your job. I'm just asking." Pacing in the sun, Mark felt the heat on his back.

"Listen, Paul. The National Insurance Agency will be calling you. They located the insurance policy Jim took out on Mary Jo Hicks. ... Got a pencil? Okay. According to the insurance reports, Mary Jo was killed in a one-car auto accident. Yep, you're right, mighty suspicious. Jim had a million dollar policy on Mary Jo. Right again, you can add insurance fraud to Jim's list of crimes."

Stepping back into the shade, Mark turned and watched Eva chatting with her brother and niece. Occasionally they all laughed.

It looks like Eva is enjoying talking to her niece and brother, Mark considered. *At least she has forgotten about Jim for a while.*

"Paul, the insurance investigators also located an old policy that Jim's father had on his mother. Yes, his mother died in a one-car auto accident and his father inherited half a million. No, Jim's parents had been married for sixteen years before she was killed. But that may be where Jimmy junior got the idea for his crime."

Paul rattled off his list of theories.

Leaning against the doorframe, Mark continued. "No, the insurance investigators haven't located a policy under Jim's alias of Hellmann. But give them some time. I just talked with them."

Waiting for Paul to finish talking, Mark studied Dennis. "I got the information through Eva's half-brother. He owns an insurance agency in Denver."

Mark turned away. "Paul, do me a favor. Check to see if Dennis has a life insurance policy on Eva. He may have a financial motive. There must be a reason he tracked down his half-sister after all these years."

A glint of light caught Mark's attention.

A spoon bounced on the deck. Eva reached for it.

"Paul, I'll call you back. Eva has had enough company for now. She's getting tired." With a click, the conversation ended.

Stepping closer, Mark watched Eva's eyelids blink slowly. *She's fighting to stay awake,* he thought. *They don't realize how easily Eva tires. Dennis has waited years to see his sister. Now he'll have to wait until she stronger. I won't have him tiring her.*

In the middle of a round of laughter, Mark stepped next to Eva. "Darling, you need to rest for a bit."

"He's right." Dennis scooted his chair back. "It's been a long day for everyone and we need to get back to our hotel."

Maggie gave Eva a big hug as they both got up. "Aunt Eva, I'm glad your alive. And I want you to know that, regardless of what Detective Galloway or others think, I have no reason to harm you." Maggie gave Mark a cold look. "I'm no aunt killer."

"I know, Maggie." Eva patted her niece's back. "You have no motive. You aren't a beneficiary in my will, so you wouldn't profit from my death."

"What do you mean?"

"You're not in my new will."

"But," Maggie's voice quivered. "I'm your only niece."

"That doesn't mean you'll inherit my estate." Eva glanced at Mark. "In my old will the university scholarship program and Princess were the main beneficiaries."

"But Princess is dead."

Eva reached into the nearby cardboard box and scooped out the two kittens. "But I now have two cats to look after and I plan to … well I hope. What I mean is, after I'm twenty-seven, I'll be free to get married, and of course my husband will then be my next of kin." Blushing, Eva looking up at Mark.

"Well." Maggie pulled back. "I thought I met more to you."

"You do. You're my favorite niece."

"I'm your only niece."

"You're more like a sister." Eva hugged Maggie. "I'll still be there for you. Besides, when you graduate, you'll be busy with a career and you'll have more than enough money."

"I didn't come all this way just for a handout, you know." Maggie flipped on her sunglasses.

"That's not what I meant." Eva rubbed her forehead. "Maybe I used the wrong word. My mind is still a little scrambled. I didn't mean to upset you. … I just didn't want you to think that I accused you of anything. You wouldn't profit from my death so why would you want to kill your Aunt Eva?"

~ 56 ~

"Watch out, Mom!" Mark pulled her aside. "Don't step in that with your bare feet."

Slipping on her sandals, Barbara stepped onto the deck from the beach walkway. Jagged shards of glass were strewn across the deck. "What happened?"

"I'm so sorry. I broke your water pitcher." Eva swept glass into a pile. *I have to be more careful*, Eva scolded herself.

Coating the deck, the shiny fragments sparkled like ice in the evening sunlight. The reddish deck beneath the glass reminded Eva of her dream. *Why do I keep dreaming of Siberia?* Eva wondered. *This broken glass looks like ice crystals. Why is there blood in my dream? I don't remember getting hurt. Or is that the accident I don't remember? No. The cold dream is just refreshing.*

"Careful, Eva, don't cut yourself." Barbara picked up pieces.

"I thought Mark could use some lemonade and a snack while he grades those final exams." Eva tossed sugar cookies into a trash sack. "But I put too much ice in the pitcher. It got top heavy."

"That pitcher was always unstable." Barbara pulled glass from under the card table. "I see you're almost done with your project."

Eva glanced at both the china doll's head and the picture puzzle she was working on while Mark graded test papers. *They both still have missing pieces like my mind,* she thought. *When I put them back together, they'll look ... what's the word? Unique?*

"Don't let a broken pitcher upset you." Barbara touched Eva's trembling hand. "I'm glad to be rid of it."

"I just don't like making a mess." Eva glanced back at the beach. The red car that had startled her was gone.

Bending over, Barbara held the dustpan. "That does it."

Eva corralled the last of the glass into the dustpan. "I'll wash the deck off. Do you have a garden hose?"

"No need."

"I insist. There was lots of sugar in that lemonade. You'll be invaded by ants if I don't wash it off. And I don't want Rex or the kittens to get any glass in their little paws." Eva picked up three lemon slices and tossed them into the dustpan. In the August sunlight, the ice cubes were melting into little puddles.

"I'll dispose of this and make us a new batch of lemonade. Fritz will get the garden hose for you." Barbara glanced at her son, rubbing his forehead. "Mark, can I get you an aspirin?"

"Make it two. Grading papers gives me a headache." Shaking his head, he checked a wrong answer on a student test paper.

"That's one thing nice about being an art teacher. No final exams to grade." Eva's voice seemed to float away with the soft evening breeze. *I don't think he heard me,* Eva mused. *Anyway, I shouldn't disturb Mark. I've distracted him enough, showering him with lemonade and glass. ... What got into me, anyway? It was just a flash of light off a car window. A red car. Why should that frighten me?*

At the deck railing, Eva studied the cars beyond the sand dunes. *I don't see anything dangerous out there. Just cars, people, and the ocean. ... Ocean. I think I'll sneak down there. I want to –*

"Don't even think about going swimming." Fritz dragged the garden hose over. A bucket of sudsy water plopped beside him.

"Who, me?" Grinning, Eva took the hose.

A spray of water showered the deck, scooting the last ice cube off the edge. With the broom, Fritz sloshed soapy water across the deck, staying clear of Mark's area. "Might as well give it a good clean. I've been thinking of giving it a new coat of paint."

"I'll help you. I love to paint." The idea of painting pleased her. *It's time I started helping out,* Eva thought. *I can't spend the rest of my life napping. And I have to find my childhood home. If the West Indies is gone, perhaps I can find Ocean Dunes. ... Then I need to get my own place. I can't burden Mark's parents forever.*

"Eva, why don't you rest for a bit?" Mark took the garden hose from her. "Dad and I will finish scrubbing the deck. I need a break from grading papers. Next term I'm switching from multiple guess to true false. That way they'll have a fifty-fifty chance of guessing the right answer."

"Sometimes there's more than one right answer." Eva picked up Mark's test papers and looked at the lounge chair, remembering snuggling there with Mark the night before. "After dinner we –"

"Eva," Barbara called from the door. "You have a phone call."

Mark turned. "Mom, who is it?"

"It's her niece."

"This may take a few minutes. Maggie is a bit long-winded." Eva took the test papers and the china doll with her.

Inside, Eva settled into a living room chair for a long chat. But the phone conversation with Maggie was unusually brief. *Is Maggie still upset about what I said?* Eva hung up the phone. *Or am I making too much of her not coming out to see me in the morning. After all, at her age going out with a few college athletes has to be more fun than visiting a sick aunt.*

Walking back out to the deck, Eva watched Mark's muscles ripple as he moved heavy deck furniture. *I wonder if Mark was a college athlete. Football perhaps. He sure has the build for it.*

"Watch it." Mark took her arm as she stepped onto the deck. "Dad got carried away with the suds."

With a grin, Fritz sloshed more soap on the decking. "I got to get all this salt glaze off if I'm going to paint. Mark, get that area rinsed before the sun dries it."

The patter of four large paws announced Rex's arrival. With a series of barks, he dashed towards the bucket of soapsuds.

Mark squirted water at his dog. "Rex. Don't –"

It was too late. Rex snatched the rope handle. Soap splattered.

"Put that down!" Mark grinned mischievously.

Rex growled and his tail wagged. With the bucket's rope between his teeth, he backed away, feet sliding on the soapy deck.

Quickly, Fritz stepped to the front door. "Eva, if I were you, I'd head for the hills. When the two of them get into a game of keep-away, there's no telling what will happen. And with a bucket of suds, you're apt to get drenched."

"I think I'll watch." Eva stepped to a neutral looking spot.

"Mark, give that dog a good bath." Fritz closed the door.

Rex dashed towards the deck's steps.

Racing forward, Mark blasted a stream of water under Rex.

Paws slid in different directions. Scrambling for stability, Rex dropped the bucket. Suds splattered skyward.

Mark slipped. Water sprayed in the air.

The hose dropped and snaked back and forth on its own.

Eva grabbed for Mark. It was too late.

Mark slid towards his dog, sprawled in a pile of suds.

Laughing, Eva grabbed the hose. "Shower time."

Rex looked at his master.

Mark nodded.

Legs scrambled. "She's it."

"What?" Eva dropped the hose.

Before she could turn, Rex dashed between her legs. His body resembled a soapy body brush fresh from a bubble bath. "Rex!"

Soapy fur tickled her legs, blue sky swirled above her, and strong arms grabbed for her.

"Eva!"

Laughing, all three crumpled onto the deck, sliding towards the bucket and a soapy doom. Splat. A wave of soapy water crested over the bucket, falling towards them. The yellow suds resembled sea foam during a northeaster but not as tasty.

"Rex, you didn't wash behind your ears." Still laughing, Eva grabbed the sponge.

His bark seemed to object and Rex slithered towards the steps.

"No, you don't. You're not running through the sand with all that soap." In a grand slide straight for the stairs, Mark tackled his slippery dog

"Mark." Eva grabbed his waist. "The stairs."

Like sliding across an icy road, there was no traction, no stopping, and no guardrails.

A yap of surprise followed Rex's slide off the steps. All three of them tumbled into the sand, dusting them like sugar cookies.

"Rex, look what you've done." Mark joked, sprawled in the sand. "Bad dog."

Rex whined for sympathy.

"Poor boy." Smiling, Eva brushed sand off Mark's chest. Her hands rippled across his strong muscles and she whipped sand from this hands that had caressed her so lovingly the night before. "Does this game have a name?"

"Rex was playing keep-away. But your game is come-hither."

"Which game do you prefer?" Eva snuggled closer.

With bodies intertwined, a roll sideways took them below the deck and out of sight. Salty kisses joined their lips. Sandy touching down wet soapy bodies intensified the pleasure of their contact.

"That feels good." Her lips whispered in his ear. His hands sliding across her slippery skin sent delightful tingles rippling through her body. Longing for more her hand slipped down his back, pulling him closer. Mark responded to Eva's encouragement.

Beyond the dunes, a flock of seagulls took flight.

Stretched out in the sand, Rex was uninterested in the new game of come-hither. It was not a game for three.

The sound of metal sliding against metal rolled over the dunes.

Rex's ears perked up. His jaw quivered. His head snapped left, aiming at the sand dunes and the beach beyond. Rex growled.

"What is it, Rex? Do you see a land crab?" Mark glanced left.

Rex hopped to his feet, snarling.

"Eva, stay down." Mark got up and slowly scanned the dunes.

Standing up, Eva tucked in her blouse. "What's wrong?"

"It's nothing." Mark winked at her. "I think we should finish this game." With a fast scoop, Mark hoisted Rex over his head and carried his squirming dog back onto the deck. Water squirted over fur, caked with sand and soap.

While they weren't looking, Eva grabbed the hose. "Next!"

Water showered over Mark. Startled, he let go of Rex.

"It's not over yet." As he pulled her body next to his, Mark squirted them with the hose. Cool water showered both of them. Soap ran down their skin like a silky bubble bath. And grains of sand slipped past, bumping into hair follicles, sending a tingling sensation in waves of excitement. Laughter roared.

He washed sand out of her blond hair.

Eva watched his sea-blue eyes and when their stares locked, she kissed him. It was shy and simple but blood rushed to her face, feeling hotter than her fever ever had. *Is this love?* Eva wondered. *Should I tell him how I feel? Is it too soon to use that word? Love.*

Mark's strong arms pulled her closer. "Eva, I love you."

~ 57 ~

Love. Eva blushed at the thought. *I love you. How can Mark say that? He's only known me for ... how many days? I'm not sure. I know women fall in love at first sight, but do men?*

"Eva, you look a little flushed. Are you okay?" Mark poured more iced tea into her glass.

Eva smiled. "Just a touch of sun."

On the other side of the dining room table, Fritz and Barbara exchanged silent glances. The evening meal was later than usual. Cleaning up after scrubbing the deck took longer than necessary. In fact, the whole front end of the house had become a casualty of splashing suds and the pursuing water fight with two garden hoses. Rex helped with water splashing from his keep-away bucket.

"Everything looks well scrubbed." Fritz chuckled, glancing at his son, Eva, and Rex. "I've never seen the deck that clean."

In their corner box, the kittens quietly licked their fur.

Barbara grinned. "It's a good head start on the fall cleaning."

"Fall?" Eva looked up. "I haven't even celebrated Memorial Day or my birthday."

"What do you on your birthdays?" Mark asked.

"I generally go down to Amish country for the weekend. I enjoy sketching and painting my watercolors directly from nature." Eva glanced out the clean front windows. Beyond the sand dunes, the ocean sparkled in the last rays of sunlight. "I wonder what salt water would do to a watercolor painting. Table salt creates some interesting patterns, but I've never tired using ocean water."

"Where did ... where were you going for your birthday this year?" Mark buttered his corn bread.

Eva stirred sugar into her iced tea. "I signed up for a watercolor seminar in Amish country. You can't do portraits of their faces but buggies and barns make interesting compositions."

"I thought the Amish all lived in Pennsylvania," Fritz said.

"Actually in north central Ohio we have more Amish than they do." Eva looked at Mark's clean-shaven face. *No beard is a sign of an unmarried man. An eligible bachelor,* she mused. *And with his strong arm, he'd have no trouble running a farm. Lots of animals, fields of wheat and soybeans.* Eva rubbed her forehead, easing the pounding inside her skull. The memory of sitting in the soybean field after her auto accident was gone, only her muscles remembered the pain.

"Is your headache back?" Barbara asked.

"I'm fine. I was thinking about the beach." Eva studied her dinner plate. On it a mound of mashed potatoes with melted butter running down it reminded her of Dennis. "My brother used most of his chemistry set making sand volcanoes on the beach."

Mark looked up. "I didn't know Dennis was into chemistry."

"Mom gave him a chemistry set for Christmas. Dennis eagerly mixed a little of everything together. But after setting his bedroom drapes on fire making gunpowder, my dad dumped all the chemicals out. Dennis was so mad at my dad that he packed up and went to live with his own father in Denver."

Mark leaned closer. "Tell me some more about Dennis and –"

The ringing of the phone interrupted.

"That's probably Maggie. She said she'd call tonight." After turning, Eva grabbed the cordless phone behind her. "Hello."

There was silence on the other end.

"Hello?"

Silence.

Mark picked up the receiver. "Hello. ... Hello!" Mark hung up. "Probably one of those telemarketing auto-dialers. Most of the time you get nothing."

"I wish they wouldn't call during dinner hour." Barbara spooned out mixed fruit into individual dishes. "Mark, sit down and eat your dessert. If it's anything important, they'll call back."

With a lull in the conversation, Eva's thoughts returned to Mark's words playing over and over in her head, like a beautiful song repeating. *I love you. He said 'I love you.' ... Mark caught me off guard. I didn't know what to say. I should have said something. One kiss couldn't tell him how I feel.*

With her fork, Eva etched a heart in her slice of watermelon. *I should have told Mark I love him.* Her mind toyed with that thought. *It's like the cat got my tongue. I don't know why. I felt like this ever since he woke me on the sand dune, it ... it was love at first sight. But that's not right. That's not the first time I saw Mark. He doesn't remember, but I do.*

"Eva, would you like some more dessert?" Barbara's voice seemed far away, although she was sitting across the table. "Eva, you're so quiet this evening. Is something wrong?"

At the bottom of the slice of watermelon, Eva toyed with a seed, smaller than a dime. "I was remembering a friend's birthday party. We were sitting at a big table and we carefully cut into our cake. It was a very special cake. At the bottom of each slice there was a treasure. ... Money wrapped in waxed paper."

Barbara's fork hit her plate. "Oh my God!"

"Barbara?" Fritz looked at his wife. "What's wrong?"

"Susan's birthday cake. I put money in the bottom of each slice for her party. She wanted a treasure cake for her twelfth birthday." Barbara took a deep breath. "I was terrified one of her girlfriends would swallow a coin."

"I don't think we could have swallowed a fifty cent piece." Eva held up a slice of watermelon that size. "Even an adult would be hard put to swallow something that large. Besides, by the time we chopped through our cake looking for money there wasn't anything left but a pile of crumbs."

Barbara twirled a large chunk of watermelon with her fork. "I watched y'all eat like a mother hawk. By the time your plates were clean, I was a nervous wreck. I never did that again. And I don't think we had any more slumber parties. With twelve girls under one roof, no one got any sleep."

"Mark did." Fritz chuckled. "If I remember rightly, he stayed with one of his friends."

"I went to Tommy's for the duration," Mark chuckled.

Barbara smiled. "Eva, were you at our Susan's party?"

Eva nodded. Fond memories floated through her mind and she didn't notice the stares from Barbara, Fritz, or even Mark. For her the sound of three words washed away the world. *I love you. That's such a pretty sound. So soft and blue like Mark's eyes. Even back then, his eyes were enchanting. He was a little more mischievous then but definitely not interested in his sister's little school friends. We all tried to impress Susan's big brother but none of us caught his eye. Ocean eyes, his sister called them.*

An anxious ring interrupted the calm.

"I'll get it." Mark grabbed the phone. "Hello. ... Hello! Oh, it's you. ... Paul, did you call earlier? ... No. Hang on a second. I want to use the regular phone."

After handing the cordless phone to his father, Mark picked up the living room phone and dragged it out on the deck, stopping when it ran out of cord.

Fritz clicked off the receiver. "So, Eva, you've been here before? At one of our daughter's birthday parties?"

"Things have changed." Eva looked around the room. "But I remember the cake. I had never seen a cake with money in it. We thought it was neat to find treasure in our food. By the time we girls got done, there wasn't any cake left for Susan's big brother." Eva watched Mark pacing on the deck, flipping the phone cord.

"Mark was always nuts about cake." Barbara spooned more watermelon on to Eva's dish. "German chocolate is his favorite."

"That birthday cake was angel food with colored candy bits. I thought they looked like little rainbow tears." Eva's smile beamed. "It was a beautiful cake. Treasure in a rainbow cake."

Studying Mark, a rush of warmth mixed with his treasured words repeating in Eva's mind. *I love you.*

~ 58 ~

"What do you mean, Jim got away!" Mark stopped at the edge of the deck. The phone cord back to the living room was stretched taught. On the other end of the conversation, Detective Paul Galloway's voice was just as tight.

"Mansfield isn't that big. You should have found him by now. Well, if you got Jim's car, he should still be around." Turning, Mark watched his mother in the living room retrieve an album from the bookcase and show it to Eva.

"Did you check with the airlines and bus depot? ... No, I'm not telling you your job. What about car rental companies? ... The man who owned the storage locker remembered seeing Jim in a red sports car. Yes, I know most sports cars are red. Could it have been Maggie's car?" Glancing back at the beach, Mark studied the cars slowly cruising up and down it, all looking grayish in the twilight.

"Whose car? ... Mary Jo's. Jim's deceased wife? I thought she died in her car. No." Mark flipped the phone's cord, listening to how Jim's wife had died in an auto accident in Jim's old car, not Mary Jo's red sports car. "Whose niece? ... Mary Jo's niece reported her aunt's car stolen. That could be how Jim got away. What's the license plate number? You found them. You're right, Jim must have switched the plate."

A tan chameleon scurried up the porch post and rested on the railing. Its little body turned a dark reddish color blending with the deck. After snatching a small bug, the chameleon scampered back into the sand, fading back to shades of tan.

"No, I'm not on a cordless phone, so you can talk. Come on, Paul, level with me. What else did you find in the storage locker?"

Mark glanced inside. Eva's back was to him but her blond hair sparkled under the dining room chandelier. "There was no body in the storage locker, just more blond hair and a chemical laboratory. Yes, you told me Jim has a degree in chemistry."

Patiently, Mark listened to Paul's long list of possibilities.

Again, the chameleon scurried onto the deck, snatched another evening bug and hightailed it back to safety. The hungry lizard finished his meal on a pile of sand, resembling a little volcano.

"Paul, I found out that Dennis had an interest in chemistry. Did you check him out?" Mark still had mixed feelings about Eva's half-brother. "How much did he inherit from his mother's estate? Half. ... I know that's not much, but that was fifteen years ago. Does Dennis have a life insurance policy on Eva?"

Sitting on the railing, Mark continued. "He does, through his insurance company. Maggie is the beneficiary. Then you can't rule them out as suspects. Yes, I'm telling you how to do your job."

Mark held the receiver away from his ear. From Mark's past experience as a Secret Service agent, he knew the local police don't like outsiders telling them how to run their departments. After a few minutes, Paul's voice quieted.

"Sorry, I didn't mean to meddle, but I have to protect Eva. How long has Jim been missing? ... Well, he could have driven down here in twenty-four hours." Sitting on the railing, Mark glanced back at the beach. A few headlights passed but it was now too dark to see the shapes of the cars, let alone distinguish their color.

"How much did Jim inherit from Mary Jo?" Mark hoped that would prove Jim's guilt. "Nothing! ... Nothing? But what about the life insurance policy? Who? ... Mary Jo's niece inherited everything. It sounds like Jim is getting careless. He should have checked his second wife's last will before he killed her. Yes, I know you haven't proved that yet."

After pawing the screen door open, Rex dashed into the sand, hot on the trail of the startled chameleon dashing into the sea oats.

"You might as well come on down. Your suspects are either here or will be shortly. Sure, you can stay with me." Mark touched his side where his old Secret Service pistol was clipped. They had given it to him when he left. "Yes, I have a gun. Eva will be safe with me. ... What flight? Delta 1129. Then you should get here about 11:30. Good, I'll pick you up."

Mark watched a figure backing out the screen door. "Eva will be fine. My father will guard the house. Yes, he taught me how to shoot." After Paul hung up, Mark put down the phone.

As Fritz strolled across the deck, his sandals squeaked. "I thought I'd sneak out before I got corralled into helping with the dishes. I've already got dishpan hands from scrubbing the deck."

"I didn't think we'd ever get the soap rinsed off. How much of that liquid stuff did you put in the bucket?"

Fritz chuckled, rubbing Rex's ears. "The whole bottle. I don't mess around when I scrub the decks. I was going to add a little water but Rex, here, snatched it away. I forgot it was his bucket."

Mark watched his mom in the living room, wiping her eyes when Eva turned away. "How's Mom taking it?"

"Taking what?"

"When Eva mentioned the birthday cake with coins, Mom dropped her fork. I've never seen her that startled. Is Mom upset because Eva knew our Susan?"

"Goodness no. There's no reason to be upset with Eva because of what happened to Susan." Fritz watched his wife, inside, flipping pages of a photo album. "Your mom was just surprised anyone remembered a birthday cake she made over fifteen years ago. That cake must have made quite an impression on Eva."

Mark studied his dad's face, his forehead wrinkled with fatherly concern. "What's troubling you?"

"Eva has good memories of her childhood here. But she seems to forget what she did a few hours ago."

"Mom said we shouldn't worry. Eva will recover." Mark turned and joined his dad looking at the ocean and the sliver of light from the new moon. "We need to give Eva a little time and all the help she needs. Remember, Dad, viral encephalitis isn't like the flu. You don't get well overnight or even in a few weeks."

"I know. I've read all those Internet articles you printed." Fritz looked down. "A few of those true life stories were frightening. Some of those folks were never the same again."

Mark glanced back at the house. Eva and his mom were clearing the dining room table and taking things to the kitchen. "It doesn't matter to me. I like Eva the way she is."

"Like? Isn't that the wrong word?" Fritz nudged his son.

"Do you remember the first time you saw Mom?"

"Yes, indeed. That was a star-studded event. I was jogging across campus to my history class when I spotted Barbara. She was a knock-out in that little student nurse's uniform. She just caught my eye. Then she did it."

"Did what?"

"Barbara's eyes locked onto mine and she smiled ever so coyly. I couldn't take my eyes off her but I continued to jog on down the sidewalk. Didn't want to be late for my history final." Fritz laughed. "Never made it."

"So you stopped to talk to Mom."

"It was more like a sudden stop. Very sudden." Fritz rubbed a small scar on his forehead. "The sidewalk turned. I didn't. I jogged right into the light pole. Smacked it a good one. Everything went dark except for the stars. Next thing I remember was looking up at the students walking by and laughing at me. Then I saw Barbara kneeling beside me, bandaging my cut forehead with her scarf. Her blue eyes looked so beautiful with stars floating around them."

"When did you fall in love with Mom?"

"The moment I saw her." Fritz's voice grew mellow. "Every time I stare into your mother's eyes, I sort of still see those stars."

Mark looked up. The stars twinkled and the moon hung low, keeping the ocean company with a ribbon of light joining them.

Fritz looked at his son's eyes, as blue as his wife's. "I hope your intentions for Eva are honorable."

Mark mused over his father's old-fashioned phrase. "Dad, I would never take advantage of Eva."

"Good. Your mom wouldn't approve of anyone hurting a friend of Susan. And I'm still strong enough to box your ears." Fritz gave his son a friendly punch.

"Yep, I know. That's the only time I saw stars." Mark chuckled, remembering the time he forgot to duck when his dad was teaching him how to box. "I've learned how to duck a blow. … And speaking of bowing out. I think you should take Mom away for a while. I don't want either of you in danger."

"Only a direct hit from a hurricane would get me to leave and your mom won't go either. I've already tried. So we're staying." After straightening his back, Fritz patted the bulge under his shirt. "Besides, you need some help defending the home front."

Mark glanced at his father's snub-nosed revolver. "Help's on the way. Detective Galloway is coming in on the late flight from Ohio. I'm going to pick Paul up about eleven-thirty. Can you watch the fort for half an hour?"

"No problem, partner. I've read enough western novels to know how to protect my homestead and the women folk."

"Hope they had a few chapters on what to do with the city slickers from back east." Mark continued in a more serious tone. "I have no idea what this Jim character is going to do. But so far he hasn't left any witnesses alive."

Turning, Fritz watched his wife closing the drapes. "I don't think Eva's testimony could put Jim behind bars for very long."

"But Dad, he doesn't know that. Jim only knows Eva is alive and he believes she knows something incriminating. It's what Jim thinks Eva knows that puts her life in danger."

Fritz patted his side. "Maybe you should have Eva get her gun out of the bank vault."

"No. No gun for Eva. It would be too dangerous."

"What?"

"Dad, think about it. Sometimes Eva wakes confused from her nightmares. It takes a few minutes for her to realize where she is. If she reaches for a gun after a bad dream, she might shoot anyone walking into her bedroom. If I gave Eva a gun I could be putting Mom's and your life in danger."

"What about Eva's life?"

"I'll protect her." A sharp pain in his chest reminded Mark of his sister's stabbing. *Rex and I both carry wounds from that knife,* he thought. *It severed a nerve in Rex's leg, ending his days as a police dog. And that knife severed my confidence. How could I trust myself to protect the President and his family? What good is a Secret Service agent that can't even save his own sister?*

Mark patted Rex, trying to stop the thoughts. But they rolled on. *After Susan died, I buried myself in teaching. Thought I'd forgotten about that emptiness until I found Eva sleeping on the sand dunes. Having Eva around makes me feel alive again. I don't want to lose her.*

"Mark, you'll need help protecting Eva. Trying to do it alone is too dangerous." Fritz put his hand on his son's shoulder. "I couldn't bear to lose you, too."

~ 59 ~

Without warning, a blast shattered the silence. A flash of light blinded her. Struggling to move, Eva's heart pounded but her body lay cold and motionless.

Only her eyelids flickered, horrified by the vision playing out in the virtual reality of her mind. In a battle of its own, her brain was burning hot in an attempt to kill the virus still lurking there. Each night her body prepared a potent mix of chemicals and heat; its weapon designed for the viral encephalitis still playing havoc with her mind. Time was running out. It had to be killed soon.

In her bed, Eva was curled like a kitten, looking peaceful from the outside. But inside was the violence of lioness fighting to save her cubs. To keep up with the battle, her blood supply had only one critical destination, the brain cells, and one mission, destroy the virus. All other organs waited, almost paralyzed.

Timing the battle was critical. If it lasted too long, parts of her mind would be destroyed from the heat. If too short, the virus would survive.

The flash of light faded and the silence returned. Eva's body remained motionless, but her mind raced, focusing on images, more real than life. Her mind slipped into a unique dimension.

Was that a gunshot? Now what? How'd I get here? Eva questioned the new image. *I was just walking through an Ohio soybean field; there was a flash of light, a shot. Swirls of red.*

Now I'm here again. But that's okay. This is my lovely Siberian dream. It's the only place I can escape the heat.

The blue summer blanket slipped from her shoulders. Eva's hands grew icy cold. Her body remained frozen in a dream.

There it is! Her thoughts recognized the image. *The Ice Palace is so beautiful in the sunlight. So sparkling and cheerful. If I could only move, I could get there. Once I reach it, it will be over. It shouldn't be long now.*

Wind whistled by her ears as she lay on the frozen tundra. Above the endless white landscape, the pale sun slipped above the flat horizon and seemed to pause. A figure walked from its light. His long black coat flapped in the cold breeze. Snow crunched beneath his boots.

He's so handsome. And he walks with such determination, always straight for me. But where's his hat? He had it on the last time. I told Mark to wear his hat in this dream.

Why is Mark in such a hurry? Is something wrong? Yes. I can feel it.

There's someone behind me, he's wheezing.

What's that?... Sounds like metal sliding against metal.

Now a click.

Who's there?

A gun slid beside her head and aimed at Mark who was still walking towards her. Mark's hand reached to his side. But it was too late. A blast and a flash erupted from the gun barrel beside Eva's head.

Mark!

The scream ripped through her mind but her lips were paralyzed. Eva could not stop the dream.

Eva watched Mark's body crumple into a snowdrift. His hand reached for her, Mark's blue eyes closed, and his head sank into the snow. With another hot flash, the blue sky and the blood red snow melted. A horrifying wave of purple rolled towards Eva, cresting and crashing over her, smacking her chest.

Breathless, Eva woke from her nightmare. *I'm not breathing! I can't feel my heart. ... I'm not breathing. I have to take a breath!* Fear flashed hot in her brain. A surge of adrenaline rushed through her veins, jumpstarting her heartbeat, expanding her lungs. Gasping for air, Eva sat up.

Beside her bed, Rex was nudging Eva. His big, brown eyes stared at her. Whines for attention reverberated with an animal awareness of another creature's distress.

"I'm okay." Eva gasped for air. "Really I'm ... I'm still alive. I think." As she petted, Rex, his attention was comforting. Eva's heart settled into a normal rhythm, but her mind bounced with odd thoughts. "Good boy. Give me a minute. I feel a little seasick from all the yucky colors swirling in my head. Shades of purple."

Rex growled.

"Smart dog. You understand the feeling of that color. Most humans don't." Eva glanced at the night-light. "Did you know magenta light can produce an intoxicating feeling in people? Don't look at me like that Rex. ... It's true. And certain flashing red lights can trigger seizures in some individuals. Parts of our mind are color sensitive. Every artist knows that." Eva closed her eyes, thinking quiet thoughts: a sparkling blue sky, the warm water at the inlet, and Mark's soft blue eyes.

Rex tugged at the sheet.

"All right. I'll get up." Slipping out of bed, Eva wrapped the blue sheet blanket around her shoulders for comfort. "Come on, Rex. I need a cup of tea and some toast to settle my nerves. That's the second time that dream turned violent. It's always been my favorite. So beautiful, white, and refreshingly cold."

After tiptoeing down the hall, the two of them slipped into the kitchen. The nightlight was all she needed to pop two pieces of bread in the toaster, heat a cup of water in the microwave for tea, and retrieve the box of dog biscuits from the cupboard.

"Come on Rex, let's eat in the dining room. We don't want to wake anyone. It's only –" Eva glanced at the kitchen clock. "Well, almost four. We don't want to wake them in the middle of the night, morning, whatever."

After ambling into the dining room, Eva quietly rested the tray on the table and made Rex beg for his dog bone. "Good boy. That will make you feel better. I hope I didn't frighten you." With her hand shaking, Eva stirred sugar into her tea. "Although I must admit that last dream got to me. I don't understand what happened, it's such a beautiful dream. Why the sudden weird ending? There shouldn't be any purple in my blue and white dream."

Outside the porch light was still on and its soft glow streamed in the dining room. Rex curled by the door and munched his dog biscuit. In the early hours of the morning, the house was silent. Even the kittens were fast asleep in their box.

At Mark's place at the table, the family photo album had been left open. Retrieving it, Eva studied the group pictures. "Susan's twelfth birthday party. It was the only slumber party I ever went to. There were twelve of us. Giggling girls. We had such fun."

Eva studied the bottom photo on the page. In it were twelve young girls, grinning for the camera. Mark's sister, Susan, sat in front of her gifts, holding one of the fifty-cent pieces pulled from the bottom of the treasure cake. Behind her were eleven friends. In the photo, a short skinny girl with blond hair looked towards the window with a shy grin. A blurred image of a young teenage boy stood outside, holding up a string of the fish for his father.

"Mark." Eva smiled at the image. "I think he wanted to swap his fish for a slice of the treasure cake."

Rex pawed at the door.

"I don't think you're supposed to go out this early. That door alarm gizmo is on. See, the red light is blinking."

Rex continued to whine and scratch at the door.

"Okay. Give me a minute to figure out how to turn it off. It's not like the one I have back home." Tinkering with the house security alarm, Eva glanced at the faint image of the sand dunes illuminated by the porch light.

"Home," she mumbled. "I wonder how far Ocean Dunes is from here? Now that Fritz has fixed my bike, I could ride up South Atlantic Avenue. I have the feeling my old home is north of here. It's near that old beacon but maybe it's gone too."

Whining, Rex scratched at the door.

"Okay. Give me a minute. This thing looks like a time bomb. I don't want it exploding in my face and I don't want to wake anyone." Eva punched a series of buttons. Finally, the alarm light stopped flashing.

"There. That did it. Now we can sneak out."

As the door swung open, the timer light blinked.

"Don't run away."

Rex dashed across the front deck and into the sand.

A frantic land crab scampered towards its hole.

Eva stepped into the night. "I wonder if I can find it?"

Her blue blanket fell across the threshold.

The door failed to close.

On the delayed timer, the number nine glowed in red.

A minute later, the number eight appeared.

The alarm warning light began to flash.

Fast red blinks.

~ 60 ~

"What the …" Mark jumped out of bed. A red light flashed. An alarm blared. Mark grabbed his gun. Adrenaline rushed into his blood. He slammed open his apartment door. A quick dash across the deck and he was at his parents' back door.

Two steps behind him, Detective Paul Galloway pulled the slide on his gun, readying it for action. "What was that?"

"The alarm on the living room door was triggered." Quickly, Mark unlocked the back door. "Be careful, my folks and Eva will be asleep."

"But the alarm –"

"I set it to ring only in my quarters." Inside, Mark rushed down the hall towards the bedrooms. His gun was raised, aimed at the ceiling for safety.

Paul followed, his gun poised.

The only sound was their footsteps.

Mark paused outside the second bedroom door, hoping Eva was sleeping safely inside. He was afraid he had failed Eva and his thoughts raced. *Who opened the front door? Did Jim break in? Is he in Eva's room? I'll kill him if he hurts her.*

With his ear to the door, Mark listened for the voice of an intruder. There was no man's voice. There was no sound at all.

Stepping to the other side, Paul nodded he was ready.

Slowly opening the door, Mark glanced inside. The nightlight dimly illuminated the bedroom. He looked for Eva. The covers were in a heap. But the bed was empty.

"Eva's gone." Mark glanced towards the dining room.

A soft slapping, like sails in the wind, echoed down the hall.

Mark pointed.

Paul nodded.

With guns raised, both headed towards the noise.

At the hall archway, they paused.

Mark stepped into the dining area, his eyes scanning the room.

The living room drapes flapped in the breeze. Light streamed in the open door. Soft blue fabric lay on the floor.

"Eva's blanket," Mark whispered, picking it up. "She must have gone outside."

"At this hour?" Paul hesitated. "Careful. Jim could have her."

Mark's chest tightened, his thoughts ran cold. *Jim better not hurt Eva. If he even gets near her, I'll —*

"Mark. Don't let your emotions get in the way."

"Never." Mark stepped onto the deck.

There was no sign of Eva. Yellow light washed over the deck chairs, creating an eerie effect.

Stepping off the deck, Mark looked for footprints on the old wooden walkway to the beach. There were none. But there were faint tracks in the sand and a streak mark like a body had been dragged away. Staying off the squeaky wooden walk, Mark followed. The yellow porch light faded beyond the deck. In the distance, red taillights flashed from a car stopped on the beach.

Pointing, Mark whispered. "Over there. Something moved."

"I'll take the right flank." With a nod, Paul stepped sideways through the sand, heading around the sand dune.

Keeping low, Mark followed the tracks towards the beach. Near the flagpole, behind the last dune, a strange noise swished. Sounds of digging and the thud of sand hitting sand rustled the night air. *Something is being buried.* Images flashed in Mark's mind. *That's where I found Eva. Sleeping beside her bike. Her little body was so still I almost thought she was dead.*

A clump of sand flopped over the sand dune. A fragment of an old bone tumbled down the slope, stopping beside Mark's foot. Crouching low, he slipped around a clump of sea oats. In the dim light, something moved south of the flagpole.

Paul's head popped over the far dune, his gun pointed at the moving shadows.

Stepping around the north end, Mark aimed his gun at the half buried image. A beach towel ended the streak through the sand. Something round, the size of a head, lay beneath it.

More sand flipped from the hole. A squatting figure heaved sand out. A smaller shadow struggled in the pit. Reaching for the towel, the figure sat up. Dim light streaked across the face.

"Eva!"

"Mark!" Startled, Eva pulled back.

Growling, Rex leaped out of the dark pit.

"What on earth are you doing?" Mark lowered his gun.

"Digging." Crouching lower, Eva whispered into Rex's ear. "Pirates. Armed pirates. They're after our treasure."

Rex snarled, but his tail wagged like in a game of keep-away.

"I can see you're digging. But why?"

"We're looking for buried treasure." Her voice faded.

Paul walked in from the other side. "What's wrong?"

Barking, Rex lunged at Paul.

"Whoa there, killer. I'm on your side. I'm a cop. Remember?" Paul backed up, hands held up in surrender.

"Easy boy. They're not really pirates." Eva pulled Rex back and sheepishly looked up at Mark. "It's too early to go fishing. And fishing poles would be better than those guns. So why are you guys prowling around in the middle of the night?"

"The living room door alarm was triggered." Mark put his gun back in its holster. "We thought someone broke in or that —" He paused. *Eva looks frightened enough*, he thought. *No need to say anything about Jim right now. And having two men leap from behind the sand dunes, aiming guns at her, must have been terrifying. Even Rex was ready to rip my leg off.*

Mark sat down beside her. "Eva, what are you doing out here alone at this hour?"

"I'm not alone." Eva petted Rex. "He needed to go out."

"But why are you digging in the middle of the night?"

"Oh." Shyly cringing, Eva looked at the sizable hole beside her. "Rex chased a land crab over here. It ducked down a hole and Rex started digging for it."

Keeping his eye on Rex, Paul squatted beside the depression. "Mighty big hole for a little crab."

"Something spooked the crab." Eva glanced at the beach. A car pulled away. "It hightailed it north."

"If the crab ran away, what are you digging for?" Paul reached into the dark sand pit.

"Treasure. Buried treasure." Eva grinned.

Mark felt her forehead. "Were you dreaming about treasure?"

"It's no dream. Looking at those old photos, I remembered we buried our treasure twelve feet south of the flagpole."

Glancing back at the flagpole, Paul shook his head. "This is a tad too far away for twelve feet."

"We took giant footsteps." Eva put her small, bare foot beside Mark's shoe.

"Our feet? I'm afraid I don't understand." Mark watched Eva, wondering if her viral encephalitis was flaring up.

"Really guys, I'm not crazy." Eva crossed her legs Indian style as she sat in the sand. "At your sister's birthday party, we saved the fifty cent pieces from her treasure cake. We all put our coins in a box along with one personal item. Susan insisted we bury our treasure chest on the beach. So, late that night, we snuck outside."

"Sounds like my sister. Susan was always reading adventure stories. *Treasure Island* was one of her favorites." Mark glanced back at the house. Although it had aged, the memories of his childhood and his little sister were fresh.

From under the beach towel, Rex pulled out his keep-away bucket and dragged it into the hole.

"Okay, Rex. I get the hint." Mark took the bucket and scooped out sand. "How deep did you bury that treasure chest?"

"We put it really deep so no one would find it except us." Eva stretched out her right leg. "It was knee deep."

Mark looked at the shapely calf of her leg. Even at twenty-seven her legs were short. At twelve, deep would have been less. "Knee deep. Well, I guess that would have been nine inches."

"Detectives use a more scientific approach." Paul walked to the flagpole and paced off mini steps. "The foot of a twelve year old is about half the size of mine. That would make it about here. Give me that little shovel."

Eva handed over a garden spade.

Rex stretched out on the sand, watching.

"We'll just watch them dig." She patted Rex.

The shallow hole Eva and Rex had made became a long trench heading back towards the flagpole and then it became wider.

Clang. Paul's shovel hit a hard object.

With the bucket, Mark scooped sand out. "Concrete. Oh no. I forgot. Dad moved the flagpole. A northeaster toppled it and Mom had him move it a little north so she could put a gazebo here."

"Now you tell us." Paul wiped sweat from his forehead and paced off twelve more mini steps, stopping near Eva's shallow hole. Now they dug towards it.

"Maybe the pirates already found the treasure." Eva grinned. "We could be wasting our time. You might not be able to find it."

Mark and Paul exchanged determined looks.

"We've come this far, we might as well finish." Paul shoveled more sand aside. "A good detective doesn't leave any stones or, in this case, grains of sand, unturned."

"Anyway, Mom's been wanting Dad to build that gazebo out here. This will make a nice foundation ditch." Mark chuckled, looking at the sandy trench. "As long as Dad gets it built before the next sand storm, he'll be cool."

Beside the trench, swishing sand flopped into manmade dunes. After sniffing, Rex hopped in, digging with his paws.

Clang. Paul's shovel stopped. "How many times did your dad move that flagpole?"

"Only once." Mark brushed sand back. White plastic covered a buried object. "I think we've hit pay dirt."

With a flurry of digging hands, a box was freed from the sand.

Pulling the plastic off, Mark stared at the rusting treasure chest. "That's my old fishing tackle box."

Eva brushed sand off the top. "The treasure chest is inside. We didn't want to it to get dirty."

Mark tugged at the lid, rusted shut. "It's going to take a crowbar to get this baby open."

"Nope. Just a little persuasion." Paul pulled out his gun.

"Don't shoot it." Eva gasped.

With a thud, the gun butt hit the side. Rust fell. Another whack and Mark pulled it open.

"That's it. Our treasure chest." Eva pulled out a cigar box. "See, we all traced our hands on the wrapping paper."

Mark watched Eva touching one handprint colored sky blue. The name Eva was printed across its palm. *She seems thrilled at finding that box. It must bring back fond memories,* Mark mused. *Twelve must have been a happy time in her life. How am I going to tell her that Jim is hunting her? I hate to tell her the bad news and break this little magic spell. But she has to know. Soon.*

"This is our treasure box." Eva carefully removed the childish wrapping paper. Her eyes sparkled like the stars above and her silky pajamas rippled in the gentle sea breeze. Beyond them, the waves lapped against the beach with a measured rhythm.

Slowly, Eva pulled out an old cigar box. Its foil-covered paper, embossed with gold coins, glittered in the first light of morning. "Look! They're all still here. Our twelve coins from the birthday cake and one treasure from each of us."

"Sort of like a time capsule." Paul looked at the assortment of trinkets from twelve-year-old girls. "It's amazing what we value when we're kids."

"Which one is your treasure?" Mark watched Eva, kindly touching each item. *I think they are all treasures to her,* Mark considered. *I wonder if Eva came back here looking for Susan. Did she recognize the flagpole? Is that why she stopped here? Did this place bring back happy memories of her childhood?*

"This is mine." Eva pulled a long thin box from the bottom. "Prang" was printed in white letters on its black metal. "It was my favorite watercolor box. It has big pans of color, except ... except I traded my purple pan for another blue one. I never use purple."

Rex growled.

"What is it, Rex?" Mark pulled his gun from its holster.

"Don't move!" Eva gasped. "Don't move your foot.

"What's wrong?" Paul aimed his gun towards his foot.

Bending over, Eva pointed behind Mark's foot.

A little creature, the size of a fifty-cent piece, struggled to climb the trench. It's little legs frantically pawed at the sand and its head stretched towards the porch light. Losing ground, its body slipped towards the edge of the trench, a dark abyss.

Eva scooped it up. "Careful there, little fellow."

"A turtle?" Paul put his gun away.

"It's trying to get to the water before sunrise." Mark touched its little shell. "Just let it go. It can find the ocean all by itself."

"I wonder how they do that? A turtle hatches and having never seen or been told about the ocean, it can find its way to the sea. Then after years of living in the deep ocean, it returns to the same beach." Eva let Rex sniff the little creature. "Hardly a day old and it knows its way. They have no maps or roads to follow. So how can they find their way home?"

Looking up, Paul rubbed the stubble on his chin. "Maybe they have some sort of built in global positioning. Or it could have something to do with that Bermuda triangle effect." He chuckled. "We didn't study turtles at the police academy."

Mark watched a car slowly roll down the beach and stop nearby. Its red brake lights glowed like evil eyes. "Eva, its time to go in. You're getting chilled."

"I'm okay. Really, I am." Holding the baby turtle on the towel, Eva glanced at the beach. "I'll just take it down to the ocean. I don't want it to get hit by a car."

"Eva." Mark touched her cool arm. "That's not safe."

"I'll watch out for cars."

"That's not what I mean."

"Mark, you worry too much." Eva turned towards the beach. "With two armed body guards and a police dog, I couldn't be safer. Now could I?"

~ 61 ~

Daytona Beach, Florida – Dawn, August 24th

"What happened out there?" Shaking his head, Fritz stood at the living room door, looking at the trench near the flagpole. "Looks like a giant mole ripped through the sand last night."

Eva watched Mark and his dad, curious about their close bond. It was so different from her brother and her father. But then Eva doubted that many teenaged boys got along with their stepfathers.

Rex dashed out the open living room screen door. With a bone clenched in his jaws, he headed towards the ditch.

"Rex, you didn't need to dig a hole that big for your bone." Fritz turned to the suspicious looking threesome sitting at the dining room table. "Mind explaining how that ditch got there?"

"Rex was digging for a land crab last night." Mark wiped rust off a thin metal box. Beneath it, newspaper protected the dinner table. Nearby was an old cigar box with girls' childhood trinkets. Next to it was a rusty kid's fishing tackle box with "M.R." painted on the side.

Sitting across the table, Paul disassembled his gun. A cleaning kit lay on a newspaper and the gun parts were neatly arranged in order. Grains of sand fell from the gun barrel as he tapped it.

Across from Mark, Eva flipped a page in her novel, anxious to find out if its fictional Eva Johnson gets her man in the end. *Why doesn't Mark just tell his dad what we were doing?* Eva mused. *Or is this bantering like the game of keep-away they play with Rex?*

Fritz stepped inside. "Land crabs. Looks more like a two-legged varmint made that. Or maybe three of them. Now, what am I going to do with that trench?"

Paul oiled the wad on the cleaning rod and slid it down his gun barrel. "It's about the right size for a foundation."

Fritz studied the ditch's location. "That's almost at the ocean edge of my property. What on earth would I build out there?"

"It has a great view of the beach." Eva flipped a page.

"She's right. And that would be a nice spot for a gazebo. Mom's been wanting one." Mark grinned at his mother walking in with coffee and rolls. His father's back was turned to her.

"I don't recall her mentioning she wanted a gazebo."

"Gazebo?" Barbara's eyes sparkled as she kissed his cheek. "Dear, that's a lovely idea. I've always wanted a picnic area out there, but a gazebo is a grander idea. I'm glad you thought of it."

Fritz took a deep breath. "Well, I guess we could put a gazebo out there, if I can get the land crabs to cooperate."

Barbara looked at everyone snickering. "Land crabs? What do land crabs have to do with gazebos?"

"They dig good foundations." Opening the door to the deck, Fritz grabbed the broom. "I just wish they wouldn't track sand all over my clean deck. Don't they know I'm going to paint today?"

"Paint?" Barbara followed her husband with his coffee and rolls. "Why don't we paint the gazebo white?"

"You'll have to wait until I build it before you can paint it." Fritz and Barbara's conversation faded.

Eva watched them on the deck. Barbara's hand pointed to the end of the walk and moved as if drawing a plan. Fritz just nodded.

They make a lovely couple, Eva mused. *What would it be like to be married? But that'll have to wait until I'm twenty-seven this June. I promised Dad and he put my money in trust until then. He said I could use it to build a beach house. My own home.*

"Is your headache back?" Mark reached across the table and tenderly touched her hand. "Eva, maybe you should lay down for a while. You shouldn't overdo it."

"Yes, dear. I won't overdo it reading my novel." Eva looked into his blue eyes. Her mind slipped to the subject of her heart. *Love. Is love the right word for what I feel for Mark? It feels more complex than that. It's ... It's stronger than the fever of viral encephalitis. What I feel for Mark makes my brain race and my heart tingle when he touches me.*

With the thoughts of romance slipping through her, Eva doodled on a blank piece of paper. The image of two turtles appeared. Nose to nose. *Do turtles kiss?* She mused.

A rush of warmth rolled over Eva as she gazed at Mark, his lips puckering as he worked on her watercolor box. "If you can't get it open, that's okay."

"Here it is." After popping open the little black box, Mark handed it to Eva. "Your buried treasure is still in good shape. It's an interesting item. Most of your little friends put in jewelry, charms, or trinkets. So is this something special?"

Her fingers slid across the eight oval pans of dry watercolors: cherry red, tangy orange, lemon yellow, leaf green, sky blue, bark brown, and midnight black. There was no purple. It had been replaced with a second pan of blue, her favorite color.

Smiling, Eva closed the hinged lid. Big white letters spelled out *Prang* on a red oval with tiny print along the edge. "Gee, I didn't know that. This was made in Sandusky, Ohio. That's on Lake Erie, just sixty miles north of where I live."

Paul glanced over at the rack of fishing poles mounted on the wall. "Sandusky, that's where we charter our boat for walleye fishing. I never knew they made art stuff up there."

Eva opened the watercolor box. "The brush is missing."

"I found one of your brushes in the creek, just upstream from where your Blazer was ... was found. It's in my room. I'll get it." Mark glanced at Paul. "Stay with Eva."

"Don't worry, I'll keep my eyes on things." With the bullets neatly setting in a row, Paul oiled the clip to his police pistol. He had dropped it in the sand. "I'm not finished cleaning this baby."

Eva smiled at Mark when he turned and winked at her, then headed down the hall towards his apartment above the garages.

He won't be gone long, Eva reassured herself. *I wonder if he really does love me? He said so, but do men really mean it? He doesn't really know me. After that fever, I'm not sure I know who I am, so how can he?*

Paul pulled the slide back on his gun. Metal slid against metal, ending in an odd click.

Startled, Eva's head snapped right, looking at the barrel of the gun. A pain stabbed her arm.

"Eva?" Paul put his gun down. "Are you okay? You look so pale. Do you want me to get Barbara?"

"I just need a glass of water." Her chair scooted back.

"No. Stay there. I don't want you to pass out. I'll get you a glass of water." As Paul headed towards the kitchen, he tucked his gun in its holster. "Don't go outside."

"I won't." Alone at the dining room table, Eva felt an uneasy emptiness. When Mark was around, she had a measure of energy. But alone, her strength drained from her and troubling thoughts seeped in. *Why did they have to tell me about Jim?* Eva sighed. *I'd almost forgotten about him. Why would Jim want to hurt me?*

Glancing out the window, Eva watched a red sports car stop. Light glinted from its window as the driver's door opened.

Looks something like my niece's car, Eva considered. *But it's too early for Maggie. When she phoned last night, she said she was going out with the college guys she met. With a bunch of handsome young men around, Maggie's mind won't be on her aunt. ...I don't know if she was more upset about not being in my will or about Detective Galloway considering her a suspect.*

Folded into the size of a bookmark was a newspaper clipping. Eva shuddered as she looked at it again. "Aunt Killer," the headline read. *Why did I keep this?* Eva wondered. *It's a grim thought: a nephew killing his elderly aunt. People do strange things for money. Maybe that's why Dad put my money into a trust fund. He didn't want anyone marrying me just to get his hands on my money. Dad said if I waited until I was twenty-seven, I'd be old enough to pick out a good husband. ... Would Mark make a good husband?*

Eva glanced out the windows at Fritz and Barbara working side-by-side painting the deck railing. Like a good team of horses, they each seemed to know where the other would move next.

A jarring ring sliced the silence.

Eva picked up the phone. "Hello. ... hello?"

No voice responded.

Only the jingle of an ice cream truck could be heard.

Eva turned to the screen door.

A jingling sound wafted in on the breeze.

Beyond the sand dunes, an ice cream truck passed.

Eva stared at the figure standing beside the distant red car.

It seemed to be looking towards her.

"Hello?" No one answered. "Hello. ... hello."

Mark pulled the phone from her. "Hello!"

The line went dead.

In the distance the red car pulled away.

Mark pulled her back from the window. His arms slid around her trembling body. "Eva, you're okay. I'm right here."

"Mark." Eva hugged him. "Jim knows where I am."

~ 62 ~

"I told you not to leave Eva alone!" Mark's voice crackled with anger. "What kind of a detective leaves a defenseless witness alone with a killer on the loose?"

Paul leaned on the deck railing. "Are you done shouting?"

"Jim could have gotten to her." Mark looked at the living room door, glad it was closed. He didn't want Eva to hear.

"Mark, I just stepped into the kitchen. Eva was in no danger. The front door was locked. No one could have gotten to her."

"But Jim did get to her." Mark touched his gun. "He called her. Jim knows where she is."

"Now we don't know that for a fact." Paul straightened his back. "The call was from a cell phone. It could have been a student playing a prank. Or –"

"It was Jim!" Mark snarled. "Eva was sure it was him. She heard wheezing and she thought he was in a car right out there."

Paul glanced back at the beach. Beyond the sand dunes, a police cruiser now sat. "If it was Jim, he won't be back. And your police friends should be able to find Jim if he's driving a red car."

"What do you mean IF? If Eva says a red car was out there, then it was. She has a good eye for colors." Mark took a deep breath, hoping to quiet his anger.

Why did I leave Eva alone? His mind taunted him. *I shouldn't have entrusted her life to anyone. Not even a police detective. Why did I go after her watercolor brush. I know better than to let anything distract me. I have to get a grip on my emotions.*

"You're right." Paul looked down. "I shouldn't have left. It's just Eva turned so pale. I thought she was going to pass out."

"Detective Galloway," Fritz called from the living room door. "There's a phone call for you."

Mark followed Paul inside and stood near the door, while he eavesdropped on the phone conversation. It was obviously Paul's captain wanting a report from his detective.

"Here, Mark. You need something to cool off." Fritz handed his son a glass of iced tea.

Taking it, Mark looked at the hallway. "How's Eva?"

"Don't worry. Your mom is with her. I think Eva was just plum tuckered out. Digging foundation ditches is hard work."

"Dad! I wouldn't let Eva do anything like that."

"Lighten up, Mark. You're snarling like an old bear."

Turning away from his father, Mark watched the beach.

A second police cruiser stopped out front and one was in the driveway in the back. Paul, his dad, and Mark were all armed. Eva was in the bedroom resting under his mother's watchful eye.

Dad is right, Mark thought. *I have to cool off. The Secret Service trained me to protect the President. I know how to handle myself. There were numerous times during the last campaign where we were concerned for the President's life. And some really tense moments during the inaugural parade. But this is different.*

Mark glanced down the hall where Eva was resting.

I'm in love with Eva. That's the difference. I always thought they were exaggerating when they said not to get emotionally involved with those you're protecting. Now I understand why. It's too easy to lose perspective and overreacting can be deadly. For Eva and my parents.

"Don't worry, Mark." His mother put her hand on his shoulder. "Eva is fine. Her blood sugar must have been a little low. She just needed something to eat and a little rest. Eva still forgets to take it easy. I think she wants to keep up with everyone. At her age, she has never had to cope with a lingering illness. It'll take time for her to get her strength back. Don't be angry with her."

"I'm angry with myself, not Eva." Mark sat his iced tea on the table. "I should take Eva away. Someplace safe. I don't want you and Dad to get hurt."

"Running away isn't the answer. And if you leave, your father and I would worry ourselves to death. We're better off if you stay. And no, we're not leaving." Barbara stepped out the living room door. Grabbing a brush, she joined her husband painting the deck.

Mom's right, Mark considered. *It's easier to defend your home turf. And Eva needs her rest. On the road, she'd get tired too quickly and it would be an emotional strain. We're staying.*

Whining, Rex nudged his master's leg.

"No. You can't go out. I don't want you playing keep-away with Dad's paint bucket." Mark shook his head, imagining what the deck and his dog would look like with paint everywhere.

"Good news." Paul hung up the phone.

"Did they catch Jim?"

"No."

"Then it's not good news."

"Jim used a credit card to buy gas."

"Where" Mark asked.

"On I-95, at one of the Savanna, Georgia exchanges."

"When?"

"Yesterday morning."

"There's nothing good about that news." Mark glanced at the cars slowly cruising along the beach. "That means Jim is here."

"We don't know that for a fact. But we do know he's getting careless." Paul tapped his police pistol. "And careless men are easier to catch."

"They're also more dangerous. Jim's not the kind of guy who's going to want to spend time behind bars. He'll try to weasel his way out and his odds are better without a witness."

"You know we can't call Eva as a witness."

"Jim doesn't know that. If he did, he wouldn't be here looking for Eva." Mark looked down the hall at Eva's closed bedroom door and was glad she was safe.

"Something is up." Paul pointed to the beach.

The second police cruiser pulled away, its lights flashing.

The phone rang.

"Hello." Mark's voice was sharp. "Oh, Bob. What's up? ... Yeah, we saw one cruiser heading north. ... No. I'll send Paul out. He can identify Jim."

Before the receiver hit the off-hook, Paul began interrogating. "Did they catch Jim?"

"They found a red car with the license plates Jim stole in Ohio. It's parked at a motel about a mile north of here. The cruiser parked in the drive, out back, will take you up there. The police want someone to identify Jim."

"Is he dead?" Paul's hand touched his gun.

"No. They don't have him yet. The police chief is having the other guests evacuated from the motel. After it's clear, they'll make their move." Mark stepped to the window. "They want someone who knows Jim to positively identify him. They don't want to grab an innocent tourist by mistake. So you'll have to go. I'm staying here to protect Eva."

Paul pulled his gun out and checked its clip. It was full of bullets. "Eva's worries will soon be over."

"She's not safe until he's in custody." Mark looked at Eva's closed bedroom door. "When you have Jim in handcuffs, call me."

~ 63 ~

"I have to leave." Eva hugged the kittens. "I'm sorry I can't take you with me. You'll be safer here with Mark, and he and his parents will be safer without me around."

Purring, the kittens snuggled closer.

"Don't worry, you'll be all right. As soon as I get Jim out of my life, I promise to come back for you." Putting the kittens back in their box, Eva looked around the bedroom.

It had homey touches. On the wall were spools of colorful thread hanging in rows, making a pattern like a homemade Amish quilt. The shell nightlight glowed with tropical colors. On the bed, the soft blue blanket was folded and laid at the end. Everything was just about as Eva had found it.

But the little blue neck pillow that Barbara had made was tucked into the backpack beside Eva's treasured watercolor box and her unfinished novel.

The doll with the cracked china head was left resting on the bed. Pinned to it was a farewell note to Mark.

"Time to go." She whispered to the kittens.

Before leaving, Eva listened one last time at the door. The sound of Mark's voice echoed down the hall. Her fingers held tight the heart shaped pendent with his name engraved below hers. She wanted to go to him, but her mind scolded. *If you stay, he'll get killed, like in your dream. If you really love Mark, you'll leave.*

After a few slow steps across the bedroom, she paused by the casement window. With a tug, the Pella window screen opened.

Her backpack flopped onto the porch outside. Stepping over the low sill, Eva glanced back into the room.

I hope they'll forgive me for sneaking away like this. Eva choked back the tears. *They've all been so good to me. I hate to leave, but I'm afraid of what Jim will do when he comes for me. Mark will try to stop him and I can't bear the thought of Mark getting hurt.*

Eva glanced down the porch that wrapped around the house. Along the front, fresh paint sparkled in the morning sun. The back porch was shady, but going that way meant someone could spot her. Slipping under the north porch railing, Eva stepped into the thick leafed grass. A quick scamper down the bank and over the retaining wall took her to the driveway. Staying close to the wall, she walked under the back deck overhang and slipped into the dark shadows of the garage.

Good, no one saw me. Eva took several deep breaths trying to quiet her racing heart. In front of Mark's Jeep, she spotted her bike. Its dents had been repaired and a fresh coat of sea-blue paint had been applied. It was ready to go.

After securing her backpack in the wire rack, Eva looked up. *I wonder what Mark's apartment is like. I didn't get a chance to see it. I wanted to, but he said we'd have to wait for that. I wonder what he was thinking of? But I'm afraid that'll have to wait until I come back. I hope Mark can forgive me for running away like this.*

The kickstand flipped back. After one last glance at the back porch, Eva rode out the driveway to South Atlantic Avenue and turned right, heading north.

I think the bridge to the mainland is north of here. I know I can't go south. The road dead-ends down by the inlet.

Peddling, Eva tried to concentrate on where she would go but her mind refused to obey. It was locked on Mark. *What will he think about my leaving?* Eva pondered. *I want to stay but I have to* go. *It makes no sense. I owed Mark more of an explanation than I wrote, but I just couldn't find the words. How do you tell someone you love that you have to leave because you love him.*

After a few minutes, a police cruiser approached her with its lights flashing.

Eva rode into a motel parking lot to avoid the cars pulling over. Stopping a moment to rest, she studied the older motel. *I wonder what happened to the West Indies? Was it torn down to make room for one of those high-rise concrete towers? Or was it altered and I don't recognize it?*

This looks like a nice older motel. Maybe I'll get a room here. Eva considered. But the motel sign read: No vacancy. Shaking her head, she rode north. *On the other hand, maybe I'll get a room on down the road. The good places always fill fast for Memorial Day weekend.*

Another motel sign read: "Low Labor Day rates, check us out." But for Eva, it was still the beginning of summer, not the end.

A police siren wailed behind her. It was heading north.

Coasting into another motel drive, Eva rested her hand on a palm tree for balance. *I'm getting nowhere fast,* Eva considered. *It'll take me days to get to where I'm going. ... So where am I going? ... Home? But, where is home these days?*

With the traffic back to normal, Eva peddled north again. *The West Indies is gone.* Her mind churned with other options. *I could ride by Ocean Dunes, but I can't stay there. It's someone else's home now.*

A delivery truck rolled past her. Its company address rang a bell: a highway home, South Atlantic Avenue by an old name.

That's it, Eva thought. *I can ride up old A1A to St. Augustine. Maybe I can find my old apartment there. It had a good view of the ocean. ... Was it Seventh Street or Sixth Street? Oh well, I'll know it when I see it. If Grace is still there, I could rent a room from her. And I wonder if they still have Atlantic augers on the beach.*

With a destination in mind, she peddled faster. St. Augustine was about sixty miles north.

"It's about an hour drive." Eva talked to herself as she peddled. Cars whizzed by her. "But on a bike, how long will it take me? At six miles an hour, it would take … ten hours! It'll be evening before I get there."

She peddled faster.

A siren grew louder, approaching from behind.

Cars began to pull over.

Getting out of the way, Eva rode into a third motel drive and stopped. *If this keeps up, it'll take me ten hours to get to the north end of Daytona and the traffic is moving too fast for me.*

Looking around, Eva spotted a ramp to the beach. Hopping back on her bike, she headed for the concrete ramp and the ocean beyond. It was a short ride through the soft area and then onto the firm packed sand. Her bike crossed the slow moving beach traffic and headed north.

This is better, she thought. *The speed limit here is ten miles per hour. I'll be safer on the beach. And with all these people around, no one will be able to find me.*

On the beach, a red sports car circled back and followed Eva.

~ 64 ~

"What do you mean, that wasn't Jim's red car?" Mark gripped the receiver tightly. "I thought they identified his license plates."

Yanking the phone with him, Mark stomped out the living room door onto the deck. The north section was still wet with fresh paint, limiting his pacing to the hot south end. Even with the heat, it was better to talk outside. Mark didn't want Eva to accidentally hear that Jim was out there, somewhere, still looking for her.

On the speakerphone, Detective Paul Galloway's voice resonated with concern. "Jim put his stolen plates on another red car at the hotel. When the officers entered the motel room Jim rented, he was gone, and it doesn't look like he's coming back. The only thing left was a discarded asthma inhaler."

"Are you sure Jim was there?" Mark hoped that he and the police were wrong about Jim being in town.

Paul continued. "It's looks like the same kind of inhaler Jim used the day we went to his Ohio apartment. They're dusting it for prints. But we know for a fact the license plates we found were the ones he stole in Ohio. That means Jim is in here."

"Tell the police to look for a red car with the new stolen license plates." Mark glanced at the cruiser sitting on the beach. "Yes, I'm telling them how to do their job. ... I know, I know. Just call me as soon as they find Jim."

Hanging up the phone didn't end Mark's worries. *Jim is smart. He'll ditch those stolen license plates as well and snatch another set; Florida plates would draw less attention.*

Beyond the dunes numerous cars meandered along the beach and the red ones all looked suspicious to Mark. Traffic always picked up two weeks before and after a major holiday. And families with children flocked to the beach for one last trip before Labor Day. Summer was coming to an end.

A second police cruiser parked near the first one.

Joining his son, Fritz pointed at the police cars. "Looks like the cavalry has arrived. They won't let any renegade cross those sand dunes. And that Jim fellow will be in the calaboose any moment now."

"Wrong, Dad. The police didn't find Jim or his car at the motel. He's still on the loose. We'll have to keep Eva inside until Jim's caught."

Rex dropped his keep-away bucket. But he found no takers in a game even after a gentle nudge at his master's legs.

Silence settled between them.

"Mark!" His mother screamed.

The screen door flung open as Barbara ran out.

"Mark! Mark! Eva is gone!"

"Gone?" Mark recognized the tremble of fear in his mother's voice, but he refused to believe the words she uttered. "Eva is in her room. Sleeping. The door is still closed."

"No! The bedroom window is open. Eva is gone." Hugging the doll with a cracked china head, tears ran down Barbara's cheek. "Eva left you a note."

With a pain stabbing his heart, Mark took the doll. A note was still pinned to its skirt. His hand trembled, not wanting to believe that she had left. Left him. Left the safety of his parents' home. Left alone with no way to protect herself and still too weak to travel far. Reluctantly, Mark removed the paper from the envelope and read the brief note.

My Dearest Mark,

I have to leave. I don't want Jim to hurt you or your parents. I couldn't forgive myself if anything happened to any of you. You'll be safer without me around.

Thanks from the bottom of my heart for being there for me. It meant the world to me. When it's safe, I'll return and explain.

I hope you can forgive me for leaving like this. With all my love,

Eva

Mark scanned the words again. *Why?* He tried to comprehend. *Why did she think leaving would protect us from Jim? He wouldn't know she had left. ... Unless Jim has been watching.*

Mark ran to the door. "Dad. Call Paul. Tell him Eva is gone."

"What's his cell phone number?" Fritz shouted.

"Just hit redial." Mark yanked the screen door open. "Rex. Find Eva."

Dashing ahead, Rex raced into the bedroom.

Inside her bedroom, the CD player was repeating "The Boxer" and its words haunted Mark. *Is she running away or going home? That's the song she was playing when she left her Ohio home. She was running from Jim then. And now she's running scared.*

Whining, Rex sniffed Eva's bed, trotted across the room, and leaped out the open window. After dashing across the deck, he ran down the bank.

Mark followed Rex. After hopping off the retaining wall, he ran into the garage. Eva's bike was gone.

"Be careful," Barbara yelled. Hugging the doll, she stood on the back porch balcony as Mark backed his Jeep out of the garage.

"Mom, tell them, Eva is on her bike. A blue bike." Shifting gears, Mark watched Rex following her scent. "Tell them Eva went north. ... Have Dad call her brother. He might know where Eva would go."

Pulling into traffic, Mark followed Rex sniffing the curb area, following Eva's trail. *Where is she going?* Mark pondered. *Surely not the West Indies, or doesn't she remember it's gone? And there isn't any Ocean Dunes motel.*

Rex detoured into a driveway of an old motel hotel with a "No vacancy" sign.

"Is she looking for a room?" Mark asked his Jeep. "No, Rex is heading north again and I doubt she'd stay this close. She left Ohio to come to Florida to hide from Jim. Now she's going back north to someplace she feels will be safe to hide. But where?"

The Jeep could not answer. And Rex continued to follow the trail, sniffing a palm tree before heading north again.

I should have asked Eva more about her past, Mark thought. *Did she live somewhere else in Florida? It would have to be far enough away to be safe and yet close enough to reach by bike. And knowing Eva, it would be near the ocean she loves.*

Mark took his cell phone and punched a series of numbers.

Police dispatch answered.

"This is Professor Reining. Is Dixie there?" Mark slowed his Jeep as Rex sniffed another driveway. "Dixie, when your team did its research on Eva, did she live anywhere else in Florida?"

Rex headed north again.

"A Florida teaching certificate. Where?" Mark turned the jeep towards a concrete beach ramp. "Eva taught art in Palatka, but it listed St. Augustine as her residence. You're right. When you find that old address, call me. And notify Bob. He and the other officers are searching for Eva. ...Yes. She left on her bike. Also tell Bob that Rex has tracked her onto the beach. Eva is heading north."

At the water's edge, Rex lost the trail.

"Rex." Slowing the jeep, Mark whistled for his dog to hop in. "Good boy. Not even you can follow a scent through the Atlantic Ocean. She's headed north to St. Augustine. Rex, look for Eva."

With his ears tilted forward and his head out the passenger side, Rex sniffed the air while he looked at the crowd of people playing in the surf.

Mark's cell phone rang.

"Paul, have they found Jim yet? Well, a red car with stolen license plates can't be that hard to find." As Mark scanned those on the beach and along the dry sand, he grew tense. The motel where Jim was last seen was less than a mile north of there.

"Yes. Tell them Eva is headed your way. She's on a blue bike. Wearing a white blouse, navy Bermuda shorts, and maybe her straw hat."

Through the salty beach haze, the distant blinking of police cars lights could be seen. They were sitting in front of the motel where Jim had stayed.

Eva was riding that way.

"I have to find Eva before Jim does!"

~ 65 ~

A flash of red caught Eva's attention.

Her bike splashed through a departing wave, knife thin.

"Trouble," she warned her bike. "We better head for the hills or at least that beach ramp. Those police cars are headed our way. We can't let Mark find us. I don't want him to get hurt."

But her escape route was cut off. A police cruiser pulled down the concrete beach ramp and stopped short of the sand. Vans, cars, and motorbikes slowly passed the waiting cruiser.

Eva peddled her bike behind a nearby food concession stand and stopped. Peeking around it, she saw a familiar looking building just beyond the police cruiser. It was a remodeled older motel. "That's it. I forgot the West Indies had a beach ramp on the south side. That's it."

"What did you say, lady?" A concession man leaned over his counter. "Y'all want a hot dog? Just made a fresh batch."

Her short ride up the beach had already taken its toll on her strength. A variety of smells floated over the counter. Food was of no interest but Eva needed some pep, a fast pick-up and something cold, sweet, and with ample caffeine. "I'll have a large Coke."

"How about a sandwich and fries to go with that?" The man stirred onions on the grill next to sizzling sausage links.

"Some fries." Looking past the police cruiser, Eva stared at the motel beyond. Old memories drifted into her mind.

"One order of fries and a large Coke." His hand reached for payment. "Lady, here's your order."

Eva handed over a twenty. "Do you know if that motel over there is called the West Indies?"

"Nope. That name doesn't ring a bell. Y'all just have to ride up there and see for yourself." He gave her change.

With her food and bike, Eva retreated to the shade behind the concession stand. Sitting in the sand sipping her Coke, she studied the shape of the motel. *We didn't have a two-story section on the front,* she recalled. *And we didn't have a swimming pool on the ocean side. But I remember that retaining wall and the way Dad built the room dividers. They tiered up instead of down.*

Swallowing the cold sweet drink, Eva's smile grew larger. *That's it. That's the West Indies. Home. My childhood home. I'll stay there. If Mark couldn't find it, no one will. I'll be safe there.*

A familiar looking beach vehicle with two surfboards for a roof stopped beside the police cruiser. Two men sat in the front.

Detective Galloway! Eva gasped and scooted back. *I hope he didn't see me. He'll tell Mark.*

A piece of trash blew past and caught in the bike's spokes.

Awkward footsteps disturbed the nearby sand.

Behind her, a man wheezed.

Fear swept through her. Eva wanted to turn but couldn't.

A hand grabbed her neck. "I've been looking for you!"

Eva was yanked from the sand like a helpless doll.

"Jim!" Eva choked on his name.

The Coke and fries hit the sand.

"You're coming with me." Jim snarled.

"No! How many times do I have to tell you to leave me alone?" Eva felt the rage in his tightening grip.

"What's this? Did your federal boyfriend give you this cheap trinket?" Jim ripped the blue heart from her neck and threw it in the sand. "He knows you're mine. ... Mine till death do us part. I'll kill him if he gets in my way again."

"Calm down, Jim." Eva trembled at the anger in his voice, as frightening as it had been in the raspberry patch when he lashed out at her. "Jim, I don't know what you want with me."

"Didn't think you would. But I have to tidy up loose ends. We're going to take a ride." Jim's grip tightened around her arm.

Eva looked over his shoulder at the black Jeep pulling beside the police cruiser and Detective Galloway in a dune buggy.

"Don't even think about calling those cops," Jim snarled.

Metal poked into her ribs. She didn't need to look down to know it was a gun. "Jim, you should go before the police see you."

"You're coming with me."

"No." Eva felt the gun barrel jab deeper.

"If you motion to those cops, I'll kill a few of those kids." Jim pointed the gun at the children reaching up for their hot dogs. They were only a few feet away, laughing and giggling.

"Leave the children out of this." Eva stepped in front of Jim.

Jim pushed her towards a parked car. "If you make a scene, someone will get hurt. And their blood will be on your hands."

Eva caught one more glimpse of the man in the Jeep sitting beside the cruiser. It was Mark. Her heart called out to him but her lips were sealed and her mind raced. *I don't want to jeopardize his life. Seeing Mark shot in my dreams is bad enough, I don't want to experience the reality. ...Reality.* The synapse in her mind burned hot, connecting emergency pathways.

Turning, she looked for an opportunity to slip away without harming others. There was none. "Where are we going?"

Jim jerked open the passenger door of a red sports car and shoved Eva. "Get in! Scoot across. You're driving."

Touching the Pontiac Firebird triggered a memory of red paint and a blast from a gun. "Whose car is this?"

"My last dead wife's. Thought I'd keep it for a getaway car. It's got a lot of horsepower. Now, get in!"

"How'd you find me?" Eva slid into the driver's seat.

"Simple. I followed your niece. Her roommate told me that Maggie went to Daytona to find her aunt. Even told me where your niece would be staying. I waited until Maggie left the hotel and followed her to you." Jim slammed the door closed and slapped the keys in her hand. "Don't do anything stupid. Just drive."

Starting the car, Eva glanced in the rearview mirror at the distant flashing lights. The police cruisers were still too far north to help. "We'll go north."

"No. South. Away from those cop cars." Jim pointed his gun.

Eva looked at the gun barrel. The opening was smaller than her revolver and Jim's handgun was a pistol: a 9mm pistol.

Eva's arm ached as she pulling the car into the southbound lane. *I have to keep calm. Buy a little time. Find out what he wants. Promise him anything. Look for a place to escape. Somewhere remote. Distract Jim. Escape. ... How?*

"The beach traffic is heavy today." Eva took her foot off the accelerator. "We'll have to take it slow and easy. The Memorial Day traffic is getting heavy."

"Memorial Day. It's Labor Day coming up. You're one dumb blond." Jim laughed. "You're more than dumb, you're stupid."

Stupid. Eva mulled over the word. *If he thinks I'm stupid, can I use that to my advantage?* She watched him take a whiff from his asthma inhaler. "The doctors say salt air is good for allergies. A nice long ride along the beach will clear your lungs."

Pushing the power button, the side windows slid down. Warm moist salt air rolled in, replacing the stale air inside the car.

Jim took a deep breath. "This time I won't miss and there's no need to make it look like an accident. Dead will do."

~ 66 ~

"Haven't they found Jim yet?" Mark's hands gripped the steering wheel of his Jeep. On the beach ramp, he stopped to check with Officer Bob White and Detective Galloway. "Did you give them a description of Eva?"

"Yes, Professor Reining. Give us time to do our job." Bob nodded. "Eva couldn't have gotten far on her bike. The cruisers coming down the beach are searching for her."

Mark shifted his Jeep into reverse. "I'll double back. Eva may have stopped to rest. She was feeling a little weak today."

"Where would she go?" Detective Galloway asked.

"St. Augustine." Mark glanced north. "She used to live there. But she's too weak to ride a bike that far. I have to find her before Jim does. Eva can't –"

Rex's barking interrupted. His ears flipped forward, aiming at something near the food concession stand. With a growl, he jumped across Mark's lap and into the sand. Dashing through traffic, he made a beeline for the concession stand.

"Look! Over there. It's a blue bike." Mark whipped his Jeep through the sand. "It's Eva's bike."

"Professor, wait." Bob flipped his police siren on. Detective Galloway, sitting next to him, held on as they spun around.

On the ramp, the police cruiser's lights flashed as it pulled across the beach approach, closing it.

Next to the concession stand, Mark's Jeep slid to a stop and he hopped out. "That's Eva's bike. But where is she?"

Eva was not in sight.

Whining, Rex pawed at the sand beyond her bike.

A shiny blue heart sparkled in the sun.

Scooping it out of the sand, Mark's chest tightened. Light bounced off the blue metallic heart. Her name was engraved above his. The broken chain left a streak of red on his hand. "Blood."

"What?" Paul stepped over the scattered French fries.

"Eva's blood." Mark touched it. "I have to find Eva."

Rex sniffed the sand, barked, and headed for the traffic.

"He's got Eva's scent." Mark slid into his Jeep.

Paul hopped in the passenger's side.

"Professor, wait," Bob shouted. "The concession man said a woman with blond hair and a straw hat left in a red sports car. The man with Eva matched Jim's description."

Mark pulled his Jeep into the southbound lane. Ahead, Rex was sniffing the ground.

"Rex, get in." Mark slowed the Jeep.

Paul pushed Rex in the back. "If Jim has her, we can't let him get off the beach."

"What do you mean, IF?" Mark pulled his Jeep around a slow moving car. "It's Jim. And I have to get to her fast."

How could I have missed her bike? Mark thought. *If I'd gotten to her sooner, Eva would be safe. ... Oh, Eva, you shouldn't have run away. You have no way to protect yourself.*

"Mark, does Eva have a gun?"

"No. She left her .38 in the bank safe."

"What good is a gun in a safe?" Paul tapped his pistol.

"It was her father's. She didn't want it to get stolen." Mark wished he had given Eva one of his spare guns. Almost did but he was concerned about his parents' safety. Giving her a gun seemed dangerous at the time. "I should have given Eva a gun."

Paul stretched to look over the cars ahead. "Having a gun and using it are two different things. I've seen rookie cops freeze in tight situations, unable to pull the trigger. I can't picture someone like Eva pumping a few rounds into Jim, not even to save her life."

"I won't hesitate."

"Mark, for your sake, leave this to the police."

"I'll do what I have to, to save Eva."

Pulling around a van, they spotted the red sports car. Two passengers sat in the front, a woman driving and a man leaning close, his hands waving as if arguing.

"Slow down." Paul hit the redial on his cell phone. "Bob, tell the other officers, Eva is just ahead of us, still heading south. Have them seal those beach ramps to the south. ... What corral?"

Mark pulled closer to the blood red Pontiac Firebird. "Do they have the corral set up?"

"Yep." Paul hung up. "I assume their corral is some sort of southern blockade. I'm game."

The red sports car slowed.

Mark glanced right.

Over the sand dunes was his parents' home.

From the red sports car, a straw hat slid out the window. It waved a couple of times and then fell to the sand.

Rex leaped out and raced to it. With a lunge, he retrieved it like a dropped Frisbee.

Mark slowed and Rex hopped back into the Jeep with the hat firmly clenched in his teeth.

"Good boy." Mark tugged for the hat, but Rex wouldn't give it up. "Keep it."

"What do you make of Eva's waving?" Paul asked.

"I think she wants us to keep away." Mark pulled closer.

The man in the red car looked out the back window. After pulling her head back, Jim held a gun to Eva's head.

~ 67 ~

Jim's gun barrel slid up Eva's neck. Jabbing under her chin, it tilted her head back. Gripping the steering wheel, her fingers felt the cold of the Siberian tundra of her dreams. Eva's heart and lungs paused. *Breathe,* her mind commanded. *Breathe. Now!* With her lungs filling, her heart skipped into rapid beats. Fear flowed through her veins. "What's wrong?" Eva gasped.

"Your federal boyfriend is following us. I want him to know if he tries anything, I'll blow your head off." Jim grinned. "It'd be a shame. It would make a mess of the upholstery."

"Then put the gun down." Driving south on the beach, Eva glanced in the rearview mirror and watched Mark motion to her.

What does he want me to do? Eva wondered. *He's pointing down the beach towards the inlet. But they don't let cars down there and it dead-ends at the jetty.*

Jim glanced out the side window. "I need to get back to my hiding spot. Take the next ramp off the beach."

"There's a cruiser at this one. We'll have to go further south." Eva remembered the boulders of the jetty forming a barricade. It was a dead-end. An escape plan began to form. "I know an old exit. They won't put a police car there. It's seldom used."

"You better be right." Wheezing, Jim grabbed his inhaler. "I want to ditch those idiot cops."

As the windows closed, the tension grew. Eva's heart felt like it was slapping her ribs like the waves smash against the jetty rocks. *That's an idea,* Eva considered. *I'll floor the gas pedal and aim for the jetty wall. That'll distract Jim and give me time to escape. ... I'll run into the ocean and swim away.*

"Where's this exit?"

"It's down near the lighthouse." Eva pointed right. The tall, dark orange tower loomed above the flat shoreline of the inlet to her right. To the left, Eva saw the long line of boulders of the jetty stretching far into the ocean. The waves smashed against them as if they were angry at being denied access to the safe harbor beyond. *Smash,* Eva considered. *I'll smash this car into them and escape.*

"Now where's that exit?"

"Near those rocks." Eva knew that wasn't true.

"It's about time." Jim glanced out the window. "Looks a little deserted down here. It's a good place to dump a body."

"I told you the tourists don't come way down here." Eva looked for barricades that should have closed off the south beach to vehicles. There was nothing between her and the jetty boulders.

"Jim, I still don't understand why you followed me here." Eva needed to keep Jim distracted. "What do you want from me?"

"How many times do I have to explain that?" Jim snarled. "I need your money to cover my losses in the commodity market. It went belly up when the stock market dropped. Your life insurance policy would have covered that with plenty left over for me."

"I don't have a life insurance policy."

"I have one on you. I always take out one on all my wives."

"Jim, you're crazy. I'm not your wife."

His gun barrel slid up her throat. "On paper you are and everything would have been okay if your federal boyfriend hadn't poked around. I should kill him just for that."

Glancing in the rearview mirror, Eva watched Mark's Jeep pull closer. "I'm the one who told Detective Galloway we weren't married. I would never marry you. So how did you expect to cash in on an insurance policy?"

"I had our marriage license, insurance policy, and all I needed was your death certificate." Jim smugly tilted his head. "You were supposed to die in that auto accident."

"What auto accident?" Eva baited Jim for another response to keep his attention off the approaching boulders.

"I should have known you were too dumb to die. You just looked at the gun I pointed at you and kept driving. It took two shots to run you off the road." Jim shook his head. "This time I'll make sure you are good and dead."

"Everyone knows we aren't married, so why would you want to kill me now?" Eva studied the line of boulders, looking for the best place to crash the car.

"You're a loose end and you know too much." Jim grabbed her hair. "Did you give the cops my Social Security cards?"

"I don't know what you're talking about." Her hand slid across the airbag warning label on the steering wheel.

"Where's that exit?" Jim snarled.

"Dead ahead. Near those rocks, you make a hard right." Eva focused on a cluster of boulders near the surf to her left. *That big boulder near the surf line.* Eva plotted. *That's the one I'll crash into. With a direct front impact, the airbags will be triggered. If I'm lucky, I'll get out before Jim grabs me.*

Eva tightened her seat belt. "I'll have to pick up speed. It takes a lot of momentum to get through the soft sand by the old beach ramp. Don't want to get stuck, do you?"

"Step on it." Leaning over, Jim slid the gun barrel down her cheek. "If we get stuck, I'll kill that federal boyfriend of yours. One round in his big chest." Jim aimed his gun at the back window, at the Jeep following, at Mark's chest.

Turning the steering wheel, Eva floored the accelerator. She aimed the red car at the rapidly approaching boulders of the jetty.

Hang on. Eva took a deep breath.

~ 68 ~

"Eva! Stop!" Mark floored the accelerator. "I've got to cut her off before she hits the jetty."

"Cut her off!" Paul shouted into his cell phone.

Police cruisers flicked on their lights and sirens walled.

"Where's Eva going?" Paul asked.

Eva aimed the red Firebird at the jetty's boulders.

Jim aimed his gun at the back window.

A flash erupted from Jim's gun. A bullet sliced through the sports car's back window.

"Hang on." Mark yanked the steering wheel right.

Police vehicles sped across the sand, towards the red car.

"Turn, Eva, turn!" Mark shouted. His Jeep was losing ground to the fast sports car. "Eva, don't."

"She'll turn, Mark." Paul gripped the roll bar. "Turn, Eva!"

A police cruiser stopped between the jetty's boulders and Eva's speeding car. The officer rolled out.

"Turn! She has to turn away from the ocean. We'll cut her off." Mark pulled right.

Abruptly, Eva turned left, showering the abandoned police cruiser with wet sand. It was a sharp ninety-degree turn. The car's hood aimed at a new target, the Atlantic Ocean.

Without a seatbelt on, Jim smacked against the passenger door. His right arm flung back. There was a blast from his gun.

"Eva." Mark whipped his Jeep into a hard turn. "Turn, Eva."

There was no turn.

The sleek red hood sliced into a wave like a speedboat. Salt water sprayed over the top. Momentum pushed the car forward, deeper into the surf. The hood jabbed into the ocean. A wave struck back. Water rolled over the back window, obscuring the view of those inside.

Mark's Jeep whipped sideways and stopped in the wet sand. "I've got to get her out."

"Wait." Paul grabbed Mark's arm. "Jim is armed."

"So am I." Pulling free, Mark raced towards the driver's side of the sports car. "Eva. Get out!"

Rex dashed into the surf.

Jim's head popped out of the passenger's side. His arm slid across the roof. His gun aimed at Mark.

Mark did a belly whopper into a low wave near the shore.

Another crack of gunfire rang out.

A hiss zinged past Mark's head. A bullet splashed into the surf behind him.

Police cars pulled to a stop. Officers took shelter behind their vehicles and aimed at the red sports car.

Rex leaped into a high wave. It knocked him back.

Mark whistled for his dog. The surf was too high for Rex to navigate. He'd only be a target.

Jim shouted. "Stay back or I'll kill her!"

Eva's head appeared. Jim's left arm was around her neck in a chokehold. "Mark. Go back. I'm okay." Eva didn't struggle.

She seems stunned, Mark thought. *Maybe she hit her head on the steering wheel. She could be hurt. I have to get to her.*

"Get back or I'll shoot her!" Pulling Eva from the car, Jim staggered back into the surf. "All of you. Get back."

Mark grabbed Rex's collar and backed away. "Come on, Rex. We can't panic Jim. It will put Eva in danger." Mark's mind flashed hot, remembering his sister's ex-boyfriend panic as the police approached. Before Mark could reach his sister, shots rang out and a knife slashed his sister's throat and him. Mark carried more than one scar from that day.

Backing towards his Jeep, Mark watched the gun barrel sliding along Eva's throat.

"Get down." Paul pulled Mark back behind the Jeep.

"We have to calm Jim down." Mark kneeled next to Paul.

"The police negotiators will be here soon. They'll try to talk him into surrendering. And a SWAT team is on its way." Paul pointed his cell phone at the police cruisers surrounding the red sports car. "They'll send two sharpshooters along the other side of the jetty. From those boulders they can get a clear shot at Jim, but they need time to get out there."

"I need to get to Eva." Mark watched the wave smashing over the red hood. "The tide is coming in. I don't want Jim dragging her into the deep water. Eva's too weak to swim very far."

"Professor Reining." Ducking beside Mark's Jeep, Officer Bob White dropped a surfboard and two bulletproof vests. "Put this on. I don't want you getting blown away before I get my final grade. I worked hard for that 'A', so put this vest on."

Mark pushed the vest away. "It'll slow me down."

"Either put it on or the chief will have you hauled off the beach." Bob shoved the vest back to Mark. "Do it! That's an order. This isn't your classroom, this is MY beach."

"He's right." Paul slipped on the spare bulletproof vest. "Only in the movies do the bullets miss the hero. And you're a mighty big target for Jim to aim at."

Slipping into the vest, Mark knew they were right but still he would ditch it as soon as possible. His plan to swim to Eva didn't include a heavy bulletproof vest. "I'm going to wade out a bit to talk to Jim. It'll distract him enough to give your officers time to move to better positions. We need to buy some time."

"Wait for our negotiator." Bob picked up his surfboard.

"Is that thing bulletproof or are you out of vests?" Paul chided.

"Neither. I'm going surfing." Bob nodded down the beach. "I'm going to paddle out and slip in behind Jim. A surfboard is silent and low in the water. If I'm lucky, he won't see me."

Mark slid a second gun in his pocket. "Then I'll distract him."

"Wait for the negotiators to get here," Bob insisted. "The chief doesn't want you or our Yankee detective getting shot."

"We can't wait. Look at Jim. He's already too nervous. Eva's life is in danger." After slipping off his shoes, Mark peered over his Jeep. He was alarmed at seeing Jim backing deeper into the surf, dragging Eva with him. "Jim will be more willing to negotiate with me than the local police."

"Why?" Bob slipped his gun into a waterproof case.

"He thinks I'm a federal agent." Mark loosely fastened the vest. "I'll try to negotiate a deal with him."

Bob glanced over the hood. "Are you crazy?"

"Mark is right." Paul pulled the slide on his pistol. "Jim thinks Mark is an FBI agent and he's more likely to talk to a fed than a local cop he doesn't know. No offense."

"The chief won't allow it."

Not waiting, Mark stood up and shouted. "Jim! Let's talk. We can make a deal. I'm going to walk closer so we can talk."

A wave smacked Jim's back in shoulder-high water. His arm gripped Eva's neck, holding her head above the water.

"I'm just going to come a little closer so we can talk." Mark slowly walked to the water line. *I need to get to a good swimming depth,* he thought. The first thin beach wave swished around his bare feet. "We can make a deal. Just tell me what you want."

"Toss your gun on the beach." Jim shouted. "If you try anything, I'll shoot Eva."

~ 69 ~

"Mark, go back!" Eva's words were muted by the chokehold Jim had around her neck. Horror swept through her as she watched Mark toss his gun on the beach. Mark walked towards her like he had in her dream. But this was different. This was real.

A wave slapped Jim, knocking him off balance.

Eva's head slipped below the surface. Salt water swished down her throat. Touching bottom, Eva forced herself up.

"Stop squirming!" Jim snarled.

"If you don't keep my head above the water, they have a clear shot at you." She looked at Jim pointing his gun at Mark. *What am I saying?* Eva thought. *I need to be below the water so the police can shoot Jim before he shoots Mark. I need to get free of Jim, soon. Mark is getting too close.*

Squirming, Eva tried to get free. "We have to move back towards the beach. The tide is coming in."

"Shut up. If you don't stop fidgeting, I'll shoot that federal boyfriend of yours." Jim pulled her higher in the deepening surf, using her body as a shield. He glanced right to Mark, then ahead at the line of cruisers on the beach, left at the jetty rocks, and then back to Mark. Jim's gun aimed at Eva's head. His hand trembled.

On the beach, police officers hunkered behind their cruisers, their arms resting on the hoods and trunks as they aimed at Jim.

"Jim!" Mark yelled across the pounding surf. "Let's talk. We can make a deal. What do you want?"

Jim slid the gun under Eva's chin. "Don't come any closer."

"Calm down. I'll stay right here." Mark stood still.

Jim stepped into a slue. "This is better. No breakers here."

"This isn't a safe place to be." Eva could barely whisper.

"Shut up! This is better without those stupid waves."

"But –"

Jim's arm tightened around her throat. Eva was speechless like in her Siberian dream, but instead of a field of frozen tundra there were the swells of the Atlantic Ocean. Fear chilled her body. Through her wet eyelashes, the light twinkled like frozen crystals.

"Get me a car!" Jim demanded. "I want a car and safe passage out of the country."

"We'll get you a car." Mark took one step closer. "It'll take a few minutes to get one here. Obviously we can't give you a police cruiser, and my Jeep is a real dog on the open road."

After checking on the beach cops and the jetty wall, Jim turned back. "Get a car here fast!"

The faster the better, Eva thought. *Jim is standing on the bank of the slue and it's giving away. We're sinking. If he steps back, he'll be in over his head. ... Will he let go of me when we go under or will he panic? Panic? Can I use that to get away?*

"Jim." Mark stepped into waist-high water. "Let Eva go. You can take me as a hostage."

"Forget it. I'm not stupid." Jim glanced towards the police cars. "Cops don't like to shoot with a woman in the way. And she's too dumb to be dangerous. I'm keeping her."

"A federal agent is a more valuable hostage," Mark argued.

"No!" Eva gasped. Neither her protest nor her thoughts could be heard. *Please Mark. Stay away. It's my fault Jim is here. I don't want you to get hurt. ... Please, please, don't come any closer.*

"Hold still." Jim jerked Eva.

"Come in closer to shore," Mark continued. "You'll be safer there. The tide is coming in."

"Forget it. I'm not falling for any dumb trick," Jim shouted. "Bullets aren't any good in deep water. I'm staying right here."

"It's not safe here," Eva whispered. Her feet dangled. She was in over her head. And one step back into the valley of the slue and Jim would be in over his head.

A tinge of panic startled Eva. But it wasn't the deep water. It was the three dark objects skimming the surface, moving closer. The color purple reflected off their balloon-like bodies. Memories of her childhood flashed back.

Purple is poison. Her mother's words still echoed in Eva's brain. *Don't touch the purple jellyfish. It's a Portuguese man-of-war. Their poison is in those long tentacles. ... Always remember: purple is poison,* her mom had repeated.

"Jim." She choked on his name.

"Shut up! I have to think of a way out. I'm not going to jail."

Pulling her hand above the water, Eva pointed to the man-of-wars. *I doubt if anyone will understand what I'm trying to tell them,* she thought. *Besides, there is nothing they can do about the man-of-wars except call the emergency squad.*

"Where's that car?" Jim shouted to Mark.

"It's on its way."

Looking south, Eva saw two men, dressed in black, dash along the jetty. With long rifles in their hands, they hopped from boulder to boulder. They would soon be behind Jim's line of vision.

The car isn't the only thing on its way, Eva considered. *Two sharpshooters are bad enough, but now I have three man-of-wars to worry about.* Her arms crossed, hoping to keep her arms free of the stings of poisonous tentacles dangling in the surf.

An ocean swell hid the sea creatures. As the water dropped, one reappeared, still floating towards Eva.

"What's that thing?" Jim pointed his gun at the man-of-war.

"It's just a little sea creature. Sort of like a jellyfish. They wash in from the West Indies." In the distance on the jetty wall, Eva saw the two sharpshooters drop down as Jim turned their way. "Don't tell me you're afraid of a little jellyfish."

"Its an ugly looking blob." Jim stepped sideways, backing away as the man-of-war floated towards him. "I don't want that slimy thing touching me."

"It's not slimy, just shiny like a balloon." Eva reached out to the man-of-war. Carefully, her finger touched only the top of its translucent purplish membrane. The poison was in the mass of long purple strings beneath its body, dangling deep into the ocean.

"What's wrong?" Mark shouted as he stepped into a wave.

"Don't come any closer." Jim aimed the gun at Eva.

"Mark, go back. I'm okay. Really." Eva pulled back from the purple strings. "It's a man –"

"I told you to shut up." Jim tightened his chokehold around her neck. As Mark approached, Jim backed away.

The other two man-of-wars floated closer.

"Here comes your car." Mark pointed down the beach. "It'll be here by the time you get to the beach."

Grinning, Jim turned his gun towards Mark. "Well then, I don't need you any longer."

Jim aimed.

Eva screamed, "Mark!"

Jim squeezed the trigger.

A blast erupted from the gun barrel.

"Mark!" Helpless, Eva watched.

Mark grabbed his chest. His head snapped up. Mark looked at Eva. His arm reached out for her. Mark sank beneath a wave.

"Mark!"

A wave rolled past where Mark had stood.

Rex dashed into the surf, dragging his leash.

Detective Galloway raced towards the surf.

Only waves rolled to shore.

Mark's body had disappeared.

Beside Eva, a swirl of purple shimmered. Anger lashed through her, her mind flamed, and her cold hand reached. Reached for the purple. Reached for the man-of-war. Grabbing only its top, Eva yanked it from the sea and flung it into Jim's face.

Hundreds of stringy purple tentacles stuck to Jim's skin. His hands clawed at the slimy mass that stuck to more skin, it's purple poison stinging. Screaming, Jim let go of her.

Curling up, Eva's body dropped into the deep surf.

A cold current pulled her down.

Long purple tentacles dangled above her.

Hitting bottom, Eva kicked against the sand, propelling her away from Jim and the long strings of purple poison.

Water churned around Jim.

Mark was Eva's only thought.

I have to get to Mark before he drowns.

~ 70 ~

Staggering in the surf, Jim clawed at the purple tentacles of the Portuguese man-of-war. As he ripped them from his face, they stuck to his hands. The poison stung his flesh. Screaming, Jim turned and aimed his gun at Eva's head sinking into the surf.

Mark's head surfaced behind Jim. His hand slipped above the water and Mark aimed his gun at Jim.

But it was too late.

Two shots echoed from the jetty wall.

Jim's head snapped back. Blood splattered across the water.

Mark glanced at the sharpshooters standing on the jetty and then at the surf, looking for Eva.

"Eva, Eva!" Mark shouted. She was not there. His heart pounded, seeing the man-of-war. *Poison,* Mark thought. *Was Eva stung? Where is she? I have to get to her.*

Swimming towards where he last saw Eva, Mark's arms sliced fast and furious into the surf. Each painful stroke took him closer.

Jim had held Eva in the deep water. If she'd been stung by the man-of-war, she might never surface.

"Eva!" Mark shouted. He couldn't see her.

Only Bob was in view. Lying on his surfboard, Bob had paddled out into the ocean to get behind Jim, sneaking in silently and low in the water. Not even Eva had noticed Bob's approach.

Bob sat up on his surfboard. "Mark, watch out. There's another man-of-war over there, floating towards the jetty."

"Did she get stung?" Mark shouted. "Can you see Eva?"

"No. She went down just beyond you." Bob paddled closer.

Mark dove under the last breaker and swam for where Eva went down. There the water was calmer but not clear enough to see well. Mark looked for any moving shapes, her white blouse, or her blond hair. He would grab anything that wasn't purple.

Eva, where are you? Mark thought. *Did you get tangled in the man-of-war? Are you ...* But, he couldn't finish the thought.

Water churned around him.

A light object and a hand moved.

Mark grabbed. But it wasn't Eva.

Bob pulled away.

Each swam in different directions.

Mark saw no trace of Eva. Adrenaline splashed through his veins. *I have to find her soon. She is too weak to swim far and she has been down too long. Even I'm getting out of breath.* His lungs ached and the bulletproof vest was like an anchor wrapped around his chest, aching from the smack of Jim's bullet hitting him.

Surfacing, Mark scanned the ocean.

Eva was not in sight.

Along the shore, police officers and paramedics were rushing into the surf. Paul was a few strokes away, swimming out to help.

"She should be right here." Paul dove.

Turning to dive, Mark saw a cluster of golden strings floating beyond him, heading back to where he had been.

"Eva!" Mark took two powerful strokes and dove for the strands of yellow, beginning to sink.

His hand slid through the shimmering threads.

Something latched onto him.

A hot flash gripped his chest.

A soft cold object touched his face.

Something slipped around his neck, pulling him closer.

Struggling, Mark surfaced, entangled with the creature.

"Eva!" He gasped. "Eva. Are you okay?"

"I'm ... fine." Eva felt his chest. "I saw Jim shoot you. ... You fell into the surf. ... Are you hurt?"

"No, darling. I'm okay." Pulling her closer, Mark swam towards the beach. "You're shaking. I have to get you ashore."

"Here, Professor," Bob called. "Put her on my surfboard."

Mark held the surfboard. "Eva. Slide on top. You can ride in."

"I don't know how to use a surfboard." Clinging to him, Eva hesitated. "I want to stay with you."

Mark saw her lips trembling and felt her cold hands. *She's too weak to ride in alone,* Mark thought. *One big wave could knock her off and the surfboard could hit her. I can't lose her again.* "We'll ride in together."

Eva held onto his heavy bulletproof vest. "Mark, how can you swim in this thing?"

Looking down, he understood why his swim had been so difficult. "I'll explain later." Mark waved to Detective Galloway just surfacing. "Paul, hang on to Eva. After I'm on the surfboard, help her get on my back. I'm going to take her in."

Bob held his surfboard steady in the gentle swells. Just beyond them the water crested and broke into high waves as they rolled across the sandbar towards the shore.

Slipping on the surfboard, the bulletproof vest was noticeably heavy. His chest ached from the impact of the bullet hitting it. The force had knocked him into the surf. But fear for Eva's life had been more pressing. It was Eva his heart ached for. "Come on, Eva. Get on my back and we'll ride in together."

Mark laid flat on the surfboard and Paul pushed Eva up on top. "Hold onto Mark."

"Hang on, Professor." With a shove, Bob pushed his surfboard into the cresting wave. "Paul and I will bodysurf in."

The voices of Paul and Bob faded from behind them. And shouts of the police on the beach grew louder.

Mark caught the front edge of the wave. "Hang on!"

As the wave curled in on itself, water foamed around them like warm champagne. The force of the churning breaker propelled the surfboard towards the beach as if it were a cork popped from a bottle of bubbly.

"Mark." Eva whispered in his ear. "I love you."

He felt her cool lips kissing his neck. "I love you. Eva." He turned to kiss her. Off balance, the surfboard tilted, dumping its passengers into the now shallow bubbling surf.

Rolling into the knee-deep water, Mark pulled Eva closer. Her soft body clung tighter and her legs tangled around his. A gentle beach wave foamed around them. Slipping under the water, their lips met. Sweet and salty was the taste. The coolness of her skin refreshed the heat within him. They tumbled over and over.

For Mark, the roll in the foamy surf could have lasted forever and her response seemed to agree.

But abruptly, a sea of hands pulled them from the surf.

"Professor Reining. Are you okay?" Bob pulled Mark up.

Mark's muscles were as limp as a wet beach towel and his body felt like an anchor. Under the bulletproof vest his ribs ached.

"You're safe now." Detective Galloway took her arm. "Eva, your neck is red. Did you get stung by that man-of-war?"

"We need help over here." Bob shouted to his fellow officers on the beach. "We need the paramedics."

~ 71 ~

"Mark, maybe you should go to the hospital." Eva watched the paramedics rip open his bulletproof vest, examine his chest for wounds, and take his blood pressure. "You know those doctors will want to take some x-rays."

On the stretcher Mark took deep breaths. "No need. ... There's nothing broken. ... How are you?"

"I'm fine." Trembling, Eva sighed with tiredness. *Or is that relief,* she thought. *I could never forgive myself if anything happened to Mark. I love him.*

With the paramedics taking over, Detective Galloway quickly walked south to where his suspect laid sprawled on the sand like a beached killer shark.

There was blood on the sand.

Near Jim's body, Bob mingled with his fellow police officers and watched attentively as the chief handled the press arriving by helicopter from the Orlando TV stations.

Away from the commotion, Eva watched Mark being treated and ignored the paramedics checking her arms.

"Ma'am, did you get stung by the man-of-war?"

"No. I know better than to touch their long tentacles." Eva repeated her mother's old warning. "Purple is poison."

Tilting Eva's head back, the paramedic examined the red scratches from Jim's gun barrel on her throat. And where Jim had ripped her chain off, there was a cut across the back of her neck. But there were no other visible signs of trauma.

The paramedic pulled his stethoscope away. "Your heart rate is a little fast and your body temperature is a little low."

"How's Mark?" Eva pulled a blanket around her shoulders.

"He's a little winded but I think he'll be okay."

Eva glanced over her shoulder. Halfway between them and the jetty's boulders, a group of police officers stood near a man lying on the sand. News cameras were pointed at the body. It was Jim.

At least the police have Jim. Eva thoughts were cold. *He'll really be angry with me now for throwing that man-of-war in his face. And he'll come after me again ... unless he's dead. Maybe the police killed him.*

Eva pointed down the beach at Jim. "What about him?"

"I'm not sure." The paramedic glanced at Mark frantically shaking his head. "They'll do what needs to be done. But –"

"Eva," Mark interrupted. "I'm going to take you home."

"Home?" Smiling, Eva began to ramble. "I found it. I found the West Indies. It's north of your place, next to a beach ramp. I should have remembered the beach ramp. But they added a new front and changed its name. They built some rooms on the beach side and a swimming pool. We never had a pool. And they repainted it."

"Slow down." After getting up, Mark joined Eva on her stretcher and kept her facing away from the action down the beach.

A morgue van pulled beside Jim's body. His head was covered by a sheet stained with blood. News cameras panned north to where Mark and Eva sat.

"Eva, we need to go home. Right now."

"But don't you have to go to the hospital for x-rays?"

"Nothing's broken." He pulled Eva up. "Let's go home. You need to rest."

"But I'm fine. Really."

"Well, I need to rest." His arm slipped over her shoulder and his weight shifted to her. "A wet bulletproof vest is heavier than I ever imagined. They're definitely no good for swimming."

"Maybe you should invent one that floats like a life vest." Eva teased. "Look, isn't that your mom and dad?"

His parents' car pulled beside the rescue squad.

"Mark, are you all right?" Barbara rushed to her son.

"I'm fine, Mom. But we need to take Eva home." He nodded down the beach at the group of camera crews strolling towards Eva. Ahead of the crowd, Rex was making a beeline back, his leash dragging through the sand.

"I see. You're right. Get Eva in the car. Your dad will drive you home." Barbara nudged her son. "After I check with the paramedics about the two of you, I'll drive your Jeep back. Now get going before they get here."

"Who?" Turning, Eva spotted the camera crews beginning to run towards them. "Mark, I don't want to talk to them. Not now."

With a hasty departure, a fast drive up the old beach ramp, over to Peninsula Drive, then north cutting through a side street back to Atlantic Avenue, no one was able to follow Fritz. The ride was silent with the weary passengers snuggled together in the back seat. It was a short ride home.

"Home," Eva mumbled to herself. At the living room window of his parents' home, she watched the flag waving on the flagpole. "What does that flag mean? Clear sailing or stormy weather?"

After a long warm shower, a change into dry clothes, and a cup of hot cocoa, Eva felt a wave of mixed emotions rolling over her. *Is it over or just beginning?* Eva pondered. *How does Mark feel now? After all, he almost got killed saving my life. Is he upset with me for running away? Will he want me to stay or should I go? But where do I go from here?*

Listening to Mark as he talked on the phone, she watched him pace, flipping the telephone cord like a fishing line.

"Eva." Mark put the receiver down. "Don't worry about Jim. He won't be bothering you anymore. Jim is dead."

"Dead? Jim is dead?" Her arms slipped around Mark as he stepped closer. "Did I kill him?"

"No. The police shot Jim."

"But I threw the man-of-war in his face."

"That's probably why he let go of you. Their poison has a nasty sting, but it didn't kill him. As soon as you slipped under the water and were free, the police marksmen on the jetty shot Jim."

Eva looked into Mark's blue eyes. "But –"

He pulled her head next to his chest. "Don't worry, darling. You're safe. It's all over."

Eva pulled back. "No. It's not over."

~ 72 ~

Dawn, August 25th – On the beach

"But it's not over," Eva repeated. The pages of the calendar flipped as she turned them back. "For me it's just beginning."

"Don't worry, darling." Sitting on the wide lounge chair, Mark pulled her closer. "If you want, we can start summer all over."

Beside them, Eva tucked the calendar under the tray. On it was a champagne breakfast with fresh fruit and almond cookies dusted with powered sugar. A bottle of bubbly sat in an ice bucket.

"Start summer over, that's a good idea. I want to have lots of good memories of our first summer together." Eva fed Mark a cookie and pulled the blanket around Mark's shoulder.

The pre-dawn air felt cool as the ocean breeze rolled across the beach and up the sand dunes. Nearby, the sea oats rustled.

Mark had moved the doublewide lounge chair out to the end of the wooden walk so they could watch the sunrise.

Under the blanket, Eva snuggled closer. Beneath Mark's shirt, she felt the strong muscles of a powerful swimmer and rubbed his shoulder where Jim's bullet hit the bulletproof vest. "Does it hurt?"

"Nope." Mark moaned in mock pain. "Never felt better."

"Poor baby." She kissed the spot on his shoulder. "I'll never forget my knight in black armor charging into the ocean to save me. … Mark, I love you."

Mark lifted her chin and his lips met hers. The moist salty mist of morning mingled with traces of powdered sugar and roasted almonds. They shared the taste.

I feel so alive, Eva thought. *I never imagined love could be so vivid. Maybe that's not the right word. Intense. Sparkling. Whatever, it's wonderful. I want to hold onto this moment forever.*

Behind them, his parents' house was still dark and quiet. The night before, it had been like Grand Central Station with police coming and going. Eva's niece and brother stayed until the wee hours, hovering around Eva, making sure she was all right.

Wrapping up the details of his case, Detective Galloway spent hours on the phone with his captain in Ohio as he sat in the Florida sun, working on a tan. Beside Paul on the deck, Rex and the kittens played a new game of keep-away with the big, brown teddy bear with the pink bow as the prize.

Fritz and Barbara had spent the evening designing the gazebo they would build over the foundation ditch that had been started by Mark, digging for Eva's treasure chest. Barbara thought it would be a lovely place for a wedding reception. Fritz agreed.

It was a time to relax and a time to plan. Everything had been resolved, almost.

Feeding Mark another cookie, Eva studied the brightening eastern sky. "Look, the sun is peeking over the horizon. A whole new day is coming."

"Speaking of days, when do you want to do it?" Mark reached in his pocket.

"Do what?" Her smile radiated with expectation. *Is this the BIG moment?* Her thoughts raced ahead. *Is he going to ask me the big question? Is he? Really? What will he say?*

"Eva, I have something for you?" Mark handed her a little blue box, bigger than a ring box and smaller that a necklace case.

In her trembling hand, the velvet-covered box was remarkably light. "Mark, is this what I think it is?"

"Maybe yes and maybe no. You'll have to open it."

As the lid flipped back, Eva saw the glint of metal, but it was not what she expected. It was long and skinny. "A key?"

"A very old key. I found it when we were looking for your treasure chest yesterday." Mark grinned as he glanced at the trench in the sand. "Could be a pirate left some buried treasure behind."

Sitting up, Eva spotted a freshly filled area. "Does this pirate have sea-blue eyes?"

"Only the good ones have blue eyes." Mark winked and handed Eva a little garden shovel with a blue bow.

After shoveling out some sand, there was the clang of metal against metal and a flash of red. Tossing the shovel aside, Eva frantically pulled the sand back with her hands. "There be a treasure chest here, mate."

"By golly, Ponce de Leon must have left part of the queen's gems behind." Mark grinned.

Brushing sand off the red metal chest, Eva found markings. "Strange, the initials 'M.R.' are painted on this chest. Isn't that a coincidence, Mark Reining?"

"A lot of things around here have those initials on them." Mark kissed the new, blue heart dangling around Eva's neck.

With a tug, Eva pulled the red metal box from the sand. "Looks like the box we found yesterday." Eva giggled.

"Well, what are you waiting for?"

"I want to cherish this moment. I'll make it the first memory of our new summer." Taking a deep breath, Eva slipped the key in the old lock. With a click, it opened and the lock pulled free. Creaking, the lid opened.

"A cigar box?" She reached in and pulled it out. *Maybe this isn't what I think it is,* Eva pondered. *I don't think anyone ever popped the big question with a box of cigars. But then cigars do have those cute little paper rings.*

Kissing her neck, Mark slid his arm around her shoulders. "Are you going to open it?"

Eva tilted the cigar box. Inside something shifted, slid, and hit the other side with a soft thud. Too curious to wait any longer, she flipped open the lid; inside was another blue velvet box.

Peeking in, Eva saw the sparkle of twinkling lights. About the size of a dime, the crown of the ring had six sides. On each side there were six sea-blue gems separated by rays of gold. In the center was a large diamond, sparkling like the morning star.

"Oh! It's beautiful."

"Let me do the honors." Mark slipped it on the ring finger of her left hand. "I know numbers and color are important to you, so I thought this would be an appropriate engagement ring. Six aquamarines and the seventh gem is a white diamond."

"It's perfect." She paused, remembering, for her six was blue and seven was white. Mark had remembered her strange theory. "Dear, it's perfect, just perfect. ... I love you."

Mark's lips joined Eva's. His arms surrounded her. Eva pulled him closer, wanting to hold on to him and the moment forever. And time seamed to understand. The sun held motionless on the rim of the horizon.

Pulling away, Mark brushed her golden hair back. "Eva, will you marry me?"

Turning away, the sunlight sparkled in her hair. "Yes, but –"

"But what?" His voice echoed with surprise.

"I promised Dad I'd wait until my twenty-seventh birthday."

"When's that?" Mark looked puzzled.

"I'll be twenty-seven this June."

"But this is August. You're already twenty-seven."

"It's August for you, but for me it's still Memorial Day. That means my birthday is next week." Eva looked at her engagement ring. "Can you wait until then?"

"If you promised your father, we'll wait. I don't want to rush you, darling. I can wait a week."

"Good. We can use the money for our first home."

"What money?"

"My inheritance. I get my full inheritance if I wait until I'm twenty-seven before I marry."

"Well, if your birthday was in June and next week it'll be September, then I think you'll be safely twenty-seven by the time we get married." Mark pulled an envelope from the box. "You forgot to open this."

She stared at Mark's aquamarine eyes, sparkling with a secret. And Eva had her own, but there would be plenty of time to explain her inheritance, later.

Eva pulled out two sheets of paper. "Tickets?"

"Yes. Tickets for our honeymoon cruise." Mark beamed. "I'm taking you on a cruise to the islands of the West Indies."

"The West Indies." The warm feeling of being home mixed with the tingle of adventure. Eva pulled Mark closer. "I would love to see the West Indies."

Their lips met in a kiss of new love that would bind their lives forever in the ebbs and flows of matrimony.

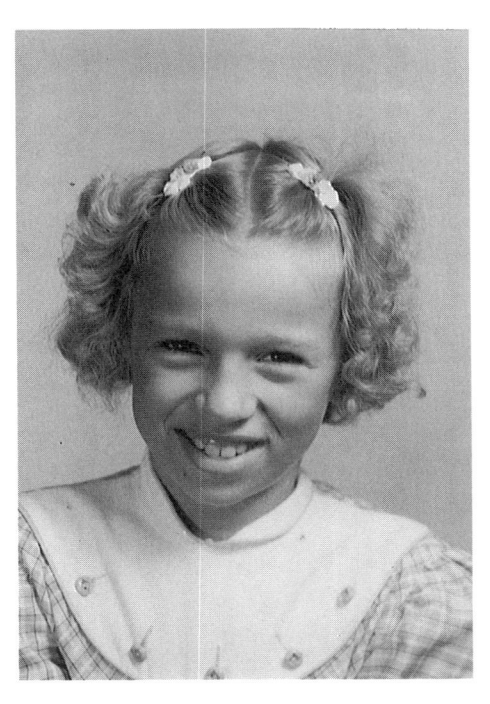